Dark Clouds Over Alabama

A Story of Struggles and Triumph in the Old South

Authré thanks! Enjoy

Carl J Barger

Carl J. Barger

Strategic Book Publishing and Rights Co.

Strategic Book Publishing and Rights Co.
12620 FM 1960, Suite A4-507
Houston, TX 77065
www.sbpra.com

ISBN: 978-1-62516-012-6

Book Design: Suzanne Kelly

Acknowledgement

I want to thank Lena, my wife, and my good friends, Paul and Jenny Nail of Conway, Arkansas, for their support in editing *Dark Clouds over Alabama.* Their encouragement and dedication in editing is deeply appreciated.

CHAPTER 1

As I entered the parlor, my mother, Catherine Bradford, was sitting in her favorite chair knitting. Knitting is one of her favorite things to do. She had taught my sisters and every female household slave how to sew and knit. My mother's first words as I approached her were, "Obadiah, you know you won't be finding anyone like our Mamie."

"I'm well aware of that, Mother."

"Just make sure she's in good health and can learn."

My mother, not like other plantation owners' wives, saw nothing wrong in teaching our household slaves how to read and write and to talk properly. In most parts of the South, this type of reasoning coming from a plantation owner would be strictly out of character.

It was the philosophy of most slave owners to keep their slaves ignorant. The owners believed if slaves learned to write and read, they would soon want their freedom and cause all kinds of problems. My parents, thank God, did their own thinking and had their own convictions and standards of living. I'm sure there were several people within Autauga County, some being our neighbors, who looked down on my parents for their attitude toward teaching our slaves. My parents also allowed our slaves to have a worship time on Sundays in our barn. I loved to hear them sing.

"One other thing before you go," my mother said. "Whomever you choose, don't have her stripped naked. That is so humiliating and disgusting."

"I will certainly honor that, Mother. You won't have to worry about that."

My father, James Bradford, entered the room and said, "Bill is here with the carriage. Are you ready?"

"I'm ready!"

"We will have Mamie's room ready for whomever you bring home. I'm sure she will be pleased with her accommodations," Mother said.

As I turned to join my father in the carriage, I thought about my mother's comment. Mamie had a room off the kitchen in our home at Twin Oaks. It had a bed, a wood floor, a table with a lamp and a fireplace to keep her warm. On some plantations, slaves live in dark shacks with dirt floors, no windows, no beds, or enough covering to keep them warm during the cold nights. I'm so thankful our slaves have better living conditions. We provide small houses for our slaves. The houses have wood floors and ample windows and doors for ventilation. Most of our slave houses have lofts. The loft is normally used as sleeping quarters for the kids. It's rather hot in the loft in the summer but nice and warm in the winter. Each of our slave houses is equipped with a fireplace for cooking and keeping warm in the winter months. We also have a new bunk house that houses several of our men slaves who are single.

Bill, our family driver, has been our driver for several years. I spent many hours teaching Bill how to read and write. In my opinion, he's probably the best educated slave in Autauga County.

After leaving the house, we traveled down the narrow dusty road that would lead us to the main road to Selma, Alabama. It was a blistering hot day, and before long I was wiping sweat from my brow.

We passed several of our slaves picking cotton. I had often wondered how our slaves could hold up working all day in this heat. Some of our male slaves, especially the boys, wore a loincloth while others wore their issued long pants. The female slaves wore skirts and loose fitting tops. Most of the females wore cloths over their heads. All our slaves went barefoot in the fields. I had always wanted to join our slaves in picking cotton, but my father would not hear of it.

"That is strictly unheard of in the South. We would be the laughing stock of Autauga County, Alabama, if we were caught laboring in the fields with our slaves," he said.

Although I didn't agree with my father, or the way of the South, I would continue to honor my father and mother.

Our slaves used straw baskets as containers for the cotton. I was always amazed how they carried the baskets. The male slaves normally carried their baskets on their shoulders while the females carried theirs on their heads.

Besides corn, cotton was the chief money crop on our six-hundred-acre Twin Oaks Plantation. On this sweltering hot day, at least eighty-five slaves were picking cotton, and several slaves were back at the barn ginning and baling cotton.

I looked at Father and said, "This heat has to be tough on our slaves."

"I agree, Obadiah. I've instructed John to give them water breaks every hour on the hour. I don't want to lose any of them to a heat stroke."

John is my second-oldest brother whom Father made overseer of our Twin Oaks Plantation. Our plantation is located about five miles from the city of Independence and about seven miles from Prattville, Alabama, in Autauga County.

Our purpose in going to Selma was to purchase replacements slaves, mostly males, for the plantation and a female replacement for Mamie, our head household slave. Mamie died of complications from old age last week, and we buried her in the slave cemetery on our plantation next to her husband, Ben. I can't remember when Mamie wasn't a part of the Bradford family. She and Ben came with us from Jones County, Georgia, when my father purchased our first plantation, Black Oaks, in Cahaba, Dallas County, Alabama, near Selma. Mamie was like a family member to all of us. She and I had a great relationship.

As part of my twenty-first birthday gift, Father was giving me the honor of picking Mamie's replacement. In my opinion, there couldn't be a rightful replacement for Mamie. She was one of a kind. She was like a granny to us all. She had been strict and firm, but honest and fair in her dealings with all of us Bradford children as we grew into adults.

I had never been to a slave sale previously. In fact, I never really wanted to be involved in seeing slaves paraded before a

3

group of rich plantation owners. From what my father shared with me, the slaves were treated like animals. Plantation owners want to know how many teeth are missing, what kind of scars are on their body, or whether they can speak, see, and hear. My father said this is a form of humiliation and torture to the slave, but necessary since teeth and scars are used as markings to iden-tify a slave who may run away or who has been a runaway. I'm sure today will be depressing.

CHAPTER 2

As we approached the beautiful city of Selma, I was reminded of the time when we first moved to Dallas County from Jones County, Georgia. Economics was the major factor in my father's decision to purchase Black Oaks, our first plantation at Cahaba, in Dallas County. Because of the large cotton production in the 1840s, Selma was a booming town. Selma was considered an export and import city because of the Alabama River and the Tennessee Railroad. In 1836, the Selma and Tennessee Railroad connected the Alabama River with the Tennessee River. This made it possible for the cotton farmers to ship their cotton by rail and steamboats up and down the rivers.

One of my favorite things as a boy when we lived in Cahaba was going to Selma and watching the steamboats dock at the city port. I loved to watch the smoke coming from the large steam pipes and to hear the loud whistles coming from the steamboats. I dreamed of someday boarding a steamboat and riding up and down the Alabama River. For some reason, I have not been able to experience that dream.

The estate sale was being held in front of Selma's town center. Upon our arrival, we were given a flyer which listed the slaves who would be auctioned off. The female slaves were listed separately from the males with their approximate ages. The information on the flyer indicated whether the slave was a house slave or field slave. I immediately started scanning the list to see who had household experience. After reviewing the flyer, I found there were five females and one male listed as having household experience.

Before the auction started, we were joined by my brother, Dent, who drove to Selma from my father's plantation in Cahaba. Dent is my oldest brother whom my father had made overseer of his Cahaba plantation when he purchased our new six-hundred-acre Twin Oaks Plantation in Autauga County. Dent informed us the auction was due to the death of Jack Thompson, who died suddenly and left everything to his wife, Charlotte, as his only heir.

According to Dent, the Thompsons had tried unsuccessfully for years to have children, but because of medical problems were unable to. Mrs. Thompson decided she no longer wanted to live on a plantation. She decided to sell the plantation, equipment, and all her slaves and move back to Atlanta where her relatives lived. She was known in the Selma area as being a gentle and kind lady to her slaves. Her guidelines for the sale included the stipulation that members of a family had to be sold together.

Dent knew we were looking for a replacement for Mamie. He had personally talked to the auctioneer and found there was a mulatto, age 36, named Mattie, who had worked as Mrs. Thompson's head household slave.

"From what I can find out, she is a very good cook and has good communication skills," he said.

"That sounds good to me," I replied.

"Yep, that's good, but there is a problem if you want Mattie as Mamie's replacement."

"What are you saying, Dent?"

"Mattie has a fifteen-year-old daughter who looks white. The auctioneer tells me she could pass as a white girl any day. She is beautiful and smart also," he said, smiling.

My father looked at me with a big smile on his face and said, "What are you thinking, Obadiah?"

I've always thought I was a quick thinker, but this was a situation I hadn't dreamt of happening. Even if I thought Mattie was the right one to replace Mamie, would my father be willing to buy both of them? I knew the price for mulattos was much higher than a pure black slave.

I looked at father and said, "If Mattie is the one to replace Mamie, are you going to be willing to buy her daughter as well?"

My father looked directly into my eyes and said, "Obadiah, it's your twenty-first birthday. If Mattie is the one you want to replace our Mamie, then so be it if I have to pay double to get her daughter. We could use another female servant."

I began to breathe normally again.

Just as we were ending our conversation about Mattie and her daughter, a caravan of wagons started arriving in front of the town hall building. The wagons were full of slaves. The male slaves had chains around their ankles. I assumed the purpose of the chains was to reassure everyone that the slaves wouldn't run away. I immediately spotted Mattie and her daughter. They were in a wagon with all the female slaves. Dent was right; Mattie was a good-looking woman, but her daughter was simply beautiful. For a fifteen-year-old, she was very mature in appearance. She was about 5 feet 5 inches, slim like her mother, and her hair was braided. She and Mattie were wearing full-length dresses made of coarse white material. Their clothes were clean. One could see that Mrs. Thompson cared about her household servants.

The auctioneer informed all potential buyers he would auction the female slaves first. Mrs. Thompson was seated in a chair near the auctioneer. She insisted she be seated where she could see who was buying her slaves and to make sure none of the slaves' families were split up and sold separately. The auctioneer started with Mattie and her daughter. They stood hand-in-hand on the platform when the auctioneer read off a list of personal information describing each of them.

He put his hand on Mattie's shoulder and said, "This here is Mattie. She is thirty-six years old; we have the official papers on her. She has been Mrs. Thompson's main household servant for several years. She works hard and is skilled in cooking, washing, ironing, sewing, and other important chores around the house. She has no signs of ever being flogged or severely punished. She is in perfect shape."

Then, he turned to Mattie's daughter and touched her on the shoulder. "This here is Penelope. She is Mattie's daughter. She's been in the Thompson's household since she was born. She is now fifteen years old and like her mother, she is a hard worker. She is every bit as good in her domestic skills as her mother. We have her official papers as well. Mrs. Thompson says they must be sold together."

As soon as he finished reading the personal information, a gentleman who introduced himself as Samuel Bishop from Haynesville, Lowndes County, Alabama, stepped forward and requested permission to examine both Mattie and Penelope.

This request was not uncommon during a slave sell. The auctioneer gave him the right to come forward and take a close look at both women. He first looked into the mouth of Mattie. It reminded me of stories my father told me about how slaves were compared to horses and cows. The buyer opened their mouths to count the number of teeth missing or the condition of the teeth. One could tell this didn't sit well with Mattie but she spoke not one word. He then did the same to Penelope. With his hands, he began to touch her body in inappropriate places. It was at this time I realized the general good will I felt for people could be offset in a minute with an angry passion to kill. I wanted to kill this guy.

My father looked at me and shook his head. He knew how much this was bothering me but didn't want me to create a scene. If this Mr. Bishop wanted Mattie and Penelope stripped, I would have to make my move upon him. I couldn't help myself. This was cruel and inexcusable. Fortunately for his sake, as well as Mattie's, Penelope's, and mine, he didn't request them to be stripped.

He stepped back and said, "Let the bidding begin."

Dent leaned forward and whispered to my father and me. "Father, you can't let that man buy Mattie and Penelope. He practices selective breeding on his plantation. He makes big money yearly by taking young slave girls like Penelope and using them for breeding purposes. Light complexion mulattos like Mattie and Penelope bring a lot of money on the open market."

I had heard about plantation owners in the Deep South practicing selective breeding but never dreamed I would actually see one of these devils. What kind of people would engage in such a heartless and hideous practice? I think my father was as outraged as I was. He turned to me and said, "Obadiah, let's wait and see where the bidding starts."

"I'll give you $1,200 for the both of them," Mr. Bishop shouted.

My father looked at me and said, "Bid $1,300." I tried to open my mouth but I was speechless. I was so mad at Mr. Bishop that I wanted to kill him. Finally, I cleared my throat and the auctioneer took that as a bid.

He looked directly at me and said, "What is your bid, young man?"

"I bid $1,300."

Mr. Bishop turned and looked at me with a grim look as though he could pounce upon me at anytime. The auctioneer asked, "Who will give me $1,400?" Mr. Bishop tipped his hat.

"Who will give me $1,500?"

I looked at my father again and he nodded it was okay for me to bid $1,500. I made the agreement nod with my head and the auctioneer said, "I got $1,500; who will give me $1,600?"

Mr. Bishop tipped his hat again and the auctioneer said, "I got $1,600. Who will give me $1,700?"

I didn't think my father would go any higher. I looked at him, but he nodded yes. This time I didn't nod; I spoke. "I'll give you $1,700." Mr. Bishop must have thought that regardless of what he bid, he was not going to get Mattie and Penelope.

The auctioneer said, "Who will give me $1,800?"

Mr. Bishop looked at me, and I looked back at him with a hypocritical smile, I might add.

The auctioneer said, "$1,700 going once, twice, and three times, sold." He pointed at me and said, "Sold to?"

I said, "Obadiah Bradford from Autauga County, Alabama."

"Thank you, Mr. Bradford. You will need to report to that desk right over there when you are ready to settle up."

"Yes sir."

As I glanced toward Mattie and Penelope, they were staring at me. A law officer escorted them to our wagon to await the trip back to Autauga County. I turned to my father and Dent and smiled.

My father smiled back and said, "You did well, Obadiah."

I looked at my father and asked, "Do you have money for the other slaves?"

He smiled again and said, "I have money!"

My father bought four strong male slaves who averaged twenty years of age. One of the slaves was a young man named Hank. He was the same age as me. He was tall, solidly built, and looked in perfect health. The male slaves cost my father $3,000, so we walked away from the estate auction spending a total of $4,700.

We said goodbye to Dent as we started across the street from town hall where Bill had been waiting with our carriage. As I was getting in the carriage, I felt someone tugging on my arm. I looked around and a young boy handed me a folded note and quickly ran away. I opened the note and read its contents.

> *August 17, 1853*
> *Dearest Obadiah Bradford:*
> *You made me proud today when you stood your ground with that devil, Mr. Bishop. I was praying hard he wouldn't outbid you for my special Mattie and Penelope. I saw compassion in both your eyes and face today. I know now my slaves will have a good home with their new master in Autauga County. May God be with you and bless you. Thank you for this good deed you did today.*
> *Sincerely,*
> *Mrs. Charlotte Thompson*

It had been a long day and my stomach felt hollow inside. I knew if I was hungry, father and our new slaves must be hungry as well. We stopped at a general merchandise store and my father bought food and drink for everyone. After we left Selma, we stopped under a big oak tree and ate our supper before heading home to Twin Oaks. It had been some time since I had watched a slave eat. They put a lot of food in their mouth at one time. It was like they hadn't eaten in days. Maybe they hadn't as far as I knew. When I handed Mattie her food, she said in a polite manner, "Thank you, Massa."

"You're welcome!"

Then I handed Penelope her food. She gracefully accepted and said, "Thank you, Massa," with her soft-spoken voice. It was then I first noticed Penelope's beautiful blue eyes. I just stood there gazing into them. I know she must have thought I was crazy. This was a first for me. I had never in my life seen anyone with any black blood flowing through their veins with blue eyes.

CHAPTER 3

O n our trip home to Twin Oaks, my father reached into his coat pocket and pulled out a legal document and handed it to me. "Son, I have a birthday gift for you. You may look at it now."

I slowly unfolded the document and began to read. The document named me the legal owner of Mattie and Penelope. I had no idea Father was going to give me ownership of Mattie and Penelope. I looked at him in surprise and asked, "Father, why did you do this? I mean, why would you do this?"

"Obadiah, your mother and I agreed that Mamie's replacement should be your choice, and she should be the first slave you owned. We didn't realize you would be getting a bonus slave along with her. When I closed the deal with the auction bookkeeper, I had him put you as the owner of both Mattie and Penelope. No one can ever punish them or buy them without your consent. You will be in full control of your slaves. Someday when I die, you will inherit part of my wealth and you will own more slaves, but today, you start with two. This is your mother's and my birthday gift to you. You are now a slaveholder, and I know you will do right by Mattie and Penelope."

I had just received the greatest surprise of my life. I never dreamed I would become a slaveholder this way. What had I done to gain this sign of respect from my parents? How could I ever repay them for such generosity? I had prayed that someday when I did officially become a slaveholder, God would give me the grace to treat my slaves with kindness and respect, just as my parents had always done over the years. I didn't dream it would be this soon. I knew in my heart, I would certainly be a good master to both Mattie and Penelope.

It was around 8:30 p.m., already dark, when we drove up to Twin Oaks. My mother, Sarah, and Miss Betsy, our other house slave, were all sitting on the front porch anxiously awaiting our arrival. They had been on pins and needles since mid-afternoon. Bill, our faithful driver, stopped the carriage in front of the steps leading up to the porch. The wagon carrying Mattie, Penelope, and the four male slaves pulled up behind the carriage. My mother and Sarah met us at the top of the stairs.

"We had begun to think you were staying over in Selma," my mother said.

"We got a late start home," Father replied.

"Well, can we take a look at Mamie's replacement?" Mother asked.

"You surely may," Father replied.

"Why don't you have George bring them on the front porch? It's lighter on the porch," Mother said.

As Mattie and Penelope made their way up the steps, my mother said, "My Lord, James, who's the white girl?"

My father and I looked at each other and smiled. "I will explain later, but first, let me introduce Mamie's replacement to you. This is Mattie and her daughter, Penelope," Father said.

"Welcome to Twin Oaks, the Bradford plantation, your new home," Mother said.

Both Mattie and Penelope gracefully said, "Thank you, Missus."

My mother turned to my father and me and gave us that look of approval. We both knew by her body language, she approved of our choice for Mamie's replacement.

My father turned to George and Bill and said, "Take the male slaves to the bunk house. Give them something to eat and drink. George, I'm placing you in charge of them tonight. Make sure they don't run away."

"Yes Sir, Massa Bradford; I's takes care of everything," George said.

"Catherine, what do you suggest we do with Mattie and Penelope tonight?" Father asked.

"Let's take them back to Mamie's room. We have one bed; however, it's big enough for two people. Maybe they can sleep together," Mother said.

After entering the room, my mother turned to Mattie and asked, "Can you two sleep together?"

Mattie said, "We been sleeping together since my Penelope was born. We don't mind sleeping together."

"Okay, that solves that problem. Betsy, take Mattie and Penelope to the kitchen and give them some food and drink," Mother said.

"Yes, Missus Bradford," Betsy said.

After everyone was settled in, I went to the bunk house to see how George was coming along with the new slaves. George was one of our most trusted slaves. Since boyhood, George had been my dearest friend. He taught me to hunt and fish. He taught me how to ride my first horse and helped me understand the ways of the slaves. He's been like a family member to me, my sisters, and brothers. George has been a big part of our lives for twenty-five years.

My father and brother John placed a lot of responsibility on George. When John leaves the plantation in the afternoon for his home in Prattville, he leaves George in charge. George is John's foreman, you might say. We have never had a runaway on George's watch. George is very talented. He can shoe horses, run a gin, and repair leather, bridles, harnesses, and all sorts of other things. I don't know anything he can't do. He's married to Minnie, and they have four children: two boys and two girls. The oldest is Tom, who is sixteen, followed by Abby, fourteen, Ben who is ten, and Joe who is eight. Minnie and the four children are good field workers. George and his family live in a two-room slave house near the bunk house. There are several married couples who live in slave houses at Twin Oaks.

I really wanted to see how our new slave, Hank, was responding to his new home. According to his legal papers, Hank was twenty-one years old, my age. I would guess he was about six feet tall and weighed around one hundred and seventy pounds. When he was sold on the block in Selma, he made no sounds nor acted up when plantation owners looked into his mouth and went through their humiliating rituals before bidding. Hank just stood there with his ankle rings on and didn't make a move.

My father had the bunk house built after he bought Twin Oaks. He was a very smart business man, one who put a lot of thought into what he did. His philosophy on building the bunk house was that it was best for all the unmarried male slaves to stay together. He believed it was more economically sound to have one building dedicated to the unmarried male slaves than trying to provide several small houses. Also, it would be much easier to supervise the male slaves in one location.

The bunk house was built to accommodate at least thirty male slaves. My father believed slaves performed better work if they had bunks to sleep on, rather than having to sleep on hard wood floors or on the ground, which was a common practice on plantations across the South.

The bunk house had a big pot belly stove in the middle of the floor with bunk beds built around the sides. There were windows put in for ventilation and two doors. To the left and right of the stove, there were several wooden tables with long benches for the slaves to have a place to eat. It was a pretty good setup for the slaves. My father assigned older men and women slaves, who were past field-laboring years, the duties of cooking, and mending and washing clothes.

My father ran his plantation differently from most plantation owners. Most owners insisted that their slaves prepare their own meals for both breakfast and supper. On most plantations, slaves had to get up early and prepare their breakfast meal. They would take their breakfast with them to the field. The slave's day started when it was light enough to work. They would work until 9:00 or 10:00 in the morning. At this time, the overseer would give them a fifteen minute break to eat their breakfast. Whenever the overseer sounded his horn, the slaves would stop wherever they were working and eat their breakfast. The breakfast meal on most plantations consisted mostly of cornbread with water. Sometimes a little molasses was added to give the cornbread a better taste.

Our slaves were not required to cook their own breakfast or supper, however. From the bunk house, Mr. John and others would prepare the breakfast meal, which was sent to the field around ten o'clock in the morning. The supper meal came when the slaves returned to the bunkhouse around 8:00 p.m. or after, depending on the season. A slave's supper meal on our plantation might consist of cornbread, hominy, potatoes, rice, meat when possible, molasses, salt, and soups. The content of a slave meal depended on what seasonal crop was being grown.

As I entered the bunk house, I spotted Hank and the other three new slaves still seated at a table. As I approached the table, I had goose bumps run up my spine. I guess I was a little nervous. I sat down across from Hank and the other three and introduced myself. I welcomed them to our plantation and explained the plantation procedures to them. I explained that George was here to help them and along with my brother John, the overseer, they would be in good hands. I asked them if they understood what I was talking about. They all looked at me as if they didn't understand what I was saying.

Finally, Hank said, "Massa, we's understands."

I asked Hank what he liked to do when he wasn't working in the fields.

He said, "Massa, I's likes to fish."

"I like to fish, too," I said. "Maybe we could go fishing sometime together." I noticed that all of the slaves looked at each other as if thinking who is this Massa that would take a slave fishing with him?

I didn't tarry long with the new slaves. My whole objective was to let them know who I was and that I wanted to be their friend, not their enemy.

The next few weeks went well. I enjoyed getting to know our new slaves and took Hank fishing a few times. He was a good fisherman. I enjoyed being with him and teaching him to read. He was smart and caught on fast.

It didn't take Hank long before he felt comfortable being around me. He enjoyed riding horses as well. On our fishing trips to the Autauga River, we enjoyed racing our horses coming home. He was a good horseman as well. In a short period of time, I had made a good friend. I felt Hank's devotion to me was more out of friendship than obligation. I was careful not to be too bossy.

CHAPTER 4

A few weeks after my twenty-first birthday, I awoke early to the smell of fresh bacon coming from the kitchen. I loved bacon and enjoyed fried eggs and bacon with some of Mamie's hot biscuits, butter, molasses, and cold milk. Betsy was a good cook, but she wasn't as good as our Mamie.

As I entered the dining room, I could see Mattie, Betsy, and Penelope in the kitchen. They were putting the final touches to our breakfast.

As I sat down, Mother said, "Good morning, Obadiah."

I replied, "Good morning."

"Now, I want y'all to be extra nice to Betsy, Mattie, and Penelope this morning. They have been working really hard on our breakfast. Say something nice after you eat." Mother went to the kitchen door and told Betsy we were ready. The three of them came in the room carrying bowls and platters of food.

My mother had found some of my sisters' dresses, and Mattie and Penelope looked really good in them. Mother never threw anything away. She said, "You can never tell when someone might need these dresses."

The dresses fit really well on both of them. Penelope entered the dining area with hot biscuits and white gravy. Breakfast is my favorite meal. I love biscuits with lots of white gravy. She carefully placed the biscuits and gravy on the table and returned to the kitchen. The breakfast meal was wonderful. Since the biscuits were so good, I asked, "Who made the biscuits?"

Betsy turned and said, "Mattie made them biscuits."

I said, "Mattie, these biscuits are the best biscuits I've ever eaten."

"Thanks, Massa Obadiah. I mean to please."

My father, who likes his eggs scrambled, asked, "Who's responsible for these eggs?"

Betsy said, "That be Penelope, Massa."

"Well, Penelope, those were the best eggs I've ever eaten. You did a good job."

"Thanks, Massa Bradford," Penelope said as she left the room to get some milk. My father and I like milk with our breakfast. My father also likes coffee, but for some reason, I've just not taken a liking to coffee.

My long-term goal was to become a medical doctor. Today, I would be starting to learn some medical procedures under Dr. John Banister's guidance. He informed me last week that he would be letting me do some stethoscope examinations, suturing procedures, bandaging, and some diagnoses. Of course, my diagnoses would not be conclusive; he would follow-up to confirm my diagnoses before any treatment would begin. I had learned so much from being Dr. Banister's apprentice and felt I was ready for this new experience in my life. It would take me another year or so to complete my course of study under his directions and then off to Augusta, Georgia, for additional schooling and training at the Georgia Medical College. I longed for the day I would pass my state boards and be addressed as "Dr. Obadiah Bradford."

After breakfast, I went to the stables where George was waiting with my horse, General. My father gave me General on my eighteenth birthday. He and I have been close companions ever since. This morning I would be riding General to Dr. Banister's in Prattville.

As I rode down the long dusty road toward Prattville, I looked toward the cotton field where our slaves were picking cotton. I stopped General and watched them carry their baskets full of cotton to the wagon. They dumped the cotton in the wagon and returned to the field.

Before I left the cotton field, I spotted Hank, our new slave that father purchased in Selma, and now my good friend. I motioned for him to come over and talk. He was hesitant at first but then walked across the cotton rows where I had stopped.

"Good morning, Hank," I said.

"Good morning, Massa Obadiah."

"How are things going for you on this blistering hot day?"

"I's just fine, Massa Obadiah!"

"Hank, I would like for you to go fishing with me on Sunday afternoon. Would you like that?"

"I love to go fishing, Massa Obadiah. Thank you, Massa Obadiah!"

"You're welcome! I'll see you Sunday afternoon," I said as Hank went back to picking.

Hank and I had already spent several hours with each other fishing and reading. He was so eager to learn. He craved knowledge and was always asking questions when we were sitting on the bank of the Autauga River fishing. A lot of Hank's questions were related to the Bible. The last time we went fishing together, Hank asked me a question that I've not been able to get off my mind. He asked, "Massa Obadiah, will there be black folks in Heaven?"

My answer to him was, "Certainly there will be black folks in Heaven. Why did you ask that question?"

"I's just wondering since we's slaves, and we's black, and we's owned by white people, I thought maybe they was the only ones to go to Heaven."

When we returned to the plantation, I got my Bible and read some scriptures to Hank regarding Jesus Christ, and how one could receive salvation. I wanted him to know who Jesus Christ was, and Christ's purpose in coming to earth. Since Hank had just started reading, I felt it was best I read and explained some of the scriptures to him. I couldn't forgive myself if I neglected his question, and he died not knowing Jesus Christ as his savior. After reading him several verses relating to salvation, I asked him if he understood.

He said, "Yessum, Massa Obadiah, I believes I's do."

I explained to him that salvation was free and was a gift to all mankind who confessed their sins and asked Jesus Christ to come into their hearts as Savior and Lord. I asked him if he wanted to be saved.

"I do, Massa Obadiah!"

I prayed the believer's prayer with Hank asking him to repeat the words after me. After we finished, I asked him if he believed what he prayed. He said, "Yes, Massa, I believe."

"That's all you have to do, Hank. Welcome to God's family."

I rejoiced with him about his new experience, and told him that he should work hard on his reading so he could clearly understand God's words, and maybe someday be able to lead several people to Jesus Christ.

He said, "I's going to work hard, Massa Obadiah."

What troubled me most was Hank's thinking that only white people could go to Heaven. We allow them to have their own service on Sunday morning in our barn but do they know God's word? One time, when I was about sixteen, I attended one of their song services. I really enjoyed hearing them sing. They sing with their hearts and appear to feel every minute of it. I did hear one man pray. I thought he did well in his prayer. I'm hoping in time, Hank's reading ability improves so he can share the Bible with other slaves.

Since I didn't have many more days at home before I left for Augusta, I decided to spend more time with Hank. I also decided to see if Sarah might have some additional time she could spend with Hank, Mattie, and Penelope on their reading and writing. Between the two of us, we could get more accomplished.

After Hank went back to his picking, I looked out over the vast field of cotton and counted my blessings. We had some of the most fertile soil in Autauga County. The ground was just right to raise cotton. None of our slaves were exempted from picking cotton. Every able-bodied man, woman, and child was involved in picking. Babies were looked after by a younger sibling who was not old enough to pick. On some plantations, the mothers of babies were limited to the amount of time they could stop for nursing. If they tarried too long, the overseer might flog them. Flogging was not permitted on our plantation, however.

Soon after arriving at Dr. Banister's, we were summoned to two plantations. These plantations were owned and operated by some of the strictest slaveholders in Autauga County. The owner

21

of the first plantation was Mr. Justin Rogers. He owned a three-hundred-acre plantation just southwest of Independence.

Upon our arrival, we were greeted by the overseer, Matt Willington, one of the meanest overseers in Autauga County. He met us at our carriage as we pulled up in front of the plantation house. He said, "Doc, I need you to take a look at one of my male slaves. He fell out of a wagon and two of his jaw teeth have been knocked out. He has a nasty hole in his left jaw. We can't seem to stop the bleeding. I'm afraid he's going to bleed to death."

"Where is your slave?" Dr. Banister asked.

"He's in the barn right now. I had him put there after the accident," Willington said.

Willington escorted us to the barn where I witnessed one of the most horrible sights of my life. The slave in question was about thirty years old. His name was Sam. He was very weak from all the blood he had lost. The left side of his jaw was torn opened. The wound was so large I could see other jaw teeth. It was apparent to me that Sam hadn't fallen out of a wagon; this slave had been hit with some kind of object.

Dr. Banister turned to me and said, "Obadiah, this is your first patient. Take a look at him and see what you think we need to do."

Sam was lying on the cold ground. I asked for a lamp for additional lighting. I also requested some hot water, towels, a dish pan, and some soap.

Willington turned to a slave nearby and said, "Go fetch some hot water, towels, soap, and a wash pan. Bring them here quickly."

I knelt by Sam's side to get a closer look at his wound. Every time I touched him, he flinched and shoved my hand away with his hand. He was delirious from the pain he was suffering. "I may need some assistance in holding him still," I said.

Willington ordered wrist restraints for Sam and ordered another slave to hold Sam's head still. Seeing Sam spread out with wrist chains reminded me of a picture I saw of Jesus Christ nailed to the cross. I knew the restraints were cruel but necessary for me to examine and repair the damage to his jaw. After cleaning the wound with a disinfectant, I discovered two upper jaw teeth had been knocked out by some object. Whatever object was used, it did lots of damage.

I turned to Dr. Banister and said, "Doc, I believe Sam needs stitches both inside and outside. What do you think?"

Dr. Banister had been watching me clean Sam's wound and quickly agreed with my assessment.

He said, "Obadiah, you are right. He will need stitches. You know what to do." I knew what he meant. Still, this would be my first experience in suturing a wound.

Dr. Banister had been letting me practice on animals but never a human being. This would certainly be my first big challenge. With my scalpel, I removed torn skin from the inside of Sam's jaw. I removed a wooden splinter along with the torn skin. I was right; Sam had not fallen out of a wagon. He had been deliberately hit with a wooden object. I stitched his torn gums and the inside part of his jaw and then proceeded to stitch the outside part of the wound.

Sam was yelling all the time I was stitching. The pain, I'm sure, was awful, but I had no pain medicine to give him. I had to rely on the slave that Willington ordered to hold Sam's head while I worked on him.

After I finished, Dr. Banister said, "Let me take a look at what you've done."

He examined both the inside stitching as well as the outside and said, "Good job, Obadiah. Now bandage him up and we will be on our way."

Dr. Banister gave Willington instructions on how to care for the wounded slave and informed him we would be checking on him in a few days.

He said to Willington, "Your slave has lost a lot of blood. I can't tell you if he will live or die. What he needs is good attention for the next few days. Can you put him some place where it's more sanitary than this barn?"

Willington agreed to move Sam to a more sanitary slave house where he would receive food and water while he recuperated.

After leaving Mr. Roger's plantation, the incident was the main conversation between Dr. Banister and me. "Obadiah, I'm sorry to say, we cannot involve ourselves with slave holders and their slaves. We are not to discuss what we see or treat on these plantations. We are doctors and we cannot discuss our slave patients with anyone but their owners. What you saw today is just the beginning of what you will be seeing in the days to come. You won't like what you see, but you must live with it."

"These plantation owners have hired me to look after their slaves. I don't like what I see, and I don't like the cruel punishment that's administered to these poor creatures, but that's not my business. My job is to repair the damage when I can. So welcome, Obadiah, to the field of doctoring!"

Our next stop was the James Manning plantation. It was mid-afternoon when we arrived. The owner, Mr. Manning, was sitting on his front porch when we drove up. He came down the steps and said, "Good afternoon, Dr. Banister."

"Good afternoon," Dr. Banister replied.

"Who is this fine looking young man?" Manning asked.

"This is Obadiah Bradford, my assistant. He's doing an apprenticeship under me."

"Welcome to the Manning plantation, young man."

"I understand you have a slave that needs looking at?" Dr. Banister asked.

"I sure do; he's a mean one at that."

"He's been setting a bad example for my other slaves. He doesn't obey and runs away. Yesterday, we found him five miles from here hiding in the woods. We brought him back here and gave him a good flogging. We lined up all our slaves and made them watch. We wanted to put the fear of life in them. I bought Buck two months ago, and I've had nothing but trouble with him since. He's a free-spirited one. We've not been able to break his spirit by depriving him of food or putting him in the stocks. After yesterday's flogging, I believe he's not going to run away again. He's been pretty much out of it since he was flogged."

"Where is he?" Dr. Banister asked.

"He's in the barn," Manning said.

On the way to the barn, we passed a large oak tree with a rope still hanging over a limb. As we passed by, I noticed spots of dry blood on the ground. As I glanced down at the blood, I was reminded of the stories my father had told me about flogging. Some plantation owners had their overseers tie a slave's wrists together by a rope and lap it over a limb, pull the rope until the slave's toes barely touch the ground. The overseer would then take a six-foot-long cowhide whip and administer the punishment of flogging. Not only did the slave have to endure the pain from being stretched out, but the pain of the flogging as well. I can't imagine the pain the slave felt. Sometimes the slave died from loss of blood or infection from the flogging.

I remember asking my father how anyone could treat another human being this way. My father's answer was, "They don't consider a slave a human being."

As we entered the barn, we noticed Buck lying on the ground with a heavy iron chain attached to his neck yoke. The chain was attached to a barn post. He was lying on his side curled up, barely breathing. He also had ankle chains. Buck wasn't going anywhere. He was just about ready to meet his maker.

As Dr. Banister examined Buck's back, I could see the deep cuts in his back from the flogging. There was blood still oozing from the deep cuts.

"Obadiah, take my stethoscope and listen to Buck's breathing. Let me know what you hear," Dr. Banister said.

I knelt down by Buck and began to listen to his breathing, which was shallow and short. I could tell that Buck was in bad shape. I turned to Dr. Banister and said, "This man is in bad physical condition. I believe his heart is about to stop."

Dr. Banister took the stethoscope from me and examined Buck. He looked at me and said, "Obadiah, I agree with your assessment. What would you do for this man if you were the doctor?"

"First, I would move him from this dark dungeon of a place, clean him up, administer medicine to his wounds, give him medicine for his fever and try to get as much fluids and food into him as possible."

"That's exactly what I would recommend."

Dr. Banister turned to Mr. Manning and said, "Your slave is about dead. You've heard what Obadiah and I recommend. If you want to save him, he needs to be moved from this barn into a suitable, sanitary place and treated. What do you want us to do?"

"We will move him into a slave house with two of our elderly slaves. They can look after him," Manning said.

I was happy to hear that Manning wanted his slave to live. It would be a shame to see Buck lie there and die. He had to be strong to endure the awful pain of his flogging and the agony afterwards. After Buck was moved to a new location, he was placed on a bed made of boards and a straw mattress. It was better than the hard cold ground in the barn. Dr. Banister gave me the responsibility of cleaning Buck and treating his wounds. I stitched several of the deep wounds made by the cowhide whip. Buck was so weak he didn't yell out or try to fight me off. I administered an ointment to his wounds and bandaged those that looked infected. Buck's life was now in the hands of God. Only he could save him.

I had never seen anything like this before. It was so hard to keep my thoughts to myself. Before I left Buck's side, I said a silent prayer for him. I wanted him to live. I wanted him to find some kind of peace: the opportunity to settle down and find a woman he could love, have some children, and find some hope of a better life, one that was better than he currently was experiencing. Regardless of whether this ever occurred, I wanted him to have that opportunity. My prayer was that he would live, that he wouldn't run away again, and that he would follow Manning's orders.

Dr. Banister informed Manning that I would be coming by in a few days to see how Buck was doing and attending to his needs at that time. I didn't realize Dr. Banister was going to give me that responsibility.

As we left the Manning plantation, Dr. Banister said, "Obadiah, what you saw today was bad. I've seen lots of floggings; none has been pleasant. This one was one of the worst."

He related to me a story of an expectant slave woman who was flogged so badly that she died during the flogging. She was only a few days from giving birth. The overseer was so mad at her that he wouldn't stop the flogging. She, being pregnant, could not endure the pain. She just gave up the ghost. The owner of the plantation dismissed the overseer because not only did he kill a working slave, he also killed her child, which would have been a future slave.

I asked Dr. Banister if he knew why the overseer flogged the pregnant slave. He said, "I was told he was angered when she failed to bring him drinking water on time."

This story made me sick at my stomach. Who in their right mind would torture a pregnant woman to death? I decided from this day forward, I would pray earnestly for God to protect slaves against such awful punishment and ultimately to outlaw floggings altogether. This abomination must not stand!

"Obadiah, I believe you are ready to make some follow-up visits. Two days from now, you will need to jump on General and do these follow-ups. This will give me time to administer to the needs of others who are coming to my office. How do you feel about going out on your own?"

"I'm excited!" I said. I felt good about Dr. Banister's confidence in me and I would not let him down.

CHAPTER 5

Both slaves, Sam and Buck, survived their overseers' brutal punishments and went back to work in the fields. I was proud of Buck. He had not attempted to run away since I prayed over him. We got to be friends during my follow-up trips. Dr. Banister assigned me Tuesdays and Thursdays as follow-up days. I worked for him on Wednesdays in his office in Prattville. That left me free to do what I wanted to do on Mondays, Fridays, and the weekends. My knowledge of medicine was improving every day I spent with Dr. Banister. I felt good knowing Dr. Banister trusted me with the follow-ups.

On Saturday morning, my father and I went to Prattville to purchase a new gin for our plantation. One of our older gins bit the dust the previous day, after undergoing several repairs over the years. After my father consulted with Mr. Brogan, who repairs gins, he discovered the parts and labor cost would be about what the cost of a new gin would be. So Father decided it made more sense to buy a new gin than to fix the old one.

My father was a good friend of Mr. Daniel Pratt, the founder of Prattville. Mr. Pratt owned a gin factory in Prattville. Almost all the cotton plantation owners in Autauga County and surrounding counties bought their cotton gins from him.

I, too, liked Mr. Pratt. In fact, I've always been fascinated by his brilliant business mind and his efforts in making Prattville the most prosperous city in Central Alabama. Mr. Pratt was known throughout Central Alabama and the Deep South as one of the most progressive and industrious businessmen of his times. According to articles I've read, he was born in Temple, New Hampshire, migrated to Jones County, Georgia, and then came here to Autauga County sometime around 1833.

My father said he first settled on Mortar Creek where he later sold fifty gins that he had brought with him from Jones County, Georgia. He later leased a water power site on Autauga Creek near Washington, which was known as McNeil's Mill. It was there he started his business of making cotton gins. For the next five years, he produced an average of two hundred gins annually. In 1835, he purchased land from Joseph May and started the town of Prattville, which is now the home of Mr. Pratt and his cotton gin. Not only did Mr. Pratt own the cotton gin, he owned a flour mill, a wool factory, an iron foundry, a sash and blind factory, a lumber mill, and several other businesses.

The little town of Prattville suddenly became a growing and thriving town. Other businesses such as a horse mill factory, machine and blacksmith shops, a wagon manufactory, and a flouring mill found a home in Prattville. The sash, door, and blind factory supplied many fine quality materials for some of the finest homes in central and south Alabama.

While living in Jones County, Georgia, Mr. Pratt was involved in construction work. He was a skilled carpenter. He built several plantation homes which proved to be some of the best in the Deep South. One can easily see his architectural brilliance in his beautiful mansion in Prattville.

Another example of Mr. Pratt's construction skills was the Methodist Church in Prattville. He was personally responsible for the building at a cost of $20,000. This was a lot of money during this time period.

He became the largest plantation owner in Autauga County. At one time, he had over one hundred field slaves and fifty slaves working in his factories. He was good to his slaves. He fed them well, dressed them well, and built comfortable housing for them. He provided them with gardens so they could grow their own food. I believe this is where my father got his idea of letting our slaves make gardens. The slaves were well behaved and counted it a blessing to work for Mr. Pratt. In their way of thinking, factory work was much better than field work. They also enjoyed the comfortable homes and the access to plenty of food. Mr. Pratt's philosophy was, if slaves are happy and healthy, they will be more productive. If it took improving their way of life, he was more than willing to make that happen.

After a thirty-minute visit with Mr. Pratt, my father bought a new gin. The new gin had fifty gin saws which cost $3.50 each. As Father and I were leaving Mr. Pratt's office, he said to me, "Obadiah, with this new gin, we will be able to gin more cotton in a shorter period of time. I have a good feeling about this new gin. It should more than pay for itself in two years. I'm excited!"

After loading the new gin on the wagon, George headed back to our plantation with instructions to put the new gin in the barn. Father and I stayed in town to accept Mr. Pratt's generous offer to buy our lunch.

While eating lunch, two young ladies came into Pratt's restaurant. One was a blonde, and the other had black hair. I could tell they were not your ordinary Autauga County girls. I politely asked Mr. Pratt if he knew the two young ladies who were seated across the room from us. Mr. Pratt knew everyone. He and Mrs. Pratt sponsored several social events at the Prattville Town Center. Normally plantation owners and their families in and around Autauga County came to the socials. My parents were not big on socializing, however, and hadn't attended many socials.

"Obadiah, the blonde is Audrey Denton, the daughter of Frank Denton who owns a three-hundred-acre plantation east of here. Her friend is Betty Simpson, the daughter of Mr. Brad Simpson. Mr. Simpson owns a two-hundred-acre plantation that joins the Denton property."

I couldn't help myself. I continued to stare at them as they sat and giggled at their table. They were having a good time. I suppose they were in town doing some shopping. All at once, Audrey looked at me and smiled. I smiled back. I asked myself, should I go over and introduce myself? I decided to play it safe and keep my distance. I had never been out with a girl on a date previously, nor had I wanted to. Audrey Denton might just be my first date someday, I thought.

After lunch, Mr. Pratt paid for our lunch and we left the restaurant. As I was leaving, I looked over at Audrey to see if she was still looking at me. She was and again she smiled. I tipped my hat at her and returned her smile with one of my own.

Bill picked Father and me up in front of the restaurant. As we climbed into the carriage, I handed Bill half of my sandwich that I had ordered for lunch. I always looked for a way to reward Bill for the good job and dedication he gave to his duty as our family driver. He was really good at what he did. Whatever I did for him, he always said, "Thank you, Massa Obadiah."

On our way home my father kidded me about Audrey. "You liked that girl back there in the restaurant, didn't you?"

I smiled and said, "She was a looker."

He laughed out loud. "I was beginning to wonder if you were ever going to show an interest in girls," he said with a smile.

"To tell you the truth, Father, the two prettiest girls I've seen around here are our Penelope and that Miss Audrey Denton."

As soon as I mentioned Penelope's name, I saw a strange expression come over his face. I could tell I had struck a nerve.

"Obadiah, I've been a little worried about how you look at Penelope. Need I remind you that Penelope is a slave? She may look white, but she is still a Negro. If you've got any future plans wipe them out of your mind right now. She is your slave, and she must always remain your slave — nothing else. Do you understand?"

"I hear what you are saying, Father, and I would never do anything that would cause shame to come upon our family. You must know that."

I wanted to tell him about the strange feelings that come over me when I am near her, but decided against it and changed the subject.

"I've asked Sarah to spend some time with Mattie and Penelope to teach them reading and writing skills. I spoke with Mother, and she gave her blessings."

"That's okay with me, but make sure that no one outside this household knows that Sarah is teaching them to read. You make it clear to both Mattie and Penelope that they are not to mention this to any of the other slaves, you hear me?"

31

"Yes, I hear you, and I will speak to both Mattie and Penelope about this. I'm sure they will honor my wishes."

We arrived back at the plantation around 4:30 p.m. I went immediately to check on Hank who had been running a low-grade fever for the past few days. I had taken Hank fishing with me on Autauga Creek on Sunday. We had a good time together and caught several fish, which I had Betsy, Mattie, and Penelope fry for our supper. Since then, Hank had been running a fever. As I entered the bunk house, I found Hank lying on his side curled up in his bed. He was burning up with fever. He had the shakes as well. When I touched him, he woke up and said, "Massa Obadiah, I am so sick!"

I called for Big John who was our head cook at the bunk house. Big John came limping out of the kitchen and asked, "What's you need, Massa Obadiah?"

"How long has Hank been shaking this way?"

"He's been doing that all day long. I's tells George, and he said he would tell you once you got back from town."

"Go to the big house and tell Betsy to send me my medicine bag."

"Yasser, Massa Obadiah."

"You are going to be all right, Hank. You just hang in there," I said as I put another blanket on him. I sent another slave to fetch George. When Big John came back with my medicine bag, I instructed him to get a bucket of cold water and to bring me a dish pan and towel from the kitchen. As I was putting a cold pack on Hank's forehead, George entered the bunk house.

"What's you need, Massa Obadiah," he asked.

"Hank is very sick with a fever. I will need to isolate him from the other slaves in case he's contagious. Where do you suggest we put him?"

"The only place suitable for Hank would be Tom and Belle's place. They are up in age and don't work in the fields no more. I use them to help me out from time to time with sick folks. Their children are all married and live in their own houses. We'll put him there, Massa Obadiah," George replied.

"Belle will need to apply cold packs to his forehead and bathe him during the night. I want her to use rubbing alcohol on him about every four hours. I've given him some quinine. Oh, by the way, I want you to take some quinine, too. If Hank has malaria, you may be exposed as well. I'll check on him before I go to bed. Come get me if you think he's getting worse."

"Yasser, Massa Obadiah," George replied.

Some might think it's out of character for slaves to address a plantation owner or a son of a plantation owner by his first name, but that's the way I wanted it. I liked the name Obadiah and informed all our slaves to address me as Obadiah and my father as Master Bradford.

I returned to the big house and wrote Dr. Banister a note. I described Hank's symptoms and asked Dr. Banister to advise me how to treat Hank. I informed him I had given him quinine in case it was malaria. I instructed Bill to take the note to Dr. Banister in Prattville and to wait for his reply. I was hoping Hank's illness wasn't malaria. I had seen a few cases of malaria while tagging along with Dr. Banister to some of the plantations. Hank's symptoms were similar in nature. If he had malaria, we could have an epidemic on our hands. Hank could die as well as others who might contract the disease.

I knew malaria was a parasitic disease that involved high fever, shaking, chills, and flu-like symptoms. It is caused by bites from the anopheles mosquitoes. If it was malaria, quinine is about the only medicine available to treat the disease. I was thankful we had a good supply of quinine in stock at our house.

I arrived back at the house in time to wash up for dinner. Since I gave Bill half of my sandwich, I was getting rather hungry. Betsy, Mattie, and Penelope had fried chicken for supper. It smelled really good. We had potatoes, greens, and hominy along with cold milk and baked bread fresh from the oven. Over supper, I informed Father, Mother, and Sarah about Hank's illness. They all shared great concern for Hank's health. They knew he had become my new friend and wanted him to be healthy again. When I told Father it might be malaria, he became quite alarmed.

"Malaria!" Father screamed. "That could be really bad, Obadiah."

"Yes, sir, Hank could die."

"Is there anything we can do for him?" Sarah asked.

"I've handled that already. We've moved Hank to Tom and Belle's house. They will be taking care of him tonight. I'm going to check on him later tonight after Bill returns from Prattville."

"Why did you send Bill to Prattville?" Mother asked.

"I sent him with a note to get Dr. Banister's advice on what to do about Hank. I described Hank's symptoms in my note and am waiting to see what Dr. Banister says."

"That's a smart move, Obadiah," Father said.

"I may be up late tonight so don't worry about me," I said as I finished my dinner.

"Obadiah, I'm really concerned here. If Hank has malaria, we could have an epidemic on our hands. I've seen plantations wiped out from malaria."

"I think everyone in this house needs to take quinine this very minute," Mother said.

"I'm in agreement with that, Mother," I said. "In fact, I've already started taking it."

I could tell that my family was taking this news very seriously. If it was malaria, we would need to isolate everyone who might come down with it. Just as we finished dinner, Bill came in with Dr. Banister's reply to my note. He handed it to me.

I opened the note and began to read, "Obadiah, from what you have described in your note, I do believe that Hank has malaria. I've seen a few cases of malaria lately in my office. I believe it's beginning to hit our county. I would recommend that you, your family, and all of your slaves begin taking quinine immediately. Instruct your slaves to keep their doors and windows closed during the night and day. I know its hot weather but they need to keep those mosquitoes out of their homes. The mosquitoes don't like the hot sun so we're not concerned so much during the day. It's night we have to concern ourselves with. I know you are fond of Hank. I'll come over tomorrow morning and check him out. You take care of yourself, you hear?"

"There will be no sitting outside on the porch tonight," my father said as he got up from the table.

"If y'all will excuse me," I said. "I'll be going back to Tom and Belle's house to check on Hank."

Before I left, I went into the kitchen and gave Betsy, Mattie, and Penelope a dose of quinine. I took time to explain to them about the symptoms of malaria. "If any one of you feels feverish, let me know." When I gave Penelope her quinine, she made a horrible face. I laughed!

I looked at her with a smile and said, "Quinine isn't the best tasting stuff in the world, is it?"

She looked back at me, making eye-to-eye contact with her beautiful blue eyes and said, "No, Massa Obadiah!"

As I stood staring at her, that strange feeling came over me again. Changing the subject, I asked her how her reading and writing lessons were coming along. "Is my sister, Sarah, a good teacher?"

"Missus Sarah is a good teacher," she replied.

"That's good!" I said. "Penelope, I want you and your mother to learn to read and write. You will learn all about history, math, and other subjects. Education makes everything you do easier and more meaningful." I didn't know if they understood what I was saying, but Sarah had already told me how smart they were, and I had full confidence in my sister.

When I got to Tom and Belle's house, I found Belle attending to Hank. "How's he doing, Belle?" I asked.

"He's been out of his head, and he's still plenty hot."

"Belle, I want you to take this dose of quinine. You don't need to come down with malaria." I sat down by Hank and took his hand in mine.

"Hank, can you hear me?"

Hank opened his eyes. His eyes looked so weak. He looked at me, and with a whisper, he said, "Massa Obadiah, I's so sick!"

"You are going to get better, Hank. You must want to get better. I don't want you dying on me, you hear." He closed his eyes. I gave Belle instructions on what to do during the night. I turned to George and said, "If he was to die during the night, you come to the big house and let me know, you hear?"

"Yasser, Massa Obadiah, I understand."

I continued to hold Hank's hand while I prayed over him. I prayed that God would spare my new friend. I wanted to spend more time with Hank. He was a good man, and he and I had fun together. I asked God to let him live.

There are some slaves who would rather be dead than to be a slave all their lives. I don't think Hank felt that away, however. I would never mistreat him, nor let anyone else mistreat him. I would make sure he had a good home on our plantation. I had just the right girl picked out for him to marry. I wanted him to be able to marry and have children. I prayed God would let this happen.

It was late when I got back to the house. My mother was waiting up for me. "How's Hank doing, Obadiah?"

"He's still running a high fever. I just don't know if he's going to make it. He's in God's hands."

"Son, God can do what we can't do. If it's meant for Hank to live, God will see to it. I want you to know how much I love you and how much I appreciate your concern for our slaves. You are a good man, Obadiah Bradford. God takes care of those whom he loves. I have a good feeling that our merciful and loving God is going to let Hank live. I think he's going to bless Hank because of your sincere compassion toward him and our other slaves."

"Thank you, Mother! You have always been my inspiration, and I'm so thankful you have taught me about God's grace. This may come as a shock to you, and please don't tell Father, but I would free all of our slaves if I thought they would be better off. I hate to see slaves treated the way some plantation owners treat them. They are treated like animals — no respect whatsoever by overseers."

"Every time I think about freeing them, however, I ask myself how they could survive here in the Deep South. Most people don't even look at them as human beings. I'm afraid they would end up in a much worse situation than being a slave on the Bradford plantation. At least we care and provide for our slaves in a humane way. Someday, Mother, I will share with you some of the things Dr. Banister and I see on some of the other plantations. It would make you sick."

"Get you some rest, Obadiah. Just know I love you and appreciate what you do for our slaves. God has a real purpose for you in this cruel world. You have a special gift from God, and you are going to be one of the best doctors in the South. You just wait and see."

My mother is a compassionate person. She loves her children and grandchildren and is a good teacher of character. Her little pep talk meant more to me than any medicine I could ever take. She came over and gave me a big hug and said, "Go to bed, Obadiah; things are going to be all right. Things always look better in the morning."

CHAPTER 6

I slept very little during the night. I prayed for Hank over and over and wondered how he was doing. George hadn't come to the big house yet so I assumed Hank was still alive. I rose early, washed my face, dressed, and took off to Tom and Belle's house. I was greeted at the door by George.

"How is he?" I asked.

"He's still alive, Massa Obadiah."

I went into the room where Belle was still applying wet packs on his forehead. She looked up at me and smiled. "I think he's better, Massa Obadiah."

Hank opened his eyes and said, "Massa Obadiah, I's feeling much better."

"That's great!" I said. His eyes looked so much better. The fever had broken during the wee hours of the morning. I checked his breathing and to my surprise, he was breathing normally.

"Thank you, God" was all I could say.

"Belle, I will send someone to spell you. How do you feel?"

"I feels okay, Massa Obadiah."

"Belle, you and Mr. Tom go to the bunk house and tell Big John to give you some food. Come back here and I'll have George get someone to spell you later. You will need to show the person who takes your place what to do."

"Yasser, Massa Obadiah."

As Belle started to leave, she turned and said, "I prayed for Hank, too, Massa Obadiah."

I smiled at Belle and said, "Belle, thank you, I believe God heard both of us. I believe Hank is going to make it."

As Belle left, my thoughts turned to the time I attended one of the slaves singing services in our barn. I think I was about sixteen years old. I remembered hearing one of the male slaves praying at the end, but never heard any of the female slaves pray. I wondered how many of our female slaves, if any, prayed in church. I wondered how Belle prayed. I guess it didn't matter because I believe God heard her prayers.

What I did remember from the service was the singing. It was spiritually uplifting. It's like they go into some kind of trance. They made music from their hearts instead of musical instruments. The Spirit of the Lord was upon them. They seemed to experience great joy from their worshipping.

"George, fetch one of the other female slaves to spell Belle so she can get some rest. I'll stay with Hank until you get back with someone."

"Yasser," George replied.

"George, wait a second. I need for you to tell Master John to come to the big house. I need to see him."

"Yes, Master Obadiah."

Hank and I visited while I waited for Belle's replacement. It wasn't long before Pansy came in and said, "Mr. George asked me to come and take care of Hank so Belle could get her some rest."

"That's right, Pansy. Belle was up most of the night. She needs rest."

I left Belle's house feeling much better about Hank's condition. After returning to the big house, I washed my hands and joined Father, Mother, and Sarah for breakfast. I was hungry after a restless night. When Penelope put my plate in front of me, I smiled and dug in like a starving dog. Penelope seemed to sense I was hungry and placed a saucer with two additional biscuits and sausage in front of me.

"Thank you, Penelope!" I said.

Just as we were finishing breakfast, my brother, John, entered the dining area. "Good morning, everyone," he said as he laid his hat on a chair.

We returned John's greeting and Mother asked him if he had eaten breakfast. "Yes, I have, but I'll take a cup of coffee if you don't mind." Mother motioned for Penelope to get John a cup of coffee. She returned to the dining area with a tray that contained a small bowl of cream, sugar, and a pot of coffee.

Betsy, or someone, had taught her well. As she poured John's coffee, I noticed she poured it with elegance, like she had been doing it for years. "Thanks, Penelope!" John said with a smile. Penelope bowed slightly and left the room.

"Obadiah, George told me you wanted to see me."

"Did George tell you about Hank being sick?"

"What's wrong with that strong buck?"

"I think Hank has malaria. Dr. Banister is coming by this morning to check him, but I believe its malaria. I thought we were going to lose him last night."

"I've been missing that boy's cotton picking skills. He's a good worker, and we need him back in the fields."

"I'm afraid it's going to be awhile before he's ready to return. He's very weak right now. If he pulls through, it will take awhile before he can come back to work."

"Well, Obadiah, you're the doctor. Just let me know when he can return. I need to get out of here and go learn how to operate that new gin you and Father bought. You got any instructions, Father?"

"Yes, I do," Father said as he got up from the table and asked John to follow him to the parlor. I expected John to throw a fit about Hank's absence, but I was pleasantly surprised by his genuine concern for Hank and his attitude on the matter.

Dr. Banister arrived at our place mid-morning. He and I immediately went to see Hank. After Dr. Banister examined Hank, he said, "Obadiah, Hank does have malaria. You need to keep doing what you are currently doing. Keep him comfortable, make sure he gets his quinine, and get as much fluid down him as possible. I do believe he's no longer in danger of dying unless he has a relapse."

I informed Dr. Banister that I had started our slaves on quinine and ordered them to keep inside at night, keep their doors and windows closed, and do everything they could to protect themselves from getting bitten by the mosquitoes.

"You have done well, Obadiah," he said. "The mosquitoes are bad this year and there have been several cases of malaria in Autauga County. Some plantation owners have already lost some of their slaves.

After a week, Hank was again up and doing well. I cleared him for picking cotton, a decision which made my brother John happy. The week was a long one because we were fearful that others might come down with malaria. We were either lucky or blessed; Hank was the only slave we had to come down with the disease.

For the next several weeks, things went well. We had a larger than usual cotton crop, and the new gin played a major role in getting the cotton ginned and baled. After all the cotton had been harvested, our slaves spent several days clearing cotton stalks and storing them in the barn to be used as kindling for fires during the winter months. After the cotton crop, John utilized several of our men slaves in preparing the fields for winter wheat.

Several of our slaves were hired out to neighboring plantation owners to help prepare their land for next year's crops.

John used the money collected from the plantation owners to purchase corn and cotton seed for next year's planting. He also used some of the money to purchase shoes, clothing, and blankets to be distributed at Christmas to our slaves. We always distributed new shoes, clothing, and blankets at Christmas and during the month of July. Besides preparing our land for winter wheat, our slaves also cut firewood for the winter months. During the winter months, my father let our slaves work for some extra money to purchase things they wanted that we didn't supply. This freedom of working for money and ownership of the things they purchased made our slaves feel important. Some bought seed to be planted in their gardens during the spring. Having fresh vegetables made our slaves happy and healthy. Some of our slaves bought pigs. This meant raising their own corn crop to be used to fatten the pigs for hog killing days.

In late October, my father received a formal invitation from Daniel Pratt to attend a fall festival event at the town hall in Prattville. The event was to celebrate the end of the cotton harvest.

Mr. Pratt had been sponsoring this event for several years, but my parents had never attended. Much to my surprise, however, they decided to accept Mr. Pratt's invitation. This would be my chance to see Audrey Denton again. I had often wondered what she was doing, and on several occasions I gave serious consideration to riding General over to her plantation and asking her out on a date. But because of my lack of courage, I always ended up talking myself out of going. This time, I was hoping things would be different. I just might get enough courage to ask her to dance, I thought.

My father was right about my lack of interest in girls. I had not been much interested in girls until we purchased Penelope. I can't explain the feelings that come over me when I'm close to her. It's like she pulls me to her like gravity. My father would consider this lusting, but it's much more than that. It's more like genuine feelings for her. I long to be near her, although, I've never let myself be alone with her. I know my father is right when he said, "Penelope is a Negro. She will always be a Negro, and you have to accept that." Not acting on my feelings for Penelope is going to be one of the hardest challenges of my life.

Sometimes when I'm in bed, I wonder what I'm going to do about Penelope. I can't deny her a life without a family of her own, but right now, I don't want her to grow up and marry a black slave. In my heart, Penelope deserves more. She may be a Negro, but she looks white and white blood is running through her veins.

There have been times I've thought about doing what other slave owners do, and that is to have her as a concubine. Several slave owners, some whom I know, have slave girls on the side to satisfy their sexual desires. They sometimes have children by their slave girls. The wives of those slave owners are aware of their husbands' infidelity, and end up hating the slave girls. They treat them with no respect and make sure their lives are miserable.

The big day for the fall festival sponsored by Daniel Pratt finally arrived. Bill arrived in front of the house with the family carriage. He helped Mother and Sarah into the carriage, and Father and I followed. We were dressed in our best clothes. Because of a chill in the air, I was dressed in a black suit, white shirt, black bow tie, and a black southern gentleman's hat. I had never been this dressed up, previously. It fact, I felt a little uncomfortable.

My mother, sensing I was uncomfortable said, "Obadiah, you will be the best looking gentleman at the town hall tonight."

I smiled and said, "Thank you, Mother. With these fancy duds, I'd better be."

I know my mother was just trying to make me feel at ease. As we traveled on to Prattville, I began to reflect on what I might say and do when I saw Audrey Denton. Then it hit me. I just realized I was making plans on assumptions. I was assuming that Audrey would be in attendance and that she would be there with her parents. But what if she wasn't there, or what if she was there but with a date. I hadn't thought she might be attending the festivities with a date. *Gosh, what is wrong with me?* Clearly it was obvious that I had never had any prior experience with such matters. *What would I do?* I thought.

Bill stopped our carriage in front of town hall. It was too late to worry about this now. I would just have to deal with whatever might come. If Audrey wasn't there, I wouldn't have to worry about it. If she was there and wasn't with a date, that would make things a little easier to deal with.

We were greeted at the front door by Mr. and Mrs. Daniel Pratt. A lady standing near Mr. Pratt had a guest list in her hands. I saw Mr. Pratt look at her and say, "The Bradford's are here." She made a check mark by our names. This reinforced my opinion of Mr. Pratt being a wise and industrious man. He would have a record of every plantation owner who showed up at his party. *A wise move on his part,* I thought. We were told to help ourselves to food and drink and enjoy the music and dancing.

My father and mother were joined by friends from the Oak Hills Baptist Church, our home church. This left Sarah and me to fend for ourselves. I looked at Sarah and said, "Sister, may I have this dance?"

Sarah with her sweet and beautiful smile replied, "I would love to dance with you, Mr. Obadiah Bradford." So we danced. I used our dance as a time to gaze around the big room to see if I could spot Audrey Denton. Suddenly, I spotted her and her friend, Betty Simpson. They were with some other girls who were standing and chatting near the punch and food area. I didn't see any men folk near her. That is not to say she didn't have a date because there were several men my age in a group nearby. *Oh,* I thought, *how is this going to turn out? Why are things always so complicated? If I had only gone to see her those times I thought about going, I wouldn't be faced with this dilemma. I could just kick myself.*

After finishing the dance, Sarah and I made our way over to the punch bowl and helped ourselves to punch and food. As I was helping myself, I glanced toward Audrey; she and the other girls were looking at me. I smiled and tipped my hat. They giggled!

Sarah and I seated ourselves in two of the chairs lined up along the wall, not far from where Audrey and the other young ladies were standing. As we sat there, Audrey and Betty made their way over to get some punch. This was it. I had to move fast. I couldn't let this opportunity pass. All three of us arrived at the punch bowl at the same time.

"May I help you ladies to some punch?" I politely asked.

"Thank you," Audrey replied.

"I'm Obadiah Bradford."

"I know who you are, Mr. Bradford," she said with a smile.

"Have we met?"

"I'm afraid not, but I've seen you around town. Don't you work with Dr. Banister?"

"Yes, I do. I'm his apprentice or assistant."

"So, you want to be a doctor?"

"Yes I do!"

"My name is Audrey Denton, and this is my best friend, Betty Simpson."

Wow! This is going pretty well, I thought. "I'm pleased to meet you, ladies."

44

"Who is the beautiful young lady you are escorting," Audrey asked.

"Oh, that's my sister, Sarah."

"She beautiful," Betty Simpson said.

"Thank you," I said. I then turned my attention back to Audrey by asking her if she had a date.

She smiled and said, "No, I just came along with my parents hoping some nice looking gentleman would ask me to dance."

The music started up again and I was ready. "May I have this dance, Miss Audrey Denton?"

"I'd be honored, Mr. Bradford." We danced and as we danced, we talked the whole time. It was as though we had known each other forever. I looked over at Sarah and winked. She knew things were going well. In a few minutes, a tall, well-dressed gentleman introduced himself to Sarah, and they began dancing. I now felt better knowing my sister wasn't dying of boredom. She now had a nice looking gentleman leading her around the dance floor as though they had done it all their lives.

During the festivities, Audrey introduced her parents to me, and I introduced my family to Audrey and her parents. *Things are going about as well as they could,* I thought. I liked Audrey and had to find a way to ask her if I could see her again, this time on a date. While our parents visited with Mr. and Mrs. Pratt, I asked Audrey if I had her permission to come calling.

She smiled and said, "Obadiah, I would love that, but it's a practice in my family for the young man to ask my father for permission to come calling."

"I can do that. When could I speak with him?"

"Before we leave, I'll tell father you have something to ask him. I'm sure it's going to be fine," she said with a smile.

What if he says no, I thought. That would be very embarrassing.

The party had ended, and I saw Audrey talking with her father, as she motioned me over. As Audrey and her mother excused themselves, Mr. Denton turned to me and said, "Audrey tells me you want my permission to call on her. Is that right?"

"Yes, sir!" I replied.

"Then you have my permission, Mr. Bradford," he said as he shook my hand and said good night.

Audrey was already in the family carriage when she waved goodbye to me. I waved goodbye to her as well. I was excited. The night had gone well. I had fun dancing with Audrey. We were relaxed with each other. We had things in common, and we were never at a loss for words.

On our way back to the plantation, my father said, "Well, Obadiah, how did things go with that lovely Audrey Denton?"

"Quite well, I think," I said with a smile.

"Your mother and I sensed you were having a good time from all that dancing and talking you were doing."

"Yes, sir, Audrey surely isn't bashful when it comes to talking."

Before he could ask me another question, I said, "I was able to acquire Mr. Denton's permission to call on Audrey at their plantation."

"Well, now, that's my son," he said shaking his head in a gesture of his approval. The news certainly seemed to perk my father up a bit.

My father's attention turned to my sister, Sarah, which was a welcome change. It took the focus off me.

"Sarah, did you have fun tonight as well?"

"Yes, I did," she said as she smiled at me.

"I was impressed with that Jim Crawford."

"Me, too," Sarah replied.

"What kind of business is Crawford in?" Father asked.

"He works for Mr. Pratt. He moved here from Atlanta, Georgia, to be the financial manager of Mr. Pratt's industries," Sarah said.

"That sounds like he's well-educated," Father said.

"Yes, he's a graduate of Harvard University, in Cambridge, Massachusetts."

I looked at Father, and he was nodding his head with the same gesture of approval he had used with me.

"I have a strong hunch we will be seeing more of your Jim Crawford," Father said as Bill stopped our carriage at the front porch steps. I, for one, was thankful we had made it home. Father's questions were about to wear me out.

CHAPTER 7

The winter of 1854 was unusually cold and snowy in Autauga County, Alabama; nonetheless, I still enjoyed making plantation visits with Dr. Banister. Although the days were cold and sometimes wet, my desire to become a doctor was still my number one goal in life. It was during the winter of 1854 that I first witnessed horrible neglect of slaves on certain plantations. Pneumonia and common colds were the two most common sicknesses we treated. Both could have been avoided if only the plantation overseer and plantation owner had shown more respect and compassion toward their slaves.

On several occasions, we found slaves sleeping on cold, damp dirt floors with no blankets to keep them warm. The huts they lived in were no better than most chicken houses. Their clothes were torn and barely covered their bodies. They had become thin from lack of food. Their rations were limited to only enough corn and potatoes to keep them alive. They had no other food.

There is one story I must tell. It's something I hope I never witness again. But because I did, I'm reminded daily of it. It was so horrible, I sometimes have nightmares about what I saw. The incident occurred in the northern part of Autauga County on Mr. James Jones's plantation. Dr. Banister and I arrived about 10:00 a.m. The overseer took us to a hut where several male and female slaves were sick and lying together on a cold dirt floor. They were trying to keep warm by lying together, using their own body temperature to keep from freezing to death. It was spitting snow outside and the temperature had to be in the high twenties or low thirties. The hut had no light or fire. After entering the hut, Mr. Mason, the overseer, lit a lantern. We now could see the awful conditions. The slaves were moaning and shaking, too weak to sit or stand. Several were coughing repeatedly. Dr. Banister looked at me and shook his head in disgust.

"When was the last time these slaves ate," he asked Mason.

"We fed them this morning, but only a few of them ate."

"Do you want these slaves to die, Mr. Mason?"

"No, sir!"

"Well, you best get some food, water, and blankets down here right away. Some of these slaves are on their last mile," Dr. Banister said. "We need to build a fire right now. These poor slaves are going to die if you don't hurry and do something."

"I'll get some help," Mason said.

Dr. Banister instructed me to start examining the slaves with my stethoscope. He had taught me how to determine if someone had pneumonia or just a common cold. The first slave I listened to had pneumonia. I was about to call out to Dr. Banister when I saw him shaking his head.

"Obadiah, we have one who's already died. I'm going to move him away from the others. Please come and help me."

As I picked up his hands, they were so cold and stiff. It appeared to me he had frozen to death. We moved him aside and resumed our examinations. Out of the twelve, one person had died and a number of the eleven survivors had pneumonia. Some were so serious they might not make it.

Mr. Mason returned with potato soup, blankets, and hot water. One of his healthy slaves built a fire. Dr. Banister informed Mason that several of the slaves had pneumonia and were running high fevers. He told Mason they needed to be moved to a place where it was sanitary and warmer. Mason didn't like the news Dr. Banister was telling him.

"Mr. Jones doesn't want to show favoritism to these slaves. He wanted them to become strong and tough," Mason said.

That was the first time I had ever heard Dr. Banister swear. He looked at Mason and said, "Damn, Mason! Damn you and Jones. You are sitting on your asses and letting these poor people die right before your eyes. How can you do that? I'm having no part in this," Dr. Banister stomped his feet and started to leave.

"Dr. Banister, please wait. Let me go talk to Mr. Jones to see what he wants me to do."

"You go talk to Mr. Jones and tell him if he wants these eleven to live and work in his fields this spring, he'd better act fast."

I was so proud of Dr. Banister. That's what I wanted to do, but because I was not a doctor, I had to rely on Dr. Banister. He did well!

Dr. Banister and I heated water and cleaned some of the filth from the slaves' bodies. They had lain in their own feces. After consulting with each other, we agreed that six of the slaves, two women and four men, were in danger of dying from a combination of pneumonia and starvation. Treatment had to start now in a more sanitary setting. The other five, three males and two females were not as sick and might make it. They had not yet developed pneumonia.

Mr. Mason returned with the plantation owner, Mr. Jones. "What's going on here, Doc?" Jones asked.

Dr. Banister gave him a report of our findings and outlined a plan of action for Mr. Jones. "Unless you provide a sanitary and warm place for these slaves, you could very well lose all eleven. I don't think you want to do that," Dr. Banister said.

"What happened to Old Joe over there?" Mr. Jones asked.

"Your Old Joe probably died of pneumonia, but I imagine freezing to death and starvation could have played a role in it as well."

"Mason, go get a wagon. We will move these heathens to the first two slave houses near the barn."

"What do you want me to do with those slaves living there?"

"Tell them to go next door. They are all family up there. Tell them we will let them have their houses back once we get these heathens well."

I could barely keep my composure listening to Jones call his slaves heathens. He was certainly the heathen, not them.

"I'm going back to my house where it's warm. After you and Mr. Bradford finish here, come by the house and I'll give you something hot to drink," Jones said.

Mason transferred the sick slaves to houses with wood floors and fireplaces. At least fires could be built to keep them warm. There were makeshift beds with straw stuffing on the floors where the slaves were laid. Blankets and food were given to each slave. The slaves with pneumonia had to be fed. They were too weak to feed themselves. I found out later from Dr. Banister that losing slaves to neglect, especially during the cold winters, was nothing uncommon in these parts or the Deep South. If I hadn't seen it with my own eyes, however, I wouldn't have believed it.

Time was getting away, and we had one other stop to make on Sam Dillinger's plantation, which bordered Mr. Jones's place. Since we were running late, we decided to decline Mr. Jones's offer of something hot to drink and move on to our next assignment. Turning down Mr. Jones's offer didn't bother either of us in the least. We'd had about all of Jones and Mason we could stand for one day.

Upon arriving at Mr. Dillinger's plantation, he met us on the steps of his front porch. "Hello, Doc! I was about to give you up!" he said.

"It took longer at Mr. Jones's place than we had counted on," Dr. Banister replied.

"This cold weather sure is putting a hurt to my slaves. I've already lost one of my older slaves."

"How many do you have sick?" Dr. Banister asked.

"I believe we have about six at the present. I've been putting my sick slaves in the big slave house over there," he said, pointing to a slave house near his barn.

"Let's go take a look," Dr. Banister said.

As we entered the slave house, we noticed a fire was going in the fireplace. We found each slave lying on a mattress stuffed with straw. The straw mattresses were on wooden beds, and each slave was covered with a blanket. Mr. Dillinger's slaves were in far better shape than Mr. Jones's.

Dr. Banister and I started examining each slave. "Mr. Dillinger, you have two with pneumonia and four who are running high fevers. I would say they are close to having pneumonia. If we get lucky, we may be able to head off the pneumonia," said Dr. Banister.

"What do we need to do, Doc?" Dillinger asked.

"They need around-the-clock attention. I see you've already got some of your healthy slaves attending them. Have them apply this ointment twice a day and once at night. They will need to take this medicine three times a day. Give them lots of fluids and hot soups, keep them warm, and no work as long as they are running a fever. Is that clear?" Dr. Banister asked.

"Yes, sir!" Mr. Dillinger responded.

"Obadiah does my follow ups. He will be checking on your slaves in a couple days."

I arrived home exhausted from a full day's work. My mind and body were equally tired. I lay back in my chair as Mother came into the parlor.

"Obadiah, you look very tired, my son," she said.

"I'm very tired."

"I'll have Penelope fill the tub with hot water. What you need is a good soaking bath," she said as she left the room. I wanted to give Penelope time to get the bath ready so I took a few more minutes in my chair.

I was just about to doze off when my mother stuck her head in the parlor and said, "Obadiah, you need to get your bath while it's hot. I believe Penelope has it ready. You have about an hour before dinner."

I went to my room, undressed, put on my robe, and went to soak in my bath. The door to the bathroom was open and I could see Penelope stirring the water to make sure it was the right temperature. She had prepared my baths before and knew the temperature I liked.

"Penelope, is my bath ready?" I asked. Her back was to me and I startled her so that she hollered and jumped as she turned around.

She took a big breath, patted her chest and said, "Massa Obadiah, you scared me right out of my shoes."

"I didn't mean to, Penelope."

"Will that be all, Massa Obadiah?"

"That will be all for the moment."

She laid a towel and washcloth on the bench by the tub, and left the room.

The bath was just what I needed. It felt so good after being out in thirty degree weather. The hot water also removed the stench I had on me from helping clean up the slaves at Mr. Jones's plantation. I must have lain there for a good thirty minutes before I climbed out of the tub. I heard a shallow knock on the door and Penelope entered the room. I had not yet put my robe on and was standing by the tub naked.

"I am so sorry, Massa Obadiah."

"Please close the door, Penelope."

"Please don't beat me, Massa Obadiah," she said as she closed the door.

I put on my robe and said, "Penelope, I would never beat you. Whatever gave you that idea?"

Penelope stood there with her head down. I think she was embarrassed to see me in the nude and thought I would punish her for intruding.

"No, I'm not mad at you. It's my fault. I should have locked the door."

"Is there anything else I can do for you, Massa Obadiah?" she asked.

"Just make sure the tub gets cleaned before someone else needs a bath."

"Yes, Massa!"

At dinner, Father asked how my day had gone.

"It's been a very interesting day," I said as I looked at Penelope.

"Anything you want to share with us, Son."

"Not really! It's been a long cold day in Autauga County, and I'm mighty tired."

I wish I could have shared the horrible neglect I witnessed today at Mr. Jones's plantation. I was clearly aware of the ethics oath between a doctor and the plantation owner. Dr. Banister made me swear an oath that I wouldn't discuss the things we experienced on other plantations. I would certainly honor that oath.

Before leaving the room, Father handed me the Selma Times newspaper. "Today's paper carried a big article on the Kansas-Nebraska Act. Obadiah, read this article. I'm afraid what's happening in Kansas will eventually present major problems regarding slave issues in the South," Father said.

The article was entitled, "How Kansas is coping with the Kansas-Nebraska Act." The article spoke of different events leading up to the passage of the Kansas-Nebraska Act. In early 1854, Senator Stephen A. Douglas, a Democrat and U.S. Senator from Illinois, proposed the Kansas-Nebraska Act. The act was passed by the United States Congress and was set in play. The act gave new territories the right, by the vote of the people, to decide the question on slavery.

In the fall of 1854, Republicans won most of the northern states seats in the United States House of Representatives. The Republicans won sixty-six of ninety-one seats. Abraham Lincoln emerged as a Republican leader in Illinois.

The article went on to describe the bitter fighting in the Kansas Territory as pro-slavery men won a majority of seats in the legislature, expelling anti-slavery legislators, and adopting the pro-slavery Lecompton Constitution for the proposed state of Kansas.

My father had been following the Kansas-Nebraska issue closely in the Selma Times. Each time something was published in the newspaper about Kansas, he would shake his head and say, "You mark my words: these slavery issues in Kansas will eventually have an adverse effect on all slave owners in the Deep South."

Knowing my father was usually right about political issues, I felt compelled to keep up with what was happening. As I've said many times, "My father is a smart man."

I spent the rest of the week doing follow up assignments at different plantations. Much to my surprise, the slaves at Mr. Jones's plantation survived pneumonia and their bad colds. I was surprised also to see the slaves were able to get better quarters to sleep in. Half of Mr. Jones's big barn was converted into slave quarters. These quarters were much better than the hut where we first found them. I'm convinced they would have died, like Old Joe, had they remained in those conditions. I thank the Lord for bringing Mr. Jones to his senses. I don't know if it was my prayers or Mr. Jones's greed in knowing if those eleven slaves died he would be out a sizeable amount of money to replace them. Whatever it was, it was still a blessing from God. Mr. Dillinger's slaves also survived and returned to work.

It was now 1855. I would soon be going to Augusta, Georgia, to college. I had enjoyed my years of apprenticeship with Dr. Banister, but now I had to finish my medical course work and do a residency at a hospital in Augusta. After I completed those requirements, I would then need to pass Alabama and Georgia's medical boards to become a full-fledged doctor. I couldn't wait. Dr. Banister had already assured me that once I got my doctor's license, he wanted me to return to Prattville and be a partner in his office. That is what I wanted as well. I love Autauga County, and this is where I would like to practice medicine as my profession.

Meanwhile my courtship with Audrey Denton had been going pretty well. We saw each other at least two times a month and sometimes on special occasions in Prattville. I had been too busy to get serious about marriage. My goal was to become a doctor first and then think about marriage after that. I cared for Audrey, but didn't know if I cared for her in a way for her to become my wife.

I know my parents cared a lot about her. They thought she was the prettiest girl in Autauga County and would welcome her with open arms into our family should we decide to get married. I had resolved in my mind our courtship would continue, but only as time permitted. I had already discussed with Audrey what the next two years could do to our courtship, and she fully understood. We would have fewer opportunities to see each other. We would spend holidays together and make the best of the time we had together. This seemed to be agreeable to her.

The thing bothering me more than anything else was my feelings for Penelope. My sister, Sarah, and I had secretly discussed how gifted Penelope was in learning. She had blossomed into a beautiful young lady who was now seventeen years old. Her English and grammar were almost perfect. Sarah had taught her everything she knew. She couldn't teach her anything else. Sarah had a friend in Prattville who told her about a place in Boston, Massachusetts, which was a prep school for young ladies. It didn't matter whether they were black or white as long as someone could afford paying their room, board, and other expenses. Sarah thought it might be good if I could send Penelope to school in Boston.

Sarah and I shared many secrets growing up. She always knew I had certain feelings for Penelope. I had given the prep school lots of thought since Sarah approached me with the idea. Two years away from each other might do us both good. If I did send her away, how could I convince my parents and Mattie this was a good thing? My parents had become accustomed to another house slave, and Mattie was as happy as she could be that her daughter was receiving a good education right here at home.

Mattie felt safe working with a nice Southern family who cared for and treated her and Penelope like human beings. How could I convince her that sending Penelope away to school was best for her?

I would have to sign papers to show she is owned by me. But what happens if she gets in Boston and meets a nice white or black gentleman, falls in love, and wants to get married? What would I do then? This could really get complicated. I want her to receive the best education and social graces, but I could also see myself becoming jealous over her. Does this mean I'm in love with her? I believe it does. As I've said many times, I've never felt this way toward another woman. *Oh, what is the right thing to do?* I pondered.

Another week went by and I was about six weeks away from having to leave for Augusta. I had to make my mind up fast. Sarah had written to the prep school for information. The information had come, and I had read its contents several times. It felt right for Penelope. If I sent her there, I would have to take her by train to enroll. This didn't give me very long to make arrangements. I decided to start with my parents, since my father would have to come up with the money for Penelope's room, board, and schooling. My parents had never turned me down for anything, and I was hoping this wouldn't be the first.

As I entered the parlor, my parents were waiting for me.

"Obadiah, what is this you want to discuss?" my father asked.

"First of all, I want both of you to know how hard this is for me," I said as I leaned forward in my chair.

"Son, what's going on?" my mother asked.

"I want to send Penelope to a prep school in Boston." I saw both of them look at each other. I knew from the expression on their faces they were not totally surprised.

"I've given it a lot of thought. Sarah has taught her everything she knows. The prep school might be the next best step for Penelope. She will learn more there, and when she completes her schooling she will be coming back here. What do you think?" I asked.

To my surprise father said, "Son, I think this is a great idea. I'm surprised you hadn't thought of it sooner."

My mother looked at me and said, "Son, we, too, want the best for Penelope. She's grown into a lovely young lady and knowing you, you want the best for her. I'm all for your idea. Have you discussed this with Mattie and Penelope?"

"No, I've not. I wanted to talk to you and Father first. Father, I wasn't certain how you'd feel about paying Penelope's room, board, and schooling."

I could tell from my father's voice, he was more than ready for Penelope to go to the school. It just struck me. My folks were too agreeable to all of this. I now know they have known for some time of my attraction to Penelope. This would buy time for all of us if she wasn't around me. I had earlier shared my feelings for Penelope with my father, not knowing he would later share with my mother. Anyway, I was happy they were in agreement with me.

I left the parlor to meet with Mattie and Penelope. This wasn't going to be easy. Mattie and Penelope had never been away from each other. Although Mattie wanted better things for Penelope, the question was, would she be in favor of sending Penelope to Boston?

As I sat down at the little round table in their bedroom, I started emphasizing how much I appreciated both of them and the good work they were doing. I caught myself trying to postpone the subject at hand, trying to build up the nerve to tell them what my plans were. I finally said, "Mattie, I want to send Penelope to a prep school in Boston, Massachusetts. I believe this is what's best for Penelope. Sarah has taught her all she knows to teach her. The prep school will give her an opportunity to grow in social graces and appreciation of the fine arts. She will be exposed to things she could never learn here in Autauga County. How do you feel about my plans?"

Mattie looked at Penelope and Penelope started shaking her head. She didn't want to go.

"I don't want to go to that prep school. I want to stay here with Master and Missus Bradford and Mama," she said.

"Penelope, I know you want to stay here but believe me, this is best for you."

"How long will my baby be away from me?" Mattie asked.

"I'm thinking it would be at least one year and maybe two. Penelope will be able to come home for two weeks at Christmas."

"Master Obadiah, please don't make me go. I want to stay here with my mama," she cried.

This wasn't like anything I had expected from Penelope. This was the first time I had witnessed her crying. This was breaking my heart. What else could I do?

"Master Obadiah, let me and Penelope discuss this in private. I'll let you know something in a few minutes," Mattie said.

"Thanks, Mattie, I'll be in the kitchen when you get through."

"Before I go, I want to congratulate both of you on your English. I noticed that you now say Master Obadiah instead of Massa Obadiah. I like that and I believe you should address both my father and me as Master. That's the correct way to pronounce Master. Thank you! I'm proud of both of you."

"Thank you, Master Obadiah," Mattie said.

In a few minutes, Mattie and Penelope came to the kitchen.

Mattie said, "Master Obadiah, my Penelope wants to talk to you in private."

"That's fine, Penelope. Let's take a walk out back."

Penelope and I went out back and sat down on a bench in my mother's flower garden. I looked at Penelope and asked, "What did you and Mattie decide?"

"Mama wants me to go. She said it's best for me to go."

"I will make arrangements for you to go to Boston."

"Master Obadiah, I will miss my mama something awful. We've never been apart!"

"Penelope, I promise you I will see that you get home during the Christmas holidays."

"Master Obadiah, will you promise me you won't ever sell my mama to anyone. I want you to promise me that."

"Penelope, I swear before God, I will never sell Mattie. I will never sell you, either."

At this news, she spontaneously threw herself into my arms. I looked around to see if anyone was watching. Oh, how I longed for this moment. Oh, how I wanted to kiss her and hold her close to me. My passion for her led me to kiss her. I couldn't help myself. After kissing her, I felt her whole body trembling. It was like a certain weakness had come over her. She looked at me with those beautiful blue eyes and smiled. She just smiled and didn't say a word.

I knew then I had to send her away. If she stayed, the inevitable would happen. I had done something I shouldn't have done. I kissed the one and only girl who ever meant anything to me. I slowly released my grip on her and apologized. "I'm sorry, Penelope. That shouldn't have happened."

"Master Obadiah, please don't be sorry. I liked it."

She was so innocent. I realized right then I had made the right decision to send her to Boston. Her innocence and my passion for her would become one of our greatest challenges in our relationship, one which I wasn't prepared to deal with at this time.

How could we relinquish this feeling and desire for each other? Oh, God, what can I do?

CHAPTER 8

It took my father and me two weeks to make arrangements to get Penelope to Boston. Since I was the owner, I would accompany her to Boston and get her settled at the prep school. The trip to Boston would give me an opportunity to see what the school was like and to know for sure this was the place where Penelope needed to be. Since it was a boarding school, she would have a place to stay and healthy food to eat. Sarah had taught her to read and write, and if she needed something, she could write back home. I suspected the hardest thing she would deal with was getting homesick for her mama. I knew Mattie would certainly get homesick for her.

Saying goodbye to each other was so hard for both Mattie and Penelope. As we watched them on the front porch, tears streamed down both their faces. I wondered in my heart if I had made the right decision in sending her away. My head told me I had done the right thing, but my heart was telling me something else. If she stayed, something might happen that could put my family in a compromising position. My parents had placed a great deal of trust and faith in me to do right before God. I had to live up to their trust. I had become an adult, and I must act like one.

Penelope came over to where my parents, Sarah, and I were standing and said her goodbyes. "Master Bradford, Missus Bradford, I want to thank you for all you've done for me and my mama. You have treated us with the utmost respect, and I will never forget your kindness," she said as she reached out to shake my father's hand.

My father reached out his hand and gave her a gentle hand shake. She offered her hand to my mother as well, but being the wise and wonderful mother she is, she hugged Penelope and said, "Go in peace, my child, and may God bless you."

Mother handed Penelope a Bible to take with her to the prep school.

"Thank you, Missus Bradford. I will certainly read this Bible," Penelope said.

Penelope looked at Sarah and said, "Miss Sarah, I owe you so much. Thank you for teaching me to read and write. I'm going to make you proud of me in that prep school."

Sarah hugged her and said, "Penelope, you've been my best student. You have learned so much, and I'm already proud of you. Good luck in Boston. I know you are going to do well."

I was so proud of Penelope. She was not only beautiful but presented herself in a gracious manner in saying goodbye to my family. I've always known she was intelligent but how much, I didn't know. She was smart, and I knew she had learned many things from my mother and sister, Sarah. Mattie and Penelope had filled a big void in our lives after the death of Mamie. They stepped right in and fulfilled Mamie's duties and responsibilities in a very effective and respectful way. Mamie would have been happy with her replacements.

I knew my parents would miss Penelope, but they would still have Mattie and Betsy to look after them. I would put Mattie and Betsy up against any maid servants in Autauga County. I know without any doubt, they were the best cooks. Mattie was a beautiful lady as well, and I had resolved in my mind that not so long in the future, I would try to find her a nice man to marry.

I needed to pay my brother Dent a visit. He recently acquired, through a trade deal, a new and handsome slave who Dent said is about the same age as Mattie. Furthermore, according to Dent, the slave was a hard worker and a good man. I also wanted to look at one of Dent's slave girls who just turned seventeen. She might be a good wife for my friend Hank. *Here I go being a matchmaker,* I thought.

Bill brought our carriage around to the front steps. He loaded our baggage, and Penelope and I were off to catch the train in Selma. Because of my father's wealth, he had taken the family different places on trains when we lived in Jones County, Georgia. I knew what it was like to ride a train, but Penelope didn't have a clue. I couldn't wait to see how she would react to the train ride.

When we arrived at the Selma train station, we were met by Dent and his family. They came to say their goodbyes to Penelope. Over the past two years, they had gotten to know Penelope well. She was well respected by Dent's family. Sara, Dent's wife, was my favorite sister-in-law. She was a good Christian lady and very good to my brother. I always reminded Dent he married above himself. He agreed! Sara presented Penelope and me with some homemade sugar cookies. I had to have one before boarding the train. We said our goodbyes. I then assisted Penelope up the steps of the train and located us a seat. I noticed several people looking at us.

Penelope had on a white dress made of satin material trimmed with white lace. She was also wearing a fashionable ladies' hat trimmed in lace. My mother wanted her to look as nice as any other young lady when she arrived at the Boston Prep School. I doubt that anyone had a clue that Penelope was mulatto. She looked white, and her blue eyes were as blue as any white person's I had ever seen. The dress Penelope was wearing was one my mother had made for my sister, Tanyua. I was wearing my Sunday church suit and hat.

Much to my surprise, Penelope seemed very comfortable with the train ride. It didn't seem to bother her that people were looking at us.

The trip to Boston was a two-day trip. Although the first day was a long one, time seemed to pass quickly with Penelope by my side. I had arranged for separate sleeping cars, for the two of us, but Penelope's room was directly across from mine. This would be her first time to sleep by herself, as she had always slept with her mother.

As I said goodnight to her at her door, I couldn't help wishing that I could stay with her.

During the night I dreamed of holding her and kissing her. When I woke, however, it had to remain just a dream.

61

The night had been pretty much uneventful other than my dream. The train attendant could be heard up and down the aisle of the train saying that breakfast was now being served in the dining car. I quickly got dressed and knocked on Penelope's door. She was fully dressed and was ready for breakfast. After we shared a good breakfast, we took a seat in the regular passenger car for the remainder of our trip to Boston.

"Penelope, I was wondering if I might ask you some questions about your past. Would you mind if I did that?"

"I wouldn't mind, Master Obadiah."

"As you know, we bought you from Mrs. Thompson. Were you born on her plantation?"

"Yes, I was born on Master and Missus Thompson's plantation, but it wasn't the one in Dallas County, Alabama."

"Where were you born?"

"Mama said I was born in Floyd County, Georgia, near a place called Rome, Georgia."

"Do you remember anything about Floyd County?"

"No. My mama said that the Thompsons moved to Dallas County, Alabama, when I was two years old."

"Did Mattie tell you who your father was?"

"Mama told me that he was a white overseer who worked for Master Thompson."

"Do you know his name?"

"No, Master Obadiah. If she knew she wouldn't tell me. When I asked her his name, she'd say, 'I want to forget about that man. He was an evil, no-good white man.'"

"So you never saw him?"

"Mama said he held me one time and said I was beautiful!"

"What else can you tell me about him?"

"Mama said that he was the father of several children born on Master Thompson's plantation."

"But you don't know what happened to him?"

"Mama didn't know, or she wouldn't tell me."

"Why is it that Mattie has light skin?"

"Mama said she had a white father, too."

"Do you know where your mother was born?"

"She was born in Putnam County, Georgia. She was sold to Master Thompson in Putnam County before Master Thompson and Missus Thompson moved to Floyd County.

"Did your mother have any family?"

"Yes, she had a mother and two brothers who lived in Putnam County."

"Do you know how they got separated?"

"Mama said they were all sold separately in Putnam County, and she has never seen them since."

"What happened to Mattie's father?"

"Mama doesn't know."

"Penelope, I'm so sorry."

"Oh, Master Obadiah, don't be sorry. Mama and I feel God has blessed us in so many wonderful ways. Especially for letting us be your slaves. You and your parents treat us good. I told Mama what you said about how you would never sell her or me."

We arrived in Boston on August 20, 1855, around 2:30 p.m. After collecting our baggage from our sleeping car, I summoned a coachman to take us directly to the girl's prep school. The school's name was Mrs. Adams's Prep School for Girls.

I asked the coachman to wait for me as I carried Penelope's baggage inside. We were greeted by an assistant of Mrs. Adams. Her name was Helen Smith. Mrs. Smith looked to be in her late thirties or early forties. She was very polite. She invited us into a conference room where she offered us a glass of fresh water. The water tasted very good after riding from the train station to Mrs. Adams's School. It was so hot that I removed my hat so I could wipe the dripping sweat from my forehead.

Penelope was holding a white handkerchief, which she used to wipe the sweat from her brow.

"I'm sorry for the heat. We've raised every window in the school, but this August heat is something we've had to put up with. Can I get you some more water?" Mrs. Smith asked.

"I'll have another glass, please," I said as I gave her my empty glass. Penelope handed Mrs. Smith her glass as well.

"Mrs. Adams will be here shortly. I've got to run to the kitchen so you make yourselves at home. I'll be back soon with your water."

I could see the nervousness in Penelope. I had to admit, I was nervous as well. The thought of leaving her here with people she had never met was a frightening thought. If I was nervous, what must Penelope be feeling?

Mrs. Adams entered the room. She was a beautiful woman in her mid-forties. She introduced herself and said she had been expecting our arrival.

"Good afternoon, Mr. Bradford," she said offering her hand of welcome.

"Good afternoon to you, Mrs. Adams," I said.

"This must be Penelope. What a beautiful young lady!" Penelope bowed slightly.

"I assume you received my father's letter, did you not?"

"Yes, I did. We have made all the necessary arrangements to get Penelope enrolled in our school and get her settled. Penelope will have a roommate. Her name is Jessica Blackman. Jessica is from upstate New York. She is eighteen years old. I believe Penelope is seventeen."

"That's correct!" I said. I was happy to hear that Penelope would have a roommate. Maybe having Jessica as a roommate would prevent her from getting too lonely after I left to return to Autauga County.

"I'm going to have Mrs. Smith, my assistant, show Penelope around the building and meet Jessica. This will give you and me time to visit over Penelope's course of study. Is that okay with you, Mr. Bradford?"

"That's fine with me, Mrs. Adams," I said as I got up from my chair. Mrs. Smith re-entered the room to escort Penelope through the building.

"Penelope, I'll see you again before I leave." She nodded as she and Mrs. Smith left the room.

"Mr. Bradford, your father explained in his letter that you are the legal owner of Penelope. I must tell you that she certainly doesn't look like a Negro. I've seen several mulattos, but none are as white as she. She could pass for white any time."

"That's the reason I want Penelope to learn about white people's ways, and I want her to become well educated. She is

64

a very intelligent girl. She learns fast and craves knowledge of different subject areas. I want you to teach her the social graces. I want her to learn about the fine arts and whatever else you teach the young ladies here."

"Mr. Bradford, we have the best prep school that the eastern states have to offer. I can assure you that Penelope will do fine in our school. Who should receive the progress reports on Penelope?"

"You can send them to my home address. My parents will be able to get the reports to me. I'm going to be attending medical school in Augusta, Georgia. I'll be in Augusta most of the time but will be going home on holidays and breaks."

"Mr. Bradford, you need to know our girls are not totally confined to this building. We believe in a well-rounded educational program. We want our girls to see what's out there. Not only is it important for them to gain academic success, but social skills as well. But let me assure you, Penelope will not go unsupervised.

"We always have someone from our staff accompany our girls wherever they go and whatever they do. The only time one of our staff members isn't present is when the girls are on their work study program. During this period, the business manager has the responsibility in seeing after his employees. We have that agreement with the participating businesses in our contract with them. One of our carriage drivers takes the girls to their work stations and picks them up afterwards. They are always under supervision. Do you have any questions?"

"I wasn't aware of a work study program. Can you tell me more about how this works into your training program?"

"The program allows the girls an opportunity to learn a trade. Also, the job gives them an opportunity to earn money that they can use to purchase items we don't furnish here at the school. The work study program gives them a sense of accomplishment. We try to place each girl in an area of interest so she can develop skills in that area. I can assure you, it builds character in the girls. Each girl's academic course of study depends on how well she scores on the four basic course content areas: math, science, reading, and English. We give each student a test to determine how proficient she is in each academic area. Each student progresses at her own rate of speed. To complete the course, each student has to score eighty percent or better on the end-of-course test. If the student fails, she will continue to study in that particular course until she scores eighty percent or better. Does that make sense?"

"Yes, it does, and let me say I compliment you on your academic program. I'm counting on Penelope to be one of your best students. Both the academic and work study program sound good, but I have a question relating to Penelope's roommate."

"What is your question, Mr. Bradford?"

"What information has been made available to Jessica Blackman in regard to Penelope?"

"That's a good question. Jessica has already been told that Penelope is Negro and she's okay with that. This is Jessica's second year with us. She is not prejudiced against Negroes. In fact, her folks are very active in New York with the abolitionist groups. No offense, Mr. Bradford, but Jessica, I'm quite sure, feels the way her folks feel about slavery."

"Did my father make it clear to you that Penelope is not free and remains a slave?"

"Your father explained that in his letter."

"I believe you've answered my questions to my satisfaction, Mrs. Adams."

"Mr. Bradford, I want to say this to you. I think this is very admirable what you and your folks are doing for Penelope. This is almost unheard of for a plantation owner in the deep South," she said.

"Mrs. Adams, I want you to know we Bradfords treat our slaves well. It's not just Penelope; we care about all our slaves. We wouldn't be where we are today without good slaves. We treat them right, and they in turn work hard for us. We recognize them as human beings, not just property."

"I can assure you, we will take good care of Penelope."

"I'm sure you will. I'll be coming back tomorrow to say goodbye to Penelope. I would also like to see her before departing today, if I may."

"I will see if Helen is finished showing her around. Mr. Bradford, it's apparent to me that you are quite fond of Penelope, aren't you?"

"Yes, I am! I want only the best for Penelope."

"From what you've shared with me about Penelope, I'm sure she will do well here at our school."

"Thank you, Mrs. Adams."

"I will send someone to get Penelope, but while we wait let me show you a few of the classrooms and the dining hall. Would you like that?"

"That would be nice."

As Mrs. Adams showed me the rooms, I felt good knowing that Penelope would be in good hands here at Mrs. Adams's school. There was no doubt in my mind that Mrs. Adams runs a good school. We went back to the conference room where Penelope and Mrs. Smith were waiting for us.

"We will leave you two alone. Let us know when you finish. We will be in my office," Mrs. Adams said.

"Well, Penelope, what do you think?"

"It's so big, Master Obadiah," she said.

"Did you see your room?"

"Yes, and it's big, too. I met my roommate, too. Her name is Jessica."

"Did you like her?"

"Yes! I do like her. Did you know she's white, Master Obadiah?"

"Yes, Mrs. Adams told me."

"Penelope, you look as white as anyone you will see here in this school."

"Master Obadiah, I know I look white, but I know I'm Negro. What if Jessica finds out I'm Negro? I'm afraid she won't want me as her roommate."

"Penelope, Jessica already knows you're Negro. She's looking forward to being your roommate. So don't you worry about her! It's going to be up to you how much you want to tell her about your background. I'm going to ask Mrs. Adams if I can meet Jessica tomorrow when I come by to say goodbye to you.

I would like to meet and visit with her. I've got to be going, Penelope. I'm going to stay at the Parker House Hotel tonight. My train leaves tomorrow at 11:00 a.m. so I'll be coming by in the morning to see you. Don't worry about anything. They will take good care of you."

I let Mrs. Adams know I was leaving. She asked Mrs. Smith to take Penelope to her room as she walked to the front door with me.

"Helen tells me she is really impressed with Penelope's English. She thinks she's very smart," Mrs. Adam's said.

"My sister, Sarah, is a teacher back in Autauga County. She's taught Penelope well. By the way, I'm coming back in the morning to see Penelope before my train leaves for Autauga County. Would it be possible for me to meet Jessica Blackman before I leave?"

"What time will your train leave?"

"It's scheduled to leave at 11:00 a.m."

"We will be doing orientation tomorrow morning, but I think we can arrange a few minutes for you to meet Jessica and say goodbye to Penelope. If you will be here around 9:00 a.m., we'll take care of your request."

"Thanks, Mrs. Adams. I appreciate your kindness."

"We will see you in the morning, Mr. Bradford."

The Parker House Hotel was everything I had heard it to be. I had never stayed in such an elegant hotel. The food was delicious, and the bed was very comfortable. The heat was the only thing I had to tolerate. I enjoyed my bath and decided to pass up the entertainment downstairs for a good night's rest. I was so tired from my lack of sleep on the train that I fell fast asleep.

I woke up around 2:00 a.m. thinking about Penelope and wondering how she and Jessica were doing. I couldn't wait to meet Jessica. Mrs. Adams described her as a fine young lady, one whom Penelope and I would like. It didn't take me long to go back to sleep. I told myself tomorrow would be a long and busy day.

I had left word with the front desk to give me a wake-up call at 6:30 a.m. I was afraid I wouldn't wake up early enough to get dressed, eat breakfast, and get to Mrs. Adams's Prep School by 9:00 a.m.

Right at 6:30 a.m., a bellboy knocked on my door. I called out, "Who is it?"

"It's your wake-up call," the bellboy said.

"Thank you!" I shouted. I quickly dressed into clothes that were more comfortable than I had worn from Autauga County to Boston. Since I had already met Mrs. Adams in my best suit of clothes, I knew I didn't have to impress her any longer.

I knew the trip back to Autauga County would be more comfortable if I could dress more leisurely. My breakfast consisted of hot biscuits, eggs, and sausage, and a big cold glass of milk. Although the breakfast couldn't compare to Mattie's, Penelope's, and Betsy's cooking, it would do. I paid my bill and checked out in plenty of time to get to Mrs. Adams's school before nine o'clock.

I again paid the carriage driver to stand by while I went inside to see Penelope and to meet Jessica. It cost me more money to have the carriage driver to stand by, but I decided I had rather pay him a little extra than take a risk of not finding another carriage to get me to the train station on time.

I was greeted in the lobby by Mrs. Smith.

"Good morning, Mr. Bradford; we've been expecting you."

"Good morning to you, Mrs. Smith."

"Penelope and Jessica are waiting for you in the conference room. Mrs. Adams is taking care of a minor problem right now and asked me to make her apologies. Please come with me."

I followed Mrs. Smith into the conference room where she made her introductions. "Jessica, this is Mr. Obadiah Bradford."

"I'm pleased to make your acquaintance, Mr. Bradford," Jessica said as she offered her hand.

I reached out and shook her hand. "I've heard several nice things about you."

"Penelope has told me nice things about you as well," she said as she sat down.

Before sitting, I looked at Penelope, who had remained quiet while Jessica and I were visiting. "Good morning, Penelope, and how are you this morning?"

"I'm doing fine, Master Obadiah."

"I'll leave you three alone for awhile. I'll be back in about fifteen minutes to get the girls for the morning's orientation assembly. Will that give you enough time, Mr. Bradford?"

"Yes, thank you, Mrs. Smith."

My short visit gave me a good impression of Jessica. Of course, I could be totally wrong, but my gut feelings were normally right. We visited a few minutes, and then Jessica excused herself so Penelope and I could have some time together alone.

"Well, Penelope, how did your night go?"

"It went well, Master Obadiah."

"Jessica seems to be a nice girl."

"I like her, Master Obadiah. She's been nothing but kind to me. Did you know she's been here a year already?"

"Mrs. Adams shared that news with me yesterday."

As we both realized time was drawing near for me to leave, there was a moment of silence before either of us spoke. I finally said, "Penelope, I want you to write me after I get to Augusta, Georgia. I want to know what's going on with you here in Boston. If you should need anything, let me know. I'll send you my address as soon as I obtain one in Augusta. I've left some money with Mrs. Adams for you to use for paper, envelopes, stamps, and other items you may need. You can check with them when you get ready for those items."

"Thanks, Master Obadiah, I promise you I will write both you and Mama."

"Penelope, I'm going to have to go. My train leaves shortly."

Penelope began to cry as she threw herself into my arms. "Master Obadiah! I don't want you to go."

I held her tightly reassuring her everything would be okay. She was trembling so badly. Saying goodbye to Penelope was one of the hardest things I had ever done. Suddenly, I heard footsteps coming down the hall. I released Penelope from my embrace and brushed the tears from her eyes.

"Goodbye, Penelope!"

Mrs. Adams entered the room and said, "Mr. Bradford, I've come to get Penelope. It's time for our orientation assembly, and she needs to be present."

"We're ready, Mrs. Adams," I said.

"Come with me, Penelope," Mrs. Adams said.

"Take good care of Penelope," I said, as my heart ached with pain. I felt my heart beating so fast I thought it might explode at any second. Seeing Penelope leave the room with Mrs. Adams was one of the hardest things I would face in my lifetime. As I stepped into the hall, I watched Mrs. Adams and Penelope walk down the hall to the auditorium. Just as Penelope reached the door, she turned and waved goodbye.

CHAPTER 9

I arrived back in Selma in mid-afternoon to find Bill waiting for me at the train station. Bill put my baggage in the carriage and asked, "Master Obadiah, are you ready to go home?"

"Not just yet. I need to go by Dent's place in Cahaba before returning home. I need to visit with him on some business."

"Yes, Master, Dent's it is."

My business with Dent was to see if he would agree to trade my friend, Hank, for his slave, Jim. This trade would be temporary in nature to give Hank and Mattie an opportunity to get to know their potential partners in marriage. If Dent accepted my plan, Hank would come to Dent's plantation to spend some time getting to know Nanny, the seventeen-year-old daughter of Dent's field supervisor, Mr. Sam.

As Bill brought our coach to a halt in front of Dent's home, we were immediately greeted by Sara, Dent, and their children who had been sitting on the front porch. "Well, little brother, I see you made it back from Boston in one piece."

"That I did. Boston is a big and exciting place to visit, but I don't think I would want to live there. I prefer Autauga County any day."

"What brings you by here this afternoon?" Dent asked.

"I need to visit with you about a business transaction."

"Obadiah, will you be spending the night?" Sara asked.

"I wish I could, but I need to get home. I have to help Dr. Banister tomorrow."

"At least stay for supper; I don't want you and Bill to travel back to Autauga County on empty stomachs."

"We would love to join you for supper."

"You and Dent go about your business, and I'll tell Minnie and Buttons to start fixing supper. We will have some of Button's Southern fried chicken," she said.

Dent and I walked out to the big oak tree located near the barn. We sat down on a bench Dent had built for the slaves to have a place to rest after coming in from the fields.

"Obadiah, before we visit about your business proposition, how did things go for Penelope at the prep school?"

"Everything went well. I believe she's going to like it there. She has a wonderful roommate. Her name is Jessica Blackman. She's from up-state New York."

"Is she white?" Dent asked.

"Yes, she's white."

"Does she know Penelope is Negro and a slave?"

"Yes, she knows that as well. Mrs. Adams, the lady who owns the prep school, believes it's for the best to share certain things about roommates. Jessica is not a prejudiced person and had no problems in sharing a room with Penelope. I got to meet Jessica. She's a lovely girl, and I believe she and Penelope will do well with each other."

"Well, that's certainly good news. To be honest with you, I was worried Penelope might have problems at the prep school because of her being Negro."

"I believe we can lay that worry aside."

"Okay, now let's talk about your business deal."

"A few weeks ago, I mentioned to you that I was looking for a nice girl for Hank to marry. You mentioned Mr. Sam's daughter. I believe she's seventeen now. Is that correct?"

"That's correct, Obadiah. She's a nice looking girl. She would make Hank a good wife."

"I have a business proposition for you."

"Okay, let's hear it."

"Since Father owns most of the slaves on the two plantations, I was wondering how you would feel if we made a slave exchange?"

"Obadiah, you're going to have to be more specific."

73

"I was thinking we could switch Big Jim to our plantation in Autauga County and let Hank come here so he could get to know Nanny. If things go well, we might be having two weddings in the near future. If Hank and Nanny like each other, they could produce several good workers for us."

"Obadiah, I think I'm going to change your name to Mr. Matchmaker! Who would ever guess my little brother, Obadiah Bradford, would come up with such an idea?"

"I'm assuming you like my plan?"

"I'm not saying yes quite yet, but it does make good sense."

"What about Jim and Mattie? Are you expecting children out of their marriage as well?"

"I have no reason to think Mattie couldn't have additional children. She's only in her thirties."

"Now, Obadiah, you must know that my Jim can do about anything on this plantation. Am I getting the shorter end of this deal?"

"Hank's a good worker. He may not know everything Jim knows, but he will make up for it with hard work. He's obedient, and if he likes you, he will do anything for you."

"As I've stated already, your proposition makes sense, but there is one flaw in it."

"What is it, Dent?" I asked.

"If both couples marry, we will have to make it a permanent exchange. Father and Mother would never agree to let Mattie come here to Cahaba and Sam will not want Nanny to move away from his family. So, little brother, have you given thought to this matter?"

"To be quite honest with you, Dent, I have considered this. I was using the temporary thing to arouse your interest. I was hoping if marriages did come from this plan that Hank could stay on here and Jim could stay on at our plantation with Mattie. I know Father and Mother wouldn't ever agree to let Mattie move away. I, too, would have a problem with that. I wanted it to be a temporary thing until we see if it's going to work. If it doesn't work out between Jim and Mattie, you may end up with both Hank and Jim. How does that sound?"

"Oh, now that's good business, little brother," Dent said as he slapped me on the back.

"When could we do this? I have only one month before I leave for Augusta."

"I'll come over this weekend and bring Jim. I want to visit with Mr. Sam and Jim about our plans. I don't think there will be a problem with Mr. Sam as long as he knows Nanny will not be leaving the plantation. For Jim, I think he would welcome an opportunity to meet a nice lady like Mattie."

"In the meantime, I'll go home and explain our agreement with Father, Mattie, and Hank. I'll be looking forward to our visit on Saturday. I've got to work at Dr. Banister's office in Prattville until noon on Saturday, but I'll be home in plenty time to have lunch with you and the folks."

"Speaking of Nanny, there she is at the well," Dent said.

"That's Nanny? She's a nice looker, as you would say," I said with a smile.

"I'll call her so you can meet her. Let's not say anything about our deal as yet. Nanny, would you please come over here?"

Nanny put her bucket down and walked briskly, almost a slow run over to the oak tree.

"Nanny, this is my brother, Obadiah Bradford. Can you say hello to Obadiah?"

"Hello, Massa Bradford," Nanny said shyly.

"I'm pleased to meet you, Nanny." I didn't want to embarrass her by offering my hand. Slave girls are not taught to meet people with a hand shake.

"Nanny, you can return to the well now and get your water. Please give Sam and your mother my regards," Dent said.

"I'm sorry about her shyness. She's not been around many strangers in her life. She's a hard worker. After she comes in from the fields, she goes to her house and normally stays there. She doesn't mix much with the other slaves," Dent said.

"Do you know if she can read?" I asked.

"I don't think so. I don't discourage my slaves from reading, but I don't go out of my way to see they learn to read either."

"If she and Hank marry, Hank can teach her to read," I said.

"Hank knows how to read?"

"I've taught him. Hank and I have spent lots of time with each other since Father bought him. He's a good reader and likes to read the Bible."

"The Bible? Hank can read the Bible?"

"He sure can. He can read about as well as I can. I'm telling you, he's smart."

"I hope this reading thing doesn't someday backfire on you."

"Dent, Nanny is a pretty girl. I believe Hank would like her," I said as I watched Nanny leave the well with her bucket of water.

Sara came to the front porch and hollered, "Come and get it before it gets cold."

As Dent and I reached the front porch, Sara said, "Obadiah, Mary Catherine wants you to sit by her at the table. I assured her that her good looking uncle would be happy to sit by her. I hope that's okay."

"That's more than okay. It's not every day I get to sit next to Mary Catherine. She's growing up so fast and is beautiful like her mother," I said with a big smile on my face.

"Well, thank you, Obadiah. I've not had a compliment like that in this house in a long time," Sara said looking directly at Dent and smiling.

"I do declare, Obadiah, are you flirting with my Sara or just trying to get me in trouble?" Dent asked in a joking manner.

"Okay, you two, let's eat before the food gets cold," Sara said as she escorted us to the dining room. As usual, the food at Dent's house tasted so good, especially after traveling on a train for two days.

It had been some time since I had eaten a meal with Dent and his family. Dent was a good Christian man, one whom I've admired and trusted. He certainly portrayed the big brother role. My sister-in-law, Sara, was good for Dent. Like my mother, Sara was a sweet lady who volunteered much of her free time at the First Baptist Church in Selma and to community affairs in Cahaba. As we ate, I couldn't help noticing how polite each of the children was.

When Dent and Sara directed a question to one of their children, the child would answer by saying, yes sir, no sir, yes ma'am, or no ma'am. I thought to myself, Dent and Sara certainly have done an excellent job in raising their children.

Marion, their first born, had grown so much in the last year. His brothers, Everett and Law, were not too far behind him in size. All of them were growing like weeds. Mary Catherine, their second born, had matured into a fine-looking young lady. She reminded me of my sister, Sarah. They had beautiful blonde hair, blue eyes, and beautiful smiles. Besides church, education was the next most important part of their lives. Dent and Sara wanted the best education possible for their children. God had truly blessed their children with the gift of learning.

Bill and I arrived home around nine o'clock. It had gotten dark on us because of staying for dinner at Dent and Sara's. Father, Mother, and Sarah were waiting up for me. I knew they would be. I also knew they would be anxious to know how Penelope reacted to the prep school.

"My goodness, Son, we thought you had forgotten your way home," Mother said as she gave me a big hug.

"I'm sorry for the lateness, but I wanted to see Dent about a business arrangement, and you know how Sara can be. She wouldn't hear of Bill and me coming home on an empty stomach. So we ended up eating supper with them. I'm glad we did because I was really hungry after traveling two days on that train. The food from the train couldn't compare to Button's Southern fried chicken."

"Let's go into the parlor where we can visit awhile. I'll have Betsy and Mattie to prepare your bath. I'll be right back so don't discuss anything until I return," Mother said.

It didn't take Mother but a minute to give Mattie and Betsy instructions to prepare my bath. "I asked Mattie to bring us some lemonade. I know you must be thirsty after that long trip from Dent's," Mother said.

"Thanks, Mother! Lemonade would taste good right now."

"Now that we are all here, we want to hear about your trip to Boston," Father said.

"Boston is a big city. It's nice, but I prefer to be living right here in Autauga County."

"We want to hear about the prep school and Penelope's impression," Father said.

I had decided to make my story as short as possible but yet detailed enough so they would be pleased to know all was well with Penelope. As I was bringing my story to a conclusion, Mattie entered the room with lemonade. I felt it important to inform her that Penelope liked Mrs. Adams's Prep School and that I left her in good hands.

Mattie was thrilled. "Thank you, Master Obadiah. I've been on pins and needles just thinking about my baby being left in Boston all by herself. I'm happy to know you think all is well," she said with misty eyes.

"All is well, Mattie. Your baby is in good hands with Mrs. Adams and her staff. I will share some other things with you later."

"When you get ready, your bath is ready, Master Obadiah," Mattie said as she gathered up the glasses and returned to the kitchen.

"It's getting late and I know you have to be at Dr. Banister's tomorrow around nine o'clock. Why don't we discuss your business proposition with Dent over breakfast," Father said.

I had literally forgotten about that subject. "Okay, good night, everyone. I will see you in the morning," I said as I left the parlor.

I could tell Sarah found my story to be intriguing. I couldn't wait to share with her the things I felt about Boston and what I saw during my short stay.

I slept well in my own bed, very tired from the trip back from Boston. Breakfast was good and Father did bring up the business issue with Dent. I fully explained my reasoning to Father and Mother and, to my surprise, they agreed after I assured them that Mattie wouldn't be leaving the plantation.

Her marriage to Jim had to be to her satisfaction. I would certainly not force Mattie to marry Jim if she didn't want to. I would introduce them, let them have time together, and if they fell in love, we could make arrangements for a lawful and proper marriage.

I didn't have time to visit with either Mattie or Hank before leaving for Dr. Banister's office in Prattville. I would have to do this as soon as possible because Dent would be bringing Jim over on Saturday. He would take Hank back with him to Cahaba if all goes well.

I arrived at Dr. Banister's office just before nine o'clock as scheduled. It was good to see him.

"Welcome back, Obadiah! Did you have a good trip to Boston?"

"Yes, I did. Penelope likes Mrs. Adams's Prep School. I think she's going to do well at the school."

"That's good news, Obadiah. I've missed you around here. We've got a busy morning ahead of us. I just heard that one of James Jones's young female slaves is having a hard time birthing her first baby. He wants us to come immediately. He sent me a note and for some unknown reason, he seems very concerned about this slave. This is not like him, as you know."

I was in total agreement with Dr. Banister. Jones had very little respect for his slaves. Why was he so concern for this one? We arrived at the Jones plantation about 11:00 a.m.

Mr. Jones met us on the front porch of his house. "Good morning, Dr. Banister and Mr. Bradford."

"Where is this young slave girl who's having problems giving birth?" Dr. Banister asked.

"Come with me, Doctor. She's in the second house on the right."

We entered the small house to find the girl's mother sitting by her in a makeshift bed. She was rubbing her daughter's forehead with a damp cloth. The girl was screaming, "Helps me, oh, please helps me. I's dying. I's hurtin' so bad."

Dr. Banister took his stethoscope and listened to the girl's breathing. He examined her to see how much she had dilated. He asked Mr. Jones and the girl's father to leave the room. He turned again to the mother and asked, "What is your daughter's name?"

"Her name is Mandy."

"What is your name?"

"My name is Millie."

"Well, Millie, I'm going to need lots of hot water and I'm going to need you to stand behind Mandy, like this, and hold both shoulders down when I start delivering the baby. Do you understand?"

"I understand, Doctor."

He looked at me and said, "Obadiah, she's in bad trouble." I knew exactly what he meant. Something had to be done and done fast.

"Obadiah, this girl is going to die if we don't get this baby out fast. She's not dilated enough to have this baby. I'm going to have to cut her. She may bleed to death. It's either cut her or lose both of them. I will need your assistance. You need to watch me so you can learn what to do if you're faced with this situation again."

Dr. Banister looked at the girl's mother and said, "Ma'am, you will need to hold your daughter down by her shoulders just like this," as he demonstrated to the girl's mother.

"Obadiah, you assist me. Get ready to see lots of blood." The screaming was really affecting me. I had never experienced birthing of a baby. The pain this girl was experiencing was just awful. I never dreamed there was so much pain in having a baby.

"Okay, Obadiah, I'm going to make a cut here and one here. Are you ready?"

"I'm ready," I said with some hesitation. As soon as Dr. Banister made his first cut, blood shot everywhere.

"Use the sponge, Obadiah," Dr. Banister said. He made the second cut and more blood came flowing from that cut.

"Squeeze the sponge out, Obadiah!" Dr. Banister shouted. I know he must have been getting irritated with me from the tone of his voice.

"Oh, my God, this is a breach baby," he said. I knew exactly what he meant. The baby was trying to come feet first. This was bad!

"I'm going to try to pull the baby out feet first. Get a towel, Obadiah. The sponge is saturated with blood. Take the towel and see if you can stop some of the blood flow. She's going to bleed more when I pull the baby out."

As Dr. Banister pulled on the baby's feet, I noticed the girl passed out. She was so weak from loss of blood and the pain. I was hoping she hadn't died.

Dr. Banister was able to pull the baby boy out feet first, but he was dead. He had died earlier from the umbilical cord being wrapped around his neck. Dr. Banister handed me the newborn baby boy. As I stood holding the baby, I realized for the first time, I was holding death in my two hands. This baby would never know life.

"There are extra towels in my bag; get one, wrap the baby, and lay it on the table," he said.

I watched Dr. Banister stitch the areas he had cut to open up enough space to get the baby out. He had a steady hand, and I could tell from watching him he had done this before. After he finished his stitching, he listened once again to the girl's breathing.

"I don't know if she's going to make it. She's really weak and has lost a considerable amount of blood."

"Come take a listen," he said handing me his stethoscope. The girl's heart was beating very weakly. She was taking short, shallow breaths, and her blood pressure had fallen considerably. Dr. Banister was right; she was in bad shape.

Millie stood crying as she continued to wipe Mandy's face. I heard Millie cry out, "Oh, merciful God, please don't let my baby die."

Dr. Banister told Millie that he would ask Mr. Jones about dispensing with the baby's body. She shook her head and let out a cry I shall never forget. It was a death cry, one I had heard before at funerals. But this time, I was touched differently because I was there. Mandy, who I'm sure was not married, would never know her baby. The pain she went though was in vain. Dr. Banister went outside where Mr. Jones, Mr. Mason, and the girl's father were standing.

"We lost the baby. It was a breach baby, and I had to deliver it feet first. The girl lost lots of blood. She will need constant attention. I would suggest you get another female slave to assist the girl's mother. She's been through a horrible ordeal today."

"What do you plan to do with the baby, Mr. Jones?" Dr. Banister asked.

"We will bury it in the slave cemetery."

"Do you know who the father was?" Dr. Banister asked.

I noticed Mr. Jones looked at Mr. Mason as Mason looked directly at him. "No, we don't know who the father is," Jones said.

I knew they were lying, but like Dr. Banister said, "It's not our affair." If I was a betting man, I would guess the father was either Mr. Jones or Mason. They were known to take liberty with their female slaves whenever they felt the urge, especially the young girls who were virgins.

As we were leaving, Dr. Banister informed Jones I would be coming back in a couple days to do a follow-up. If Mandy was to die, they were to let Dr. Banister know.

As we left Jones's plantation to return to Prattville, Dr. Banister quizzed me on my understanding of delivering a baby.

"Obadiah, when you become a doctor, you will deliver many babies. Most of the time, delivering a baby is no problem — not like the one today. That girl's body frame was not made right to have children. She was too closely built. She won't be the last one you will see with a small build."

Before today, I had never witnessed a woman giving birth to a baby. I had no knowledge other than seeing cattle, hogs, and horses giving birth to their offspring. This is one area I would need lots of help. I'm sure I will get plenty of knowledge, understanding, and practical experience during my schooling in Augusta.

After arriving back at Twin Oaks, I made arrangements to meet with Hank and Mattie. I first met with Hank and informed him that he would be going with my brother, Dent, to our plantation in Cahaba near Selma. I described Nanny to him and told him that if things worked out between them, she might become his legal and lawful wife for life. Hank was excited and looked forward to his move to Cahaba.

I later met with Mattie and explained to her what my plans were for her. Mattie wasn't as receptive as Hank. She looked at me and said, "Master Obadiah, I'm perfectly happy with the present arrangements without a man."

I asked her to give it a try. "If you don't like Jim, you won't have to marry him, I promise."

"You are my master, and I'll do what you want me to do."

I assured Mattie that if she and Jim fell in love and got married they would continue to live at the big house in Mattie's room. She would also continue to be our head house servant. That seemed to perk her up some. I left Mattie feeling good about our visit. I appreciated the dedication she gave to our family. She truly loved being our head house servant. She was such a nice lady. *Jim would truly be blessed to have a wife like Mattie!* I thought.

CHAPTER 10

My last month in Autauga County was spent doing follow-ups for Dr. Banister. One of my follow-ups was attending to Mandy, the slave girl who lost her baby during childbirth. Much to my surprise, she survived the horrible ordeal of trying to give birth to a breech baby. During my last visit to see Mandy, I discovered she had healed and regained most of her strength. I released her to go back to work on the farm, a decision that I'm quite sure pleased Mr. Jones and Mason.

I began to see more of Audrey Denton. I found her company both pleasant and enjoyable. She was more of a tomboy than I had imagined her to be. She loved to ride and race her horse, Millie. We ran races, went on picnics, went dancing in Prattville, and went fishing in the Autauga River.

Audrey's horse, Millie, was a beautiful black mare with a long white blaze running from the top of her head down to her nose. Millie and my horse, General, got along well, too well on one occasion. Millie had come into heat, and Audrey and I were having a hard time keeping them apart. We finally decided to let nature take its course by putting them together in the corral at the Denton plantation. If nothing unforeseen happens, Millie should be foaling in about eleven months.

Dent sent me a message that all was going well between Nanny and Hank on his plantation. He said, "I believe Hank is bringing out the very best in Nanny."

Big Jim and Mattie seem to be doing well together, too. Jim works part time in the cotton field and part time at the barn running the new cotton gin. Mattie cooks Jim something every night after he gets through with his job responsibilities. After he spends time with Mattie, he returns to the nearby bunk house where he sleeps.

As Dent said, "Big Jim can do about anything on our plantation." We've noticed he's very knowledgeable about our new ginning machine. If something goes wrong, he seems to know what to do to get it up and running again. My brother, John, plans to make Big Jim foreman over the ginning and baling of our cotton.

I've seen Mattie teaching Big Jim to read on more than one occasion. He appeared to be enjoying reading. I believe if all continues to go well, we will be having a wedding soon. I would like to see my plans for Hank and Mattie finalized before leaving for Augusta. Since I only have two weeks left here in Autauga County, I have to get busy and make this happen.

After arriving home from a full day's work with Dr. Banister, my mother handed me a letter from Penelope. "This letter came for you today," she said as she went back inside the house.

I sat down in my favorite rocking chair on the front porch. I didn't open the letter immediately, but just sat there and stared at it. The envelope was addressed to Master Obadiah Bradford. The handwriting was beautiful. I had never seen her writing previously, but Sarah had told me how well she could write. I opened my pocket knife and gently opened the envelope, being careful not to rip it.

> *Dear Master Obadiah,*
>
> *It's been three weeks since you brought me to Mrs. Adams's school in Boston. I'm learning so much here. Everyone has been very nice to me. Jessica has been wonderful and is taking good care of me. She's a lot like my mama. She's a little bossy, but I think that's because she's been here for over a year and knows how things are to be done around here. I don't mind her help. She means well.*
>
> *I miss my mama, you, and all the Bradford family. I wish I could be home in Autauga County but am satisfied I need to remain here in Boston to learn. I am learning. I have been placed in a tailor shop near the Parker House Hotel where you spent the night while you were in*

Boston. I like my job. The owner said I am a good seam-stress and am doing a good job. I'm saving my money for something special.

How are Sarah and Missus and Master Bradford doing? Please tell them I send my regards. I hope you don't get mad at me for writing my mama. I will mail her letter today when I mail yours. To my knowledge, Mama has never received a letter from anyone. I wanted it to be special for her. I hope you understand, Master Obadiah.

We have been practicing writing letters in our language class, and I enjoy writing. I hope you like the letter.

I would like for you to write me sometime. Please let Mama write me. I am sending her money to purchase stamps, paper, and envelopes. I hope you don't mind. Mama has never written a letter. It would be nice to get a letter from her.

Sincerely yours,
Penelope Bradford

The letter made me cry. I was so proud of Penelope's ability to write such a nice letter. The letter assured me, even more, that my decision to send her to school in Boston was the right thing to do.

I had just finished reading the letter when my mother stuck her head out the door and said, "Obadiah, dinner is ready. Come wash up."

"I'll be right there."

As I took my seat next to Sarah, I whispered in her ear, "Read this letter later. It's from Penelope to me. You are going to be very impressed with her writing." I wanted Sarah to see Penelope's accomplishment in writing since she was the one responsible for teaching her to read and write.

"Catherine tells me you got a letter from Penelope today. How is she doing in Boston?" Father asked.

"She's doing very well. She sends her regards to all of you. She misses everyone but is enjoying being at Mrs. Adams's school. Her letter was well written. After Sarah reads it, I want you and Mother to have an opportunity to read it as well. I think you will be very impressed with Penelope's ability to write." My offer to let Father and Mother read Penelope's first letter seemed to satisfy my father's curiosity.

After dinner, I asked Mattie if she had received a letter from Penelope.

"Yes, I did, Massa Obadiah. I was so happy to hear from my baby."

"I got a letter from her as well. I was very impressed with her writing."

"Master Obadiah, Penelope's letter is the first letter I've gotten from anyone. I am so proud of her. She's doing well, isn't she?"

"Yes, Mattie, Penelope is doing really well. We are all proud of her."

"Will you permit me to answer her letter, Massa Obadiah?"

"Certainly! You write Penelope anytime you wish."

"She sent me some money to buy stamps, paper, and envelopes. She's got a job, you know."

"Yes, she told me in her letter."

"She's good at needlework. I'm really proud of my baby."

"Mattie, how are you and Big Jim doing?"

"Just fine, Master Obadiah."

"I was wondering if Big Jim had asked you to marry him."

"Yes, he's asked."

"Well, Mattie, what did you say?"

"I said it's not my decision."

"What did you mean by that?"

"I'm your slave; you own me, Master Obadiah."

"Mattie, I thought I made it clear that if you two wanted to get married it would be perfectly all right with me."

"I do love Jim. I just didn't know what to say, Master Obadiah."

"Mattie, it would make me proud to see you marry Big Jim. We all like him, and I think he would make you happy."

"If we marry, will Jim be able to move in here with me?"

"You wouldn't want him to keep sleeping in the bunk house would you?" I said laughing.

"Oh, Master Obadiah, you're so funny!"

"Mattie, I'm going to talk to Big Jim tonight. If you are ready to accept his offer, we are going to have us a wedding before I leave for Augusta."

"Thanks, Master Obadiah. Can I write and tell Penelope that I'm getting married?"

"Certainly, you can," I said, laughing as I walked away.

I didn't know what I would have said or done if she had said no to Big Jim. I really think Big Jim will be good for Mattie and can't see why a young lady like Mattie should live her life without someone to love and care for her. I felt good as I entered the bunk house.

"Big Jim, could I have a word with you?"

"Yes, Massa Obadiah," Big Jim said showing a little nervousness.

"I just finished visiting with Mattie and she said you had proposed marriage to her."

"Yes, Massa Obadiah, I's did ask her. She said, 'Master Obadiah owns me. You will have to ask him.'"

"Well, why haven't you asked me?" I could see that Big Jim was getting a little anxious.

"I's wanted to, Massa Obadiah, but I's was scared."

"Big Jim, I've given Mattie permission to marry you."

"You's really have?" Jim asked with excitement.

"Yes, I have, and we are going to have a wedding really soon."

"Can I go over and talk to her now?"

"Yes, you may! Go!"

I left the bunk house feeling good about Mattie and Jim's upcoming wedding. Now, I needed to get in touch with Dent and let him make the arrangements with Hank and Nanny. If all goes well, we will have a double wedding before I leave for medical school.

I informed Father and Mother of Mattie's and Jim's commitment to each other and my plans for a double wedding at our plantation. My mother immediately offered to plan the wedding. All of our slaves would be invited as well as Nanny's family from the plantation in Cahaba. Of course, all my brothers' and sisters' families would be invited as well.

I sent Bill to Cahaba with a letter from me requesting that Dent make the final arrangements for Hank and Nanny to be married at our plantation. The plan was to have a double wedding ceremony on Saturday before I leave for Augusta on Monday.

CHAPTER 11

The double wedding ceremony was the biggest thing that ever happened at the Twin Oaks Plantation. It was a perfect day, one of jubilee, you might say. My mother had involved our slaves in planning the wedding. Since she is a woman of wisdom, she didn't want the wedding to be too formal. She wanted to include Negro culture and traditions into the ceremonies and celebration.

Dent's family, who lived on our plantation in Cahaba, arrived early enough on Friday to join the family for dinner. My brother John and my sisters, Mary Ann Shadrack, and Tanyua Ballard, all lived in Prattville and would arrive sometime during the morning.

At dinner, Mother was the center of attention. "I'm telling you, planning these weddings has worked me into a frazzled state," she said panting.

"Catherine, you know you've enjoyed every minute of it," Father said laughing.

"You're right! I haven't had this much fun in years. I'm telling you, I've learned a lot about Negro culture and traditions these past few days. You will be surprised when you see them celebrating," Mother said as she continued to pass bowls of food around the table.

My mother wanted the weddings to have a spiritual meaning as well. Mattie requested the tradition of jumping the broom be part of her wedding ceremony. Hank and Nanny made that their request as well. In most parts of the old South, the marital rite had neither sacred nor civil sanctions worth anything, so far as the Negroes were concerned. There were few opportunities for slave marriages to include any of their traditions. The common procedure for slave marriages was

90

the male slave went to the slave owner and requested that the female slave become his wife. That was about all it was to getting married. They lived together as husband and wife until death did them part.

"You will love Mattie's dress," Sarah said.

"What color is it?" Dent asked

"It's white! Of course," Mother said.

I knew where Dent was coming from. He knew Mattie had never been married, yet she had given birth to Penelope. I think he just wanted to see how my mother would react. As I've said many times, my mother is one of the kindest ladies I've ever been around. She strives to see good in every situation she's confronted with. Her spirituality is unquestionable. She is a lady of character, one who loves her family and cares about the welfare of our slaves. My mother doesn't see colors. She sees beauty in each and every person she knows or meets.

The big day arrived. One couldn't ask for a prettier day. The sun was shining with no sign of rain clouds. As I stepped out on the front porch, I could smell the aroma coming from the fire pit where fresh pork loins were roasting.

My father's role was to make sure there was lots of food and drink. He was quite good in making those types of arrangements. Today, we would all eat together, plantation owners and their slaves, something which doesn't occur often in the South.

The weddings went off without a hitch. Mattie, Jim, Hank, and Nanny chose the tradition of "Jumping the Broom" as part of their wedding ceremony. Jumping the Broom was a symbol of sweeping away the old and welcoming the new, or a symbol of new beginnings.

My mother invited the Dentons to the wedding. Audrey and I enjoyed seeing the different slave traditions. In fact, at some time during the festivities, all of us Bradfords participated in dancing, clapping, and singing. Whatever our slaves did, we tried to do so as well. I was amazed to see how good a dancer Hank was. I had never seen anyone do some of the things he could do. He was loose as a goose as the saying goes. My body just didn't work that way, although it was fun trying.

Our slaves had never eaten so well. I could tell they were having fun, not fearing any reprisals from anything they did. This is the way it should always be, I thought.

It was good having the Bradford family together. We rarely were able to get together more than once or twice a year. Christmas was the only holiday we regularly celebrated together. My nephews and nieces were quickly growing into adulthood. As I looked around watching them visit with each other, I realized my parents were responsible for several Bradford descendants who would carry on the Bradford name.

The wedding was a big success. I had been successful in accomplishing my goal to get Mattie and Hank happily married. I felt good about how things had worked out. If what I have done brings happiness to Mattie, Jim, Hank, and Nanny, that is what counts. Nothing else matters.

I spent my last Sunday attending the Oak Hill Baptist Church in Prattville with my parents and Sarah. What time I had left was spent with Audrey Denton. Saying goodbye to Audrey was difficult. I never dreamed it would be so hard. As we kissed goodbye, I was surprised to see tears coming from her eyes. Audrey really cared about me and this was the first time I had seen her cry. It really bothers me to see women cry.

"I'm going to miss you, Obadiah Bradford."

"I'm going to miss you as well."

"You will write me, won't you? I want to hear everything about Augusta and what's going on with you in school."

"I will write you."

"You promise me?"

"Yes, and hope to die if I don't."

"That's good enough for me, Obadiah. Oh, by the way, I have a going away present for you," she said handing me a beautifully wrapped box.

"What is it?"

"Open it and find out."

I carefully opened the package to find a painting of Millie and General. The horses were standing side by side with General kicking up his heels. I believe she had captured this moment in time when they were in the corral together.

"Audrey, this is beautiful."

"I wanted you to have something to remind you of the good times we spent together riding our horses. Every time you look at the painting maybe you will think of me as well," she said with a big smile.

"Thank you so much, Audrey. You couldn't have given me a better present. I will find just the right spot in my room for this beautiful painting."

"This painting can be your good luck charm. Touch it daily and think about the girl you left behind. That's all I want!" she said giving me another hug.

The day had come for me to say goodbye to Father, Mother, and Sarah. I didn't realize it was going to be so hard to leave. Although I would be coming home from time to time, it would be my first extended time away from home. Bill was waiting in the carriage while I said my goodbyes.

"You take care of yourself, Son," my father said as he gave me a big bear hug.

"I love you, Father. You take care of yourself as well."

"Here is your first Augusta newspaper and a copy of our newspaper. I've subscribed to both papers for you. I want you to keep up on what's going on both here and in Augusta."

"Thank you, Father. I really appreciate this."

"You will be receiving both papers at your new address in Augusta," Father said.

I turned to Mother and almost lost it when I saw tears streaming down her cheeks.

"Son, I had Betsy bake you some fresh oatmeal raisin cookies for your trip."

"Thank you, Mother! Please tell Betsy I said thanks. I'm sure I'm going to enjoy them."

"You be a good boy. You write often, you hear."

"I promise you, I will write."

"I love you, Son," my mother said as we embraced.

I stood there hugging the most wonderful mother in the world. When we finally released each other, I was crying, and my mother was using her handkerchief to wipe away the tears streaming down her face.

Sarah was the last one I said goodbye to. She hugged me and said, "Obadiah, I'm counting on you being the best student in the Medical College of Georgia, you hear?"

"I'll do my best," I said as I kissed her on the cheek.

I climbed into the carriage, closed the door, and waved goodbye as Bill and I headed to Selma to catch the train to Augusta. It was sad to leave my family, but I knew my future of becoming a doctor depended on how well I performed at the medical college. My main goal was to be a good doctor, one of the best to come out of Alabama.

CHAPTER 12

After boarding the train in Selma, I decided to read from the copy of the Augusta Chronicle newspaper, which Father handed me as I left the plantation. Father felt it important for me to have a weekly local newspaper that would keep me current on the happenings in Augusta, Georgia, while attending school there. He also subscribed to the Selma Times, which carried newspaper stories from Autauga, Dallas, Montgomery, Elmore, Lowndes, Perry, and Bibb counties, as well as national news. Having two newspapers would certainly take care of any boredom should there be idle time while in medical school.

My father knew I liked reading newspapers. He always read his paper as he ate breakfast. He used this time in educating the rest of us about what was going on locally as well as nationally. After he finished his newspaper, he would hand it to me and say, "Obadiah, when you find some time, you might want to read that article," pointing to a particular story.

Father wanted me to be a well-rounded citizen, one who could talk to anyone, about anything, at any time. He believed newspapers were the best source of current events. He felt it was the duty of all citizens to be knowledgeable about what was occurring, both locally and nationally. As I've said many times, "My father is intelligent as well as a man of wisdom."

The Augusta Chronicle had in recent months covered slave stories told by slaves who had successfully escaped to freedom in the North. These slave stories were being promoted by abolitionists from the North. I found the articles to be most intriguing.

In this edition of the Augusta Chronicle, there was an article, "The slaves are overworked." The article dealt with witnesses who gave testimonies of what they had observed while living in the

Deep South. The article dealt with cruelties to the slaves during cotton harvest time, which occurred between the months of October and December. The comments came from people from all walks of life, from religious leaders, Southern plantation owners' relatives, and missionaries from the North. The comments were short testimonies from people being interviewed by the abolitionists.

"The slaves go to the field in the morning. They carry with them cornmeal wet with water, and at noon build a fire on the ground and bake it in the ashes. After the labors of the day are over, they take their second meal of ash-cake."

"The breakfast of the slaves was generally about ten or eleven o'clock."

"The slave is forced to pound or grind his own corn and make his own bread, when already exhausted from toil."

"The main food for a majority of slaves is corn. At every meal, from day to day, from week to week, from month to month, corn. In some states, the sweet potato is substituted for corn during part of the year."

"The quantity of food allowed to a full grown field hand is a peck of corn a week, or a fraction over a quart and a gill of corn a day. Eight quarts of corn a week is utterly insufficient to sustain the human body, under such toil and exposure as that to which the slaves are subjected."

"Most Southern plantation owners gave their slaves white gourd seed corn, instead of flint corn. A peck of the white corn generally given to the slaves would be only equivalent to a fraction more than six quarts and a pint of the corn commonly raised in the New England states. What would be said of the northern capitalists who should allow their laborers but six quarts and five gills of corn for a week's provisions?"

"A slave's laboring day consists mostly of fifteen hour days. Little time is given for sleep and rest. When slaves return home from the field, they normally have to grind their own corn by hand and cook their own meal for breakfast which starts about 10:00 a.m. somewhere in the cotton patch."

"During the cotton-picking season, they usually labor in the field during the whole of the daylight and then spend a good part of the night in ginning and baling. The labor required is very frequently excessive and speedily impairs the constitution."

"It is the common rule for the slaves to be kept at work fifteen hours in the day, and in the time of picking cotton a certain number of pounds are required of each. If this amount is not brought in at night, the slave is whipped, and the number of pounds lacking is added to the next day's job; this course is often repeated from day to day."

"It was customary for the overseers to call out the gangs long before daylight. Such work was done by fire light that came from pitch pine, which was abundant."

"Slaves are not allowed to talk to each other during the day."

"The corn is ground in a hand mill by slaves after their tasks are done; generally there is but one mill on a plantation, and only one can grind at a time. The mill is going sometimes very late at night."

As I sat there reading these testimonies, I felt shame in my heart. I could not discredit anything they had said. I've witnessed some of these very same things on plantations in the county where I grew up. Right now, my only justification of owning slaves is that we treat our slaves well. We recognize them as human beings and treat them accordingly. Thank God for that! But I could not help thinking: *Is it really right to continue to benefit from a system where so many slaves are treated so inhumanely?*

I was about to put down the newspaper when I noticed a headline that read, "Probate Sale." As I started to read, I quickly realized this was another testimony from an abolitionist who witnessed cruelty toward the slave. The following information was part of Mr. Tom Johnson's testimony of two probate sales he had witnessed.

There were two different probate sales ordered by Judges of different Louisiana parishes. The first advertisement was from the estate of Mr. James Logan.

Mr. Johnson started out by saying, "All slaves being sold belonged to the estate of Mr. James Logan, deceased, and advertised by T. J. Gleeson, Judge of Concordia, Louisiana. The sex, name, and age of each slave were contained in the advertisement, which filled two columns. The whole number of slaves was one hundred and thirty. Of these, only three were over forty years old. There were thirty-five females between the ages of sixteen and thirty-three, and yet there were only *thirteen* children under the age of thirteen years!"

"It is impossible satisfactorily to account for such a fact, on any other supposition than that these thirty-five females were so overworked, or underfed, or both, as to prevent child-bearing."

The other advertisement is that of a "Probate Sale," ordered by the Court of the Parish of Jefferson, including the slaves of Mr. Bill Tomalley.

"The whole number of slaves was fifty-one, the sex, age, and accustomed labors of each were given. The oldest of these slaves was thirty-nine years old. Of the females, thirteen were between the ages of sixteen and thirty-two, and the oldest female was but thirty-eight, and yet there are only two children under eight years old!"

"Another proof that the slaves in the southwest states are over-worked is the fact that so few of them live to old age. A large majority of them are old at middle age, and few live beyond fifty-five. In one of the preceding advertisements, out of one hundred and thirty slaves, only three are over forty years old! In the other, out of fifty-one slaves, only two are over thirty-five, the oldest is but thirty-nine, and the way in which he is designated in the advertisement is an additional proof that what to others is "middle age" is to the slaves in the southwest old age. The thirty-nine year old is advertised as Old Jeffrey."

"A document released by the Agricultural Society of Baton Rouge, Louisiana, shows the annual death rate of slaves on plantations in the South is so high that the slave population decreases at a rate of two and half percent per year."

After finishing the article, I slowly folded the newspaper and laid it on the seat beside me. My heart grieved from reading these testimonies. My thoughts turned to Penelope. She is my slave, and as God is my witness, I will someday set her and Mattie free. This I can and will do at the appointed time.

My thoughts were interrupted by the passenger car attendant who was coming through the car saying, "Coming into Augusta, Georgia. Everyone prepare for departure."

CHAPTER 13

My father had made arrangements for me to stay at the Milton Boarding House located at 322 Jackson Street in Augusta. The Milton House held the distinction of boarding several students who attend the Old Medical College of Georgia, which is located one block over on Telfair Street. There would be no need for any type of transportation.

As I stepped down from the horse-drawn carriage, I was impressed with the beauty of Jackson Street and the Milton House. Father had done well.

After making two trips from the carriage to the lobby of the boarding house, my driver and I successfully accomplished the task of manually transporting every stitch of clothing I owned. I tipped him and thanked him for his help, and he was on his way. I turned to find Mr. James Milton standing behind the check-in counter. I walked up to him and said, "I'm Obadiah Bradford. I believe my father, James Bradford, has made the necessary arrangements for my stay in your nice establishment."

"That's correct, Mr. Bradford, and welcome to Augusta, Georgia. I believe you will love Augusta," he said with a smile. "If you will just sign your name on this line, I'll show you to your room and give you a quick tour of the house. You will be located on the first floor."

After carrying in my heavy luggage, I was happy to hear my room was going to be on the ground floor instead of the second floor.

"Come with me, Mr. Bradford, and I'll show you to your room."

I followed Mr. Milton. He unlocked the door and handed me the key.

"All our rooms are big and comfortable. I'm sure you are going to enjoy your stay with us. I understand you will be studying medicine?"

"That's correct," I responded.

The room was big. It had a study table with a lamp, a bed side table and lamp, a wash basin with a mirror hanging above it, a table and four chairs, and a large throw rug. In the corner of the room was a fireplace. The wall was covered with blue wallpaper. The room had everything I would need to be comfortable.

"Mr. Bradford, all ten of our guests attend the Old Medical School. You will have lots in common with each of them. If you will follow me, we will take a look at the entire house."

Mr. Milton showed me the door that led to his and Mrs. Milton's living quarters. He explained that his living quarters were off limits to the guests unless there was an emergency. He showed me the dining area and explained the meal schedule. We walked up stairs where there were six rooms for guests. As he had already stated, all these rooms were occupied by college students, as well as the four downstairs. After returning downstairs, he showed me a large room off the entrance that was used as a recreational room for the residents of the boarding house. He then showed me a large room with a sign that read, "Toilet."

"I'm sure you will be interested in knowing we do have indoor plumbing. Since you will be sharing this toilet with other guests on the first floor, we would ask you to show respect and courtesy in sharing this facility," he said as he smiled.

"Yes, sir! I fully understand."

"Do you have any questions, Mr. Bradford?"

"When will the other students be arriving?"

"Oh, most of them are here already. Including you, we have four new students with us for the first time. Two of you have checked in, and we expect the other two later on today.

"What is there to do around here?"

"There are several things to see and do in our downtown district. We have a theater, taverns, restaurants, a city library, saloons, grocery stores, general merchandise stores, banks and lots of other things. There are several restaurants along the

Savannah River. If you like walking, we have a beautiful city park where one can go and feed the pigeons and squirrels. Just don't be mean to the animals. There is a big fine if you are caught being mean to the animals. Mr. Bradford, you are going to like Augusta!"

Since there was still daylight, I decided to walk over to the Old Medical School on Telfair Street. On my way, I met several other people walking. To my surprise, they were very friendly. The medical school was part of the city hospital, as the hospital and the medical school were partners. When students finished a certain number of college credits, they would be assigned to one of the hospital doctors as a student intern. This would be similar to my work with Dr. Banister in Autauga County, but much more intense.

When I arrived back at the boarding house, several of the guests were socializing in the large recreation room. As I walked in, I was greeted by Henry Dotson, a second-year student at the college and my next-door neighbor in the Milton House.

"You must be Obadiah Bradford from Autauga County, Alabama?" he said, reaching out to shake my hand.

"Yes, I am Obadiah."

"My name is Henry Dotson from Atlanta, Georgia. I'm pleased to make your acquaintance."

"Please to meet you, Henry."

"Let's go into the recreation room, and I'll introduce you to the other gentlemen."

I followed Henry into the room, and right away everyone got quiet.

"My friends, say hello to Mr. Obadiah Bradford, from Autauga County, Alabama."

Almost in unison, they said, "Welcome to Augusta, Obadiah." Then they began to come around to introduce themselves to me. I had not expected such a warm welcome.

"We are just one big family here," Henry said.

All ten guests were together in the recreation room. I was able to spend some time with everyone who was present. I was the only one from Alabama. The others were from Georgia, Louisiana, Mississippi, and South Carolina.

Mrs. Milton came to the door and said, "Gentlemen, dinner is being served in the dining room."

Mrs. Susan Milton was a nice looking lady. She was somewhat younger than her husband. She was in charge of feeding us hungry men. The Miltons had a Negro cook and a maid who also lived in the house. Their names were Kissy and Martha. Kissy was much younger than Martha. I was impressed with their cooking. It was good old Southern-style home cooking, just like back in Alabama.

After dinner, Henry continued to make me feel right at home. It was like he had been assigned as my buddy. I liked him and appreciated his orientation time. He was able to answer all my questions. I learned that the street we lived on was named after the famous Revolutionary War General, James Jackson. General Jackson had also been governor of Georgia.

Several of the streets around Jackson were named after famous people like General George Washington, who became the first President of the United States. McIntosh Street was named after General Lachlan McIntosh and Elbert Street was named after General Samuel Elbert. There were several other famous streets, but they were too much for me to remember at one time.

"Will you need someone to wake you up in the morning, Obadiah?" Henry asked.

"I brought a clock with me; I think I'll be okay," I said, with appreciation to Henry.

"Well, it's been a long day, and tomorrow we report to Old Medical School. I'm going to turn in. I'll see you in the morning for breakfast," Henry said, as he left for his room.

I, too, decided to go to bed. Tomorrow would be one of the most important days of my life.

CHAPTER 14

Our first day at the Old Medical School was spent in orientation. We were given our schedules and room assignments. We went through a short schedule for the purpose of meeting our teachers, obtaining our textbooks, and getting a list of supplies we needed for each of our classes. It was a busy day to say the least.

One of the events I enjoyed most was getting to tour the two-story brick building that housed both the medical school and hospital. The building was built in 1835 after the Georgia General Assembly approved the official name for the college. The building was equipped with lecture rooms, dissecting rooms, a library, and several hospital rooms. As we entered one of the dissecting rooms, the smell of formaldehyde was very strong. This would be my first experience in dissecting animals, one I was not too excited about.

As I was leaving the building to return to the Milton House, I heard someone call my name. I looked around to see my new friend, Henry Dotson.

"Hello, Henry," I said.

"Are you heading back to the Milton House?" Henry asked.

"Yes, I am!"

"You mind if I walk with you?"

"Certainly you may!"

"Well, Obadiah, how was your first day?"

"It was exciting! I got to meet my teachers and was able to hear a short speech from each of them. I really think I will like them. I know my course of study is going to be more structured and demanding than anything I'm used to, but I believe I can handle it."

"Obadiah, I've taken those first year medical courses you named. If you think my notes could be of help to you, you are more than welcome to borrow them."

"That's very nice of you, Henry. I'm going to take you up on that offer."

I didn't want to reject Henry's offer to use his notes. Although I will be taking my own notes, I still could use Henry's as an extra study aid. I certainly didn't want to hurt Henry's feelings. He was trying really hard to be my friend. I liked him, and I was sure we were going to have lots in common during my first year in Augusta.

"Now, tell me about your day, Henry."

"Well, Obadiah, I've been assigned to Dr. Matthew Tolskey, a teaching surgeon from Atlanta. Here at the college, he's gained a reputation for being very strict and demanding. He expects the very best from the students under his supervision. To be honest with you, I'm a little intimidated around him."

"Henry, I'm sure you are going to do well."

"Thanks for your encouragement, Obadiah."

Upon arriving at the Milton House, we went inside where we found several Milton House residents visiting over snacks and lemonade. We had all come to Augusta for the same purpose: to obtain a doctor's degree in medicine. We were excited and ready to meet the challenges of tomorrow and each succeeding day.

As I visited with each of the first-year students, I suggested we form a study group. It made good sense, since we were all enrolled in the same courses and had the same teachers. Each of them quickly agreed that it was a good idea. We had Henry to thank. Henry had previously shared with me his experience with a study group during his first year of medical school. He said, "It was a complete success. Not only did we benefit from each other's knowledge, but great friendships came out of it as well." If a study group had been successful for Henry and his group, why wouldn't it be successful for us as well?

We ended our first day by enjoying a great dinner cooked by Kissy and Martha. As I pushed away from the table, I felt full as a tick, an old expression I'd heard our slave, George, say. I had a hard time getting up. I thought, *if I continue to eat like this, I will surely gain weight.*

After our first day, we had settled into a rigorous, taxing, daily schedule. I was spending every waking moment doing something in relation to my class work. The assignments were both demanding and time consuming. Each night, I was joined by my study group, which consisted of Ben Murphy, from Atlanta, Georgia; John Peters, from Lafayette, Louisiana; and Jim Boroughs, from Columbus, Mississippi. We quickly became good friends. We were engaged in long hours of individual study as well as group study. The weekends were the only days we had any time for relaxation and recreation away from our study. At times, I wondered if my brain would be able to handle any additional knowledge.

During the first few days of school, I managed to get off letters to my parents, Sarah, Audrey, and Penelope. I had received a reply from all four. My mother was the first to write. She said all was going well with her and Father. She said Mattie and Big Jim were just made for each other. She wanted me to know that Sarah's relationship with Jim Crawford was developing just as we had hoped. They were seeing each other at least two times a week. She thinks something serious might be coming out of the relationship. She said that Father approves of Jim Crawford and is very kind to him when he comes calling.

Audrey was the second person to reply to my letter. She said she misses me something awful. She reported that Millie, her horse, was getting fatter by the day. She couldn't wait to see what the colt will look like. She wonders if the colt will be black or red, since Millie is black and General is red. She asked me which was dominant. *She's already giving me medical questions to answer,* I thought. She had taken a job in Prattville working for Mr. Daniel Pratt at a ladies dress shop he owns. She said if Mr. Pratt lives long enough, he will eventually own every business in Prattville.

The next to write was Sarah. She wanted me to know that she was getting serious about Jim Crawford. She's just waiting until he pops the question of marriage to her. She said she had gotten the idea Father really approves of Jim Crawford. She said she had received a letter from Penelope, and she is enjoying

Mrs. Adams's Prep School. She bragged about Penelope's sentence structure and her ability to express herself.

Finally, I received Penelope's letter. She apologized for the delay in writing but wanted to wait until she got her first report card. She was so happy about her performance. She wanted to share with me that she had received all Bs in her general education courses. She also stated that she misses me and thinks of me every day. She had written Mattie two times and had received two letters from her. She was really happy to see her mother writing letters. She said, "I'm the first one Mama has written to. I'm so very proud of her." She went on to say her mother was very happy in her marriage to Big Jim. Penelope described her friendship with her roommate, Jessica, as being wonderful.

Although Penelope was the last to write, her three-page letter was filled with lots of news. I could tell she was happy at Mrs. Adams's school.

After reading Penelope's letter, I decided I would take Sunday afternoon to answer all four letters. Sunday afternoon was about the only free time I had.

My Saturday mornings were dedicated to reading the two weekly newspapers that Father had provided for me. The abolitionists continued their objective to end slavery. Their goal was to publish testimonies throughout the Northern and Southern states through weekly newspapers to bring about an awareness of the atrocities of slavery. They were certainly doing a wonderful job!

I found some of the testimonies interesting. The one from Rev. Joseph Belton, a minister of the Methodist Episcopal Church in Marlborough, Massachusetts, who had lived for a number of years in Georgia, said: "Another dark side of slavery is the neglect of the aged and sick. Many, when sick, are suspected by their masters of faking, and are therefore whipped and forced to work after disease has taken fast hold of them. When the masters learn that they are really sick, they are in many instances left alone in their cabins during work hours; a few of the slaves are left to die without having one friend to wipe off the sweat of death. When the slaves are sick, the masters do not, as a general rule, employ physicians, but *doctor* them themselves, and their mode of practice in almost all cases is to bleed them and give salts. When women are about ready to give birth, they have no physician but are committed to the care of slave midwives. Slaves complain very little when sick. When they die, they are frequently buried at night without much ceremony, and in many instances without any. Their coffins are made by nailing together rough boards, frequently with their feet sticking out at the end. Sometimes they are put into the ground without a coffin or box of any kind."

Another testimony caught my eye. This one was shared by Bill Payton, a native of Richmond, Virginia, who was once a slaveholder. For several years, he had been a merchant in Richmond. He finally emancipated his slaves and removed to Hamilton County, Ohio, near Cincinnati, where he is a highly respected elder in the Presbyterian Church. He said, "I am pained exceedingly, and nothing but my duty to God, to the oppressors, and to the poor downtrodden slaves, who go mourning all their days, could move me to say a word. I will state to you a few cases of the abuse of the slaves, but time would fail, if I had language to tell how many and great are the inflictions of slavery in its mildest form."

Mr. Payton gave testimony to the following event: "I once knew a man by the name of Benjamin Drake, a wealthy tobacco farmer of Richmond, Virginia, who whipped a slave girl to death. She was fifteen years old. While he was whipping her, his wife heated a smoothing iron and pressed it on her body in various places, burning her severely. The verdict of the coroner's inquest was, 'Died of excessive whipping.' He was tried in Richmond, but acquitted. I attended the trial. Some years after, this same man whipped another slave to death. The man had not done as much work as was required of him. After a number of protracted and violent scourging, with only short intervals between, the slave died under the lash. Drake was tried, but again acquitted, because no one but blacks had witnessed the events. Afterwards, Drake severely whipped yet another slave for not working hard enough. After repeated and severe floggings in quick succession for the same cause, the slave, in despair of pleasing Drake, cut off his own hand. Mr. Drake soon after filed for bankruptcy and went to New Orleans to regroup his finances, failed, removed to Kentucky, went insane, and died."

The third testimony was from Mr. Lon Turney, a regular and respectable member of the Second Presbyterian Church in Springfield, Virginia. He was born and brought up in Caroline County, Virginia. He said that slaves should not be considered to be, nor treated as, human beings. One of his neighbors whose name was Carr said on one occasion that he stripped a slave and lacerated his back with a bull whip, and then washed it with water with salt and pepper in it. Mr. Turney saw this. He further remarked that he believed there were many slaves there in advanced life whose backs had never been well since they began working.

He stated that "One of his uncles had killed a slave woman — broke her skull with an ax helve because she had insulted her mistress! No notice was taken of the affair." Mr. Turney said further that, "Slaves were frequently murdered."

He mentioned the case of one slaveholder, who he had seen lay his slaves on a large log, which he kept for the purpose, where he stripped them, tied them with their face downward, then had a kettle of hot water brought. At this point, he would take a paddle made of hard wood and perforated with holes, dip it into the hot water and strike, before every blow dipping it into the water. Every hole at every blow would raise a whelk. This was the usual punishment for running away.

Another slaveholder had a slave who had often run away and often been severely whipped. After one of his floggings, he burned down his master's barn. This act so enraged the owner that when he caught the slave, he took a pair of pincers and pulled the slave's toenails out. The Negro then murdered two of his master's children. The slave was hunted down, shot through the shoulder, and hanged.

I couldn't stand reading anymore. The abolitionists were certainly getting their message out to the whole world. This method of propaganda, which was mostly true, was surely working. It was disturbing! I told myself I would stop reading these testimonies because it made me feel so bad.

CHAPTER 15

My first semester proved to be everything Henry Dotson said it would be. My study group and I averaged five hours a night studying for our final exams. There were times I felt I couldn't cram anything else into my brain or it would explode. I can't say I looked forward to the final exams, but I was definitely looking forward to Christmas break. I would be returning home to Twin Oaks for a two-week break. The break would allow the opportunity to see Penelope, Audrey, Sarah, and my folks. My medical school obligations had been so demanding that I wasn't able to make it home for Thanksgiving.

My first semester had given me an opportunity to become good friends with Henry Dotson, John Peters, Ben Murphy, and Jim Boroughs. I learned so much from Henry Dotson. Being a second-year student, he is presently at the top of his class, and will finish his course of study this year, provided he passes his state medical boards. I have no doubt he will pass with flying colors. Much of what we do, we do together. Right now we all have a competitive spirit that stimulates all of us to want to learn and succeed. We are always sharing ideas and asking each other medical questions. This is one way we learn. Although we work hard, we still leave some time to play. Since we all like the theater, we normally spend our Saturday nights at the theater. Some of the other medical students who live at Melton Place are involved in dating girls. The four in our group, however, only hang out together. It's not that we don't like girls; we decided early on that girls were not the most important thing in our lives at this time.

Last week, I made arrangements for Penelope to come home from Boston on the train. This is her first time to ride by herself on a train and her first train trip since I accompanied her to Boston. She's excited about being home for Christmas. Like me, she hasn't had an opportunity to come home since going to Boston.

In my last letter to Audrey, I told her I wanted to spend some quality time with her during my two-week Christmas break. She still works as a sales clerk at Daniel Pratt's ladies dress shop in Prattville. Every time I look at General and Millie's painting, I'm reminded of Audrey. This was Audrey's objective to keep me focused on her every time I looked at the picture.

Our semester exams were easier than I had expected. In fact, I feel pretty good about my performance. My instructors have scored my work as A's all through the semester. I feel I am learning things that will equip me to be the doctor I have always dreamt of being.

On December 18, 1855, I said goodbye to my friends and bordered the train home to Autauga County. The train ride to Selma took one day. As soon as I stepped off the train in Selma, I heard a familiar voice.

"Master Obadiah! Master Obadiah! It's so good to see you," Bill said as he came walking up to me.

"Bill," I said, as I gave him a big hug.

"Master Obadiah, let me get that bag for you."

"Thanks, Bill! It feels good to be back in Selma. How's everyone at Twin Oaks?"

"Everyone is doing just fine, Master Obadiah. Everyone is waiting for your return home. Mattie, Betsy, and Penelope are cooking your favorite meal, fried chicken with all the trimmings."

"I can't wait. I'm glad Penelope got home safely. I was worried about her coming home alone."

"I don't think you have to worry about Miss Penelope, Master Obadiah. She's really blossomed out since leaving Twin Oaks."

"I swear, Bill! You are using some big words. What does blossom mean?"

"You know what blossom means, Master Obadiah, don't you?"

"I know, but I want to hear what you think blossom means."

"Master Obadiah, blossom means Penelope is really beautiful and talks and acts like a southern lady."

"Now, Bill, I think you have been studying those books I asked you to read while I've been gone."

"Yes, I have, Master Obadiah. I wants to speak properly, too."

I laughed out loud at Bill. He was so funny. I complimented him on his reading and speaking ability as we left the depot in Selma. As I've said several times, Bill just might be the best educated black man in Autauga County. I want to think I've had a little something to do with his education.

As Bill headed home to Twin Oaks, my thoughts turned to Penelope. I wondered if I would still have strong feelings for her. I can remember clearly the night I kissed her in my mother's garden and the morning I held her in my arms in Boston before saying goodbye to her. If these feelings were still present when we are around each other, these two weeks may get rather complicated.

As Bill turned off the main road and headed toward Twin Oaks, the lush green wheat field caught my eye. Green had always been my favorite color, just as spring was my favorite season. It seemed like yesterday I was looking at a field of white cotton at the same location. The tall cotton stalks had been cleared away, and winter wheat had been planted. My father believed in utilizing every acre of our six-hundred-acre plantation to grow seasonal crops.

As Bill stopped the carriage in front of Twin Oaks, my parents, Sarah, Mattie, Betsy, and Penelope were standing on the front porch waiting for my arrival. I didn't wait for Bill to open the carriage door as I normally would have. I opened the door, stepped down, and quickly climbed the eight steps leading up to the top of the porch where everyone was waiting.

"Welcome home, my son!" my mother said, as she threw herself into my arms.

"Oh, Mother! It's so wonderful to see you."

"Welcome home, Son," my father said, as he gave me a hug.

Sarah was waiting her turn as usual. She threw herself into my arms and said, "Great to see you, Obadiah. I can't wait to hear all about your first semester."

After greeting my family, I turned and walked toward the door where Mattie, Betsy, and Penelope had been patiently waiting. I first hugged Betsy, and then Mattie. I then turned to Penelope. She was so beautiful. As I reached out to hug her, she offered me her hand instead. I knew immediately she had learned this social grace at Mrs. Adams's Prep School. I knew she wanted me to acknowledge it as well. Not to embarrass her, I bowed slightly and kissed her hand, and she smiled. Then before I could say anything, she jumped into my arms just as Sarah had done. It didn't take long for me to realize that my feelings for Penelope were still very present. I could feel Penelope's heart beating as I held her in my arms. How was I to react to this burst of affection? I knew everyone was watching us. I put her down and took a step back and said, "Look at you! I can't believe you're all grown up." I wanted to say, "You are so beautiful!" but decided this was not the place or time.

"Thank you, Master Obadiah!" Penelope said with those beautiful blue eyes sparkling along with her beautiful smile.

"It's cold out here," I said. "Let's go inside where it's warm."

I enjoyed my short visit with my folks before supper. We talked about the Georgia Medical School, the Milton House, my new friends, and my college course work. I answered one question after another. They wanted to know a full semester's agenda in a short time. I decided to save my questions for them for a later time.

Mattie came to the parlor and announced supper was ready. As we got up from our chairs, I noticed my father getting up a little slowly from his chair. I had never seen him get up so slowly. Normally, he springs up and out of his chair with ease.

"Are you feeling okay, Father?" I asked.

"Just arthritis setting in, I suppose," he said.

"Have you seen Dr. Banister about that?"

"No, not yet, but I will if it gets worse."

Mother was right; Mattie, Betsy, and Penelope had done a great job on the meal. It was very good. I ate so much I literally thought I would burst. As old George would say, "I'm as full as a tick!"

After supper, we all returned to the parlor for coffee, dessert, and fellowship. Several more questions were asked and answered. I was informed that my good friend, Hank, was going to be a father. He and Nanny were expecting a baby in April. Big Jim had turned into a strong assistant for my brother John and Mattie was pregnant with Big Jim's baby. A lot has been happening, I thought. Father was still very concerned about what was going on in Kansas.

"What happens in Kansas will certainly affect all of us," he said. "I'm hoping they can get control of some of the violence up there."

What my father was referring to was that Kansas was to have been forever free under the Missouri Compromise of 1820, but in 1854, the Kansas-Nebraska Act established "Popular Sovereignty." This new law required residents of the territory to vote its land free or pro-slavery. In the lingering hope that the North and South might again share federal power, Kansas would have had to become a pro-slavery state. The abolitionists wouldn't accept this because Kansas Territory was the only land then available to balance the slave power. There was a famous quote coming out of Kansas that said, "As goes Kansas, so goes the nation!"

I had been keeping up with the events in Kansas by reading both the Augusta Chronicle and the Selma Times. I'm afraid my father is right. What happens in Kansas could very well affect the slavery question throughout the South. It had been some time since we both were interested in the same subject.

As Father and Mother excused themselves for bed, I again observed Father having problems getting out of his chair. This bothered me. Arthritis might be the problem, but it could be something else. I decided to have Dr. Banister give him a good examination before I returned to Augusta.

Sarah shared with me her love for Jim Crawford. They had set their marriage date for June 29, 1856. After they are married, they will be making their home in Prattville. I felt good knowing Sarah was happy. She deserved the very best, and from her description of Jim Crawford, she may be getting the best. I had only met him once, and he did seem to be a nice man. He is highly educated and is presently the head financial officer for Daniel Pratt's businesses. I was happy for Sarah. She and I are more than just sister and brother. We are the best of friends.

Mattie came to the door and said, "Master Obadiah, your bath is ready."

I excused myself and bade Sarah goodnight.

After finishing my bath, I decided to take a stroll in my mother's garden before turning in for the night. As I was sitting on the bench, I heard a noise from behind me. I turned to see Penelope approaching.

"Penelope, what are you doing out here this time of night?"

"Mama wanted me to run some food over to Big Jim at the barn. He's working late tonight on some farming equipment."

"Come sit with me," I said, scooting over to make room for her to sit down by me.

"Do you still like Mrs. Adams's Prep School?"

"Oh, yes! I'm learning so much at the school. I'm doing math, studying history, choir, writing themes, doing drama, and even doing some science."

"It appears you're learning some of the same stuff I'm learning."

"Learning is fun for me, Master Obadiah."

"What do you like best about the school?"

"I believe I like writing the best. I may want to be a writer someday."

"You express yourself well in your letters, Penelope."

"Thank you for saying that, Master Obadiah."

"What about Jessica? How is she doing?"

"Jessica is wonderful! We've become good friends. She looks after me like a big sister."

"That's good, Penelope!"

"Master Obadiah, what are you learning in medical school?"

115

"Sometimes more than I think my brain can stand. If I keep doing well, maybe I can graduate in two years and start my practice back here in Autauga County."

"That would be nice, Master Obadiah."

"Since your mother and Big Jim are sharing Mattie's room, where are you sleeping?"

"Your mother has been so nice to let me sleep in Tanyua's room."

"That's very nice of my mother."

"Your folks have treated me like family, Master Obadiah. I know I'm still a slave, but they treat me like I'm special."

"What do you hear in Boston about the abolitionists?"

"I read a lot and hear a lot from Jessica. Her parents are active abolitionists in New York. They believe slavery should end. They believe slavery is cruel and inhumane."

"How does Jessica feel?"

"She feels the same as her parents."

"I'm curious, has Jessica encouraged you to run away and not return to Autauga County?"

"Oh, no, Master Obadiah! She would never do that. She believes you are a good person and you will do right toward me."

"Penelope, I promised you that I would never sell you or your mama. Do you remember me telling you that?"

"I do remember your promise, Master Obadiah."

"Have you ever given thought to what you'd do if I made you free?"

"Yes, I have. In fact, I think about it often, Master Obadiah."

"What do you think you would do?"

"I think I would stay in Boston where people are free. I believe with additional schooling, I could make me and my mama a decent living."

"Have you met any nice men in Boston?"

"I've met a few, but I'm not interested in any man right now."

"Penelope, I want to say something to you. This has to remain between you and me. Okay?

"I promise you, Master Obadiah. I won't tell a soul. What is it?"

116

"Someday, I will set you and your mother free. I'm convinced it is the thing to do, but right now isn't the time. I've seen freed slaves who are experiencing great hardships because of the hatred of people in the South. They barely make it. I don't want that to happen to you and Mattie. I want you to continue your studies and make something of yourself."

"I understand, Master Obadiah."

"Penelope, during the next two weeks, I'll be seeing Audrey Denton. Do you remember Miss Denton?"

"I've seen her with you."

"My folks want me to marry her."

"What do you want to do, Master Obadiah?"

"I'm not ready for marriage right now."

"Do you love her?"

"I'm not sure about that either."

"I think I need to go, Master Obadiah."

I saw tears running down Penelope's face. I reached over and put my arm around her. "What's wrong, Penelope?"

"It's nothing, Master Obadiah!"

"Have I said something to hurt you?"

Penelope shook her head no, as she laid her head on my chest. I could feel my heart beating faster and faster. As I sat holding her tight, my burning passion was taking over my mind and heart. I kept thinking, "This is okay. She's my slave. I own her, and I should be able to do whatever I want with her." It's okay, but it's not okay. I released my grip on her and scooted away to look at her. She was so beautiful, and so very innocent. Who was I fooling? I had to stop this and stop it now. She looked at me and said, "Its okay, Master Obadiah," as she slowly stood up and ran toward the house. Oh, what have I done? I felt like a complete idiot. Should I have waited awhile before talking to her about Audrey? I felt awful and ashamed.

I got very little sleep during the night. All I could think about was Penelope and how I had hurt her. Bringing Audrey into the picture must have crushed her spirits. I hated so much that I hurt her. As I got ready, I wondered if she was helping with breakfast. As I went by the kitchen, I stuck my head in and said good morning to Mattie and Betsy. Penelope was not there.

I decided to go to the parlor to see if Father was there. He was and Penelope was pouring him a fresh cup of coffee. She looked at me and asked, "Master Obadiah, would you like a cup of coffee?"

"I do believe I will have a cup, Penelope. Thank you!"

Penelope placed the coffee cup on a saucer and asked, "Would you like sugar or cream?"

"I'll have both cream and sugar, please," I said.

Penelope smiled as she put cream and sugar in my coffee and stirred it. She handed me the coffee cup as she excused herself to help Mattie and Betsy with breakfast.

"I'm impressed!" Father said.

"What do you mean?"

"Penelope! I was sitting here reading the paper and she came in carrying a pot of fresh coffee. She asked me if I would like some. I said, 'Yes, please.' She poured a cup and asked me the same thing she asked you. 'Sugar or cream?' I answered by saying both. She put both sugar and cream in my cup of coffee, stirred it, and passed it to me. It was some of the best coffee I've drunk in this house. I'm telling you, Obadiah, that prep school has done wonders for that girl."

"I'm impressed as well, Father."

My mother came into the parlor to announce that breakfast was ready. We took our coffee cups to the dining area in hopes of more of that good coffee. I was relieved to see Penelope happy, and not sad, as she served my father and me fresh coffee as we sat down at the table.

After breakfast, I had George to saddle General for a trip into Prattville. I decided to surprise Audrey who was working at Daniel Pratt's dress shop. While in Prattville, I would try to see Dr. Banister as well. I wanted to talk to him about Father.

As I tied General to the hitching post near the dress shop, I spotted Audrey assisting a lady who was looking at hats. She had not yet noticed me. As I entered the store, Audrey was checking her customer out at the counter. I made my way over to the opposite side of the store where I continued to watch Audrey and her customer. Audrey's beautiful smile and her long blond hair were two things I greatly admired in her beauty. As the lady exited the store, I slowly walked toward the checkout counter. I was within ten feet of the counter when Audrey looked up and spotted me. "Oh, my goodness, Obadiah, is it really you?"

We met in front of the counter where she threw her arms around me and we kissed.

"Obadiah, I've waited a long time for that kiss," she said.

"Me too!" I said with excitement as I stepped back giving her a good look.

"You are so beautiful," I said.

"For that flattering remark, I'm going to let you take me to lunch."

"I would love to, Audrey."

"It is so good to see you, Obadiah."

"When does your lunch break start?"

"In about forty-five minutes."

"Good, that will give me time to visit with Dr. Banister."

"Why are you going to see Dr. Banister? Are you sick?"

"No, I'm not sick. I just need to talk with him about Father. He's not doing well."

"What seems to be wrong?"

"I don't rightly know. He's getting around really slowly. He says it's arthritis, but I want to make sure."

"You go see Dr. Banister. I'll be right here waiting on you when you get back."

Upon arriving at Dr. Banister's office, I found myself waiting for ten minutes as he finished with one of his patients. His receptionist, Maxine, had informed him I was waiting. As the patient left, Dr. Banister came to the door and motioned me back to his office.

"Obadiah, welcome home! How long have you been here?"

"I just arrived yesterday."

"Well, it sure is good to see you. Are you ready to go to work?"

"I wish I could, Doc. I'm learning a lot, and I do love the Georgia Medical School. I can hardly wait until I can join you here in Prattville."

"I wish you were here right now. Maxine has appointments set up for me two weeks in advance. I've got too many patients and too little time. You study hard and make sure you finish in two years. I'm killing myself here.

"I'll do my best, Dr. Banister."

"What about some lunch, young man?"

"Oh, I wish I could, but I have a luncheon date with Audrey Denton."

"Oh, so I'm getting passed over for that lovely Denton girl?"

"I'm afraid so."

"Well, I guess I can live with that."

"When would be a good time to visit with you?" I asked.

"Why don't you go with me out to James Manning's plantation this afternoon around 1:30?"

"I would love that. By the way, what's happening at the Manning plantation?"

"I just got word that one of Manning's slaves needs medical attention from a flogging."

"It sounds like Manning is up to his old brutal tactics."

"I'm afraid you may be right. Be here at one-thirty and we'll drive out, to see what's going on. You can tie General to my carriage so we can visit on our way out to Manning's."

"Doc, I'll see you around 1:30."

Lunch with Audrey was really special. There wasn't a minute of silence other than when we had a mouth full of food. We had so much to catch up on. She gave me a report on Millie, her horse, who, in a few months will be giving birth to General's offspring. She was excited, and had been putting together a list of possible names to call the colt. Since I had been gone for almost six months, she brought me up-to-date on happenings around Prattville. "I see lots of new faces around town," she said. "I've heard several abolitionists from up north are here looking for stories on the treatment of slaves in our county."

"The abolitionists are everywhere," I said. "The newspapers need the money, so the abolitionists don't have any trouble getting their stories published."

I walked Audrey back to the dress shop where we made a date for Saturday night's dance in Prattville. I mounted General and rode directly to Dr. Banister's office.

On the way to the Manning plantation, I visited with Dr. Banister about Father.

"How old is your father now?" he asked.

"Father is sixty-nine."

"Obadiah, it could very well be arthritis. I will give him a thorough examination."

"I'll make sure Father knows you're coming."

We arrived at the Manning plantation around two o'clock. We were greeted by Mr. Manning at the front door.

"Mr. Manning, I understand you have a slave who needs medical attention," Dr. Banister said.

"I do!" Manning said.

"Where is he?"

"He's in the barn. I don't think he's going to be running away anytime soon."

"So he is a runaway?" Dr. Banister asked.

"Yes, he is. He's worse than Buck ever was. He was missing for several days before the federal authorities found him at a farm thirty miles from here. He and six others were being hidden by some underground organization. He was returned to me because of the Fugitive Slave Act."

As we walked toward the barn, I was reminded of another incident involving the flogging of Buck, another runaway who was severely flogged by Mr. Manning a year ago. Buck was beaten so badly that Dr. Banister and I didn't give him much of a chance to live. I prayed for Buck every time I came out to check on him, and by the grace of God, he lived.

We entered the barn and found the slave in the same area where we had found Buck. He had ankle irons attached to his legs, and his wrists were tied with a rope and stretched over a rafter. The rope was stretched so tight that his feet barely touched the ground. His back was filled with deep cuts and blood was oozing from the cuts. The flies were swarming all over his back. It was a horrible scene.

Dr. Banister said, "Manning, get him down from there. I need to be able to examine him. Do you have a blanket we can lay him on?"

"Yes, sir!"

Manning directed his overseer to get a blanket. After placing the slave on the blanket, Dr. Banister examined the slave, looked at Manning and asked, "Do you want this slave to live?"

"Doc, if I didn't want him to live, I wouldn't have sent for you."

"Then move this poor soul to a more sanitary place so we can work on him." Manning ordered Caleb Burns, his new overseer, to move the slave to a house next to the barn.

"What's his name?" Dr. Banister asked.

"His name is Nate," Burns replied.

"Obadiah, would you like to help me with Nate?"

"Yes, sir!"

"Let me see what you remember. You take charge!" Dr. Banister said.

I ordered hot water and soap to clean Nate's back. Some of the cuts needed suturing so Dr. Banister let me stitch the deep ones. I applied a disinfecting ointment over his entire back and then applied a bandage to cover the deep cuts. I told Dr. Banister that Nate was severely dehydrated.

"How do you know that?" asked Dr. Banister.

"He has a low blood pressure, a dry sticky mouth; his eyes are sunken, and he's in shock! He needs constant attention and fluids immediately. Nate may die of dehydration instead of flogging," I said.

"Obadiah, I agree with your diagnosis," Dr. Banister said with praise.

"Mr. Manning, you've heard what Obadiah said. I would suggest you carry through on this treatment starting right now."

"We will follow your directions, Dr. Banister."

As we were getting into Dr. Banister's carriage, I heard a voice say, "Master Obadiah is that's you?"

I turned and saw Buck running up to me. "Buck, how are you doing?"

"I'm doing okay, Master Obadiah. Did you fix Nate up like you did me?"

"I believe Nate will live. You need to talk to him about not running off again."

"I's going to do that, Master Obadiah. Did you'd pray for him like you'd did for me?"

"I did pray for him, Buck. Just as I did for you! You need to pray for him, too."

"I's best get back to my chores, Master Obadiah. I's don't want another flogging!"

"It's been good talking with you, Buck. I'm glad things are better for you."

"Master Obadiah, I have got me a woman now. We's got us a baby coming. I love my woman. I's never going to run away again! No sirree!"

"Buck, I'm so glad to hear you're so happy. Congratulations to you and your wife on the baby. I know you will be a good father."

"Thanks, Master Obadiah. I am always being thankful for you. You saved my life!"

"You take care of yourself, Buck," I said, as Dr. Banister and I left the plantation.

As we drove away, Nate became the focus of our discussion. "What can be done to stop flogging?" I asked.

"Obadiah, I agree that flogging should be stopped, but you know what the law of the South is. It's left up to the slave owner how he punishes his slaves. There isn't anything we can do. I know this is awful, but, Obadiah, this is just the way it is."

"This is the part I don't like, Dr. Banister. I don't like for my hands to be tied when it comes to doing nothing about such inhumane treatment. There is nothing right about flogging, nothing! Something has to be done!" I said, trying to hold back my anger.

Dr. Banister arrived at Twin Oaks around 9:30 in the morning. Mother invited him to the parlor where my father was reading his paper.

"James, Dr. Banister is here to see you," she said.

"Come in here, John David," Father said.

My father and Dr. Banister were the best of friends so Father always addressed him as John David instead of Dr. Banister.

"What's troubling you, my friend?" Dr. Banister asked.

"I don't think it's anything to worry about, but Catherine and Obadiah, my soon-to-be doctor son, insist I have a good physical examination. They won't leave me in peace until it's done. So, John David, let's get it done. The rest of you can leave and let the good doctor do his thing."

"James, I would like for Obadiah to stay if it's all right with you?"

"Well, since he's going to be a doctor someday, I suppose it's all right."

Dr. Banister gave Father a thorough examination. As I watched him, I observed him doing things I had never seen him do. I could tell from his facial expressions and questions that he was trying to piece together a diagnosis.

"Well, James, I think this will do it for now. I've taken some mental notes that I want to think through. Your blood pressure is elevated some and I want to make sure I'm making the right diagnosis. I'll let you know in a few days what I think is ailing you."

"Like I said, I think it's just arthritis setting in," Father said.

"Well, I best be on my way. Obadiah, when will you be returning to Augusta?"

"I'm heading back on January fourth. Classes start on January sixth."

"Good, maybe we can see each other before you leave for Augusta."

"I'll walk you to your carriage, Doc."

"James Bradford, I'll see you in a few days."

I followed Dr. Banister to his carriage. I was curious about what he thought was ailing my father.

"Obadiah, I think your father has some arthritis, but I'm not sure that's his real problem."

"What do you mean?"

"Obadiah, I'm afraid that anything I say would be purely speculative at this point. You have a good time with that Audrey Denton," Dr. Banister said as he smiled and got into his carriage.

CHAPTER 16

My Saturday night with Audrey was most enjoyable. I picked her up early so we could dine in Prattville. We ate at Pratt's Restaurant, which was the same restaurant that I first laid my eyes on her and her friend, Betty Simpson. Again, we had no problem talking to each other. As I looked across the table at Audrey, I could see she enjoyed being with me. I enjoyed being with her. It was like we had known each other all our lives. Audrey was a beautiful lady, one any man would appreciate having a date with.

Later at the dance, Audrey was a hit. Several of my friends wanted an opportunity to dance with her. Being the gentleman I was, I graciously stepped aside to let them have their short period of glory with my lovely date. As my friends twirled her around the dance floor, her long blonde hair bounced around her shoulders. Although I wasn't jealous of my friends, Audrey somehow wanted to assure me that she knew who she came to the dance with. She would look at me and smile and give me a wink. I had never been winked at by anyone. It was so cute. I liked her sense of humor.

While visiting with my friends, I learned that several of them were keeping up with what was going on in Kansas. One of my friends said, "I'm telling you guys, the outcome of what happens in Kansas will certainly affect us here in the South. You better hope Kansas doesn't come in as a free state."

I found it amusing that these guys, too, were interested in Kansas and had expressed basically what my father had been saying about Kansas. Maybe I had best start keeping a closer watch on Kansas myself. When the band decided to take a break, Audrey and my friend Bill Walters joined us for punch. Audrey immediately asked if we could sit down.

"My feet are killing me," she said.

"I can understand why. You've danced with about every friend I have in this room."

She smiled and asked, "Are you jealous, Obadiah Bradford?"

"No, I'm not jealous. I just know that you must be getting tired from all that dancing."

"I love to dance, Obadiah, but the rest of the night is yours. We can leave any time you wish."

On the way to Audrey's home, we enjoyed a full moon so bright it lit up the whole sky. We could see a far distance down the road. As we turned off the main road to the Denton plantation, I could clearly see the mansion a way off. The plantation mansion was a beautiful two-story house with large white columns that supported a full porch on the second level. The house was built by Audrey's father in the 1820s. It was located near Blue Creek, a beautiful creek running down the middle of the plantation. As we crossed the wooden bridge to get to the mansion, Audrey pointed toward the corral and said, "Look, Obadiah, its Millie.'"

Millie was running around the coral with her tail sticking straight up. I think she knew Audrey was coming home. "Let's go see her," Audrey said.

"She is getting big!" I said.

"She eats all the time. I think she will have a male colt."

"What makes you think that?"

"Our Old Joe, who looks after the horses, tells me when a mare eats and eats and still wants more, she will likely give birth to a male colt."

"Well, let's hope Old Joe is correct," I said with a giggle.

After petting Millie for a few minutes, we walked over to the big oak tree and sat down on a large white bench. We loved this location because it faced the creek that flowed through the plantation. As we sat on the bench, we snuggled closely to each other to stay warm. It wasn't a really cold night, but there was just enough chill in the air for snuggling. This was the first night we had been out this late. It was our first time to hear the frogs croaking from the creek nearby. Because of the still of the night, the frogs were making all kinds of sounds. The night was full of laughter as we tried to imitate the frogs. I don't think I ever before laughed so hard. It was fun to be silly. It was easy to enjoy time with Audrey. She always had something going that was interesting or funny. We were like two teenage kids out to have a good time, being silly and enjoying every minute.

That would be the last date we would have for awhile. I had made no plans to return to Autauga County during the second semester. We spent the last few minutes together snuggling and saying goodbye to each other with an occasional kiss. When it came to kissing, we refrained from getting overly passionate with our feelings for each other. Audrey was strictly a southern girl who believed that passion came after marriage. I certainly would honor that. It was late when I left Audrey's plantation for Twin Oaks. It would take me about thirty minutes to get home. I was tired and knew I wouldn't have trouble sleeping.

It was now Christmas Eve, a little chilly, with a slight drizzle, but a perfect night for a stroll in the garden. The moon was full and the stars were twinkling throughout the sky. I had seen Penelope come and go most nights through the garden to take big Jim his dinner. She used the trail through the garden as a short cut from the house to the barn. I had decided I needed to see Penelope before Christmas. I had purchased her a scarf for a Christmas gift and wanted to present it to her in person. I had also purchased one for both Mattie and Betsy. I didn't want them to feel left out. I took a seat on the big white bench my mother had placed near a section of her roses. Mother loved her roses and was blessed with a green thumb in raising them. During the early spring, she always kept our house smelling like roses. She, too, loved sitting in her garden smelling the roses and admiring her other beautiful flowers. Gardening was truly one of my mother's favorite hobbies.

As I sat there waiting patiently for Penelope to return from the barn, I began to question if this was a good idea. I had considered the risk involved in meeting Penelope alone in the garden but resolved in my mind that the risk was one I was willing to take. I heard Penelope coming up the trail so I stood up, not wanting to startle her as she approached the bench.

"Master Obadiah, what are you doing out here on this crisp cold night?"

"To tell you the truth, Penelope, I've been waiting for you."

"For me, Master?"

"Yes, for you. I have a gift for you and one for Mattie and Betsy. I would like for you to give them their gifts on Christmas Day," I said handing the two gifts to Penelope.

"Let's sit down so you can open your present," I said as I handed her the gift.

Penelope gently unwrapped the present and took out the scarf. She put it to her face and said, "It's so warm! Thank you, Master Obadiah. I love the scarf! May I try it on?"

"Sure! It will keep your face warm on this chilly night."

Even with the scarf draped over her face she still looked so beautiful. Her smile melted my heart.

"It's cold out here, Master Obadiah."

"Yes, it is. I guess we need to go inside where it's warm."

"Before we go inside, I have to share something with you, Master Obadiah."

"What is it, Penelope?"

"I really don't know how to properly say this to you, but I'm going to try. Please bear with me. Jessica tells me I have to learn to tell people what's on my mind, even though it may turn out badly. Anyway, Master Obadiah, I think I'm in love with you. Please forgive me for just coming out and saying that, but I need to get it off my chest. I know deep down that you can never love me as I love you. I know also that white folks would never approve of you loving me and even marrying me, but I have to tell you something. It's so hard for me to be around you without touching you and telling you how much I love you. You are the best thing that ever happened to me and my mama, and I will always appreciate you for your honesty and respect for us. You are just wonderful! Please forgive me for how I feel. I promise you, I will never do anything to put you to shame. I would do anything for you, and I want you to know that I would willingly be your mistress should you want me to."

"Stop, Penelope! Please stop. I'm not mad at you. You have just described to me how I've felt for you all these years. I'm in love with you as well. I think I've been in love with you since the first day I looked into those beautiful blue eyes of yours. You are right about how society would look upon our relationship. It wouldn't work between us as husband and wife. I've thought many times we could run off together to New York or even Boston and get married where no one would ever know you are a Negro. You don't look like a Negro, so we could pull it off. That's not the solution either. I'm not sure there is a solution. I want your love very much. My heart and body ache for you. I appreciate your willingness to make me happy, but right now, just knowing you love me and I love you has to be enough for both of us."

"Will you please hold me, Master Obadiah?"

I reached out and pulled her close to me. She was shivering so hard. I couldn't tell if it was the cold or if it was emotion. It had to be hard on Penelope to share her love for me. I was flattered! I love her and it breaks my heart we can't be together. Her offer to be my mistress would be what most slave owners dreamed about and would welcome with open arms. How can I explain to her that this can't happen? How can I explain to her that I can't accept her love and affection for me? Lord, help me!

As I continued to hold her, her shivering seemed to leave her body. She looked up at me and smiled. I told myself that one last kiss wouldn't be wrong. I drew her near and kissed her soft lips. Those same feelings again surfaced. My passion for Penelope was so real. I tried to convince myself that this was right. She was enjoying it as much as I, but one of us had to stop it. It had to be me. She had already described how she felt, and if I didn't stop, something was going to happen that I would regret, or would I? I gently released my grip on Penelope, looked her in the eyes, and said, "My dear Penelope, I do love you. I will always love you. I'm going to ask you not to ever forget this night."

"Master Obadiah, I'll always remember this night. I believe that someday God will make it right, and please know that I will be there for you. I believe this with all my heart," she said as she stood and then ran to the house.

I must have sat there for another hour after Penelope left to return to the house. I can't describe in words how I felt. It was like I was in some kind of trance. I felt empty, barely able to hold my head up. I felt depressed, something I had never experience in my entire life. I finally convinced myself I would freeze to death if I didn't get in out of this weather. I slowly motivated myself to stand up and head for the house. I found my room warm with a fire going in the fireplace. I needed to get some sleep. Tomorrow was Christmas day and Christmas day was always a big day for the Bradfords. My brothers and sisters would be coming for Christmas dinner and some would be staying the night. This was a custom my parents started several years ago, one that we would continue as long as my parents lived.

It was the custom of the Bradford family for my father to read the Christmas story. Since we had family coming from Prattville and Cahaba, the Christmas story would be read after lunch. Our family had grown so big that smaller tables had to be brought into the dining area so everyone would have a place to be seated. Betsy, Mattie, and Penelope had prepared a delicious Christmas dinner. Big Jim was present to carry the heavy meat trays to the big table. He looked very becoming in his white apron. As I looked at him helping Mattie, I decided I had picked just the right man for her. Most men wouldn't like to be bossed around, but Big Jim didn't seem to mind at all. As usual, the Christmas dinner went off without a hitch. Penelope was her lovely self. We made eye to eye contact several times during dinner. At one time, I noticed my sister Sarah looking at me shaking her head as if to say, "Obadiah, don't make things so obvious."

After dinner, we congregated in the parlor for Father's reading of the Christmas story from Luke, Chapter Two. My father had done this so many years that he actually ended up telling the story instead of reading it word for word. This year, there was something different in Father's voice. I sensed a certain emotional tone to his telling the story. It was like he was saying goodbye or something. I couldn't wait for Dr. Banister to give us a report of his findings in regard to Father's health.

The exchange of presents took most of the afternoon. The Bradford house was full of Christmas spirit and thanksgiving. Our Lord and Savior had been good to us. His blessings had been many and we were all thankful we could be together for another year. The family members who lived in Prattville returned home while my brother Dent and his family spent the night. Cahaba was just too far away to travel home in the dark.

After dinner, Dent and I went for a walk in Mother's rose garden. I shared with Dent my feelings that Father may have some serious health issues facing him. I told him that Dr. Banister was analyzing his physical examination results of Father, and that we should know something in a few days.

"Obadiah, Father is getting up in age. He's been through a lot during his lifetime. I've seen him do work you've not seen him do. You were too young to see some of the things that man could do. Arthritis may be his problem. Let's hope so at least."

"I do hope you're right, Dent. I want to believe you are, but something in Dr. Banister's eyes tells me that he suspects something else is wrong."

"Obadiah, can we change the subject and talk about another concern I have?"

"Okay, big brother, what's on your mind?"

"I don't know if anyone else in our family saw how you and Penelope were looking at each other today, but I certainly did. What's going on between you two?"

I scratched my head trying to figure out how to answer Dent's question. I knew Dent was very observant, but hadn't expected him to question me about Penelope.

"Well, Obadiah, are you not going to say anything?"

"Dent, there isn't anything serious going on between Penelope and me," I said looking away. I knew I couldn't look him in the eye and say that.

"Obadiah Bradford, my little brother, oh, how you are lying to me!"

"I'm sorry, Dent. You must know I have feelings for Penelope. I've had feelings for her since I first laid eyes on her. If you want to know the gospel truth, I'm crazy in love with her."

"Obadiah, I can't say I blame you. You've got a big problem. It's very obvious."

"You are right about that. What's worse is knowing I have to go through life not having the woman I cherish. What should I do about Penelope, Dent?"

"It's obvious she feels the same way about you."

"Well, what do you think I need to do?"

"What I think goes against God's teachings, Obadiah, but Penelope is your slave and she loves you. I think she would do anything for you. Why not see her on the side like lots of slave owners do?"

"Dent, I couldn't do that and I won't. Furthermore, I would not put our family in any compromising position that might cause embarrassment. What if Penelope came up pregnant like hundreds of other slave girls? Big brother, I can't believe you are advising me this way."

"Obadiah, all I know is you've got it bad. I mean bad! It's written all over your face. There will come a time you will have to face this head on. If I was in your shoes, I'm not sure I could resist Penelope. That girl is head over heels in love with you, little brother."

"I know you're right. I'm finding it very difficult to resist Penelope. I keep telling myself it's all right to have a relationship with her on the side, as you said, but, Dent, I love her too much not to have her in a Godly way. If I can't have her in a Godly way, I'll have to distance myself from her unless God works things out for us."

"Obadiah, I hate to burst your bubble but the Godly way is not going to work here in Autauga County, Alabama. It will never happen!"

Dent put his arm around my neck and said, "Obadiah, your secret will remain our secret," as we walked back to the house.

Dr. Banister's visit to Twin Oaks on January 3, 1856, brought news of the worst kind. What I had feared was about to be revealed to my father. Mother, Sarah, Father, and I met in the parlor with Dr. Banister as he informed us of his findings.

"James, you do have some arthritis settling in your knees and hips joints, but my friend, what I'm concerned about is your heart."

"I don't understand what you're saying, John David," my father said.

"James, I'm afraid your heart is wearing out. You are going to have to take it easy around here. No riding horses, no physical exertion, eating right, and light exercising. I'm going to give you a list of things you are not to do. I know this is going to be hard on you, my friend, but all of this is important if you want to continue living."

"That's a big order, John David," Father said.

"Don't you worry, Dr. Banister; we'll see that he behaves himself," Mother said.

Dr. Banister took my father's hand and said, "If you do as I say, you could live several more years, but you have to do what I say. Do you understand that, James?"

My father acknowledged Dr. Banister by saying, "I'll do my best."

I walked to the carriage with Dr. Banister. I thanked him for being truthful with all of us about Father's heart condition. We said our goodbyes, and he left to return to Prattville for a busy day at his office.

After Dr. Banister left, Sarah and I wrote our brothers and sisters to bring them up-to-date on Father's health issues. I sent George into Prattville and Bill to Cahaba to deliver our letters. After George and Bill left, Father called a family meeting.

"Obadiah, I just got word from Sarah that you don't plan to return to Augusta for school. What's going on here?" Father asked.

"Father, I think I'm needed here right now. I can go back to school later."

"That is out of the question, Obadiah. You are returning to school and that is it!" Father said quite emphatically.

"But, Father, hear me out."

"Obadiah, I agree with your father. You go ahead with your schooling. Sarah and I will take care of your father. We have lots of help. Bill can move in here and be here at night. Big Jim is just a shout away. We will be just fine, so you go ahead and make your plans to return."

"Father, I don't feel right returning to school when I know I could help out here."

"Son, you've always wanted to be a doctor. You've dreamed about it since you were a boy. This is what your mother and I want for you. We want you to honor our wishes. Furthermore, I'm not going to die until I see my son walk down that aisle to receive his doctor's degree. You can just count on that!"

I knew it wasn't going to do any good to argue this subject with Father and Mother. If that was what they wanted, I would certainly honor their wishes.

I was up early making the final arrangements with Bill to take Penelope to Selma on January seventh for her return to Boston. I knew I could count on Bill to get her on the train. Mattie, Penelope, and Betsy had prepared an extra special breakfast. We had pancakes and maple syrup, eggs, bacon, sausage, and hot biscuits. It was a breakfast that would stay with me for the entire day.

It was hard for me to say goodbye to my family. To see my father in the condition he was in really hurt. I still felt guilty going back to Augusta. I just hoped and prayed that Father will take care of himself. I have every bit of confidence in my mother, but at times my father can be quite contrary. I didn't like saying goodbye. Everyone was standing on the front porch getting last minute hugs and crying as usual. I had said goodbye to everyone but Penelope. She had been standing off to the side crying. She handed me a box of oatmeal raisin cookies, my favorite.

"I baked them myself," Penelope said.

"Thank you, Penelope. I'm sure I'm going to enjoy these all the way to Augusta."

"If you have some left, you can share them with your friends at the Melton House."

"I'll do just that," I said hugging her and wishing her well in school during her second semester. "You take care and write me."

"I promise, I'll write, Master Obadiah."

"We love you, Son!" my mother said as I waved goodbye to everyone.

CHAPTER 17

My train ride from Selma to Augusta was uneventful. When I arrived in Augusta, I took a carriage from the train station to the Milton House where I found my friends engaged in a card game. After quietly placing my bags on the floor, I went to the parlor and yelled, "Is that all you guys have to do?"

"Come on in here, Obadiah. We've been waiting for you to show up," Henry Dotson said.

"Welcome back, Obadiah," John said as he, Henry, Ben, and Jim got up and came over to give me a welcome back hug.

"We were wondering if you had decided against coming back," Ben said.

"Indeed! We were wondering if that lovely Audrey Denton had persuaded you to stay in Autauga County," Henry said.

"No sir, Audrey wanted me to come back and take care of my buddies," I said with a laugh.

"After you get settled in, come back and join us. We have about an hour before dinner," Henry said.

"I'll do just that," I said as I left the room to check in with Mr. Milton at the counter.

"Welcome back, Obadiah Bradford," Mr. Milton said.

"Thank you, Mr. Milton. It's good to be back in Augusta."

"I trust you had a good Christmas break with your folks."

"Yes, I had a wonderful time, but I'm ready to get back to my schooling."

"You will need to get washed up. Kissy, Martha, and Mrs. Milton have cooked Southern fried chicken for dinner. I know you must be hungry after a long train ride."

"You're so right about that!"

I went to my room, washed my hands and face, and went back to join the others in a game of cards.

It was so good to be back with my friends. Their friendship meant everything to me. My success in my course work during the first semester was due to their encouragement, studying together, and sharing ideas. We spent time helping each other in one way or another. Ben Murphy was one who we had to help most. He had an awful time waking up and getting ready for breakfast. One of us had to take on the responsibility of getting him up and getting him to breakfast every morning. After he ate breakfast, he was good for the rest of the day.

It was good seeing Kissy, Martha, and Mrs. Milton again. Mr. Milton was right about his assessment of the dinner. The Southern fried chicken and all the trimmings were great, second only to Betsy's and Mattie's fried chicken back at Twin Oaks.

Although I was worried about Father, I'm glad he insisted I come back for my second semester. On the train ride here from Selma, I had time to reflect on my two weeks at home. Father getting sick had convinced me I needed to hurry and finish my doctor's degree. I need to get back to Autauga County and help my mother with Father. By going to school during the summer, I could finish my course work in the spring of 1857. I could take my board exams and hopefully be able to practice medicine with Dr. Banister in Prattville during the summer of 1857. I will pray that God will allow this to happen.

I also have some big decisions to make concerning Penelope and Audrey. I love both of them in two different, distinct ways. Being away from both of them for almost two years would give me time to resolve what would be best for me and them.

My second semester will certainly become more of a challenge. The course work is projected to be harder and more time consuming than the first semester. I'm satisfied I can do the work, but it doesn't leave much time to do anything else I like to do. My friends are experiencing the same feeling. Henry tells us we shouldn't be worrying. He says, "You guys are smarter than I am and look at me. I'm making it."

We are well aware of Henry's status here at the medical school. He is very intelligent and if something unknown doesn't occur, he will probably graduate with one of the highest grade points of anyone who's attended this school. We all agree it's good to have Henry around.

After two weeks into the second semester, I got my first letter from Penelope. She was back at Mrs. Adams's Boarding School in Boston. She made it back without any trouble and was enjoying school. She and Jessica were having a great time. She said Boston newspapers were full of the Kansas conflict over slavery. She said the abolitionists were currently having their national conference in Boston. She had met Jessica's parents who were strong leaders in the abolitionist movement. "They have treated me like family by inviting me to some of the best restaurants in Boston. Can you believe that?" she asked. "I want you to know; I was on my best behavior and acted just like a southern lady would act in the big city of Boston." She ended her letter by telling me how much she enjoyed the Christmas break and that she would hold true to her promise. Her letter ended by saying, "I love you."

I slowly put the letter back into the envelope and placed it inside my desk where I kept all her letters. I couldn't bear destroying any of them. I had just lain back on my bed when Henry knocked on my door. "Obadiah, are you in there?"

"Come in, Henry!"

"I was wondering if you might be up to a stroll down to the Sylvania River Park. I need some fresh air and thought we might have a cup of Madison's fresh brewed coffee."

"Let me get my coat, hat, and scarf," I said.

As soon as we reached the river walk, we stopped in at Madison's coffee and bakery shop, our favorite place in Augusta. The heat never felt so good. We seated ourselves at one of the white, red, and black checker top tables. The colorful tables were always clean and refreshing. The fresh fragrance of the coffee brewing added to the warmth and personality of Madison's. After ordering our coffee, I looked at Henry and said, "What's on your mind, my friend?"

"Obadiah, I have a problem."

"What's going on, Henry?"

"Have you noticed I've been coughing a lot lately?"

"Well, come to think of it, I have. I just thought you had a cold."

"It may be more than a cold. I went to see Doctor Mark Bradley yesterday and he did a tuberculosis test. Some people refer to tuberculosis as consumption. I may have tuberculosis, Obadiah."

"Oh, Henry, I pray not! When will you know for sure?"

"Dr. Bradley is running some tests and I'm to report back to him tomorrow."

"I'm going with you tomorrow. I don't want you to face this alone."

"That's kind of you, Obadiah. I really need your prayers. If I have tuberculosis, I'll have to drop out of medical school. Tuberculosis is a horrible disease. Hundreds of people die yearly from this dreaded disease."

"I'm going to pray you don't have it. When we get back to Milton's, I would like to check your breathing with my stethoscope. Can we do that?

"I don't mind, Obadiah."

"When I worked with Dr. Banister, I gained experience listening to people who had pneumonia, flu symptoms, and tuberculosis. I got pretty good in telling the difference in the three."

"Let's have another cup of coffee before we return," Henry said.

"Why don't we cheat a little and get a piece of our favorite apple pie as well," I said.

"I was craving a piece of apple pie, Obadiah. By all means, bring it on."

Upon arriving back at my room, I listened to Henry's breathing. The sound coming from his lungs was somewhat confusing to me. I couldn't tell if it was a bad cold, pneumonia, or tuberculosis. It didn't sound like pneumonia nor did it sound like tuberculosis. When Dr. Banister wasn't completely sure, he would make his patients drink a home remedy concoction made from a mixture of green tea, honey, and whisky. If it wasn't tuberculosis, the patient normally got well.

"After dinner, I'll make you a drink. It won't hurt you and should make you relax."

I was right; he went off to sleep and slept like a log. He slept so soundly that I had to wake him up to get ready for breakfast.

"My cough is better, Obadiah."

"That's good news, Henry. Now let's hope you get good news today."

We didn't say anything to Ben, John, and Jim. We didn't want to worry them with Henry's problem. Since Henry's test was being conducted at the hospital, we wouldn't have to miss any classes. I could tell Henry was really nervous and worried. I suppose I would be, too, if faced with the same situation. I had been praying hard that Henry wouldn't have tuberculosis. This would literally destroy Henry's dream. He wanted to be a doctor as much as I did. He would certainly be one of the best doctors in the nation if given a chance.

Dr. Bill Bradley was a pulmonary specialist with the hospital and an instructor at the college. When we arrived at his office, Henry asked Dr. Bradley if I could attend the conference with him. The good doctor said, "Sure, come on in, Obadiah."

Dr. Bradley got right to the point. "Henry, I don't think you have tuberculosis. What you do have is a fungus in your lungs that acts similar to tuberculosis. The good news is that it's treatable."

"Thank God," Henry said, as he sat back in his chair.

"We can give you some medicine which should clear this fungus up. It's a concoction loaded with whisky and other ingredients that will make you drowsy and sleepy. You should sleep soundly, and rest is what you need," Dr. Bradley said as he winked at me.

"Dr. Bradley, you have given me the best news of my life. How can I thank you?"

"You have thanked me already by being our star student here at the medical school. We can't afford to lose students like you."

The medicine worked and it wasn't long before Henry was back to normal. It was good to see him returning to his old self. God had answered my prayers once again.

My time in the next several weeks was spent in study, reading, and having fun with my buddies. The fun part didn't occur often because of the demand of our time toward our studies. I was receiving letters from Mother and Sarah, and each time they reported my father was doing well. He was cooperating with my mother's every wish and seemed to be getting stronger as the weeks passed.

Audrey was right about the colt. Millie gave birth to a male colt. She said the colt looked a lot like General. He was red and had a white blaze down his forehead just like General. She was excited. "I'll never sell this colt. He will be my constant reminder of the good times we had together," she said. Her work was going well and she loved her job. She always ended her letters with, "I love you."

My ego wanted to tell me I was some special man to be loved by two special women, but in my case, it was confusion. It was something that continued to tear at my heart. I couldn't get peace regardless of how much I prayed to God.

Both the Selma Times and Augusta Chronicle were still carrying short testimonies of how slaves were being treated by their owners. The abolitionists were still hard at work. I found some of the testimonies in today's Augusta Chronicle interesting.

"In most of the southern states, the clothing of the slaves is wretchedly poor and grows worse as you go south. During the winter months, most slaves are frequently seen with nothing but a tattered coat, not sufficient to hide their nakedness. Their clothing seldom serves the purpose of comfort, and frequently not even of decent covering. In most states, the slave gets one pair of shoes a year. Stockings are seldom issued to slaves. A small poor blanket is generally the only bed-clothing, and this they frequently wear in the field when they have not sufficient clothing to hide their nakedness or to keep them warm. Their manner of sleeping varies with the season. In hot weather they stretch themselves anywhere and sleep. As it becomes cold, they nestle together with their feet towards the fire. As a general fact, the earth is their only floor and bed — not one in ten have anything like a bedstead, and then it is a mere bunk put up by themselves."

"Their bed clothes are a nest of rags thrown upon a crib, or in the corner; sometimes there are three or four families in one small cabin. Where the slaveholders have more than one family, they put them in the same quarter until it is filled, then build another."

"Their houses were commonly built of logs, sometimes they were framed, and often they had no floor. Some of them have two apartments, commonly but one; each of those apartments contained a family. Sometimes these families consisted of a man and his wife and children, while in other instances persons of both sexes, were thrown together without any regard to family relationships."

"A slave owner in Alabama who owned about three hundred slaves ceased to employ a physician to attend to his slaves because he alleged that it was cheaper to lose a few Negroes every year than to pay a physician."

"In recent days, a slaveholder in Alabama shot a Negro woman though the head; and put the pistol so close that her hair was singed. He did it in consequence of some difficulty in his dealings with her as a concubine. He buried her in a log heap; she was discovered by the buzzards gathering around her."

At the bottom of the testimonies were two quotes. The first quote was from the Honorable William H. Fitzhugh, Esq. of Virginia, a slaveholder. He said, "Slavery, in its mildest form, is cruel and unnatural; its injurious effects on our morals and habits are mutually felt."

The second quote was from the Hon. Samuel S. Nicholas, late Judge of the Court of Appeals of Kentucky, and a slaveholder, in a speech before the legislature of that sate. "The deliberate convictions of the most matured consideration I can give the subject are that the institution of slavery is a most serious injury to the habits, manners, and morals of our white population — that it leads to sloth, indolence, dissipation, and vice."

I had come to the conclusion after working side by side with Dr. Banister in Autauga County that slavery was wrong. Although I believed it was wrong, I couldn't do anything about it. I couldn't go against hundreds of slave owners who lived in the South — especially my father! At least my parents treated our slaves like human beings. Our slaves didn't go naked, nor did they go hungry. We equipped them with good housing compared to how other slaves lived on other plantations. We attended them when they got sick by calling Dr. Banister. We treated them like human beings. I will continue to honor my father's wishes and support slavery until the law changes it. I do pray that someday slaves across this great nation will be free. If the abolitionists continue their work, my prayer may be answered sooner than I realize.

Looking back on years past, I can remember when I first heard about the abolitionists. I remember quite well reading *Uncle Tom's Cabin*, by Harriet Beecher Stowe, a devout abolitionist. *Uncle Tom's Cabin* was written by Stowe to show the evils of slavery. When the book was released to the public in 1852, it caused a rumble of discord across the South toward Stowe. She was called everything in the book by slave owners throughout the South. Her book played a major impact on the way Northerners viewed slavery and was the beginning of a push in the northern states to do away with slavery. Thousands of Northerners joined the abolitionist organization to push for the end of slavery.

Just as I was getting ready to touch base with Henry, Ben knocked on my door.

"Come in!" I said.

"Hey, Obadiah, the gang is going out tonight to the theater. You want to go?"

"I need a night out. Yes! When are we leaving?"

"About six o'clock. That will give us time to eat and still have time to catch the show."

"We'll see you later," Ben said as he closed the door.

The gang, as Ben described us, loved doing things together. We all had girl friends back home so we weren't out looking for girls. We just enjoyed each other's company. What we were actually doing was building a life-long relationship, one we would cherish for years to come.

CHAPTER 18

Henry was right when he said, "Time goes fast when one is busy." It was now May 20, 1856, and Henry was one of twenty students graduating from medical school. As we expected, he was number one in his class and was graduating with the highest grade point of any student who had graduated at the Old Georgia Medical School. We were all proud of our good friend, Henry. Henry's speech was one I will not forget. His words of wisdom gave me hope in mapping out the remaining part of my schooling.

I shall always remember Henry's parting remarks of his wonderful speech. He said, "To our president, Dr. Thompson, staff, parents, students, and close friends: when I came here two years ago, I came with one goal in mind, to prepare myself to become one of the best doctors in our country. I've always dreamed of being a doctor of medicine, and with the help of my Savior, Jesus Christ, the staff's untiring dedication to teaching, my parents support, loved ones, and close friends' encouragement, I can stand here today as a witness that the first part of my goal has been accomplished.

"I'm not going to stand here today and say it was easy, because it wasn't. But what I want to emphasize to you is that hard work and determination, and one's faith in God are key ingredients in reaching one's goals. Before taking my state boards, I prayed to God that he would give me the ability to recall the broad scope of knowledge I've learned in these past two years. My goal of returning to my home city of Atlanta, Georgia, and practicing medicine is now a dream come true. Today, I share this platform with nineteen others who have achieved the same goal. Today is our day! But next year, for you who will be graduating, it will be your day, my friends. Don't let up; work hard and dream of greater rewards ahead. Thank you for listening!"

Henry was given a standing ovation by the entire assembly, including the teaching staff, and college president, Dr. Jeffrey Thompson, who was seated on the platform as well.

After the graduation ceremonies, our gang joined Henry and his family at Madison's for a time of celebration. We enjoyed getting to know Henry's family and as usual, Madison's wonderful apple pie and fresh brewed coffee.

Jim Boroughs and Ben Murphy decided to join me and remain in Augusta for summer school. Our friend Jon Peters chose to return home to Lafayette, Mississippi, for the summer. He would be returning to Augusta for the fall term.

Since there would be a two-week break before summer school, I decided to return home for a few days to see my folks and Audrey. I would not be seeing Penelope who would be continuing her schooling and working at her job in Boston. Her friend and roommate, Jessica, was also staying in Boston. Jessica's parents had moved to Boston and started a hardware business. Jessica would be helping with the family business as well as working part time at Mrs. Adams's Boarding School. It put me at ease when I found out that Jessica would be nearby should Penelope need anything. Like me, Penelope hadn't been home to Twin Oaks since Christmas. I knew she must miss Mattie and be anxious to someday see her new baby brother, Jim Jr. Mattie had given birth to a healthy baby boy in April, and she and Big Jim named him Jim Jr. I also received word from Dent that my friend Hank and his wife, Nanny, were parents of a baby boy as well. They named him Obi, after me. I felt very honored and looked forward to seeing him while I was home for summer break.

On my train ride back to Selma, I reviewed some articles about what had been going on in Kansas. I knew without doubt my father would be quizzing me about the happenings in Kansas. I needed to be ready. One of the things I figured he would ask my opinion about was the Border Ruffians incident in Lawrence, Kansas, in May. The event was one of the most publicized events in Bleeding, Kansas. The May twenty-second editions of the Augusta Chronicle and the Selma Times printed the Border Ruffian's story on the front page of their newspapers. The headlines were so big a reader couldn't possibly have missed it. After this story occurred, Kansas was the talk of the school. Students were concerned that civil war might begin over this incident.

The story was about pro-slavery looters from Missouri known as Border Ruffian's, ransacking Lawrence, Kansas, which was known to be a staunch free-state area. During the raid, Lawrence was sacked and burned. Several citizens were killed and millions of dollars of damage was done.

One day after the incident, the papers covered the story of a fight on the U.S. Senate floor. The story reported that pro-slavery Congressman Preston Brooks attacked Congressman Charles Sumner with a cane after Sumner had given a speech attacking the pro-slavery forces for the violence occurring in Kansas. Kansas had become a hotbed of violence as pro- and anti-slavery forces fought over the state's future. I must confess I'm finding this issue in Kansas very interesting. In my opinion, the citizens of Kansas should be given their rights under the Kansas-Nebraska Act to decide whether Kansas is to be a free or slave state. If my father should ask my opinion, that will be my answer.

I also figured my father will want to know who I plan to vote for in the upcoming United States presidential election. The Republican candidate, John C. Fremont, is crusading against slavery. His slogan is "Free speech, free press, free soil, and free men."

The Democratic Party's candidate, James Buchanan, accuses Fremont of trying to start a civil war and tells people that Fremont's election as President would lead to civil war.

At the present time, I'm leaning toward Fremont. Of course, I will not be telling my father that.

I had fallen asleep and was dreaming about Penelope when I was awakened by the car steward saying, "Selma, Alabama!"

As I stepped off the train, I heard that familiar voice that always meets me at the train station. It was Bill, my friend and reliable driver.

147

"Master Obadiah, it's so good to see you!"

"Bill, I'm so glad to see you as well. How are you?"

"I'm doing just fine, Master Obadiah. My Lord's been good to old Bill," he said with a laugh.

"How's everyone at Twin Oaks?"

"Everyone is just fine. Your daddy is doing much better. Missus Bradford makes him behaves himself. She cracks the whip, if you know what I mean?"

"I do know what you mean, Bill. She's good at that!"

After Bill put my bags in the family carriage, he looked at me and asked, "Are you ready to go home, Master Obadiah?"

"I want to run by Dent's place in Cahaba. I want to see Dent and his family and Hank, Nanny, and the new baby."

"I was hoping you'd want to do that. I would also like to see our friend Hank and his new son."

As we pulled up in front of the plantation house, Mr. Jake, Dent's house servant, came out to meet us. "Master Obadiah, it's good to see you. Is Master Dent expecting you?"

"No, Jake! They didn't know I was coming by. Are they here?"

"Missus Sara and the kids are here, but Master Dent's in the barn right now."

"I'll say hello to Sara and the kids. Why don't you go fetch my brother?"

"Yes, Master Obadiah, I'll be right back!"

"Bill, come up here on the porch, and I'll have Sara send someone out to get you a fresh glass of water. Have a seat over there."

"Yes sir, Master Obadiah!"

I went inside where I found Sara and Mary Catherine in the parlor working on altering Mary Catherine's dress.

"What a pretty dress on such a pretty lady," I said.

Both Sara and Mary Catherine quickly turned toward me and smiled.

"Obadiah Bradford, where did you come from?" Sara asked as she came over to hug me.

"I had Bill bring me by to see everyone before going on to Twin Oaks."

Mary Catherine was now sixteen years old and was probably the prettiest sixteen-year-old in these parts of Dallas County. She came over and hugged my neck and said, "It's so good to see you, Uncle Obadiah."

"It's good to see you, too!"

"How long can you stay?" Sara asked.

"I'm thinking a couple hours. I want to get home before it gets dark."

"That's good! We will have an early dinner. How's fried chicken sound?"

Sara knew the answer to that. She knew fried chicken was my favorite. "Fried chicken will be wonderful," I said.

"Where are the boys?" I asked.

"Marion's with a friend, fishing on the Alabama. Everett and Law are riding their horses somewhere on the plantation. They will be here for dinner," Sara said.

"I hope you don't mind, but I sent Jake to fetch my brother from the barn."

"Good, Dent's been out there too long. He and some of our workers are busy getting the gin ready for cotton season."

"We want to hear all about what's been going on with you in Augusta," Sara said.

Sara had no more gotten those words out of her mouth when Dent came walking in.

"I hear we have a very important, unexpected guest in our home, Sara," Dent said, smiling and winking at Sara.

We embraced as Dent welcomed me to his home. "What brings you by here, Obadiah?"

"I wanted to see Hank and his family. I hope its okay."

"It's perfectly okay. I'll send Jake to the fields to get them. Meanwhile make yourself at home."

"Obadiah, I'll have Daisy bring you some lemonade. If you will excuse Mary Catherine and me, we'll go to her room and get her out of this dress."

149

In a few minutes, Daisy entered the parlor with a big glass of lemonade. Dent came in and asked Daisy to bring him one to the front porch.

Dent and I went to the front porch where Bill was sitting waiting for me.

"Bill, I bet you are thirsty, too, aren't you?"

"I'm okay, Master Dent."

Daisy came out carrying a pitcher of lemonade and an extra glass. "I brought an extra glass for Mr. Bill, Master Dent."

"Well, thank you, Daisy. That was very thoughtful of you."

"Bill, come and get you a glass of this lemonade."

"Thank you, Master Dent."

Bill took his lemonade to the other end of the porch where he found a chair and seated himself out of the sun.

Dent and I took a seat in the middle of the porch. We were enjoying our visit when we saw Hank and Nanny walking toward the plantation house. Hank was carrying his baby boy.

As they approached the steps leading up to the porch, I got up from my chair and met them.

"Master Obadiah, it's so very nice to see you."

"I'm glad to see you and Nanny as well. Now let me see that baby boy."

Hank carefully handed me his baby boy.

"His name is Obi. We named him after you, Master Obadiah."

"Obi's a nice name, Hank. You and Nanny did well. This is a beautiful baby. I know you both are extremely happy with him."

"Oh, yes sir, we are!" Nanny said.

"How are your parents, Nanny?"

"They are doing well, Master Obadiah. They are really happy to have Obi as their first grandchild."

"Well, I can see why. He's a big one, and good looking like his mother," I said winking at Hank.

Hank was beaming with joy showing all over his face. I knew he was a proud father. I always knew he would be a good father as well. He and Nanny would raise Obi in the spirit of love.

"What have you been doing for yourself, Hank?"

"I'm preaching, Master Obadiah."

"You've become a preacher?"

"Yes sir! You always told me I could preach to my people, and Master Dent lets me preach to them on Sundays. We have us a nice place in the barn where we meet for service."

"Hank, I'm so happy for you. I'm so proud of you."

"It's because of you, Master Obadiah. If you and Missus Sarah hadn't taught me to read, I couldn't ever been a preacher. I know the Lord is blessing us."

"The Lord will bless you and your people, Hank. He loves you, and he will bless you and your ministry. I do believe that."

"Missus Sara got us some hymnals. We sing some good old southern gospel hymns."

"I wish I could attend one of your services, Hank, but I don't think my short time here will allow it. Someday when I come back to Autauga County to live, I'll attend one of your services. That's a promise!" I said as I handed Obi back to Hank.

"May God go with you and bless you in what he has in store for you and your family," I said as Hank and Nanny left the porch.

"Dent, I'm so very proud of you, big brother!" I said.

"Why are you proud of me, little brother?"

"Because you have opened up your heart to your slaves. You have given them the opportunity to know God and to worship him. You've given them hope. I love you even more than I did before."

"Obadiah, Sara is mostly responsible for all of this. She convinced me that we should do this for our slaves. Since Hank had pretty much educated himself to read, we saw his leadership to be an important part of our slaves' needs. I have to admit he's good, Obadiah. He's got our slaves singing and rejoicing all the time. They seem to be happier than they have ever been. It's like God has given them hope. They work hard and play hard. I'm hoping these are good signs."

"I believe they are, my brother!"

As we started into the house to get ready for dinner, Marion, Everett, and Law came riding up on their horses. Marion had a

Carl J. Barger

string of fish hanging out of his saddle bag. The boys tied their horses to the hitching post under one of the big oak trees, and Marion instructed two of the slave boys to take the horses to the barn. After seeing me on the front porch, Law shouted out to the other two, "Uncle Obadiah is here."

What a great welcome from Dent and his family! Bill and I enjoyed our visit, and then we were on our way to Twin Oaks. We were both in agreement that Daisy's fried chicken was almost as good as Betsy's and Mattie's. Almost!

CHAPTER 19

I felt good walking up the steps of our plantation home in Twin Oaks. As usual, I was greeted with open arms by my parents, Sarah, and others. The first thing my mother said to me was "Welcome home, Obadiah; we've planned a big homecoming party for you this weekend." My mother knew how to throw a party. Her news was good news to me. The family get-together would mean I wouldn't have to spend a lot of time during my two weeks going to see brothers and sisters. That extra time would allow me more time with my parents, Sarah, Audrey, and Dr. Banister.

Sarah also gave me some good news. She and Jim Crawford moved their wedding date up two weeks so I could be present for the wedding. I had previously notified my folks I would have to miss her wedding because of my classes starting before June twenty-ninth. Since everyone who would be coming to the wedding lived nearby, there was no problem in changing the wedding date. My mother and father had always taught us to practice the principle of accommodation. To my knowledge, that principle has always been a strong practice in our family, one which I truly appreciated.

"Obadiah, you must be starved," Mother said.

"Not really, Mother. We stopped at Black Oaks to see Dent, Sara, Hank, Nanny, and little Obi. You know how Sara is; she fed us an early supper. But if you have some of Betsy's famous apple pie, I might have room for pie and coffee."

"Betsy has baked two fresh apple pies. Those pies are sitting on the kitchen table just calling out your name," Mother said taking my arm and escorting me to the dining room.

It was good seeing everyone. Mattie brought her baby boy in to introduce me to him. He was a strong and healthy looking child.

"You and Big Jim have done well, Mattie."

"Thank you, Master Obadiah. We are mighty proud of Little Jim."

"What are you calling him?"

"Little Jim! I call his father Big Jim, and the baby Little Jim."

I smiled! Mattie was such a sweet lady. After giving birth to Little Jim, she was still a pretty lady. She seemed to be very happy being married. I talked to her about Penelope, and she said that Penelope was homesick and would like to come home to see her new baby brother.

"I will make arrangements for her to come home for Christmas. I promise you!"

"Thanks, Master Obadiah. How's your schooling?"

"The course work is demanding, but I like it a lot."

"I look forward to calling you Doctor Obadiah Bradford."

"I am looking forward to that day as well."

The family took coffee and pie in the parlor where we enjoyed visiting with each other. Father had given me a reprieve from politics. We talked about everything but politics. I wondered if my mother had asked Father not to discuss politics with me during my first night at home. We discussed how well the plantation had done financially and Father's thinking of increasing the cotton acreage this year. None of our slaves had died, so we weren't going to have to replace any.

When things settled down, Mother said, "Obadiah, let's go for a walk in my garden. I want to show you how pretty my roses are this year. We've had just enough rain for everything to be in full bloom."

"Okay, I'm ready!"

My mother's garden was simply beautiful. All the flowers and rose bushes were in full bloom. She wasn't kidding; her garden was awesome! I don't think I have ever seen her roses look any better. My mother is a stickler about raising pretty roses. She spent lots of time working with them. She always says, "Roses are like babies. You have to give them lots of attention and tender loving care."

"Let's sit down for a spell," Mother said.

We sat down on the bench that Penelope and I normally used when we met in the garden. I couldn't help thinking about Penelope as we sat down.

"Obadiah, I know you've been anxious to know how your father's doing."

"Yes, I've wanted to ask."

"He's doing very well. The only time I have trouble with him is when he wants to ride his horse. I don't let him ride alone. I always send George with him. Sometimes he talks George into riding longer than I like. When he gets home, he's always worn out. I don't want to stop him from doing things he loves, so I've been flexible."

"I think you're doing the right thing. If he's denied doing things he enjoys, he might become depressed, and we don't want that."

"Don't be surprised if he hits you up with political talk sometime in the near future. He's always complaining about what's going on in Kansas with the abolitionists. He thinks we are headed toward a civil war between the South and North."

"I do hope not, Mother. I know it's getting bad, but I would hate for our country to be torn apart over the issue of slavery. However, I do think the abolitionists are right in their overall assessment of how poorly slaves are treated. I want to believe our governmental officials can work through issues regarding slavery. They need to do what's good for our country and quit thinking about what's good for them."

"Please watch what you say to your father about slavery. He thinks the abolitionists are at fault for all the discord."

We picked roses from Mother's garden before returning to the house. We were met at the back door by Mattie who announced that my bath was ready. The bath was what I needed. I was very tired from a long train ride from Augusta and my carriage ride from Selma. I knew I wouldn't have any problems sleeping.

I awakened the next morning to the smell of fresh bacon cooking. It was such a wonderful smell, one I enjoyed all through my early years. I missed Twin Oaks and longed to return home. I didn't want to be late for breakfast so I immediately dressed and went to the dining room where Father, Mother, and Sarah were waiting for my arrival.

"Good morning, Obadiah," Father said.

"Good morning, Father, Mother, and Sarah," I said while giving Mother a kiss on the cheek.

"Did you sleep well?" Mother asked.

"I slept like a log. I don't think I turned over once."

Mattie and Betsy entered the room with the food.

"Everything smells so good. I'm really hungry this morning."

My father laid his newspaper down and said, "There's an article in the paper this morning that you might want to read, Obadiah."

"What's it about?"

"Oh, it's a story of more killing in Kansas. I'm telling you, they need to get that issue of being a slave state or free state resolved. Everyone in Autauga County is talking about what's going on in Kansas. I'm telling you, it's going to get worse if things aren't resolved soon."

"I've been keeping up with the articles in the papers as well. I'm in agreement; the Kansas issue needs to be resolved."

"Who's going to be our next President of the United States?" Father asked.

I knew this one was coming. I needed to be careful how I answered Father's question.

"I'm finding the presidential race very interesting. It appears John Fremont is crusading against slavery; James Buchanan is advocating that if Fremont wins, there will be a civil war; and Millard Fillmore doesn't seem to be a threat to either."

"Obadiah, you sound just like a typical politician. What kind of answer is that?" Father said.

"I guess you can say I don't know who I will vote for at this time. I'm assuming Father that you have your mind made up."

"You bet your boots I do. I think Fremont is crazy. Buchanan is our only hope. Fillmore is wasting his time."

"I guess we'll know pretty soon," I said. "The election is only a few months off."

I wasn't about to let my father know I was going to vote for the Republican, John Fremont. If I revealed my selection to him, it might upset him so badly that he would keel over with a heart attack. I was going to be very careful talking politics with Father.

Father and I continued to have some interesting talks during my two weeks at home. I felt good about his health condition, and I knew in my heart that he was doing quite well.

I had sent Bill over to the Denton's with a note to let Audrey know that I was home and would be coming to her house on Friday night. She sent me a note saying, "We want you to come for dinner. Dinner will be served at five o'clock. We can go to the dance in Prattville after dinner if you like."

As I pulled up in front of Audrey's home, she raced down the front steps and met me head on as I stepped down from the carriage. "Obadiah, Obadiah, it's really you. I've missed you so much." She threw herself into my arms, and we kissed. She looked at me with her beautiful blue eyes and said, "Welcome, Obadiah Bradford."

"It's so good to see you, Audrey."

"It's been too long, Obadiah. I've missed you so badly. Come, dinner is about ready."

We went inside where I was greeted by the Dentons. We visited in the parlor until Mrs. Denton came to escort us to the dining area for dinner.

After dinner, Audrey and I drove into Prattville for a community dance held at the Prattville town center. As we entered the center, we were encircled by friends. It had been a long time since we had been to a social event. Audrey passed up opportunities to attend the local dances because she didn't want to date other young men. As father had already told me, most of the talk revolved around Kansas and the effect the conflict over slavery was having on the South. Several of my friends hated the abolitionists. They blamed them for all the discord in Kansas and across the South.

Politics was certainly alive and healthy in Autauga County. After the dance, we said goodbye to our friends and left for the Denton plantation. After arriving back at the plantation, we sat down on the big white bench facing the stream flowing through the plantation. This was, and still is, our favorite place on the plantation.

We took a stroll out to the corral to see Millie and her colt. The colt looked exactly like General. "General and Millie did okay, didn't they?" I asked.

"They certainly did! I'm never going to sell Millie or the colt. I'm calling him Patience."

"Patience! What kind of a name is that for a horse?"

"Patience is what I've had to endure waiting on you, Obadiah Bradford. I thought it was most appropriate to name him that."

I laughed! Audrey was so funny. Only she could come up with a name like that for a horse. When I started laughing, she laid her head on my chest. I held her in my arms. This was the first time I had experienced this type of passion for Audrey. It was at this moment I realized I really cared for Audrey. This time I was feeling the way I felt with Penelope when I held her. What did this all mean? Did this mean my love for Penelope was gone? Did this mean Audrey now had my heart? Oh, what was going on here? Maybe it was the distance and time that was creating this emotion and passion I was feeling. I was feeling too good to try to figure this all out.

As she pulled her head from my chest, I looked down at her and kissed her again. A feeling of passion raced through my body. I could tell it was happening to Audrey as well. This is serious stuff, I thought. Audrey looked up at me and said, "Obadiah, I think I'm going to pass out." I picked her up and carried her back to the bench.

"I'm sorry, Obadiah; I don't know what came over me."

"You don't have anything to apologize for, Audrey Denton. I'm really enjoying this!"

"Maybe we should call it a night," Audrey said, as she took my hand.

Although I was enjoying my time with Audrey, I knew she was right. It was late, and I needed to get home. What Audrey and I had just experienced was special. We had had a good time together and there would be other times together before I had to go back to Augusta. In fact, Audrey and her parents would be at my homecoming party tomorrow at Twin Oaks. Maybe between now and then, I could figure out what was going on between the two of us. Whatever it was, I liked it!

By noon, all of my brothers' and sisters' families had made it to Twin Oaks. Everyone was hungry. Dinner was served under the twin oak trees that stood in our front yard. Bill, Betsy, Mattie, George, and others had cooked up some mighty good food. I don't think I ever saw anyone eat as much food as Dent's three boys. It was good seeing everyone. Dent and Sara brought Hank, Nanny, and Obi with them to the celebration. Hank and I worked out a time, with Dent's approval, for us to do some serious fishing in the Alabama River while I was home. I would go to Black Oaks at Cahaba and pick Hank up one day next week. I looked forward to our fishing trip.

I was able to visit with Jim Crawford and felt good about him. I believe he will make Sarah a good husband. I could tell that he loves my sister and wants to provide a good life for her. I looked forward to being one of his groomsmen at the wedding. Jim had lots of ambition to do well in Mr. Daniel Pratt's business organization. Mr. Pratt pays him well for being his financial director. My parents would miss Sarah as she would be moving to Prattville after the wedding.

I enjoyed spending some time with my brothers, Dent and John. We talked about plantations, Black Oaks and Twin Oaks, and how well they were doing in returning a good profit. We felt lucky to be a part of our father's farming organization. Although I've spent less time dealing with the day by day running of the plantations, I still was concerned about the productivity of the plantations. I always appreciated my brothers for their hard work and dedication to the Bradford plantations. Someday, when I become a full-fledged doctor, I can give back to the plantation through my skills as a doctor as I take care of the needs of our slaves.

159

The celebration party lasted until seven o'clock. My brother John and sisters, Tanyua Ballard and Mary Ann Shadrack, and families returned to their homes in Prattville. Dent and his family spent the night with my folks. Audrey and I had a few minutes alone before she and her parents left for their home. We arranged to meet each other for lunch in Prattville on the following Monday. We also agreed to attend the Friday night dance in Prattville, and would see each other again at Sarah's wedding at the Oak Hills Baptist Church on the following Saturday. The wedding would be the last time we would be together until my Christmas break. I would be returning to Augusta on Sunday.

CHAPTER 20

After Dent and his family left for Black Oaks, I decided to spend some time with Father. It had been a long time since we had gone fishing, and I felt today was a good day. Father was sitting in the parlor having more coffee as he read the newspaper.

"Father, I was thinking this would be a great day for us to go fishing. We've not gone fishing together in years. Do you think you'd be up to a trip to the Little Autauga River?"

"It might do me good to get out of this house for a few hours. Sure, let's go!"

"I'll have Bill get the carriage, bait, and fishing poles ready. We should be able to leave within thirty minutes."

"I'll have Mattie and Betsy fix us a picnic basket. By the way, Obadiah, have you cleared this trip with your mother?"

"Not yet, but I don't think she will object."

Mother entered the room as I was finishing my statement. "What might I not object to?" Mother asked.

"I've invited Father to a fishing trip with me today on the Little Autauga. It's a beautiful day, just right to catch a big mess of fish for dinner."

"That sounds like a marvelous idea, Obadiah. That should do your father good."

On our way to the Little Autauga, Father started laughing.

"What are you laughing about?" I asked.

"You always get your way with your mother. If I had suggested going fishing, she would have found some reason to keep me at home. That woman has become somewhat of a pest!"

I couldn't help laughing at Father. He was dead serious. I know Mother has been very restrictive on what Father does. Ever since Dr. Banister's diagnosis, she has been overly protective. That's the main reason I wanted to get him out of the house for a time. I also wanted to see how he reacts to walking and having fun. Between Bill and me, we will make sure he doesn't over-extend himself.

During the early part of our fishing trip, we talked politics, shared in a nice picnic lunch, and caught some nice eating size fish.

Before returning to Twin Oaks, my father informed me that he wanted to discuss something of a serious nature with me.

"What is it, Father?"

"Obadiah, it's about Penelope."

"What about her?"

"Where do you stand in your relationship with her?"

"I'm not sure I know where you are coming from, Father."

"I think you do, Obadiah!"

I shook my head, not knowing what to say.

"I've seen how you and Penelope look at each other. I also know about you kissing her in your mother's garden."

"Father, how could you know about that?"

"I was walking around that night and spotted the two of you in the garden."

"You've never said anything to me."

"That's right, I haven't, but I feel compelled to say what's on my mind today. Obadiah, I can see you love that girl, and that scares me."

"Father, I'm going to be honest with you as well. It scares me, too, but I want you to know I've always respected Penelope. We've done nothing wrong in the sight of God."

"Obadiah, I believe you. What's bothering me is your future. I only want what's best for you and Penelope. In my opinion, what's best for you is to marry Audrey Denton and have me some grandchildren."

"Father, I don't know if you can understand how much I love Penelope. It's not lust, as you once told me. It's a genuine love, a passionate and true love, which, in all practicality, may never develop into a husband and wife relationship. It tears away at my heart knowing our love is in vain. We will never be able to spend the best days of our lives together. Southern values and standards will continue to dictate to us what we can and can't do. I'm telling you, Father, I hate this part of Southern culture."

"Obadiah, I do understand where you're coming from. I can understand how you could love Penelope. She's a beautiful lady. Yes, I said lady. She's probably one of the prettiest women I've ever laid my eyes on. I guess what I don't understand is why you and she haven't already had sex."

"Father, I can't believe you said that. You and Mother have always taught me to respect women. According to God's word, sex outside of marriage is wrong. I can assure you, I've honored your and Mother's religious teachings on this subject."

"Obadiah, as I see it, you are going to have to find a way to distance yourself from Penelope. Every time you see her, especially alone, will be another temptation."

"Father, I know that, all too well. What do you suggest?"

"Let me first ask how you feel about Audrey Denton? Do you love her?"

"I do care for Audrey. I think she would make anyone a great wife. I enjoy being with her, but our relationship is nothing like mine and Penelope's. It's been strictly southern courtship."

"Obadiah, you need to foster this relationship with Audrey and distance yourself from Penelope."

"Just what do you think I need to do with Penelope?"

"We need her to stay in Boston. You could tell her she has your permission to date respectable young men. If she falls in love with someone who would make her happy, you could free her as a slave and let her have her freedom. Obadiah, you would be doing her an injustice by keeping her hopes set on you."

"Father, I don't want to do that right now!"

"Think about it, Obadiah. You need to do this as a favor to Penelope. Let her have her freedom in Boston. She is a beautiful and smart lady, one whom I feel certain will have no problem finding a young man to love and marry. If that should occur, you could make her free. You need to do this for Penelope and yourself."

"You're serious, aren't you?"

"Obadiah, you've already admitted it. The love you have for Penelope is indeed in vain. It can't develop into a husband and wife relationship. You've got to get on with your life."

Our trip home to Twin Oaks was not what I had expected. Things had gone so well until Father brought up Penelope. Now, I was riding home with my father who had dampened my spirits to the point I felt sick at my stomach. I know my father loves me and wants the best for me, but right now, my feelings toward him are undesirable to say the least.

After returning to Twin Oaks, Bill took the fish to be dressed for our dinner meal. I was certainly not hungry after the episode with Father. I dreaded facing Mother and Sarah at dinner. I knew I had to work on getting my spirits back into focus or Mother would guess that something unpleasant had happened on our trip. A good hot bath helped. While soaking in my bath, I realized I had at least a year to work out a solution about Penelope and Audrey. A year was a long time. A lot of things can happen in a year, I thought.

On Thursday morning, I arose early, dressed, and ate breakfast. I had sent word to George to get General saddled for my trip to Black Oaks in Cahaba. Today, Hank and I would be going fishing together on the Alabama River. I had prearranged the fishing trip with Dent during my homecoming celebration party. Hank would get a day off from laboring, and I would have the pleasure of visiting with him. It had been several months since Hank and I had spent any time together.

I arrived at Black Oaks around 9:30 in the morning. After saying hello to Dent and Sara, Hank and I headed out for a day of relaxation and fishing. The fish were biting well, and it wasn't long until we had caught a big string of fish. Mattie had made sandwiches for our lunch. We set our fishing poles in the sand as we lay back and enjoyed our lunch.

"Hank, you and Nanny sure did well when you created Obi," I said.

"Thank you, Master Obadiah. He's our pride and joy."

"How do you like living on the Black Oak plantation?"

"It's okay, Master Obadiah. I'm happy because I have Nanny, Obi, and Nanny's family here. My family is my life.

Master Dent and Missus Sara have been so nice to us. We get to make a garden and Master Dent lets me work for a neighboring farmer to earn a little money when things are slack here on the plantation. We are lucky to have Master Dent."

"I'm happy to hear that, Hank. Dent's a nice man. He wants the best for his slaves."

"I hear you, Master Obadiah! Did Master Dent tell you he made me supervisor over the field hands?"

"Yes, he did. I told him he couldn't have picked a finer man."

"It's not a hard job because our field hands work hard, and I don't have to get after them."

"I can see that. Dent is a fair man, and he knows you are well-respected among your people."

"Thanks, Master Obadiah! By the way, what's Augusta like and how is your schooling going?"

"Things are good, Hank. If I'm lucky, I'll finish up this next year and I will realize my lifelong dream of becoming a doctor. Augusta is a large city, similar to Selma. It's a pretty city that's built along the Sylvania River. It's warm in the summer and cold in the winter."

"It's going to be nice calling you Dr. Obadiah Bradford. I want my Obi to grow up and be smart like you. Who knows, he might be a doctor like you someday!"

"Well thank you, Hank. But from what Dent's been telling me, you're a smart man, yourself."

"What's Master Dent been saying about me?"

"He says you are a great preacher. It takes a smart man to read the Bible and then get his point across to his congregation. I'm really proud of you, Hank."

"The Lord has really blessed me, Master Obadiah. I can really feel the Holy Spirit working inside me. My peoples enjoy studying and praising the Lord through God's Holy Word and hymns. I'm telling you there's been times during our song ser-vice that the Holy Spirit has been so strong I thought Master Dent's barn roof was going to blow right off. I'm telling you, I could hear the rafters squeaking."

"Hank, that's wonderful! I'm so very proud of your leadership. I've known all along, God had something special in mind for you. Now I know what it is!"

"It's because of you and Misses Sarah that I've learned to read. If it hadn't been for y'all, I wouldn't be able to do what God is allowing me to do. I have you to thank for leading me to Jesus Christ. Thank you, Master Obadiah!"

"When we first started building our friendship, you asked me if I thought slaves and blacks would be in Heaven. Now that you've studied God's word, what do you think?"

"God's word tells me regardless of whether men are black, white, yellow, red, or purple, they can be saved. All they have to do is believe and trust in our Lord and Savior, Jesus Christ. God's word says we are saved by God's grace, not of our works, but by his grace. Christ promised us if we are believers, he will make us a home in Heaven. I believe in Jesus Christ as my savior, and I have faith that he has built me and my family a home in Heaven."

"Hank, you said I was a smart man; you are the smart one! You have grown so much in your understanding of God's word. I'm so happy for you."

After returning to Black Oak, I said my goodbyes to Hank and his family, Dent, Sara, and their family and headed home to Twin Oaks. The ride home on General was enjoyable. I felt good about my day with Hank. Just knowing how God had blessed him and his family meant everything in the world to me. What a marvelous God we have!

The special day for Sarah and Jim Crawford had arrived. Everyone at our house was busy getting ready to leave for Oak Hills Baptist Church. The wedding was at two o'clock. I've never seen my mother look so beautiful. She was wearing an elegant full-length blue dress. Father had bought him a new suit, and looked really nice in it. It had been a good while since this family had enjoyed a family wedding. I was wearing a black tux, white dress shirt, and a black bow tie. Jim Crawford had asked me to be his best man, and I had agreed. It was going to be a big wedding. Sarah had six bridesmaids. I had never seen so many people at the wedding rehearsal dinner.

Sarah and Jim scheduled the town center for the wedding reception. There would be a lot of dancing going on, and Oak Hills Baptist Church was not a suitable place for dancing. After the wedding reception, Jim and Sarah would stay at the Granville Hotel in Prattville before leaving for Selma, Alabama, to catch the train to New York. The honeymoon in New York was Mr. Daniel Pratt's wedding gift to Jim Crawford.

The wedding and reception went off smoothly. A few tears were shed by my mother when Sarah said goodbye as she and Jim climbed into the carriage to go to the Granville Hotel. Sarah had been looking forward to New York ever since Jim told her of Mr. Pratt's wedding gift. She had never been out of the state of Alabama since arriving here from Georgia as a young girl.

I know my parents would certainly miss her at Twin Oaks. She had been such a permanent fixture in our family. When Mother and Father needed something outside of the home, they would ask Sarah to do it. She could be described by some as their business associate. I was happy that Jim and Sarah bought a home in Prattville. Their new home was located at 301 Madison Street, not far from the First Methodist Church.

After their honeymoon, they would return to Prattville so Jim could continue his job as Mr. Pratt's financial business manager. Prattville was only a short distance from Twin Oaks. If either Mother or Sarah got homesick, they could jump into a carriage and be at each other's home in just a short time.

My last date with Audrey was the night of Sarah's wedding. We danced several times at the reception, and I later accompanied her home. We again took a seat on the big white bench overlooking the creek that ran through the beautiful valley on their plantation. The first thing Audrey wanted to talk about was Sarah's wedding. Although I had never officially asked Audrey to marry me, I think she just assumed I would eventually get around to it.

"What did you thank of the wedding, Obadiah?" Audrey asked.

"I thought it was a beautiful wedding."

"I want my wedding to be just like Sarah's. I want six bridesmaids. I, too, want to be married at Oak Hills Baptist."

I believe Audrey was deliberately throwing a marriage proposal my way. I wasn't ready to do that just yet. Although I believe I could love her as a wife, I didn't want to commit to her at this time. I know without a doubt she would be a good wife. I know she loves me and would say yes should I ask her to marry me. I asked myself if I was being selfish in not going ahead and asking her. But something just kept saying to me, "Don't do it right now."

Our last night together was both enjoyable and sad. There was a sense of sadness coming from Audrey. I don't know if it was because I didn't propose marriage to her, or if she was sad because I was leaving. We kissed and held each other tight with long periods of silence. I wish I knew what was going on in her head. I resolved in my mind that if God means for us to be husband and wife, then he will work it out after I receive my Doctor's degree in medicine. One year isn't too long to wait, I thought.

All at once I was getting sleepy. It was getting late, and I was a good thirty minutes from Twin Oaks. I said goodbye to Audrey and headed home. I was glad Dan, my loyal and trusted carriage horse, knew his way to Twin Oaks. I caught myself falling asleep several times during the journey home. I set my alarm clock, skipped my bath, and fell into bed. It felt like the shortest night of my life when my alarm clock went off at 6:00 a.m. I jumped out of bed, got dressed, and met Mother and Father in the dining room at 6:30 a.m. My train was leaving at 11:45 a.m. I would have to put everything into high gear to make it to Selma on time.

CHAPTER 21

On the train trip back to Augusta, I had plenty of time to read the newspaper Father handed me as I left Twin Oaks. The abolitionists were still at it. They continued to pound away, driving their point across that slavery was evil and inhumane. Their goal was not to stop until our governmental officials adopted laws to end slavery. The Kansas issue was still to be resolved of whether it would become a free state or a slave state. The issue was causing a lot of unrest in Kansas.

The presidential race was not too far off. The Republican, John C. Fremont, was still crusading against slavery, and James Buchanan was advocating that if Fremont won there would be a civil war. The third party candidate, former President Millard Fillmore, didn't seem to be a threat to either Fremont or Buchanan. It was going to be interesting how all this played out.

Because of my lack of sleep, I decided to take advantage of the long trip to Augusta and take a much needed nap. My eyes were so heavy. I quickly found myself falling into a deep sleep, which triggered a dream about Penelope. I dreamed I had gone to Boston to see her. We dined in some of the best restaurants in Boston and danced in some of the best dance halls.

Mrs. Adams's Prep School had truly groomed Penelope into a beautiful and elegant young lady. I was so impressed with her social graces and how she conducted herself with others. If I hadn't known her background, I would have never guessed she wasn't from a prominent upscale Boston family. I never once thought of her being a slave. At this moment in time, I was convinced a life with Penelope would surely be like living in heaven. On the last night in Boston, I took Penelope to my room at the Parker House Hotel. She had wanted to see what my room looked like. I had convinced myself this was all right. It was risky to be alone with Penelope, but one I was willing to take.

The first thing Penelope did after entering my room was make a quick dash to the window. My room was located on the fifth floor, and Penelope wanted to see what it looked like looking down on the street below. From my window, she could also see the Boston Bay area. She and Jessica Blackman visited the Bay area every chance they got. The Bay area offered several little shops and delis, as well as a pier and a small park where they could sit and feed the sea gulls and pigeons. It wasn't long before Penelope was sitting on the edge of my bed.

"I've always wondered what kind of bed you slept on in this hotel room," she said, bouncing on the edge of the bed.

"It's very comfortable," I said as I found amusement in watching her bouncing on my bed.

"Our beds at Mrs. Adams's place aren't nearly as comfortable. In fact, they are quite hard."

I went over and sat down on the bed by her. As I turned to her she was smiling. Her beautiful blue eyes gave off a glow that took my breath away. She was so beautiful.

"Why are you looking at me like that?" she asked.

"Penelope, you are beautiful!"

"Master Obadiah, that's nice of you to say."

"I mean it, Penelope. You get better looking each time I see you."

"Oh, Master Obadiah, I've missed you so!" she said as she laid her head on my chest.

"I've missed you as well." I put my arms around her.

It wasn't long before our passion for each other kicked in. I told myself this was all right. No one would know what went on behind closed doors. We loved each other and this was meant to be. She was willing, and I was willing to face the consequences. All of a sudden, I felt someone tugging at my shoulder. I opened my eyes to find the train car porter asking me, "Sir, are you all right?"

I looked around, still half asleep, and asked, "Where are we?"

"We just arrived in Augusta, sir," the porter said.

"I'm so sorry! I guess I had fallen asleep."

"That's all right! Some passengers sleep so hard I have to shake them. That's one reason they've got me around to wake up people like you."

I smiled, offered my thanks, and exited the train to catch a ride to the Milton Boarding House. I was looking forward to seeing my good friends, Jim Boroughs and Ben Murphy. I would certainly miss my good friend Henry Dotson who was now practicing medicine in his home city of Atlanta.

Upon arriving at the Milton House, I was greeted by Mr. and Mrs. Milton. I took my bags to my room and got ready for dinner. I was told by Mr. Milton that Jim and Ben had gone down to Madison's but would be returning for dinner. Since I had a little time on my hands, I went to the reception room where I met Frank Thompson and John Matthews, two new medical students who would be attending the Old Georgia Medical School.

I learned from Frank that he was from Montgomery, Alabama, whereas John Matthews was from Charleston, South Carolina.

Jim and Ben returned from Madison's just in time for dinner. It was so good seeing them. After a fine dinner prepared by Kissy and Martha, we went to the recreation room to play cards with Frank and John.

The first day of summer school was exciting. I had already gotten to know Dr. Bill Bradley, the pulmonary specialist whom Henry had for several of his courses. Dr. Bradley was one of the best in his field and I had looked forward to having some courses under him. Henry had loaned me his notes and I was ready to learn all I could from Dr. Bradley. Another thing I liked about summer school was it was more relaxing. The days were longer. We had more time to study. The Augusta town center was busy with tourists and there were lots of new shows at the theater. One of my favorite things to do in the afternoon was going to the Sylvania River Park to study. The park had several large oak trees that provided shade from the hot sun. I loved to lean back on one of the big oak trees and read. If I wanted to take a nap, I did that as well.

It wasn't long after school started that Frank and John joined Jim, Ben, and me in a new study group. Like Henry, I shared my class notes with Frank and John. This, too, was a big help to them. When the summer term ended, I had achieved my goal. My grades were all As. At this point in time, I had achieved an accumulated grade point of 4.0, the same grade point that my friend Henry Dotson had when he graduated. I wanted to be like Henry. I wanted to be the best. With God's help, I wanted to graduate with highest honors, just like Henry.

Back home in Autauga County, my father's health was still good and holding. Mother was missing Sarah, but managed to see her every two weeks either at Twin Oaks or in Prattville. Audrey still enjoyed her job at Henry Pratt's dress shop in Prattville. She kept me up-to-date on what was happening in Autauga County. She also kept me informed about Patience, Millie's colt. She was bound and determined not to let me forget about her. She told me that she'd be sending me a painting of Patience any day now.

Due to the short break between summer school and the fall semester, Ben, Jim, Frank, John, and I decided to go to Atlanta to visit Henry.

Our trip to Atlanta was one of the most enjoyable trips of my life. Henry was in business with two well-established doctors in Atlanta who graciously covered for him during the two days we were in Atlanta. We found Atlanta to be a booming town, full of southern hospitality and excitement. Its population was around ten thousand, the twelfth largest city in the South. It served as a vital transportation and logistics center with several railroads, including the Western Atlantic, which connected Atlanta to the city of Chattanooga, Tennessee.

Henry introduced us to his fiancée, Helen Anderson. Helen was the daughter of Mr. Frank Anderson, mayor of Atlanta, a wealthy southern gentleman whose goal was to someday be governor of the state of Georgia. I liked Helen immediately. I always knew Henry would pick a lady who was intelligent, pretty, and wanted a family. Henry shared with me on several occasions that he wanted a large family and that he planned to pick someone who shared his dreams. I believe that Helen will meet his expectations.

We arrived back in Augusta in time to enjoy one day of relaxation before starting the fall semester. I found out the day we arrived back that Dr. Matthew Tolskey, the noted surgeon and instructor at the Old Georgia Medical School, was going to be my supervisory teacher. Dr. Tolskey was Henry's supervisory teacher during his last year in medical school. Henry felt intimidated at times by Dr. Tolskey. He told me on several occasions that Dr. Tolskey was the hardest and most demanding teacher he'd had in school. Because of Dr. Tolskey's expectations, Henry did well. In fact, Henry made the highest grade ever made in Dr. Tolskey's class. New challenges have always been good for me. I've always welcomed each challenge as it came my way. I would look upon Dr. Tolskey as a new challenge, one that would enable me to develop my surgical skills, which would later benefit me in my practice.

Henry was right about Dr. Tolskey. He expected a lot from his students and was very demanding. Although I wasn't intimidated by him, I did get tired of all the work he assigned. There were some days I questioned whether I would be able to complete his assignments on time. But somehow, I managed to complete the tasks he gave me. It was mid-way through the first semester that Dr. Tolskey gave me my first medical case. A young boy was admitted to the hospital with a broken arm. My task, under Dr. Tolskey's supervision, was to set the boy's arm back in place. I had watched Dr. Tolskey teach the procedural methods of setting broken bones, but hadn't actually set a bone, other than what Dr. Banister let me do back in Autauga County. My heart was beating faster than normal because I knew Dr. Tolskey was watching each step I took. I was able to complete the task without Dr. Tolskey intervening in my work. I assumed he approved of the job when he said, "Good job, Obadiah!"

I performed several minor operations under his supervision, and each time he would say, "Good job, Obadiah!" One day we had watched Dr. Tolskey perform surgery on a man whose appendix had ruptured. The man would have died if Dr. Tolskey hadn't operated when he did. I watched him carefully, analyzing each step he used during the surgery. The man lived. A few days later, a young boy was admitted to the Old Georgia Medical Center with severe stomach cramps. Dr. Tolskey called me and three other students into the boy's room where he explained the boy's symptoms. He said, "I want each of you to examine this young man and let me know what you think the problem is."

Henry had warned me about Dr. Tolskey's tendency to put his students on the spot. He already knew what the problem was, but he wanted to see if we could diagnose the problem. He stepped back and had each of us examine the young man. After I completed my examination, I stepped back to make way for other students to do their examinations.

"Okay, students, what's wrong with this young man?"

The answers went from an appendix attack, infection of the bowels, to diarrhea. When he got to me, he asked, "Obadiah, what is your diagnosis?"

"Dr. Tolskey, if I may, I would like to ask the young man one more question before I answer your question."

"Please precede, Obadiah!" Dr. Tolskey replied.

I first asked him his name, and he said it's Johnny.

I said, "Johnny, what was the last thing you ate today?"

"I ate some wild berries in the woods."

"Do you know what kind of berries they were?"

"No sir, I don't," was his reply.

After pressing on Johnny's stomach again, I felt confident that it wasn't appendicitis. My educated guess was his problem was the result of the berries he had eaten from the woods. He already had diarrhea and was holding his stomach tight. If his pain was localized in the area of his appendix, and if he was suffering from an appendicitis attack, he would have been running a fever. There was no fever, however.

"Dr. Tolskey, I believe Johnny's problem is due to the wild berries. His pain appears to be coming from his lower abdomen. Also, if it was appendicitis, he would be running a fever. I believe he needs to be treated for an upset stomach and watched for a few hours."

"Well, students, I'm in agreement with Obadiah. Johnny doesn't have an appendicitis problem. As Obadiah has said, I believe Johnny's problem is related to the wild berries. At this time, we will treat him accordingly and keep a close watch on him. Students, you may go back to what you were doing."

As I was walking away, Dr. Tolskey touched me on the shoulder and said, "Obadiah, may I see you in my office?"

"Yes sir," I responded with some tension in my voice.

"Good work back there, Obadiah."

"Thank you, Dr. Tolskey."

"Obadiah, you remind me of your good friend, Dr. Henry Dotson. He was one of the best students ever to graduate from this college. Have you seen him since he left us for his practice in Atlanta?"

"Yes sir! My friends and I just returned from visiting Henry in Atlanta."

"How's he doing?"

"Very well, Sir!"

"Obadiah, you and Henry Dotson have similar qualities as doctors. You both are very observant of what's going on around you. Your accuracy in diagnosing problems speaks highly of your knowledge and understanding of different diseases. You have a special gift of relating with your patients. Only God gives those qualities and gifts to a person."

"Thanks, Dr. Tolskey! I must confess that my prior training as an intern under Dr. John David Banister, from Autauga County, has been a great asset to me. During my two-year internship, I had the opportunity to see and experience several different diseases and trauma situations relating to plantation slaves."

"I've heard about Dr. Banister. He certainly has a good reputation in Alabama."

"He's asked me to be a partner in his medical practice in Prattville after I complete my graduation requirements."

"You will certainly be an asset to Dr. Banister and the people of Autauga County. I wish you well, Obadiah."

"Thanks, Dr. Tolskey. Oh, by the way, I want you to know I'm enjoying my training under your leadership."

"Before the year is over, you may want to take that comment back. We have lots of hard work ahead, work that will involve amputations, surgical procedures, and life-threatening situations that we've not yet tackled. Get ready for more to come," Dr. Tolskey said with a subtle smile.

The newspapers were full of political ads relating to the presidential race. I had the opportunity to meet both the Republican candidate, John C. Fremont, and the Democratic candidate, James Buchanan. I liked what both men had to say, but I still leaned toward Mr. Fremont. On the day of the election, my friends and I went to the polls to cast our vote for the next President of the United States. I believe I was the only one who cast a vote for Mr. Fremont. When the election was over and the votes were counted, Mr. James Buchanan was elected. Mr. Buchanan carried five northern and western states and all the southern states except for Maryland. Our former President Millard Fillmore won in Maryland. I decided then and there that I must not know too much about politics. I resolved to listen to my father more in the future.

I know when I go home for Christmas break that my father will certainly remind me of our last conversation about who would be elected as President. I certainly wasn't going to tell him that I wasted my vote.

CHAPTER 22

As soon as the first semester ended, I packed my bags and headed home to Autauga County for a two-week Christmas break. I was tired of school. Dr. Tolskey had warned us that the last semester in school would be the most taxing period of our lives. In my opinion, that was an understatement. I needed a break from school. I needed a time to relax and get revived.

I boarded the train from Augusta to Selma at 7:30 a.m. My train was to arrive in Selma at 3:30 p.m. I brought along two newspapers that I hadn't gotten around to reading. Because of time restraints and demands on my class assignments, I had put reading newspapers on the back burner. I knew Father would want to talk politics and issues when I got to Twin Oaks, so I thought I'd better catch up on current events.

The first newspaper article that caught my eye was, "U.S. Supreme Court issues decision on Dred Scott Case." As I read the article, I discovered that Dred Scott and his family were slaves and were moved by their owner to a free state. Mr. Scott claimed he and his family should be free because he had been held as a slave while living in a free state. The United States Supreme Court ruled by a vote of six to three that his petition could not be seen because he did not hold any property. The ruling stated that even though he had been taken by his owner into a free state, he was still a slave because slaves were to be considered property of their owners. The Supreme Court further ruled that Congress lacks the power to exclude slavery from the territories where slaves are property and have no rights as citizens and that slaves are not made free by living in a free territory.

The article went on to say that the Supreme Court ruling had just furthered the cause of the abolitionists as they increased their efforts to fight against slavery.

The abolitionists continued to use the newspapers to further their agenda of getting slavery abolished. The paper was full of stories of slave abuse across the Deep South as well as estate sales. As I read some of the articles, my thoughts went back to the day I first saw Mattie and Penelope standing on the platform in front of the town hall in Selma, Alabama. I can still see the fear in their eyes as they stood hand-in-hand together not knowing what the future would hold for them. As it turned out, they were some of the fortunate ones. Many slave family members are separated through estate sales, never again to see each other, and never knowing what happened to each other. Mattie is a good example. She was separated from her entire family. If she had been separated from Penelope, I don't know if she could have survived the pain and agony she would have suffered from losing her precious daughter.

As usual, Bill was waiting for me as I got off the train in Selma.

"Master Obadiah, let me gets those bags," Bill said after we greeted each other with a hug.

"It's great to see you, Bill!"

"It's good to see you, too, Master Obadiah. You sure do look handsome."

"Thank you, Bill. How are things back at Twin Oaks?"

"Everything and everybody is just doing fine, Master Obadiah. I heard Missus Catherine tell Mattie and Betsy to cook lots of fried chicken for dinner. Everyone knows that's your favorite meal."

"You got that right, Bill!"

"Do we need to go by Master Dent's?"

"Not today, Bill. I want to get home to that fried chicken."

"Yes sir, Twin Oaks it will be."

As we pulled up in front of the house in Twin Oaks, Mother came running out on the porch yelling, "He's home; Obadiah is home, James." Father was not too far behind her.

I quickly ran up the porch steps into the arms of my wonderful mother. "Oh, Obadiah, it's been too long. Welcome home, son."

"Thanks, Mother. It's good to be home. I've missed you all a lot."

Father was patiently waiting his time for his hug. "It's good to have you home, Obadiah."

"It's great to be home, Father."

"Let's go inside. It's cold out here," my mother said as she grabbed my arm.

As we entered the parlor, I could smell the fried chicken cooking. It brought back old memories. We went to the parlor to visit before dinner. Mother excused herself to go and check on dinner, leaving Father and me to visit. Father looked good. His color was good, and I believe he was moving about better. In a few minutes, Mother returned, followed by Mattie and Betsy with coffee.

"Look who I found in the kitchen, Obadiah."

I stood and greeted both Mattie and Betsy as they served us hot coffee.

"We's been preparing your favorite meal, Southern fried chicken, Master Obadiah," Betsy said.

"Betsy, fried chicken is no longer my favorite meal. I like steak better now."

Betsy looked at Mattie and Mattie just smiled. "We's didn't know, Master Obadiah," Betsy said.

"I'm kidding with you, Betsy. Fried chicken will always be my favorite. Especially yours and Mattie's!"

"We best be getting back and seeing to dinner," Mattie said.

"How are you feeling, Father?"

"I'm doing well, Obadiah. Even if I wasn't, I wouldn't tell your mother. She would start depriving me of everything I enjoy doing."

"Now, James Bradford, you know that's not true," Mother said.

Mother left the room to go check on dinner. Father and I had just started talking about the upcoming presidential race when Mother returned to announce that dinner was ready.

"Obadiah, you have time to wash up first. Go wash up and join us in the dining room," Mother said.

After dinner, I had an opportunity to speak with Mattie.

"Have you heard from Penelope since I sent her the train ticket?"

"I have, Master Obadiah. You know she's planning on being home Friday."

"I'm looking forward to seeing her, Mattie."

"Me, too! I'm so excited. I've not seen my baby in such a long time. You know she's never seen her baby brother. It will be good to have all my family together here in Twin Oaks."

"How's Big Jim doing?"

"He's doing well. He enjoys his work here at Twin Oaks. Master John lets him do lots of things on his own. My Big Jim likes your brother. Master John depends on Big Jim, and Jim wants to please Master John."

"You're right about my brother John liking Big Jim. John told me himself how much he depended on Big Jim. John says Big Jim knows more about running a cotton gin than anyone he knows."

"I got me a good man in Big Jim. He treats me like a lady. Did you know he's been saved since we've married? I'm so happy he's accepted the Lord as his savior."

"I didn't know about Big Jim being saved. Please tell me how Big Jim got saved. I'm interested in that."

"Well, Master Obadiah, I taught Big Jim to read. We read the Bible together every night. I helped him to understand how he could be saved. We go to church every Sunday in the barn. You'll have to come and hear us sing. We are having a special service this coming Wednesday night. We will be singing lots of good ol' spiritual songs. I'm going to sing one myself. If you can make it, please come by."

"Mattie, I just might take you up on that invitation."

"Master Obadiah, I have a favor to ask you."

"What is it, Mattie?"

Would it be possible for me and Little Jim to ride over to Selma with Mr. Bill on Friday to pick up Penelope? I just can't wait to see her!"

"I'll tell Bill you and Little Jim will be making the trip with him. Your presence at the train station would certainly be a nice surprise for Penelope."

"Oh, thank you, Master Obadiah. You are such a nice man!"

"How about getting my bath ready? I'm really tired and will be going to bed early tonight."

"Yes, Master!"

After my bath, I met Mother and Father in the parlor for coffee. They brought me up-to-date on what had been going on with family members. They talked mostly of Sarah and Jim Crawford expecting a baby and how that was going to change Sarah's life.

My first full day back to Twin Oaks was busy. I started the day off with a wonderful breakfast. I had a nice visit with my brother John. He had come by to see me. He gave me an excellent report on the productivity of the plantation. He said we had the best crops we've had in some time. Two of our older slaves had died during the month of November. He thought we needed to replace them in the spring with younger male slaves.

I decided to ride into Prattville and surprise Audrey. While in Prattville, I planned to take her out for lunch at Pratt's restaurant and try to see Dr. Banister before returning to Twin Oaks.

Due to the wintery conditions, I decided not to ride General into Prattville but took the carriage instead. As I pulled up in front of the dress shop, I tied the reins to the hitching post and went inside. The store was warm, and the smell of the fragrances coming from the scented candles and perfumes was just heavenly. As I closed the door behind me, the bells jingled, and I saw Audrey look up from the checkout counter. She smiled big and made her way around the counter toward me. Since I didn't see anyone in the store, I picked up speed and headed toward her. We embraced and kissed right under some mistletoe. We couldn't have picked a better spot in the store.

"Obadiah, when did you get home?"

"I made it home yesterday, late afternoon!"

"I've thought of nothing else but you in the past few days. It's so good to see you."

"Audrey, it's good to see you as well."

"Are you Christmas shopping?"

"Yes, I am, but mostly I wanted to take you out for lunch. Are you going to be free for lunch?"

"I'm always free for you, Obadiah. What time is it?"

"It's eleven o'clock," I said.

"Do you have something you could do until twelve?"

"I thought I might run by to see Dr. Banister."

"Why don't you do that and come back around twelve. I'll be ready."

As I entered the reception area, Dr. Banister was coming from his examination room with one of his patients. He saw me and immediately came over to shake my hand. "Obadiah, when did you get home?"

"Yesterday afternoon!"

"It's great to see you, young man, and Merry Christmas!"

"Merry Christmas to you as well," I said shaking his hand.

"Well, Obadiah, tell me, how many more months before I can call you Dr. Obadiah Bradford?"

"Six months, I hope!"

"What a great accomplishment for you. I can hardly wait. Please come with me; I want to show you something."

He led me past the receptionist's desk to a door that opened up into a hallway. He had added some additional rooms since I had last visited his office. The first door to the left was my office. There was a note on the door that said, "Future office of Dr. Obadiah Bradford."

"What do you think about all of this, Obadiah?"

"Dr. Banister, this is just wonderful!"

"I was hoping you would like it. We've worked hard trying to get the addition ready for you to see while you were home for Christmas break."

"I had no idea you were doing all of this."

"I wanted it to be a surprise. Are you still maintaining a 4.0 grade point?" he asked.

"Yes, sir, I am."

"Obadiah, I've always known you were very intelligent."

"Thank you, Dr. Banister. I owe most of my success to you. My apprenticeship under you has helped me more than books ever could."

"Well, thank you, Obadiah, for that compliment. By the way, what are you doing for lunch?"

"I'm taking Audrey to lunch, but you are certainly welcome to come join us."

"Thank you, Obadiah, but I guess I had better decline your invitation. It appears I'm always playing second fiddle to your beautiful Audrey Denton."

"I'm sure Audrey wouldn't mind."

"That's all right, Obadiah. You go ahead and have a nice lunch with Audrey."

Dr. Banister handed me a large envelope and said, "Take this proposal with you, and if it meets with your approval, we can finalize the agreement upon your graduating from the Old Georgia Medical School."

The document was in regard to the partnership that we had discussed earlier on. He felt it important for us to have every-thing in writing and in order when I come into his medical prac-tice. I took the document and placed it in my side coat pocket.

"Thank you, Dr. Banister. I'll look over the document and get back with you. Please tell Mrs. Banister I said Merry Christmas."

Audrey and I had a wonderful lunch together. We ate at Pratt's restaurant, which was owned by Daniel Pratt. Mr. Pratt owned about every establishment in Prattville. The food was excellent, and my hour with Audrey went too fast. We made a date for the Christmas dance and social on Christmas Eve night at the Prattville Town Center.

After lunch, I drove by Sarah's home to visit with her before returning to Twin Oaks. It was a pleasant surprise to find my sis-ters, Tanyua Ballard and Mary Ann Shadrack, at Sarah's home. They had gotten together to compare their Christmas gift lists. Since there were so many Bradfords to buy for, they wanted to avoid buying the same present for the same person. As I've mentioned before, Christmas at James and Catherine Bradford's home was a big family affair. It was more than a one day's affair. After Christmas dinner, father always read the Christmas story, and then we opened presents. It took most of the afternoon to open Christmas presents and clean up afterwards. Since I was terrible at buying Christmas presents, I decided to sweet talk my sisters into shopping and buying my Christmas presents for me.

My sisters had spoiled me. I guess being the baby in the family has some advantages. With a few sad stories of why I hadn't done any Christmas shopping, my sisters agreed to bail me out and do my shopping for me. There were only two people whom I wanted to personally shop for and that was Penelope and Audrey. I assured my sisters that I would richly reward them for shopping for me by buying them a nice present. Of course they laughed, knowing that I was terrible at picking something out for them. I assured them I would solicit Mother's help in purchasing their gifts.

When Sarah, Tanyua, and Mary Ann agreed to do my Christmas shopping, my stress level was lowered tremendously. What a blessing they were to me. I hated shopping, and I knew they loved it. How many sisters would do the same for their little brother? Only mine, I thought! I really appreciated my family. I know without doubt that all of them sacrificed one way or another to see that I got an opportunity to fulfill my dream of becoming a doctor. Dent and John are every bit as intelligent as I am but they chose to help Father run the plantations, a job that sometimes became a twenty-four-hour job!

The next few days passed so fast. I was able to accept Mattie's invitation to attend the special Christmas program at the barn. My mother and father accompanied me to the service. I didn't realize our Mattie was so talented. Her voice was beautiful, and the song she sang was so very touching to my heart. She truly presented Christ in a very special way through her body language and voice.

Bill, our family driver, gave a short devotional from the Bible. Again, I was very proud of Bill. I had taught him to read and write, and he had become a very educated slave. We enjoyed every minute of the program. At times, I looked over at my father and could tell he was having a good time. Mother was just thrilled to see our slaves worship our Lord and Savior with so much emotion. She had always wanted the best for our slaves. We came away feeling really blessed from attending the Christmas program. What I liked most about the service was how the slaves sang from their hearts. They seemed to reach deep down in their souls and deliver the message in such a way that was both entertaining and uplifting. *What a tremendous experience!* I thought.

Christmas Eve was a big day for Mattie, Bill, and Little Jim as they prepared to go to Selma to pick up Penelope. I had explained to Mattie that attending the Christmas Eve event in Prattville would prevent me and my parents from being at home when they arrived back to Twin Oaks. "Please make my apologies to Penelope, and tell her I look forward to seeing her at breakfast on Saturday morning."

Penelope and Mattie had already prepared Sarah's room for Penelope. Penelope always loved Sarah's room and enjoyed the many hours she spent with Sarah learning to read and write.

It was mid-afternoon when George brought one of our three family carriages around for me to use to pick up Audrey. George would later bring Father and Mother to Prattville in another carriage. *The Bradfords are very blessed with having good transportation,* I thought. By the time I picked up Audrey and got to Prattville, the Christmas Eve party had started.

Daniel Pratt always went out of his way to make the event a memorable, entertaining night. He and Mrs. Pratt loved to entertain and money never appeared to be an object. As I looked around the large ballroom, I spotted several members of the Bradford family; in fact, I think everyone in my family had arrived except for Father and Mother. I'm sure they would be showing up at any minute.

As Audrey and I were finishing our punch, the band struck up our favorite song, and we began a long night of dancing. As I've said many times, Audrey loves to dance. She had rather dance than eat. I was just the opposite.

As we were visiting with Audrey's friend, Betty Simpson, and her new fiancé, Grant Johnson, we were joined by Jim Crawford and my sister Sarah. I learned from Grant that he was new to Prattville and was employed as one of Mr. Pratt's factory overseers. He seemed to be a nice guy.

As I was visiting with my brother-in-law, Jim Crawford, Mr. Daniel Pratt came over to visit.

"Obadiah, welcome home!"

"Thank you, Mr. Pratt. It's certainly nice to be back in Autauga County."

"Dr. Banister tells me in six months you will be finishing your medical degree and will be joining him in his medical practice."

"That's the plan, Mr. Pratt."

"Well, congratulations. We need another doctor in Autauga County. Dr. Banister is working himself to death."

"He sure is! I'm looking forward to relieving some of his demanding schedule."

"After you get back to Autauga County, I would like to visit with you and Dr. Banister on a hospital project I've been thinking about."

"Yes, sir, I'll look forward to visiting with you."

It was getting late when Audrey looked at me and said, "Obadiah, I think I've had all the dancing tonight that I can stand. If you are ready, I'm ready to go home."

"I'll go pull the carriage around. Give me a few minutes."

Our trip back to the Denton plantation was so cold, too cold for us to sit outside on our favorite bench. After arriving at the plantation, we went inside where we found a nice fire in the fireplace in the parlor. Audrey asked one of the house maids to bring us a pot of hot coffee. Hot coffee was what I needed. I was still shivering from the trip from Prattville. Audrey's parents had already gone to bed so we had the parlor all to ourselves. We visited about everything from Betty Simpson getting married to the abolitionists invading Autauga County. "I'm telling you, Obadiah, those abolitionists are sure stirring up things here in

Autauga County. If half of what they say is true, I'm afraid there will be some kind of uprising someday."

"Audrey, I can assure you that some of the things they are saying are quite true. I've seen some of this abuse with my own eyes."

"Why do they treat their slaves in that manner, Obadiah?"

"I think most of them want to show their supremacy over their slaves. They want the slaves to be scared of their authority. They like to see pain inflicted upon slaves. I wish I could tell you some of the things I've seen right here in Autauga County."

"Why can't you tell me?"

"Audrey, I just can't! I swore an oath to Dr. Banister that I wouldn't talk about the different situations we see on some of these plantations. It's a matter of ethics."

"That's just awful, Obadiah!"

"I agree, Audrey, but unfortunately that's the way it is in the Deep South. I do think the abolitionists won't stop until they get slavery abolished. You can remember I said that."

"I heard some ladies talking in the store that their husbands are afraid that the Southern states and the Northern states may go to war someday to settle the slavery issue. Have you heard anything about a war?"

"What I'm hearing in Augusta is the South is getting tired of the North poking their noses in our business. I do hope the issues can be resolved in Congress rather than going to war. That would be disastrous for our country."

"Let's change the subject. Tell me what you are expecting from your last semester?" Audrey said.

"I'm thinking it will be my hardest semester. I'm taking some hard courses and will have to spend several hours in studying."

"You will do well, Obadiah Bradford. You know why I know that?"

"Why?"

"Because you are good looking, intelligent, and got the faith to move a mountain."

"Wow, is that the way you see me?"

"Exactly, and I know you will be successful in achieving your goals. You are determined to succeed, and you will succeed. You can remember I said that, Obadiah Bradford," she said with her beautiful smile.

"Audrey, I believe you are a little prejudiced."

"I might be a little bit, but I know you, Obadiah. You can do anything you set your mind to do. I have faith in you."

"Thanks, Audrey! You deserve a big kiss for that compliment."

"I'm ready, Obadiah!"

"Obadiah, I need to ask you a very important question."

"What?"

"How do I fit into your plans after you return to Autauga County?"

I was certainly not ready for her question. I had never proposed to her because of the uncertainty of my schooling and my feelings toward Penelope. Now she had confronted me with one of the most serious subjects in life. I needed to choose my words carefully.

"Audrey, you know I care for you a lot. I've liked you from the first day I set my eyes on you at the Pratt's restaurant. My folks think you hang the moon."

"But how do you feel, Obadiah? I need to know where our relationship is headed."

"Audrey, my lifelong dream of becoming a doctor has been my number one concern since moving to Augusta. I understand your future concerns about us, and I want you to know that I sincerely appreciate your patience with me, but I would like to be fully on my feet as a doctor before proposing marriage to you. I know that's probably not what you want to hear, but right now that's my position."

"Oh, my dear, Obadiah, my dearest, Obadiah, I appreciate your honesty, but I must let you know, I can't wait on you forever. I'm getting older. My friends are calling me the old maid in Autauga County. Most of my friends have gotten married, or are getting married. My best friend, Betty, is getting married in a few weeks. All I'm asking is do you plan to marry me once you become a doctor?"

"The answer to your question is yes. If you will have me?"

Audrey threw herself into my arms and we kissed. She had never kissed me like this before. I believe I had just made her the happiest person in Autauga County. I wish it could have been more romantic for both of us, but she needed to know. I had put her off too long. I didn't want to lose Audrey. Any single man in Autauga County would give his eye teeth for her. I'm glad it's done. I'm relieved! I will still have to deal with Penelope, but knowing I had made a commitment to Audrey would help, or at least that's what I hoped.

I had been carrying around with me an engagement ring that I had planned to give to Audrey should the right opportunity present itself. Since this was Christmas, I decided this would be my Christmas present to her.

"Audrey, I have a Christmas present for you."

"I have one for you as well. Let me go get it. I'll be right back."

When she returned she was carrying a large box wrapped in gold Christmas paper.

"You open your present first," she said.

The box contained a painting of Millie and her colt, Patience. Patience had grown to be half the size of his mother. It was a beautiful picture, one she had promised me that I would be getting. As I dug deeper into the box, I pulled out a large black coat. It had a furry collar to keep my neck warm against the cold wind.

"Do you like it?"

"I like both of them," I said.

"Audrey, I didn't wrap your gift. You will have to forgive me. Please close your eyes and don't open them until I tell you."

"This is so exciting!" she said as she closed her eyes.

"Now you can open your eyes," I said as I opened the ring box.

"Oh, my Lord! Obadiah, it's so beautiful!"

"You like it?"

"I love it. It sparkles so," she replied as she waved it in front of me.

She kissed me and told me how much she loved me. I could tell that things were working out for the good. Audrey was happy, and I was happy to finally make a commitment.

The clock on the wall let out eleven chimes. I looked at Audrey and said, "I've got to head home to Twin Oaks. I didn't realize it was getting this late."

"Obadiah, you've just made me the happiest girl in the whole wide world. I promise you I will make you a good wife. I look forward to spending the rest of my life with you. I'll have as many children as you want."

"I'm going to hold you to that promise in about six months," I said with a hug and kiss.

"I'll see you to the door. Will I see you in church Sunday?"

"Yes, my entire family will be there."

"Can I tell my folks that we are engaged?"

"I don't see any reason why not."

"Oh, I can't believe it!"

We kissed goodnight, and I left Audrey waving goodbye from the porch.

After arriving at Twin Oaks, George was waiting to take the carriage to the barn. It was one of George's responsibilities to handle the horses, and he was good at it. I'm only sorry that I caused him to be up so late.

There was a nice fire going in the parlor as I entered the house, so I decided to warm up a few minutes before going to bed. I had no sooner sat down and was tugging away at my right boot when I heard a familiar voice. "Master Obadiah, let me help you with that boot."

She walked across the room and knelt down at my feet. "Now hold your feet up and let me get those cold boots off," she said with a smile.

"Thank you, Penelope! I thought you would already be in bed."

"I wasn't sleepy, and I knew you would need a hot bath coming in from a cold night like this. So, I fixed you a hot bath. It's ready when you get ready for it."

"Penelope, it's good to see you."

"It's good to see you, too, Master Obadiah."

"Did you have a good trip from Boston?"

"Yes, I did. It was a wonderful surprise to see my mama and Little Jim walking toward me and greeting me at the train station in Selma. That meant the world to me. Little Jim is a good looking little brother. We love each other already."

"Have you got settled in?"

"Yes, I have. I love Sarah's room. Everything is just as I remembered."

"Penelope, I wanted to tell you that we aren't expecting you to do scheduled work while you are home for the holidays."

"Oh, Master Obadiah, I want to. I wouldn't feel right not helping Mama and Betsy. I really need to brush up on my cooking skills. As you are well aware, we don't do much cooking at Mrs. Adams's place."

"I think I'm going to take you up on that hot bath. I can't seem to get rid of this chill."

"I put some towels on the counter next to the bathtub. I'll go and let you get your bath."

"Penelope, please wait a minute. I want to thank you for helping me with my boots. I also want to thank you for making my bath."

"You are most welcome, Master Obadiah."

"I look forward to seeing you tomorrow. Merry Christmas, Penelope!"

"Merry Christmas to you as well," she said with her beautiful smile.

The bath water was just right. It wasn't long before the chill had left my body. It was just what I needed. I just lay there thinking about Penelope and how very beautiful she was. She had blossomed into a beautiful woman.

After my bath, I went straight to my bedroom. There was a fire in the fireplace, but it hadn't knocked out the winter chill within the room. I felt cold once again. I jumped into bed and pulled the covers over my head in hopes I would soon get warm. I must have gone right to sleep for it wasn't long before I was awakened by a knock on my door, and I heard my mother's voice say, "Obadiah, I need to see you."

I pushed back the covers, bounced out of my bed, and opened the door to find my mother in a panic. "Obadiah, your father is having trouble breathing. Please come quickly."

Father was having an asthma attack. I asked Mother to wake Mattie. I needed her assistance in the kitchen. I had Big Jim start a fire to boil some water. I needed it as hot as we could get it. I fixed an old-time potion made of a vapor ointment, including vinegar and other remedies. I soaked cotton stockings and wrapped them around my father's throat. I used the vapor to open his breathing cavities. I also used a paper sack for him to inhale and exhale. This helped him with his hyperventilation. It wasn't long before he was calm and began to breathe normally again. Breathing the cold night air coming from Prattville hadn't been good for him. Because of his age and health conditions, we would have to limit his outside activities. He would not like it, but it was either slow down and stay inside or get pneumonia and die. My mother would have to crack the whip, so to speak.

I asked Mattie to stay with Father so Mother could get some rest. I informed her to come get me should he have another attack.

CHAPTER 23

On Christmas Day, one wouldn't have guessed that Father had an asthma attack during the night. He was up as usual having his breakfast and was as cheerful as he could be.

"Obadiah, I appreciate you taking good care of me last night," my father said as I sat down at the table.

"You gave us a little scare, Father. How are you feeling this morning?"

"I'm feeling pretty good. I have to admit, it was a little scary last night. That's the first time that's happened to me."

"We are going to try to make it the last time. You will need to stay in out of the cold and damp weather."

"I don't think I want to hear that."

"If you don't want another attack, you will need to do as I say."

"Well, let's have some breakfast. I'm hungry, and we have a big day ahead of us."

When Father didn't like someone's opinion or direction, he would find some way of changing the subject. I just hope Mother will be able to talk some sense into him.

Penelope entered the room wearing a beautiful white dress. She had an apron covering the front so not to get it dirty. She poured coffee for Father, Mother, and me and went back into the kitchen to help Mattie and Betsy with breakfast.

The second time she came out, my mother asked her how her night went in Sarah's room.

"I had a good night, Missus Bradford. I have always loved Sarah's room."

"That's good, Penelope. Sarah would be happy you are staying in her room. When the time permits, we would enjoy hearing about your experiences in Boston. Do you think you could do that?"

"I would love to share my experiences. I can't thank you enough for your generosity and hospitality."

Mother and Father looked at each other with amazement. Penelope's vocabulary of words surely had increased since leaving Twin Oaks. I was amazed at how well she handled herself in answering questions and carrying on a conversation. Indeed, Mrs. Adams's Boarding School had taught Penelope well.

Since Father was still a little weak from his asthma attack, he asked Dent if he would read the Christmas story. Dent, of course, was glad to do so. Once again, we were blessed to have one hundred percent of the Bradfords present for the Christmas festivities. Everyone enjoyed a fine family dinner prepared by Mattie, Betsy, Penelope, and Big Jim.

After dinner, we crowded into the large parlor where Christmas presents were handed out and opened. As I looked around the room, I wondered what was going to happen when my parents were no longer the nucleus of this family. My guess is these grand occasions would become a thing of the past. But right now, we are all together. We are building memories — memories that will be with us as long as we shall live.

I pray someday, if God blesses me with a family, we will build family traditions just as my parents have done.

Another tradition Father started after all the presents were opened was a time of sharing with everyone. This gave everyone who wanted to an opportunity to share with the entire group something that had occurred in their lives that made them both happy and thankful.

I had already decided that this would be a good time to share the news about Audrey and my engagement. I always wanted to be last because I wanted to hear what everyone else had to say. Finally, it came my turn. I stood up from my chair and said, "Last night, I asked Audrey Denton to marry me, and she said yes. I'm thankful for that!"

Applauding and shouting sprang up throughout the room. I didn't see anyone who looked disappointed. Dent yelled, "When is the big date?"

"Not immediately, but sometime in the fall after I get settled in my practice with Dr. Banister," I replied.

My father rose from his chair and asked, "Where's that eggnog? I want to make a toast!"

Mother asked Sarah if she would step in the kitchen and ask Mattie and Betsy to bring eggnog to the parlor. It wasn't long before everyone had a glass or cup in their hands.

"I've been waiting a long time for Obadiah to make this announcement. We love Audrey Denton, and we know she will make him a wonderful wife. I congratulate you, Son. We wish you and Audrey a wonderful life together. Remember, I want the Bradford name to keep on growing in numbers." Everyone laughed!

After Father ended his toast, several came up to me to offer their congratulations. Just as I finished hugging Sarah, I glanced through the big French door leading to the hallway. There I spotted Penelope. She was removing glasses from a table in the hall where my family had placed their empty eggnog glasses. She turned and looked at me. Tears were streaming down her cheeks. *Oh, my God, she must have heard my announcement,* I thought. She had the most pitiful look on her face.

Sarah, my sister, noticed me staring straight ahead and saw Penelope crying as well. "I'll go help Penelope. Let's meet later. We will need to talk."

About mid-way through the afternoon, several of the family members started back to their homes to carry on some family traditions they had started with their family members. Dent and his family would spend another night at Twin Oaks.

When things settled down, Sarah came to the parlor and motion for me. I excused myself and met her in the hallway. She asked if we could go to my room and talk. I said yes.

"Obadiah, I admire you in asking Audrey to marry you. That had to be hard knowing how much you love Penelope. Please know you made the only rational decision you could make. I know you'd rather had been with Penelope, but Southern cultural values would have never allowed that. You and Penelope both would have been miserable."

195

"I know exactly what you mean, Sarah. You don't know how I've searched my soul for an answer from God. God wouldn't give me a sign. Penelope will always be my first love. I don't know what it's going to be like without her. What am I to do, Sarah?"

"Let Penelope stay in Boston. If you feel led, free her and give her freedom to find someone to love her. That's exactly what I would do."

"How is she, Sarah?"

"Broken hearted right now, but deep down she knows why you are marrying Audrey."

"I need to talk with her."

"Not now, Obadiah. Let's give this a little time. Thank about what I said about her freedom in Boston. I really think that's best for her right now."

"I know you may be right about giving her freedom, but to tell you the truth, I can't do that right now."

"Then, you've got to get her back to Boston. I see how you two look at each other. Your marriage to Audrey won't last if Penelope is around. You've got to think about that, Obadiah."

"I'm more concerned about my own weakness and temptations toward Penelope. It's so hard for me not to want to take her in my arms and hold her."

"Then you have to keep Penelope in Boston. She can't move back here after she graduates. That will not work, Obadiah."

"Don't you think I know that?"

"Oh, my dearest, loving, kind brother! I feel you're hurt. I wish I could say the right words to help you, but I can't. I've got to go. Jim will be wondering where I am."

"You're very happy with Jim, aren't you?"

"I'm very happy, Obadiah! I'm carrying his child and loving every move he is making inside of me."

"God bless you, Sarah. I'll see you at church tomorrow."

I decided to joined Dent and Father in the parlor where I found both of them in a heated political discussion.

"What's going on here?"

"Oh, Father thinks that if John C. Fremont had won the presidential race that we would have had a civil war. I told him that was ridiculous."

"What do you think about that, Obadiah?" Father asked.

"Don't drag me into this. I'm going to trust you guys will work this out. I've got a few things I need to do. Please excuse me."

As I walked by the kitchen, I stuck my head in and asked Penelope if she would meet me in Sarah's room. She looked at Mattie and Mattie nodded her approval for her to leave what she was doing. I went on to Sarah's room and had just closed the door when Penelope knocked. I said, "Come in."

"You wanted to see me, Master Obadiah?"

"Yes, Penelope, I do. How much of my announcement did you hear?"

"I heard everything, Master Obadiah," she said as she sat down on the bed, bent over and began to cry.

"Penelope, I'm sorry you overheard my announcement. I had planned to tell you privately."

"Master Obadiah, I want you to be happy. If marrying Audrey makes you happy then so be it."

"Penelope, I will always love you. It's just too complicated for us. As I've said many times, we can't be together as husband and wife. Our society won't support that."

"I hate our society! I wish I was dead!"

"Oh, no, Penelope, don't you say such foolish things. Don't ever wish to die. You have too much going for you."

"What have I got going for me, Master Obadiah? Just what do I have going for me? I've lost the only man who meant anything to me."

"Penelope, you've not lost me. I don't care how far away you might be, I'll come if you need me."

"What are your plans for me, Master Obadiah?"

"I want you to return to Boston and finish your course of study."

"You're aware I'll finish my course of study in one year. Then what?

"I don't know yet, Penelope!"

"Why don't you free me?"

"I've been thinking a lot about doing just that."

"You said to me once that someday you would free both me and Mama. When I finish my course of study, why not then?"

"We will decide then, Penelope!"

"May I be excused, Master?"

"Wait just a minute. I have something for you," I said, handing her a present.

She was trembling all over as she opened the present. The package contained a silver bracelet that I had purchased in Augusta. I was hoping she would like it.

"It's beautiful, Master!"

"Why are you not saying, Obadiah?"

"I'm sorry, Master Obadiah! Right now, I'm just hurting!"

"Oh, my dear Penelope! I'm so very sorry it's turned out this way."

"I have something for you as well. I made it myself."

Penelope pulled a large package from under the bed and handed it to me. As I opened it, I felt so ashamed. What had I done to this amazing, beautiful lady? Why had I fallen in love with her, and why have I ended up hurting her so badly?

The package contained a beautiful navy suit. It was well made and was made for a southern gentleman.

"I hope it fits. I measured one of your suits before going back to Boston the last time I was at home. I hope you like it."

"Penelope, you actually made this for me?"

"Yes, Master Obadiah, for you!"

"Thank you so much. I'll wear it to church tomorrow."

We said good night to each other, and I left the room to return to the parlor. Dent was sitting all alone when I arrived.

"Where have you been, little brother?"

"I had something I had to take care of."

"It wouldn't have had something to do with Penelope, would it?"

"How did you know?"

"Obadiah Bradford, I, too, saw Penelope crying in the hall. I knew she must have overheard your engagement announcement. Why didn't you tell her prior to your announcement?"

"I was going to, but there wasn't time to visit with her."

"Well, needless to say, I'm sure you've broken her heart. That girl loves you, you know!"

"Indeed, I know, and I will always love her."

"Obadiah, you might want to consider what we've talked about earlier. If you can't marry her, then see her on the side."

"Dent, I can't do that. I won't do that; furthermore, that's crazy!"

"You are a better man than I, little brother."

Mother came to the door and said, "Dinner will be served in about thirty minutes. We're having leftovers!"

I don't think I slept a wink. I lay awake thinking of both Audrey and Penelope. I never wanted to hurt Penelope. Sarah is right. I must keep Penelope at a distance after marrying Audrey. If I brought Penelope back to Twin Oaks, Audrey surely would suspect something. I don't think I could have the two of them in the same household. That could be disastrous!

One other tradition we Bradfords observed after Christmas was to attend church together at Oak Hills Baptist Church in Prattville.

Father wouldn't hear of staying home and letting us go to church without him. Mother dressed him in his warmest clothes and I made him a mask to cover his nose and mouth.

Audrey and I sat together during the church service. She held my hand throughout the service. The ring I gave her sparkled. I could tell she was very happy about the ring and our engagement. In my mind, I knew that marrying Audrey was the only thing I could do that would be acceptable to my parents, family, and the community.

Rev. Bishop's sermon went on and on and on. I tried to concentrate on his message, but my thoughts of Penelope and

Audrey kept running through my mind. How could I possibly resolve this dilemma?

The next few days went fast. I was able to spend quality time with Audrey, but for many reasons I was looking forward to returning to Augusta.

CHAPTER 24

My trip back to Augusta was uneventful. I slept most of the way. I was tired from the rigorous schedule I kept back in Twin Oaks. My relationship with Penelope and Audrey continued to be a burden on my mind. I had to find some way to resolve this in my mind. I can't afford to be tormented by these constant annoying thoughts. These thoughts are putting my whole career in jeopardy. I need to find peace, but how?

It was good to see my friends Ben, Jim, and John. They were all sitting in the reception room playing cards with our new friends, Frank Thompson and John Matthews.

Ben spotted me first and hollered, "Come on in here, Obadiah. We've been waiting for you."

"Good to see you guys."

"We thought you had decided to stay in Autauga County," Jim said.

"Nope, I'm ready to hit the books again."

"Tell us, Obadiah, did you get yourself engaged to that lovely Audrey Denton?" John asked.

"How did you know?"

"Actually, we've been talking about it, and we took some bets whether you did or didn't get engaged. So you really did get engaged?" John asked.

"Yes, I'm engaged. We will be married sometime in the fall after I get settled in at Dr. Banister's medical practice."

"Pay up, boys! I win!" said John.

Mr. Melton came to the door and announced that dinner was being served. We enjoyed a good dinner together and returned to the reception room for coffee and more cards. Since school was starting back, this would be one of the few nights we would be free to visit and relax together.

On the second day back, Dr. Matthew Tolskey asked me to assist him in amputating a man's leg. Gangrene had set in, and the leg had to come off. I observed closely the step-by-step procedure Dr. Tolskey used in removing the leg. He used ether as an anesthetic to ease the man's pain. He looked at me and said, "You won't always have ether to fall back on to ease pain. That's when things get really interesting," he said as he gave me a wink.

I could tell the poor man still felt pain by the way he cried out. Dr. Tolskey looked at me and said, "Obadiah, we just saved this man's life."

In the next few weeks, I assisted Dr. Tolskey in several operations. He had yet to let me do a major operation under his supervision. I expected this would change sometime in the near future; however, I didn't have to wait long. There was a young man admitted with an appendicitis attack. Dr. Tolskey sent for me. "Scrub up, Obadiah; this one is yours," Dr. Tolskey said.

I quickly scrubbed and met Dr. Tolskey in the operating room. He looked at me and asked, "Do you remember the procedure?"

"Yes, sir!"

"Then I'll assist and let you perform the operation."

This was my first time to make a delicate incision. I felt confident as I took my scalpel and cut through the muscle to get to the appendix. Making the incision didn't bother me in the least. I had seen much worse situations back in Autauga County. I was in and out and sewing up the small incision within a few minutes. Dr. Tolskey looked at me and said, "Good job, Obadiah."

The boy recovered nicely with a very small scar. I don't like scars and was determined to try to be as perfect as I could when cutting on my patients.

Time was quickly passing. My friend Dr. Henry Dotson told me I could expect a whirlwind of a last semester. Although it's been busy, I had time to answer some letters I received from my mother, Audrey, and Penelope. All is going well with them. Father has a cold, but mother says it's not bad.

Audrey has been showing her ring off to everyone in Prattville. She is so happy about our engagement. She had waited patiently while I held out and deserves the attention she's getting.

Penelope is back in Boston and has gone back to work at the men's shop where she made my suit. I love the suit. She has turned into a skillful seamstress. The letters I've received from her have been short. I know she is still hurt.

Everyone who is interested in politics is talking about Kansas. It appears there is still a big problem in determining the fate of Kansas as whether it will enter the union as a free or slave state. This morning's Augusta Chronicle carried a story about another recent development. The article contained a story of the Lecompton Constitution that has come about in response to the anti-slavery position of the 1855 Topeka Constitution written by James H. Lane and other free-state advocates. The territorial legislature, consisting mostly of slave-owners, met at the dedicated capital of Lecompton in September to produce a rival document. The document was boycotted by a vote of the free-state supporters, who comprised a large majority of actual settlers in Kansas.

President James Buchanan supported the Lecompton Constitution and appointed Robert J. Walker as territorial governor with the understanding that Mr. Walker would enforce the Lecompton Constitution. Mr. Walker was a strong defender of slavery, but opposed the blatant injustice of the constitution and resigned rather than implement it. The Lecompton Constitution enshrined slavery in the proposed state and protected the rights of slaveholders. In addition, the constitution provided for a referendum that allowed voters the choice of allowing more slaves to enter the territory.

When the Lecompton Constitution was voted on, over half of the 6,000 votes cast were deemed fraudulent. As a result of the vote, President Buchanan endorsed the Lecompton Constitution before the U. S. Congress. The President received the support of the Southern Democrats, but many Northern Democrats, led by Stephen A. Douglas, sided with the Republicans in opposition to the constitution. Douglas found help from Thomas

Ewing Jr., a noted Kansas Free State politician and lawyer, who led a legislative investigation in Kansas to uncover the fraudulent voting ballots. A new referendum over the fate of the Lecompton Constitution was proposed, even though this would delay Kansas's admission to the Union. This brought on a new constitution, the anti-slavery Leavenworth Proposal, by a vote of 10,226 to 138. This put a hold on any enforcement of the early vote on the Lecompton Constitution.

It appears now that a vote will be taken by the federal House of Representatives sometime early in 1858. This vote most likely will resolve whether Kansas will be a free or slave state.

I have become very interested in Kansas. That's all people want to talk about around here. I've never witnessed a better political issue than Kansas. Most of the Southern states are hoping that Kansas will become a slave state. Most Southerners are fearful that if Kansas is admitted as a free state, it will be perceived as a defeat for slavery. This was my father's thinking when I was home. He always said, "If Kansas is admitted as a free state, so goes the union." I hadn't given that a lot of thought until the last few days, but my father may be right.

We were well into April when Dr. Tolskey called me into his office. "Obadiah, I'd like for you to make rounds with me at the hospital today. I've got a patient I want you to look at. I'm not sure what's wrong with him. I'd like your opinion."

I met Dr. Tolskey at 4:00 p.m. in his office. While waiting for him, I begin to wonder whether this was another one of his tests, or was it legitimate. As we entered the patient's room, I smelled a terrible odor. I first thought it was formaldehyde.

"Obadiah, I want you to look at Mr. Gaston's feet."

I pulled back the bed linens, and I almost gagged when I saw his feet. His feet and his right leg had huge sores that were infected.

"You need to use gloves, Obadiah."

I put gloves on and begin to examine his feet. The sores were everywhere. I looked at Mr. Gaston and asked, "How long have you had these sores?"

"For about two weeks, I reckon!"

"Can you give me a little background information about when you first noticed the sores and what you were doing at the time?"

"I had been pulling stumps from a low area on my property and had cut my foot on something sharp. The cut is on my right foot."

"Yes, I can see the cut. Were you barefoot?"

"Yes, sir, I was. I didn't want to ruin my good working shoes."

"Where do you live, Mr. Gaston?"

"I live about three miles south of Augusta, near the Sylvania River."

"You hang in there, Mr. Gaston! We're going to see what we can do to help you. Do you mind if we take some water samples from the swamp area on your property?"

"No, sir, Doc. I don't mind."

"We'll be getting back with you soon."

"Thank you, doctor!" Mr. Gaston said, as we left the room.

After leaving the patient's room, I turned to Dr. Tolskey and said, "I've seen similar sores on plantation slaves in Autauga County. I believe what Mr. Gaston has is impetigo. If it is impetigo, it's treatable."

"How do we determine if it's impetigo, and how do we treat it?" Dr. Tolskey asked.

"I would like to go out to Mr. Gaston's farm and test his water. If it's impetigo, the infection most likely started from the cut on his foot. The water may be contaminated."

"Before you leave, I need to tell you something."

"What is it, Dr. Tolskey?"

"I'll be honest with you. I've never seen impetigo. I was afraid we were going to have to cut both of his legs off to save his life."

"I believe its impetigo. If you noticed, his sores contained a yellow colored substance. The areas of his feet and right leg will need to be cleaned with soap and water and the crust on his sores will need to be removed, allowing the sores to dry in the air. We will need to treat Mr. Gaston's sores with fusidic acid.

Dr. Banister uses something called flucloxacillin. If Mr. Gaston's problem is impetigo, he's got a bad case of it."

"It sounds as though you have a good plan. What time period are we talking about to get rid of this impetigo?"

"It normally takes about three weeks."

"You go on and get your water sample and let me know what we need to do next."

"Yes, sir!"

My diagnosis was correct. The swamp water was contaminated, and that's how Mr. Gaston's impetigo got started. I informed Dr. Tolskey how I thought we should treat Mr. Gaston, and he agreed. After two weeks, Mr. Gaston had shown a tremendous improvement. In another week, he should be completely free of impetigo. I have not seen a case as bad as his. Again, I have Dr. Banister to thank for things that I learned from him when we were going from plantation to plantation treating the slaves. My experience with him has helped me in so many ways.

I had done about every operation that Dr. Tolskey had done except for amputations of a body limb. Since we were down to six weeks of schooling, I thought maybe I'd get lucky and not have to do an amputation. After observing and assisting Dr. Tolskey during surgical amputations, I found no enjoyment whatsoever in participating in that type of surgery.

It was now four weeks before graduation. After a long day at the hospital, I returned to the Melton place, picked up my mail, and opened a letter from my mother. As I opened the letter, I said a silent prayer, "Please, God, don't let this letter bring bad news from home."

Much to my relief, Mother was bringing good news in her letter. She wanted me to know that every member of the Bradford family was planning to be in Augusta for my graduation. She informed me that Father was telling every member of the family that, "A team of wild horses wasn't going to stop him from being at his son's graduation."

My father and mother have been nothing but supportive, financially as well as giving moral support, since I decided I wanted to be a doctor.

Besides the Bradford clan, Audrey wrote that she and her folks planned to be present for my graduation as well. "What better support could one want?" I thought.

Two weeks before the end of school, a man was admitted to the emergency room of the hospital with a severely crushed and mangled arm. His arm had been caught in a machine press. It was broken in several places and torn badly. I was summoned along with my friends Ben Murphy and John Peters to the emergency room by Dr. Tolskey. We arrived just in time to see Dr. Tolskey applying a tourniquet to slow down the bleeding. As we entered the room, Dr. Tolskey looked up and said, "We are going to have to act quickly on this one to save his life."

"Obadiah, you will do the amputation, and Murphy and Peters will assist you. Are you ready for this?"

"Yes, sir!" I said.

"Let's scrub! We need to act fast."

The thing I feared most had occurred. This was something I had hoped I wouldn't have to do. I knew Dr. Tolskey well enough to know that he would fail me if I didn't perform up to his standards. As I was scrubbing, I said a silent prayer. I dried my hands and headed back to the operation room. I was confident I could do the operation, but the thought of sawing a limb from a man's body shot pain through me. Cutting off this man's arm wasn't all I had to do. I would also have to cauterize the area where I removed his arm. This was not going to be an easy task. "God help me," I prayed as I started sawing through his upper arm.

As expected, the man was experiencing a lot of pain. John held his shoulders down while Ben held the lower part of his body. I found the ether to be of little help in curtailing the man's pain.

The procedure took a good thirty minutes. He was very weak from the loss of blood and the trauma of the surgery. I wanted to believe he would live, but the next twenty-four hours would be a critical time.

I looked at Dr. Tolskey and asked, "Is there something else I need to do?"

207

"Obadiah, you did well. Come by tomorrow and check on him."

"Yes, sir," I said as I left the operating room.

I was exhausted! I had not been this exhausted in years. I knew part of my exhaustion was due to stress. After I washed up, I went back to the Melton Place where I enjoyed the evening meal and went to bed early.

The next several days passed without any major crisis. We had three more days before graduation. Unless something unexpected happened, I was going to graduate and receive my diploma. Last week, on Tuesday, I found out I had passed both the Alabama and Georgia medical board exams, which would allow me to legally practice medicine in those two states. All I had to do now is to get that diploma in my hands.

Two days before graduation, Dr. Tolskey called me to his office.

"Obadiah, I have some great news for you!" he said with excitement.

"What is it, sir?" I asked.

"I'm happy to inform you that the governing board of the Old Georgia Medical School has voted you our number one graduate. You now join the ranks of your good friend, Dr. Henry Dotson, as being the most outstanding graduate of your class."

"You're not joking around with me, are you?" I asked with excitement.

"Obadiah, it's true. You've been selected the top graduate of 1857. All you have to do now is prepare and make a speech. I'm so proud of you!"

"Dr. Tolskey, I don't know what to say. I can't thank you enough for all you've done for me."

"It's been my honor to have you as a student. I will be introducing you on the platform at graduation. I will try to do you justice."

"Dr. Tolskey, I've been blessed having you as my supervisory teacher. I've learned so much from your teachings. I'll try not to let you down."

"I know Autauga County is getting the best we can offer. You will do well in your practice there. May God bless you, my friend!"

I left Dr. Tolskey's office feeling a sense of pride, which I'd never felt before. I had achieved another milestone in my life. I immediately went to the telegraph office and sent the following telegram to my parents.

"Dear Father and Mother. Stop. Good news! Stop. Your son is receiving the top honors award at graduation. Stop. I'm proud to share this news with you. Stop. I look forward to seeing you. Stop. Love, Obadiah Bradford."

CHAPTER 25

My graduation day finally arrived. My folks, as well as Audrey and her parents, were present. Because of limited seating at the hospital auditorium, the graduation ceremonies were being held on the lawn of the Old Medical School Campus. Due to my being named top honor student, the first two rows on the right side of the speaker's podium were reserved for my family and friends.

Dr. Tolskey did an outstanding job introducing me to the audience. One would have sworn he was introducing his own son. As I rose from my chair to make my speech, a sense of nervousness fell over me. I had never experienced this type of nervousness before. Maybe it was stage fright, or maybe it was just the thought I might mess up. Whatever it was, I needed to shake it off fast. It was time for me to focus on the task at hand.

As I began to welcome and greet our many guests, I found my eyes focusing directly on my family. The looks on their faces reassured me I was doing fine and they were proud of me. As I looked at Audrey, she gave me her usual sweet and lovely smile, as if to say, "I love you!" I kept thinking about some of the things my speech teacher had taught me in class. One was to scan the audience and not to look down. As I looked straight ahead, I was pleased to see my old friend, Henry Dotson, in the crowd. He had fulfilled his promise. He had come from Atlanta to see his buddies walk across the platform to receive their diplomas. It was such an honor for me to see Henry in the audience, as well as his lovely wife, Helen.

Another thing my speech teacher had taught was to make eye to eye contact with my audience. If the audience laughed or nodded in agreement, then they were still with me. If they were quiet, non-responsive, dropping their heads as if they were sleepy, then normally, this meant they were bored and not interested in what I was saying.

My speech teacher always emphasized that a speech needed to be short. She said, "If you can't make a speech less then fifteen minutes then you'd better be a good comedian." My speech lasted fourteen minutes and fifty-eight seconds. I received a standing ovation. I guess they liked what I had to say.

My father had reserved the train's dining car for a time of celebration on our way back to Selma, Alabama. There was standing room only with all the Bradfords and Dentons present. There were several speeches given by members of my family. I kept wondering what Father would say when he stood to address the family. My father is a good speaker. He knows how to choose his words and how to express himself through body language as well. He waited patiently as he gave everyone an opportunity to voice their congratulations. When no one else chose to speak, he took a spoon in hand and loudly tapped on his glass. Everyone turned in his direction to give him their undivided attention.

"I've certainly enjoyed listening to everyone's remarks and congratulations to Obadiah. I believe we may have some potential and promising politicians in our midst here today. Obadiah, please come and stand by me. Audrey, if you will, come and stand by Obadiah."

Father didn't realize it, but I was more than honored to be standing beside him. He meant everything to me.

"Obadiah, I want to offer my congratulations to you. You have made me and the whole Bradford family very proud. You have accomplished your goal. You didn't quit when things got tough. Your return to Autauga County will be a big help to my friend, Dr. Banister. Autauga County will have two of the best doctors in Alabama attending to the health needs of our families and our slaves.

"Oh, by the way, Obadiah wanted me to announce that he has a special gift for each of us. He is offering his medical services to each member of the Bradford family, and to every slave on our plantations at Cahaba and Twin Oaks. The best part of this gift is that his service will be free. Did I get it right, Dr. Bradford?" Father said with a chuckle.

"That's right, Father!" I said as I nodded my head in the affirmative as everyone laughed.

Father wasn't kidding. He and I had made a gentleman's agreement and sealed it with a hand shake before I left for Augusta, Georgia, some two years ago. This agreement was my idea. I felt it was only fair since Father had paid for my medical degree expenses, as well as Penelope's schooling and board in Boston. This was the least I could do to repay him for his generous financial support.

"Again, we are very proud of you and wish you and Audrey the very best as you embark on a long and enjoyable life together as husband and wife."

Everyone raised their glasses and said, "Here, here!"

We celebrated all the way to Selma. Upon arriving in Selma, Bill, George, and others were there with carriages and wagons to take the Bradford clan home to Cahaba, Twin Oaks, and Prattville. It was getting late so we hurriedly said our goodbyes at the train station and headed out to our designations. I would be seeing Audrey in Prattville on Monday when I reported for my first day of work as Dr. Bradford.

The trip to Twin Oaks was short. I was still celebrating in my mind. I couldn't help noticing my father dozing off and on as Bill drove a steady pace along the dusty road home. I was so very proud of my family. The closeness we shared was very important to all of us. I couldn't stand the thought of my father and mother dying. Because of their age, I knew God would someday call both of them to his heavenly home. A big part of the Bradford traditions would come to an end when they died.

After a nice bath prepared by Mattie, I jumped into bed and fell fast asleep.

I started my practice with Dr. Banister on Monday. I spent the first day just getting organized in my new office that Dr. Banister had built for me. Before leaving for the day, Elizabeth Benton, Dr. Banister's scheduling nurse, went over my appointments for the remaining part of the week. She had me scheduled to see patients on Mondays, Tuesdays, and Wednesdays in the office and out in the county on Thursdays and Fridays. I noticed she had me traveling to Mr. James Jones plantation on Friday. I was scheduled to spend most of Friday at the Jones plantation. My memories of Mr. Jones and Mr. Mason, the overseer, were not pleasant. The way Jones and Mason treated their slaves was a disgrace. The living conditions were horrible. I'm hoping these conditions had changed for the better.

My working in Prattville afforded me the opportunity to see Audrey on a daily basis for lunch. We enjoyed eating at our favorite Pratt restaurant. The more I saw her, the happier I became. In a few weeks, she would become Mrs. Audrey Bradford, wife of Dr. Obadiah Bradford. *That has a nice sound to it!* I thought.

On Friday morning, I left Twin Oaks for the Jones plantation, which was about ten miles from Twin Oaks. As I approached the plantation, I had a strange feeling as I glanced toward the old shed that once housed the half-starved and half-frozen slaves during the winter of 1853. On that particular trip, Dr. Banister and I found one slave, old Joe, dead. Eleven other slaves were malnourished, some had pneumonia, and some were about to freeze to death. It was a horrible sight.

Mr. Max Mason was still the overseer of Mr. Jones's plantation. I didn't have any respect for him. I was in hopes I would get the opportunity to express these feelings to him during this visit. As I pulled up at the hitching post, I was met by Mr. Mason.

"Welcome back to Autauga County, Dr. Bradford."

I certainly hadn't expected to be welcomed in such a friendly manner. Especially from a guy who was known throughout the county as a mean, vicious, and uncaring white trash of a man. I decided I would be as professional as I could as I stepped down from the carriage.

"Thank you, Mr. Mason," I said, not offering my hand.

"I always knew you would be a doctor someday."

"Who needs my attention today?" I asked.

"Well, we've got four slaves who need you. The first one is in the barn in chains. He's a mean one. We bought him last month, and we've had to give him floggings at least once a week for his rebellious moods and running away. We've not made a believer out of him yet. We have two of our female slaves who are about to drop babies. The other is a young girl who got herself knocked-up. She's been having some problems."

As soon as he mentioned the young slave girl, I immediately thought to myself that he was probably the expectant father.

"Let's take a look at the one in the barn first," I said.

Again, I found the barn dark and damp. Mason had the poor man chained to a post near the middle of the barn on some hay. At least he wasn't lying on the damp ground.

"Mason, I'm going to need some light. Can you get me some lanterns?"

"I can!" he said in an agreeable manner.

"What is his name, Mason?"

"We call him Hercules."

"Why Hercules?"

"He's very strong! He's already broken two of our chains."

I found Hercules lying on his left side. He was very stiff. I knew he wasn't dead for I could see him breathing.

"Can you help me turn him over on his back?" I asked.

Mr. Mason didn't answer me. He knelt down and proceeded to turn Hercules over on his back. As he did, I couldn't believe what I was seeing. Both of his eyes were swollen shut. Not only had they flogged him, they had beaten him severely in the face. His lips were busted, and lacerations were present on both his face and back. He was in bad shape.

"Mr. Mason, did you do this to Hercules?"

"I don't see that's any of your business, Dr. Bradford."

"Mr. Mason, I'm making it my business. I've waited a long time to tell you and Mr. Jones how I feel about how you treat your slaves. Don't you know your slaves would do you more good if you treated them right?"

"Slaves don't understand goodness, Dr. Bradford. You have to show them who is boss. You got to scare the devil out of them."

"Oh, Mason, you are so wrong. If you were to treat them with kindness by giving them ample food, clothing, rest, and proper living quarters, your slaves would work for you harder and your plantation would be more productive. Don't you know that?"

"You do your job, Dr. Bradford, and I'll do mine."

"I'll need some hot water, soap, and a couple of towels. Do you think you can manage getting those items for me?"

"I'll get you the water and towels, but I don't appreciate you jumping all over me about how we treat our slaves. They are our slaves, and we can do whatever we want with them."

He left the barn in a rage. I had struck a nerve in him. I didn't care. I've wanted for years the opportunity to confront him about his cruel treatment of his slaves. I felt better getting it off my chest, although it probably won't make a difference in how he will treat his slaves in the future. He is just a mean man!

I cleaned Hercules body as well as I could and bandaged the infected areas on his back and face. If Mason would move him to a sanitary place, I believed he would live.

"Mr. Mason, if you want Hercules to live, you need to get him off this hay and out of this barn. He needs a dry and sanitary place with a cot or bed to lie on. He needs food and lots of fluids. He's at the point of being dehydrated."

I could tell I had struck another nerve by the way he looked at me. I know Mason would probably want Mr. Jones to fire me, but I didn't care. He had to know how I felt. If he lets Hercules die, he would be the responsible party and not me.

"I'll have to talk to Mr. Jones about that. He won't like moving him," Mason said.

"Mason, can I ask you a question?"

"It depends on what you're asking, I reckon!"

"How much did Mr. Jones pay for Hercules?"

"I don't know if that's any of your business, Dr. Bradford!" Mason said with anger in his voice.

"Well, let me say this. I figure Mr. Jones paid around six hundred dollars for him from the way he's built, and as young as he is. His teeth are in excellent condition and he's got a well-built body. Regardless of the beatings you've given him, he's still strong. If I was Mr. Jones, I would hate for him to die and have to be replaced with another six hundred dollar slave."

Mason mumbled something under his breath and then said, "I guess I could make a space for him in Old Milton's shack. He and his wife are getting up in age, and they could take care of him until he gets well enough to work."

"Now that sounds like a great idea to me. I'll tell you what I'll do for you. If you will move Hercules in with old Milton, I'll see what I can do to get Hercules not to run away again. I've been successful before in getting runners to calm down, behave, and work hard for their owners. It's the way you treat them, you know."

Again, he looked at me with anger in his eyes. I knew then that he had taken about all he was going to take from me, so I handed him the medicine for Hercules's back, picked up my medical bag, and headed out of the barn.

At my second stop, I examined the two expectant female slaves who were due at any time. After examining both of them, I informed Mason that the babies could come as early as the next five to seven days. I asked Mason if he had a midwife on his plantation that had experience in birthing babies.

"Yes, we do! We have Minnie. She lives at the big house and is one of Mr. Jones's house maids. Minnie has delivered several babies on this plantation."

"That's good to hear, but if Minnie runs into any trouble, you send for me."

The last patient was the young slave girl who was pregnant with her first child. She couldn't have been more than fifteen years old. Her name was Teshia. As I was examining her, I was reminded of another young slave girl named Mandy, who Dr. Banister and I attended a few years earlier on Mr. Jones's plantation. Teshia was just like Mandy: close built. Mandy ended up losing her baby, which was breached. She was in critical condition for several days, but pulled through the awful ordeal.

"Mr. Mason, whatever happened to Mandy, the slave girl who almost died trying to give birth to a breached baby?"

"Mr. Jones sold her at a slave sale in Selma."

"Why did he sell her?"

"Mandy went crazy. No one could handle her. She became a real problem."

"I'm sorry to hear that, Mason. The last time I attended her, she seemed normal."

"Why are you asking all these questions?"

"Well, Mason, I'm afraid Teshia may have some real problems when she goes into labor. I don't think she can have this baby on her own. I'm afraid Minnie won't be able to give Teshia the medical assistance she may need."

"Hell, what do you mean?"

"I'm saying she is going to have a rough time giving birth. The baby is big and she's built close. That will be a problem when she goes into labor."

"What do we need to do?"

"As soon as she goes into labor, you send for me. I guess I'm finished unless you have someone else who needs my attention."

"I don't know of anyone else, Dr. Bradford."

"I'll come by next week and check on Hercules and the ladies. If you should need me before Thursday, you send for me."

As I left the Jones plantation, my thoughts turned to Hercules. Most men couldn't have survived the floggings and beatings he'd withstood. *God must have a plan for him,* I thought. I'll do what I can to try to convince him to settle down and do his work at Mr. Jones's plantation. I will never understand how one human being can treat another human being the way Jones and Mason treated Hercules. I wasn't too concerned about the two older slave ladies who had previously been successful in giving live births. The one I was most concerned about was Teshia. I fear for both her and her baby.

On Saturday night, Audrey and I attended a dance at the Prattville community center. We were able to visit with several of our old friends as well as Mr. and Mrs. Daniel Pratt. While visiting with Mr. Pratt, he brought up his plans to build a hospital in Prattville.

"Obadiah, I would love to visit with you and Dr. Banister about my idea of building a nice hospital here in Prattville. When do you think we could have lunch together to discuss this venture?"

"Let me discuss this matter with Dr. Banister, and we will let you know."

"I'll be looking forward to our visit."

On Sunday, I picked Audrey up at her house, and we rode together to the Oak Hills Baptist Church. In two weeks, we would be married. I stayed for Sunday dinner at Audrey's home before returning to Twin Oaks for a relaxing afternoon. While relaxing on the front porch, Mattie came out and sat down by me.

"Master Obadiah, this is a beautiful afternoon, isn't it?"

"It is certainly a nice day, Mattie. How are you?"

"I'm doing fine, Master Obadiah. I was wondering if I might speak with you about Penelope."

"Is something wrong?"

"Her health's fine, but she's dealing with a troublesome problem. A problem she doesn't want you to know about, but I felt you needed to know."

"You must tell me, Mattie!"

"My Penelope has met a nice young man in Boston. He's white and he's proposed marriage to her. She's told him she needed time to think about it, but he's become very persistent. He doesn't know she's black and that she's a slave. Master Obadiah, I think Penelope has gotten herself in big trouble. She didn't want me to speak to you about this."

"Mattie, is Penelope with child?"

"Lord's a mercy, Master Obadiah! No, she's not with child. She's never been with a man."

"There's something else you need to tell me, isn't there?"

Mattie took a big breath and said, "I guess not."

I could tell there was something else that Mattie wanted to tell me but was finding it hard to say.

"Come on, Mattie. I can tell there is something else you want to say. Just say it!"

"Oh, Master Obadiah, I don't know how."

"Come on, Mattie. You must tell me!"

"Penelope is in love with you. She's so broken-hearted over you marrying Miss Audrey. She thinks you love her, but knows you can't marry her. She's so troubled with all of this. I believe this is why she's seeing this young man."

"Mattie, I do love Penelope with all my heart. I've loved her since the first time I laid my eyes on her in Selma, Alabama. That's the reason I sent her away. Penelope and I can't be together as husband and wife. Do you understand why we can't be together?"

"Yes, Master Obadiah, I do understand. I know you're right, but what can we do to get Penelope out of this problem?"

"Mattie, I want you to write Penelope and tell her I'm bringing her home to Twin Oaks. Don't tell her we've had this talk. Audrey and I are getting married in two weeks. I want to have some time with Audrey before I bring Penelope back to Twin Oaks. Since Audrey and I are planning to live in Prattville, Penelope will be a big help to my mother in caring for the needs of my father. Mattie, by the way, do you know the name of this young man Penelope has been seeing?"

"I do have his name. His name is Marcus Lane."

"Mattie, I've considered giving Penelope her freedom many times. I've already told her that someday I planned to free both of you. Right now isn't the time to do that, however. Furthermore, my folks wouldn't understand why I suddenly freed both of you. If I knew for sure that this Marcus Lane would be good to her, and love her as she should be loved, then I might consider doing this in the future. Another thing we'd have to consider is the truth. Once Penelope's secret of being a slave and being black is revealed to Marcus Lane, all hell may break loose. He might not even want her. There is too much at risk right now, a risk I'm not willing to take at this time."

"Oh, Master Obadiah, it's going to be so nice to have Penelope back here with us. Thank you so much!"

"You're welcome, Mattie. Let's not say anything to anyone right now about Penelope coming home. We will let that be our secret."

Just as I thought things were going well, a barrel of dynamite exploded right in my face. Oh, was I doing the right thing? How could I do anything else? I couldn't give Penelope her freedom.

I couldn't let her marry this Marcus Lane. If he were to find out that she was owned by another man and that she was black and a slave, he might even hurt her. I couldn't take a chance on that happening. I had to bring her home. My thoughts were going into all sorts of directions. My troublesome times had returned. I had to get focused. There were too many things to plan out in the next two weeks.

Father had made arrangements for Audrey and me to go to New York on our honeymoon. We would be back in Autauga County and settled in at Prattville before Penelope returned to Twin Oaks. Another comforting thought was that I would be busy in my medical practice and wouldn't have to be around Penelope every day. Maybe this wasn't going to be as bad as I first thought.

CHAPTER 26

Today, Audrey Denton and I stood before our Lord and Savior, Jesus Christ, and repeated our vows, committing ourselves to a lifetime partnership in holy marriage. Our vows were repeated before one of the largest crowds ever reported at the Oak Hills Baptist Church in Prattville. The Bradfords alone took up at least a third of the sanctuary, while the Dentons and our friends took up the remaining sections.

As I watched Audrey walk down the aisle of the church, my knees began to knock. I hadn't been this nervous since making my graduation speech at the Old Georgia Medical School. I had given much thought to my vows, especially the part that said I would take Audrey as my lawful and wedded wife, to love and cherish, till death do us part. I had peace about marrying Audrey, although another woman possessed my heart and soul. Nevertheless, I resolved that I would be a good husband, and Audrey would never know that I loved Penelope.

When the pastor finally said, "I pronounce you husband and wife," I lifted Audrey's veil, and we sealed our marriage with our first kiss as husband and wife. I was marrying one of the very best women in Autauga County. She was pretty both inside and outside. She was one of the kindest ladies I had ever known. Audrey would be a good wife. She and I wanted basically the same thing. We wanted to start our family as soon as possible. We wanted a large family, and we wanted to raise them in the Oak Hills Baptist Church. We had previously agreed that both of us would continue our jobs until we started our family. After that, Audrey would become a stay-at-home wife and mother.

The wedding reception was held at the community center in Prattville. I've never seen so many people. My mother, sisters, and Audrey's mother were in charge of the wedding reception and Father and Mr. Denton provided the financial means necessary to purchase the food, drinks, and decorations. Our wedding cake had five layers with thick white frosting. I loved it. I guess you could say sweets are my weakness. The cake was so good that I asked my mother if she could pack a big piece of it away in a box so that Audrey and I could share another piece on our train ride to New York City.

As tradition would have it, I led my bride to the middle of the dance floor where we enjoyed our first dance together as a married couple. We also got to show off our dancing skills, or I should say Audrey had an opportunity to show off hers. She loves to dance and is very good at it. I am average. We didn't get to dance long before my father cut in to dance with Audrey. I looked around and found my mother, and we danced. I don't remember ever dancing with my mother previously. She danced quite well. I had seen her and Father dance before but never really watched them closely. I felt good leading my mother around the dance floor.

As the reception ended, Audrey and I were showered with rice as we walked to the family carriage. Bill, our trusted and faithful driver, had pulled our family carriage close to the front door where we stepped into it and waved goodbye as we headed out to Selma, Alabama, for our long journey to New York City.

My father had arranged for us to have the honeymoon suite on the train for our journey to New York City. Our two-day and two-night trip from Selma to New York City was far too short. Our stay at the Desoto Hotel, located on Broadway Street, was just wonderful. We attended several Broadway shows and dined at some of the best restaurants in New York City. We had the time of our lives.

Upon returning to Autauga County, Bill drove us by Twin Oaks for a visit with Mother and Father before taking us to our house in Prattville.

As we stopped in front of the house, Mother came running out of the house to meet us on the front porch. "Thank God you're here, Obadiah. I need your help with your father."

"Where is Father?"

"He's in the parlor. Obadiah. I don't know what's gotten into him. After he read today's newspaper, he got really upset and became very agitated. He has worked himself into a state of anger. I'm afraid he will keel over with a heart attack."

"Today's paper carried a big story about the United States Congress rejection of the Lecompton Constitution and how it would affect Kansas. Would you please go into the parlor and check on him? Try to get him to see that getting upset is not good for his heart."

Father could easily get upset when it came to politics. He had been following the Lecompton Constitution issue closely for the past year. The Lecompton Constitution was first passed in 1857 by the Kansas territory. Since Kansas had not yet become a state, the United States Congress had to vote on the Constitution as well.

I found Father sitting in his chair near the fireplace. He wasn't asleep. He was just sitting with his newspaper across his lap looking off to the right.

"Father, how are you?" I said, hoping to arouse him.

He turned, looked straight at me and said, "Obadiah, you're back."

I went over to him and asked, "Are you doing all right?"

He responded loudly, "Hell, no, I'm not doing all right! Obadiah, do you know what has just happened to Kansas?"

"I've not seen the paper today, Father."

"Well, take a look at this article," Father said as he handed me the newspaper.

The article confirmed what I thought might upset Father. The Lecompton Constitution, which had been supported by President James Buchanan, would have made Kansas a slave state. In a vote of the U.S. Congress yesterday, however, the approval of the Lecompton Constitution was defeated by a majority of anti-slavery congressmen and was sent back to Kansas for a vote. Father was certain that this action would kill the Lecompton Constitution and force Kansas to come up with another constitution that would eventually allow Kansas to be a free state.

"Father, I know this upsets you. I must remind you that this issue is not over yet. You have to stay calm. Your heart can't take much more of this excitement."

"I'm telling you, Obadiah. If Kansas comes in as a free state, we are going to have a civil war. The South will not stand for this!" he said, shaking his head.

"Let me see how that heart is doing," I said, as I pulled my stethoscope from my medicine bag.

"I'm all right, Obadiah. I think I've scared Catherine, but I'm all right."

"I still need to listen to your heart."

"Well, all right! Get on with it."

My father's heart was beating fast and erratic. In fact, it was beating much too fast.

"Father, I'm going to give you something to help you relax. Your heart is beating too fast."

"Well, suit yourself!"

I gave Father medicine that should help to calm him down. He needed to get some rest.

"I'll come back tomorrow and check on you," I said as I put my stethoscope in my bag.

"Mother, I need to see Mattie a few minutes before we leave. Why don't you and Audrey stay with Father?"

I needed to find out if Mattie had heard from Penelope. I found Mattie in the kitchen working with Betsy on dinner.

"Mattie, how are you and Betsy doing?"

"We're doing just fine, Master Obadiah," Betsy answered for her.

"Betsy, I need to borrow Mattie for a few minutes. Do you think you can handle things here?"

"You two go right on. I'll do very well by myself."

"Thanks, Betsy!"

I learned from Mattie that Penelope was excited to be coming home to Twin Oaks to help take care of Father.

"Did she say anything about Marcus Lane?"

"She didn't say anything," Mattie replied.

No one knew at this time that I was bringing Penelope home. I planned to tell Father and Mother tomorrow. I'm sure this would be welcome news to my mother. Having Penelope at home will allow her more time to spend in Prattville with family members as well as time to play bridge with her friends. Since I'm now married to Audrey, I don't think my father will mind for Penelope being at Twin Oaks, especially since I won't be living under the same roof.

Upon arriving back at Prattville, I carried my beautiful wife over the threshold into our first home. The privacy of living all alone in our first house was a great feeling. We both were enjoying our extended honeymoon. We decided if Audrey got pregnant on our honeymoon, so be it. We would certainly rejoice in having a little one crawling around our feet.

I awoke early for a delicious breakfast, which was prepared by my wonderful wife. Audrey didn't want a slave girl doing all the work. She wanted to cook our meals, wash our clothes, and do what many other wives who don't have slaves do.

My trip to Twin Oaks was refreshing. I stopped and watched our slaves pick cotton. We had another bumper crop. As I was sitting in my carriage, my brother John rode up on his horse.

"Good morning, Little Brother. How are the newlyweds doing?"

"Good morning, John. The newlyweds are doing great."

"I was just at the big house. Father appears to be better today. He gave Mother quite a scare yesterday."

"Indeed he did!" I said.

"What do you think of Father's health?"

"John, Father has a bad heart. Any agitation and excitement could cause him to have a heart attack. We've got to find some way to keep him calm, and that's going to be next to impossible."

"That's an understatement. Mother is about the only one who can handle him and she wasn't so successful yesterday."

"John, I'd like to stay and visit, but I've got a busy schedule today. We need to get together some night for dinner."

"You know where we live, Little Brother. Just let us know when would be a good time for you and Audrey."

"Good deal! I'll talk with you later."

As soon as I reached the house, Mother met me at the door.

"How did it go last night?" I asked.

"Oh, he was restless, but I believe he had a good night. He's in the parlor drinking his coffee and reading the paper."

"Good morning, Father!"

"Well, good morning to you, too, Dr. Bradford," Father said, with a big smile.

"I can already tell you are doing better than you were yesterday."

"I'm telling you right now, I'm all right."

Much to my surprise, Father's heart was back to normal, and he appeared to be his normal self.

"Good news! You're a hundred percent better this morning. Let this flare up be a lesson to you, Father. Maybe you should take a break from reading newspapers. You can't do one thing to change what's going on in Kansas."

"Now, Obadiah, you know darn well I'm not going to stop reading my newspapers. I'm telling you, if Kansas is admitted to the Union as a free state, there will be trouble. You mark my words, Obadiah."

"Let's not worry about Kansas right now. Let's concentrate on you. By the way, I've got some news to share with you and mother. Mother, why don't you sit down?"

"What is this news?" Father asked.

"Penelope will be coming home to Twin Oaks in two weeks. She will be staying here permanently and helping Mother with your care. Mother can use the free time to visit with family and friends in Prattville."

"I think that's a good idea, Obadiah. James, don't you think that's a good idea?"

"I like Penelope, and yes, I do think it's a good idea. Maybe I'll finally get some good hot coffee," Father said with a chuckle.

"Good, then consider it done. I'm making arrangements for her to be home two weeks from tomorrow. Mother, do you think she can have Tanyua's room?"

"I don't see why not. She seemed to enjoy the room when she was home last. I'll make sure everything is ready for her when she gets here."

"There is one other thing I need your approval on in regard to Penelope's return to Twin Oaks."

"What is it, Obadiah?" Mother asked.

"I would like for Penelope to teach our young slaves reading and writing skills. She is gifted in this area, and I feel it would be nice if our young slaves were given the opportunity to learn to read and write."

"Obadiah, you may be opening up a can of worms doing that. When other plantation owners find out we're teaching our slaves to read and write, they are going to think we're crazy."

"Father, I don't care what our neighbors think. What we do for our slaves at Twin Oaks is no business of theirs. What I do know is that Daniel Pratt requires that his slaves be taught how to read and write. His slaves make up the majority of the work force in his factories. The slaves are able to read and write, making them more productive in their work skills. I believe we can accomplish the same here at Twin Oaks. Please trust me with this!"

"Are you saying John should pull the children from the fields and not work them?"

"No, I'm asking John to make them available for instruction on Saturdays and Sunday afternoons. We normally don't work our slaves on weekends. It will be a requirement for them to attend school under Penelope's supervision."

"Well, in that case, I guess I can go along with your recommendation. Penelope is smart, and this new job would give her a sense of importance. She's very talented, and I agree, we should utilize her talents," Father said with sincerity.

"Good, then it's settled. Thank you for supporting my plan. I'll make the arrangements."

"I'm betting this reading and writing won't stop with just our young slaves. Before you know it, I'm betting our whole plantation of slaves will be reading and writing. Then what are we going to do with the most educated group of slaves in Autauga County?" Father said with a bit of irony.

"Well, I think it's a wonderful idea. I'm one hundred percent in support of it," Mother said as she got up from her chair.

"I've got to get out of here. I have lots of work to do today. Mother, send Bill for me if you need my service."

Before leaving, I visited with Mattie in regard to my plan. She said, "I can't wait! My Penelope will be excited. It will be so good to have her teaching her little brother. I believe Little Jim is going to be smart, just like his sister."

I left Twin Oaks in a good frame of mind. I knew Penelope would enjoy teaching. I didn't want her to develop an attitude that everything she learned in Boston was in vain. I wanted her to be able to use her talents for the good of others. Penelope is an intelligent lady. Her talents could be far reaching if only we channel them in the right direction. Thanks to my parents, Penelope will have an opportunity to bloom at Twin Oaks. Lord, thank you, thank you!

CHAPTER 27

I accompanied Bill to Selma to pick up Penelope at the train station. The trip back from Selma would give Penelope and me time to visit about Father's care and her new responsibility of teaching our plantation slaves to read and write.

It was early spring, and there was still a chill in the air. When Penelope exited the train, she was wearing a beautiful burgundy dress and a fashionable black hat. She was so very beautiful. She was no longer the young girl I sent away to Boston. She left as a young girl but has returned as a lady. As Bill and I approached her, she spotted us and waved.

"My goodness, Miss Penelope, you sure do look good," Bill said.

"You always say the nicest things, Bill," she said, as Bill picked up her bags.

"Welcome home, Penelope," I said, as I reached out my hands to touch hers.

She grasped both my hands, and we stood staring into each other's eyes. Her blue eyes were still as beautiful as ever, and her pretty smile melted my heart. Finally, she said, "It's good to see you, Master Obadiah."

"It's good to see you, too! Are you ready to go to Twin Oaks?" I asked.

"I'm ready, Master Obadiah. I've been ready for months."

I helped Penelope into the family carriage as Bill climbed into his seat to drive us home to Twin Oaks. On our trip back, we talked continuously. There was no stopping us. We had so much to talk about. Penelope wanted to know how the wedding went and how Audrey was doing. She talked about how things in Boston were and how she had gotten really homesick to see her mother. I kept waiting for her to mention Marcus Lane but for some reason, she avoided mentioning him.

We talked about what I wanted her to do in caring for father, as well as my thoughts on her role as teacher to the slaves on the plantation. She wanted to know where she would be teaching. I informed her that my mother suggested Sarah's room in the big house. The room was large and had plenty of good lighting and a large fireplace. It would be an excellent room to work with children.

Penelope was thrilled about teaching. She informed me that next to writing, teaching would be her second choice as a profession. I let her know that my sister Sarah, although heavy pregnant, had volunteered to come over and help her set up her room. She was also bringing several textbooks and some teaching supplies that she no longer needed since she wasn't teaching.

As we turned off the main road onto the small road leading to Twin Oaks, I cleared my throat and said, "Penelope, I need to ask you a personal question. I would like a straight answer from you."

"What is it, Master Obadiah?"

"I understand you were seeing a Marcus Lane in Boston, and he had asked you to marry him."

"Yes, that is true."

"Did you love him?"

"I first thought I did, but I realized Marcus wasn't for me."

"So Marcus Lane is out of your life?"

"Yes, he and I will not be communicating anymore."

"May I ask how he responded when you broke off with him?"

"At first, he didn't understand. I finally convinced him that I was in love with someone back in Autauga County. I didn't mention who but I was persuasive enough that he got the message."

"I need to ask you one other important question."

"What is it?"

"If you had been free, no longer a slave, would you have said yes to Marcus Lane's marriage proposal?"

"No, Master Obadiah. Marcus and I had some good times together. He was good to me and treated me like a lady, but I couldn't marry him. I love you, Master! There will never be a man in my life but you."

"Penelope, I need you to promise me something."

"What, Master?"

"Audrey is to never know that we love each other. Do you understand?"

"Master Obadiah, I would never hurt Audrey. I will treat her with the utmost kindness. I just want you to know you can always count on me."

"Thank you, Penelope."

After arriving at Twin Oaks, we went inside where we were greeted by Father, Mother, Betsy, Mattie, Little Jim, and Big Jim. It was like a Bradford homecoming.

Mother had made arrangements for Betsy, Mattie, Bill, Little Jim, and Big Jim to join us for dinner to celebrate Penelope's homecoming. I can't remember any occasion where any of our slaves were guests at the Bradford dinner table. As I took my seat next to Penelope, I felt good knowing that Father and Mother had opened their hearts to make Penelope and her loved ones guests at our dinner table. If our neighboring plantation owners knew about this, what would they say and do? I couldn't help laughing inside as I thought about it.

"We are honored tonight to have Penelope back home with us. Now let's all enjoy this nice meal that Mattie and Betsy have prepared for us," Father said as he began to pass the food around.

After dinner, I checked Father's heart before leaving for Prattville. His heart was still beating normally and he appeared to be feeling well.

It was good getting home to Audrey. She had prepared dinner for both of us, not knowing when I would get home. I didn't want to hurt her feelings so I pretended I was hungry. I had no sooner sat down when our doorbell rang. The person at the door was a messenger from James Jones's plantation. The note said,

"Dr. Bradford, please come quickly. Teshia is having her baby. She needs your help! Mason."

I apologized to Audrey about the emergency. She fully understood the urgency of my going to help Teshia. It took me thirty-five minutes to make the trip to Mr. Jones's plantation. After arriving, I went immediately to the slave house where I found Mason and the girl's father on the front porch.

"Doc, Minnie is inside with Teshia. Please go on in," Mason said.

Minnie turned and looked at me as I approach. Teshia's mother was standing at the head of the bed rubbing Teshia's forehead with a cold damp rag. A female slave was boiling water in a big cast iron pot.

"Doctor, this girl is in trouble. She shouldn't ever got herself with child. She's a child herself!" Minnie said.

"Let's see what's going on, Minnie."

"Please help me, Doctor! I's dying! It hurts so badly!" Teshia said as she continued her screaming.

Teshia hadn't dilated nearly enough to have this baby. This is what I feared most from the first time I examined her. I would need to make some incisions to help get the baby out. I had never done this but remembered the way Dr. Banister did when he delivered Mandy's baby a few years ago.

I was thankful that I brought some ether along with me. The ether would be helpful in lowering the pain threshold during the delivery. I was praying that Teshia would be able to push the baby through the birth canal or at least to the point I could reach the baby's head.

I tried to keep the incisions as small as possible to keep down the bleeding. It was still going to be a tremendous task to get the baby out. I wasn't sure Teshia was strong enough to push the baby through the birth canal. If she wasn't, I would have to try pulling the baby through the canal, a task that could injure both Teshia and the baby.

We were lucky. Teshia's baby was in the birth canal with its head coming first — a blessing. At least it wasn't a breach baby like Mandy's. Once I started the delivery procedure, Teshia continued her screaming. That was okay. At least she was trying to help me. If she fainted that would make things more difficult. I talked to her as I was doing my procedure. I wanted her to push with every ounce of energy left in her. Minnie was right. Teshia was only a baby herself. Whoever got her pregnant should be flogged. The delivery procedure took about thirty minutes. We were able to save both the baby boy and Teshia. The suturing of the cuts I made turned out to be quite an ordeal. It took several stitches to close the incisions. Teshia would be weak for several days from loss of blood and exhaustion, but she and the baby should survive.

I washed my hands and stepped out on the porch where I found Mason and the girl's father.

"Your daughter, Teshia, has a baby boy. She and the baby are alive, and if nothing unforeseen happens, I believe they will live."

"Can I see her?" her father asked.

"Yes, but don't stay long. She needs her rest."

I turned to Mason and said, "If you are the father of that baby, you should be ashamed of yourself!"

"Now you wait just a minute, Dr. Bradford. You have no business talking to me like that."

"Mason, people like you make me sick."

"I don't know why you get yourself all excited. Slaves are meant to be bred, don't you know that!"

"You're not worth talking to!"

"Is that baby white looking?" Mason asked.

"Why don't you go see for yourself? But first, how's Hercules doing?"

"Oh, you'll be happy to know he's doing just fine."

"I'll be coming back in a couple of days to see Teshia and the baby. While I'm here, I'll check on Hercules as well."

"Doctor Bradford, I want to say something to you. It's no secret that I dislike you, but I do appreciate you coming and taking care of Teshia. That baby is mine, and I'm going to see both Teshia and my baby get good care, you hear."

"That's the first positive thing I've heard you say tonight. You certainly owe it to both of them to see they get good care."

It was all I could do to keep my composure as I drove off from the Jones plantation. How could Jones tolerate such a mean, selfish, trashy overseer as Mason? Furthermore, how could our laws protect a person like Mason? Unfortunately, I already knew the answer to both questions. As long as slaves are considered property of their owners, they will be treated in whatever manner the owner chooses. These acts of cruelty will continue to exist until slavery is abolished. People like Mason will continue to take advantage of poor innocent slave girls for their sexual gratification.

CHAPTER 28

It was now October 1858; the cotton crops were being harvested throughout Autauga County. Dr. Banister and I were extremely busy attending the sick. We had an unusual number of slaves with impetigo, which always reared its ugly head during the fall of the year, mostly during cotton season. Dr. Banister and I were not popular with the plantation owners during cotton picking time. In order to be cured of the impetigo, the slave had to be removed from the cotton patch and treated with medication and rest. This didn't set well with the plantation overseers or the owners. Although they didn't like it, most of the owners followed our recommendation. For those who didn't pull their infected slaves, the problem got worse, and sometimes the slave died from the infection.

As I made my rounds from plantation to plantation, I discovered that Mr. James Jones wasn't the only plantation owner who neglected his slaves. Due to the plantation owner's legal powers over his slaves, I had no way to enforce my medical advice upon them. Therefore, I decided to pray that God would give the slave owners a change of heart and they would take my advice. I prayed especially hard for the slaves living on their plantations.

As I made my weekly trips to Mr. Jones's plantation, I found Teshia and the baby doing well. It appeared Mason was keeping his end of the bargain in providing good care for both Teshia and his illegitimate baby boy. Each time I examined Teshia, I wondered how many more young girls Mason had abused on the plantation, and if he someday would abuse Teshia, again.

Time was passing much too fast for me. I found myself with little free time. Audrey understood my lack of time with her. I assured her that things would soon settle down, and we could spend more time with each other.

My parents hosted a party at Twin Oaks to celebrate the birth of James Daniel Crawford, son of my sister Sarah and Jim Crawford. My sister named her son after my father, an honor he deeply appreciated. Much to my disappointment, I was unable to attend because of medical emergencies. I was thankful that Audrey was able to represent us at the celebration.

Penelope's presence at Twin Oaks has been a blessing for my mother who has had time to visit family and friends in Prattville. Mother and her friends play bridge every Wednesday. Wednesday is the day I go to Twin Oaks to check on Father. While I'm there, Penelope gives me a day by day accounting of how Father has done during the week. I try to spend most of my time with Father while I'm there. The last time I visited Father, Penelope asked me if I could take time to see what she had done to her classroom. I agreed to give her a few minutes of my time. I was certainly impressed with how she had arranged her room. It had several teaching cubicles and teaching stations for group teaching. She got really excited telling me and showing me how she taught the children reading skills. It was obvious that Penelope enjoyed her work tremendously.

"Master Obadiah, I'm telling you we have some good readers here at Twin Oaks. Our young slaves and some of their parents are working hard to learn to read and communicate. May I show you some of their writings?"

"Of course, I would love to see some of them."

She handed me a short story written by a thirteen-year-old boy named Sam. She said, "Sam is one of my best students. He is very bright. He not only likes to write, he loves to read as well."

She went on to say that he has read everything in her room. She looked at me and said, "If you can get your hands on some additional books in Prattville, I sure would appreciate it. I could use them for students like Sam."

"Penelope, I'll make it a point to get you some new books. I'm really impressed with what you're doing."

"Thank you, Master Obadiah. I do love what I'm doing. By the way, how is Audrey?"

"Audrey is doing well. She's still working part time at the Pratt's Ladies Wear Store in Prattville."

I didn't want to tell her about the news that Audrey was pregnant. I didn't think she needed to know that right now.

As I started to leave the room, Penelope touched my arm as to get my attention.

"Is there something else you need from me?"

"Master Obadiah, I just want you to know that I'm so happy you brought me back to Twin Oaks. Just being close to Mama and family means everything to me. I also look forward to our visit every Wednesday."

"Oh, Penelope, I'm so glad to have you home as well. My father loves you. He tells me all the different games you two play. I can't remember my father settling down long enough to play any game. You are special to him!"

"He's special as well. He treats me really nicely. He likes his coffee hot, and I make sure he gets all the hot coffee he wants."

"I'm afraid you are spoiling him."

"Oh, I don't mind. He loves to talk politics, and I do, too. I must confess something to you. I take his discarded papers and read them all the time. I try to familiarize myself with the political issues he brings up. I want to be able to carry on an intelligent conversation with him. Sometimes, I think I get more out of the articles than he does. He's really concerned whether Kansas will be a free state or a slave state."

I couldn't keep from laughing at Penelope, and for a moment I thought about taking her in my arms. Finally, I came to my senses and said, "Penelope, I'm sorry, I have to go. I've got an appointment in Prattville I've got to get to."

"You take care, Master Obadiah!"

As I drove back to Prattville, I couldn't get Penelope out of my mind. I almost made a big mistake, one which would have caused me a great deal of grief.

I know what I've got to do. I have to focus on Audrey and not Penelope. Last weekend, Audrey gave me the best news I could ever hope to hear. We were going to have a baby. If all goes well, Audrey will give birth somewhere around the last of May or the first of June. I have to stay focused on Audrey's needs. When I left this morning, Audrey had just lost her breakfast due to morning sickness. I tried to be helpful, but she looked at me with that awful expression on her face and said, "I don't like this part of being pregnant!" I held her and tried to convince her that this, too, would pass.

My medical practice is everything I thought it would be. I love being a doctor and helping the sick. Dr. Banister and I have committed to be administrators/doctors of the new hospital that Daniel Pratt is building in Prattville. We will be in charge of hiring additional doctors and nurses to staff the hospital upon its completion. My agreement with Daniel Pratt and Dr. Banister is that I will continue to make plantation calls in the county.

The hospital is expected to be finished in December of 1859. I have been in touch with my good friends with whom I graduated. Jim Burroughs, from Columbus, Mississippi, has agreed to become one of our doctors. We will need one more doctor and several nurses. Jim has been practicing in three medical clinics in Columbus but hasn't been happy with the situation there. He's ready to pull up stakes and move to Prattville. It will be great having one of my best friends as a colleague working with me here in Prattville.

The newspapers in the last few days have been full of articles about Kansas. It appears that the Kansas territorial government is working on another constitution that would be voted on sometime in 1859. The constitution is being called the Wyandotte Constitution. I wish the Kansas governmental officials would hurry and get things settled. It's been a long drawn-out process, one that keeps everything unstable.

We had a big snow three days before Christmas, but the snow melted before Christmas day, and the Bradfords were able to carry on their annual Christmas tradition at Twin Oaks. This year, we added a new addition in attendance at Twin Oaks. Jim and Sarah Crawford's little boy, James Daniel, was the hit of the party.

Audrey and I spent Christmas day at Twin Oaks with other members of the Bradford family. I intentionally avoided being alone with Penelope. I stayed pretty close to Audrey during the whole time. Penelope was very helpful to Mother in providing food and drink for everyone. She looked great in her burgundy dress. Her long black hair fell below her shoulders. She was so beautiful. A few times while serving coffee in the parlor, she would give me a look and smile. I don't think Audrey noticed, but the one who did was my big brother, Dent. I should have known he would notice her looks and smiles.

"Hey, little brother, what's up?" Dent asked as he put his arm around my shoulder.

"All is going well, Dent. How are Hank and his family doing at Black Oaks?"

"Hank has got him another baby on the way."

"Really!" I said with excitement.

"Yep, he and Nanny are expecting their second child sometime this spring."

"I would certainly like to see Hank."

"Why don't you ride over and take Hank fishing? I know he would love to go fishing."

"I, too, would love to do that, but with the schedule I'm keeping, I have little time to do anything except for doctoring sick folks."

"Hey, let's take a walk out to Mother's garden. I need to talk to you."

"All right, Dent, what's on your mind?"

"Well, first of all, how much time have you been spending at Twin Oaks?"

"I'm here once a week to check on Father. That's about all the time I have."

"I saw how you and Penelope were looking at each other."

"Oh, come on, Dent. You've got to be kidding me. I swear there isn't anything going on between Penelope and me. I could never betray Audrey. You should know that."

"I believe you, Obadiah, but it will never change. Penelope will always be in your heart and mind. To tell you the truth, I can't figure out why you brought her back from Boston. I thought maybe you had decided to, you know, see her on the side."

"Oh, Big Brother, you are pathetic!"

"Come on, Obadiah! You know I'm not going to say anything to anyone else."

"There were two reasons I felt I had to bring Penelope back to Twin Oaks. First, our mother needed help with Father. She was about to the point of exhaustion. The second reason was Penelope was seeing a man by the name of Marcus Lane. He had proposed marriage to her, but she had turned him down. I had to get her out of Boston."

"Well, I'll be darn! All this time, I've been trying to make something out of something that wasn't there."

"You're right about that, Big Brother! Penelope and I have an understanding of her role here at Twin Oaks. She is very happy taking care of Father and teaching our slaves how to read and write."

"Mother shared with me about Penelope's teaching. How's that working out?"

"Penelope tells me the kids are doing very well. She's increased her work load by letting some of the adult slaves attend sessions to learn to read and write."

"Lord have mercy! I can't believe this is going on right under our father's roof. Do the neighbors know what's going on here at Twin Oaks?"

"No, and if I want them to know, I'll tell them. By the way, why don't you let Hank teach your slaves at Black Oaks?"

"Are you serious, Obadiah?"

"I'm serious, Dent. We are seeing good results from Penelope's teaching. The kids and parents are thankful that we are letting them learn to read and write. You should see them when they read. It's so exciting to see them smile and see their eyes gleam with joy when Penelope brags on them."

"I'll tell you what, Little Brother. I'll give it some serious thought, but don't count your chickens until they're hatched."

"Dent, I'm getting cold! Are you ready to go back inside?"

He shrugged his shoulders and said, "I guess so."

Again, our Bradford traditional Christmas was a success. We had been truly blessed as a large family. We had gone for several years without a death in the family. My parents are both aging and have some health problems, but their spirits are high, and they are enjoying life. I feel I'm the luckiest duck in the pond.

Spring has arrived in Autauga County. We were blessed with a mild winter, and the fields are now coming alive with our slaves preparing the soil for spring planting.

Audrey is getting bigger by the week, but she is still as beautiful as ever. Since the terrible morning sickness is past, her pregnancy has gone well.

The baby's heartbeat is very strong. I think it's going to be a boy. Audrey and I have spent several nights lying in bed discussing boy and girl names. I think we've decided if it's a boy we will name him Obadiah Charles Bradford II. If it is a girl, we will name her, Catherine Elizabeth Bradford. Elizabeth is Audrey's middle name.

In early June, Audrey started having some false contractions. This went on for about three days before the real contractions started. Sarah, my sister, had been staying with Audrey during the day and came for me at the office. I was just finishing with a patient when Sarah came into the main office. I heard her tell Mrs. Daniels, our receptionist, that she needed to see me. It was an emergency. I quickly met Sarah at the reception counter where she informed me Audrey was having frequent labor contractions.

"The baby is coming!" she said, with excitement.

I told Mrs. Daniels to let Dr. Banister know I was leaving and to say a prayer for me. I had delivered several children since becoming a doctor, but this would be different. I would be delivering my own. This is what Audrey and I had looked forward to for months.

Sarah had sent word to Mother that the baby was coming, and when we arrived at my house, Mother, Father, Mary, and Tanyua were all there. I hadn't expected the whole family, but I certainly wasn't going to send them away, especially my mother. My mother had lots of experience in delivering black babies, especially when we lived at Black Oaks in Cahaba. I knew she could be of valuable

241

help to me. After examining Audrey, I knew it wouldn't be long before she would go into hard labor. We didn't have much time to get things ready. Mother took charge, while my sisters followed her directions.

As the contractions continued, I wasn't prepared for what was happening to Audrey. Her blood pressure was dropping to a dangerous level. For some reason, Audrey had lost her strength and wasn't able to push the baby to the birth canal. She wanted to but was so weak that she couldn't. I asked Sarah to go get Dr. Banister. I wanted him by me if I had to alter the normal course of action. Audrey was in great pain. I tried calming her by talking to her, but it did little good.

Dr. Banister entered the room and I briefed him on what was going on. He examined Audrey and pulled me to the side and said, "Obadiah, Audrey's in trouble."

"What do you think is going on, Doc?"

"Her blood pressure is not good. We need to get the baby out, and fast."

I asked him if he had heard of a new procedure of delivering a baby called C-Section.

He said, "I've read about it in a recent medical report. Did you learn to do it in medical school?" he asked.

"I assisted Dr. Bailey in doing one, but personally I've never by myself done one. But if it will save Audrey and the baby's life, I'm willing to do it."

"Obadiah, I would encourage you to do it now. Audrey's blood pressure is dropping."

"Will you assist me?"

"Of course! I will."

I gave Audrey a large dose of ether to help her relax and hopefully put her to sleep while I made an incision in her abdomen and uterus. After making the incisions, I reached in and lifted the baby through the walls of the uterus and out through the abdomen incision. "It's a boy," I said loudly.

"Indeed!" Dr. Banister said with a chuckle. I tied the umbilical cord, cut it, and handed my mother my son and said, "Mother, meet your grandson."

Mother took our boy, and with the help of my sisters, began cleaning him up. I immediately began closing the uterus by suturing the area as fast as I could. Audrey had lost a lot of blood. After closing the uterus, I closed the larger incision in her abdomen. Audrey was now breathing better and her blood pressure was getting back to normal. As we waited for Audrey to wake up, Dr. Banister and I gave my son a thorough examination. He was a big boy, weighing in at eight pounds and seven ounces. He had some strong lungs as well. He was healthy and strong. I announced to everyone present that Audrey and I had chosen Obadiah Charles Bradford II as his name.

Dr. Banister was complimentary of the Cesarean Section procedure I used to bring my son into the world. He said, "Obadiah, if we had known how to do this procedure a few years ago, we might have saved Mandy's baby."

Mandy was the young slave girl who lived on the James Jones Plantation who couldn't give birth to her baby. Dr. Banister was right. If we had known how to do the C-Section then, we might have saved Mandy's baby.

Audrey finally came out from under the influence of the ether and wanted to know where her baby was. I motioned for Mother to bring our son to Audrey so she could hold him.

"He looks like a boy," she said in a weak whisper.

"He's a strong boy!" I said with a big smile.

"I had some problems, didn't I?"

"Yes, but you and the baby are doing just fine now. I had to take him by Cesarean Section. I'll explain to you later what I did."

My sisters Tanyua and Mary volunteered to rotate on a daily basis during the first week to help. It was nice to have them available during the day, but I soon realized that we needed someone around the clock. Mother and Father agreed to let Betsy come and live with us until Audrey got back on her feet. The Cesarean surgery had left Audrey very weak and sore. It would take a good month for her to recover. I didn't want her to try to lift Charles, who was growing and eating like a newborn piglet. All he wanted to do was nurse. He was wearing Audrey out. I knew Betsy was good with babies, and since she was a good cook as well, she would be a welcome guest in our home. Betsy's presence allowed Tanyua and Mary to return to their homes to provide for their families needs.

By July, things really began to heat up in Kansas. The territorial legislature, which was controlled by free-state supporters, approved a fourth constitutional convention. They are presently meeting in Wyandotte, Kansas, for the purpose of studying the Wyandotte Constitution. The article quoted several legislators as saying that they believed the document would be strongly approved, and if so, Kansas would be admitted as a free state.

Everywhere I went in Prattville, people were talking about Kansas. I knew my father must be boiling mad about this article. I hope he stays composed. I don't want him to have another run away heart. Tomorrow is Wednesday, and I'll be checking on him at Twin Oaks. For the first time, I felt my father might be right about Kansas. He always said, "If Kansas is admitted as a free state then we will have a civil war. Slavery as we know it in the South will be on its way out."

I can't imagine what a civil war would do to our country. It would be horrible! The South would never be the same again. I personally don't think the South could win a civil war. The South does not have the manpower, or the financial resources to win a war. "Lord, help us all!"

Upon arriving at Twin Oaks, Penelope met me on the porch.

"Master Obadiah, I'm so glad you're here."

"What's happening, Penelope?"

"It's your father. He's not doing well. Missus Bradford stayed home today. She didn't want to leave your father the way he's acting."

"Does this have something to do with all this mess in Kansas?"

"I do believe it does."

"Where is Father now?"

"Your mother insisted he lie down. She and Mr. Bradford are in the master bedroom."

"Come with me, Penelope. I may need your help."

I went inside and knocked on my parents' bedroom door. Mother came to the door and said, "Thank God you are here. Your father isn't feeling well."

"That's what Penelope just told me. Let me take a look at him."

As I approached Father's bed, I could see he was breathing pretty hard. I put my hand on his forehead to see if he might have a fever. As I did, he opened his eyes and looked up at me but didn't say a word.

"Father, how are you doing today?"

He just stared at me without any response.

"How long has he been this way?"

"He was fine at breakfast, but after he read his newspaper, he started raving, stomping, and got himself into a big tizzy. I shouldn't have let him read that article on Kansas," Mother said.

I began a thorough examination of Father. I placed my stethoscope on his chest and found his heart was racing and beating erratically, just like the last time he had an attack. After looking closely into his eyes, I realized Father had had a stroke. I turned to Mother and Penelope and said, "Let's step out in the hall."

Mother was frantic. I could tell she expected the worst. "What's happened to him, Obadiah?"

"Mother, I'm afraid he's had a stroke."

"Oh, God, no!" Mother cried out.

"Did he take his medicine this morning?"

"Yes, Master Obadiah, I gave him his medicine," Penelope replied.

"Okay, we need to keep a close eye on him. He's running a low-grade fever. We will need to apply cold packs to his forehead. Penelope, do you think you can do that?"

"Yes, of course."

"Mother, is Bill around?"

"Yes, he's probably at the barn."

"Please send for him. I need Bill to ride into Prattville and tell Dr. Banister that I'll be here the rest of the day. I also need Bill to carry notes to Audrey, Mary, Tanyua, and Dent."

"Oh, Obadiah, is it that bad?" Mother asked.

I took Mother in my arms and whispered softly, "Mother, I'm afraid it's bad!"

She let out another cry and squeezed me tightly. "What will we do without your father?" she asked.

"Why don't you go back and stay with him while I write the notes to the family. I'm sending Penelope to get Big Jim."

It wasn't long before Bill and Big Jim came into the parlor.

"Jim, I need for you to find Master John and bring him here as soon as possible."

"Yes, sir! Master Obadiah."

I could tell that Mattie had been working on Big Jim's grammar. That "yes sir" was a pleasant surprise.

"Bill, I need for you to ride into Prattville and take these notes to the Bradford family and to Dr. Banister. As soon as you finish delivering in Prattville, ride over to Cahaba and give this note to Dent. This is going to take you awhile, and time is of the essence. Saddle General and ride him. He will be faster than the carriage, and he needs to be ridden anyway."

"I'll be back as soon as I can," Bill said.

As Bill was leaving, my brother John came through the door of the parlor. "How bad is he?" he asked.

"It doesn't look good, John."

"He was fine when I came by this morning."

"According to Mother, he was fine until he read his newspaper. I'm afraid that article on Kansas got him upset."

"What about Kansas?"

"Oh, according to the article, it appears the Wyandotte Constitution will be ratified, and if so, Kansas will be admitted to the Union as a free state."

"Father always takes these things too serious," John said.

"John, I'm afraid Father might be right about Kansas. You know he always said, 'If Kansas goes, so goes the South.'"

"Do you really think that will happen?"

"I don't know, but according to the talk in Prattville, several Southern states may secede from the Union."

"I can't believe that's going to happen. I've heard the same talk, but how could something like that happen?"

"Father surely believed it could happen. I didn't want to believe it, but now, I'm not sure."

"Lord, help us all if our nation falls apart over slavery!" John said.

"Right now, let's get with Mother and pray for Father."

Mother entered the room and we prayed. The Bradfords are a praying family — a family who prays together sticks together. Our faith has always been one of our strongest assets. We love the Lord!

Each time I examined Father, I became more convinced that he had suffered a bad stroke. He no longer opened his eyes when I touched him or talked to him. I believed he was slipping into a coma. I asked Mother to see if she could rouse him. If anyone could get through to him, Mother could. She sat down in a chair near the bed and held Father's left hand. She began talking to him and patting his hand. He did not respond. She asked him to squeeze her hand if he could hear her, but he made no attempt. She looked at me with tears streaming down her face and shook her head as if to say, "Obadiah, I think he's leaving us."

I put my hand on her shoulder to try to comfort her. I looked across the room and tears were running down Penelope's cheeks as well. I looked at John who was standing near the door. He looked pale. I wanted to cry, too, but my mind was telling me that I had to be strong. I was a doctor, and doctors couldn't cry before people. They had to remain calm and private with their feelings. I put my stethoscope on Father's chest once again. His heart had quit racing and was now barely beating. I could barely hear the faint, slow beats of his heart. Mother was right. It wouldn't be long before Father's soul would be with our Heavenly Father.

Within fifteen minutes, Father slipped from this life to his eternal home in Heaven. He didn't have the chance to say goodbye to any of us. His death is a good example of how fast God can take one of us out of this life. One day we're here, and the next day we're gone. We can't pick our time to die. My father lived a good life. He was healthy most of his life and truly enjoyed life. He had a kind spirit about him. I never observed at any time a mean spirit about him. His legacy in being generous to all will certainly live on in all of the Bradfords.

John and I escorted Mother to the parlor where she sat down to wait for the arrival of the other family members. Penelope went to the kitchen to fix tea for our guests. I told Penelope to tell Mattie that we would have extra mouths to feed for supper. Penelope said she would help Mattie.

It wasn't long after Father passed that the family started arriving. My sisters, Mary, Tanyua, and Sarah, arrived about the same time. They were shocked to hear how fast Father went to be with the Lord. Mother had regained her composure and joined the family as my sisters paid their last respects to our father. I always hated to be around crying women. I was emotional myself but stayed calm as John and I comforted our sisters.

About three hours later, Dent and his family arrived from Black Oaks. Dent, too, was surprised that Father died so quickly. I assured my siblings that Father didn't have to suffer. I praised God for taking him so quickly so that he didn't have to linger and suffer from the result of a stroke or coma. Giving up a loved one is always hard, but our faith and trust in Jesus Christ, our savior, gave us assurance that we would one day be with our father in Heaven. What a glorious day that will be.

The funeral service was two days later at the Oak Hills Baptist Church. We buried Father in the family plot at the church's cemetery. Our pastor, Rev. Bob Jacobs, preached a wonderful sermon on what makes a good father and brother in Christ. His analogies pretty much described our father. After the funeral, my mother came to me and asked if she could talk to me in private. I assured her that my time was hers.

She informed me that the Oak Hills Baptist Church had prepared a meal for the family and wanted everyone to stay and eat. I told her Audrey, little Charles, and I would stay.

After we ate, Jonathan Beckard, our family lawyer, asked to speak to Mother and the family. He informed us that he needed to meet with the family in regard to Father's last will and testament. He apologized for the intrusion but told us that our father left strict instructions that he wanted his will read within a week of his passing. He was putting us on notice that he needed to carry through on Father's wishes. Since we were all together at the church, we all agreed to meet with Mr. Beckard on Thursday of the following week.

The church did a wonderful job of providing more than enough food for our large family. Several of our friends joined us for dinner. After dinner, Mother asked me if we could have our private meeting.

"Obadiah, I really appreciate you taking time to visit with me."

"Mother, how can I help you?"

"Obadiah, I have a special request to ask of you."

"What is it, Mother?"

"Obadiah, I want you, Audrey, and little Charles to move in with me at Twin Oaks."

Mother's request completely caught me off guard. I hadn't expected this at all. Audrey and I were just getting used to our little house in Prattville. We loved it. I knew I owed Mother an answer, but this was something I was completely unprepared for.

"Mother, you've caught me completely off guard. I don't know what to say."

"Obadiah, I love Twin Oaks, and I know your father wants me to stay there, but I don't want to be there by myself. All my children are gone. I don't know how much longer our Lord will let me live, but I don't want to live at Twin Oaks without you living there with me."

"Mother, I love Twin Oaks, too, but my medical practice is here in Prattville. It's much more convenient for me to live in Prattville."

"Obadiah, I was going to wait until Mr. Beckard read your father's will, but I guess I need to go ahead and tell you what I know. You must not tell any of your sisters and brothers. Will you promise me that?"

"I can promise you that anything you tell me will remain between you and me."

"Before your father dictated his instructions to Mr. Beckard, he and I agreed that Twin Oaks and half of the plantation would become yours, along with half of the slaves. You will hear all of this again next Thursday. We want Twin Oaks to remain in the family and we wanted it to be under your ownership."

"May I ask who's getting the other three hundred acres?"

"Your father is leaving the other three hundred acres to your brother John. John will be getting half of the slaves."

"What about Dent?"

"Dent's getting the Black Oaks plantation with its three hundred acres.

"What about the girls?"

"They are getting a great sum of money. He wanted you boys to have the land. He knew the girls didn't care for farming."

"Mother, thanks for sharing this with me, but I can see some significant problems if I move back to Twin Oaks."

"May I ask you a personal and private question Obadiah?"

"I guess! What is it?"

"Wouldn't you jump at the chance to return to Twin Oaks if it wasn't for Penelope?"

Again Mother's wisdom was coming into focus. How was I going to answer that question? I can't ever recall lying to mother, and I wasn't going to start today. I would be truthful with her. I knew that anything I said to her would be between the two of us. I trusted her with my life.

"You're right, Mother! You are seldom wrong. That's what I love about you. I've known for some time that you and Father must have known about my love for Penelope. You were always supportive of the school in Boston and other matters relating to Penelope. You, above anyone else, must know how hard this is going to be on me and Penelope should I move my family back to Twin Oaks."

"Oh, Obadiah, I understand fully, but we can make this work. I love Penelope, and I love Audrey, too. I believe that Penelope could be a big help to Audrey in her recovery and in helping with little Charles. I really don't think Penelope would ever do anything intentionally to cause a problem between you and Audrey."

"It's not Penelope I'm worried about. I don't know if I can live under the same roof day in and day out with Penelope without something happening. Mother, this is all too much, too fast. I need some time to think."

"You have until next Thursday. Mr. Beckard is going to read your Father's will, and he will want to know what you plan to do with Twin Oaks."

"I want to ask you a question. Will I get Twin Oaks if I chose not to live there?"

"I would like to say no, but I would be lying to you. You will get Twin Oaks regardless. There is a stipulation in the will that says that I will be able to live on the plantation and be cared for as long as I shall live. Oh, Obadiah, I need for you to come home to Twin Oaks."

"Mother, Audrey is a very perceptive person. What if she finds out that I love Penelope? What if someday in my weakest moment I surrender to my temptations. What then?"

"Stop it, Obadiah! I know you. You are stronger than that. God will show you a way out and you know it."

"Let me talk to Audrey and get her reaction. I may have to tell her that Father is leaving me Twin Oaks. I'll make sure she doesn't say anything to anyone about it. We will keep quiet until after next Thursday."

Mother gave me a kiss on the cheek and brushed my hair back. She told me she loved me and for me to pray hard about it. On the way back to the fellowship hall, I could think of nothing but her request.

For the next several days, I was terribly troubled over Mother's request. I had tried to rationalize it in every way I knew but couldn't get any peace of mind. Since I had yet to have an opportunity to talk to Audrey, I decided tonight over dinner, I would discuss the matter with her.

Betsy had cooked a delicious dinner for Audrey and me. I was hungry from a long and busy day of calling on different plantations in the county. As we sat down at the dinner table, I looked at Audrey and said, "Audrey, there is something very important that I need to discuss with you."

"What is it, Obadiah?"

"First, you need to promise me you won't say anything about this conversation to anyone."

"Obadiah, you know if you ask me to keep my mouth shut about something, I can do that. So what is this very important thing you need my input on?"

"Mother told me in confidence that Father left me Twin Oaks in his will, along with three hundred acres, and half the slaves."

"He did what?"

"I'm serious! He left me Twin Oaks."

"Oh, Obadiah, I love Twin Oaks. When can we move out there?"

"You're telling me that you would be willing to move to Twin Oaks?"

"You bet your boots, I would. You know how much I love the country, and I love Twin Oaks. It's one of the prettiest plantations in Autauga County. You know how much I love being outside. Twin Oaks would give me a chance to ride Millie. I've not ridden her in a long time. I could get back to my tomboyish ways," she said with a chuckle.

"In his will, Father stipulates that Mother can live at Twin Oaks for as long as she lives or until she decides to move somewhere else. She is entitled to five percent of the profits from the plantation. How do you feel about sharing a house with my mother?"

"Obadiah, you know I love your mother. She's one of the kindest ladies I've ever been around. I wouldn't have any problem living in the same house with her."

"Well, I guess that resolves that!"

"Obadiah, do I sense reluctance from you about moving back to Twin Oaks? I've always thought you'd jump at the opportunity to live there."

"No, there's no reluctance. I, too, love Twin Oaks. I just want you to be happy wherever we live."

"When can we move?"

"We will have to wait until the will is completely probated; then we can move."

"Oh, Obadiah, I'm so excited! This means I can keep my Betsy. She will be happy to get back to Twin Oaks."

"You do know that Mattie, Big Jim, Little Jim, and Penelope will be there as well. We will all be living under one roof."

"Oh, I love Mattie and Penelope. I'm sure we will become good friends, and Penelope can help Charles learn to read and write. I'm afraid I'm not going to be good at those things. There is something else I just thought about."

"What?"

"Charles will have Little Jim to play with. I'm sure they will become good friends."

"I hadn't thought of that. You do know Big Jim and Mattie are expecting another baby don't you?"

"No, I didn't know that. Why haven't you told me?"

"I just found out a few days ago. I examined Mattie one day when I was at Twin Oaks."

"Well, Charles will have two friends to play with."

"Audrey, you do know Mother can be a little bossy at times, right?"

"Twin Oaks is her home. She's entitled to be a little bossy in her own home. I'm going to be happy there, Obadiah. When I get my strength back, I'm going to start riding Millie and training Patience," she said with excitement.

Oh, what a relief! Why hadn't I talked to Audrey sooner? It would have eliminated all of this grief I've been going through. It appears that Audrey likes Penelope, and from all indications, she doesn't suspect anything between her and me. Maybe Mother is right. We can work this out.

CHAPTER 29

Thursday finally arrived, and all the Bradfords crowded around Mr. Beckard's law firm's conference room for the reading of Father's will. Everyone was able to be seated around the table, except some of the younger ones who chose to stand. Mr. Beckard greeted everyone and passed out copies of Father's will.

He started by saying, "I appreciate everyone's attendance. Sometimes with a family of this size, it's hard to get everyone together. James Bradford was one of my best friends. I miss him and know you do as well. His wishes were very specific. He wanted his will read within five days of his burial. I promised him that I would follow his wishes. As I read through the will, if you have questions, please don't hesitate to stop me and ask questions. I'd rather get the questions answered as we move through the will instead of waiting till the end. Is everyone ready?"

Everyone answered in the affirmative. It didn't take Mr. Beckard long. Father's will was five pages long and very precise in what he wanted everyone to have. Over the years, Father had been very observant of each of his grandchildren. He knew exactly what interested them. Each Christmas, he would present them with a gift that represented their interest. He wanted them to know he was watching them. In his will, he left several personal items to his grandchildren. The personal items were historical in nature and value. He wanted his grandchildren to keep these items to preserve Bradford history. In fact, with each item, father had a narrative that explained why the item had historical significance.

As Mother had already shared with me, Father left Dent the Black Oaks Plantation. Dent also inherited all the slaves on the plantation. He left Twin Oaks Plantation, house, and three hundred acres of the western half of the plantation to me. He also left me half of the slaves.

My brother John received the eastern part of the plantation, which also contained three hundred acres. He also received half of the slaves at Twin Oaks. To my sisters, Tanyua, Mary, and Sarah, Father gave five thousand dollars each in cash, as well as bonds that would later mature.

To my nephew, Zachariah George Bradford, son of my deceased brother, Zachariah Bradford, he gave five thousand dollars. To my mother, Catherine Bradford, he gave ten thousand dollars and some bonds. Mother also inherited both Bill and Betsy as her own slaves. The will went on to say that Mother would be able to live at Twin Oaks as long as she lived, or until she chose to move somewhere else. She would also receive five percent of the plantation's proceeds as long as she lived or as long as a Bradford held ownership.

Father further rewarded his grandchildren with an educational endowment that would pay for a college education should they choose to pursue a college degree. These funds were not to be used for any purpose other than to pursue a college degree. This was Father's way of encouraging each of his grandchildren to make something out of themselves.

As I expected, everyone seemed to be supportive and pleased in regard to Father's generosity. Mr. Beckard asked, "Are there any questions from any member of the family?"

"Jonathan, I would like to ask one question, if I may?" Mother said.

"Of course, Catherine," Mr. Beckard replied.

"How much time will it take to probate James's will?"

"Catherine, that's a good question. It normally takes from two to six months to probate estates as large as James Bradford's. If there are no challenges then I would say it shouldn't take over two months. I don't see any major problems for anyone to worry about."

"That's good news. Now, before everyone gets away from here, there is one thing I want everyone to know. When I die, I want to be buried by James Bradford in the Oak Hills Cemetery, and I want Betsy and Bill to become free slaves. If they want to stay on the plantation, then I want them to be paid regular wages. I will put these things in my will," Mother said.

Everyone looked at each other as if to say, "Okay, Mother, we heard you; why are you telling us this now?" Mother was in good health and very active physically. I certainly didn't know where she was coming from. There had to be a reason, but what?

In the month of October, two events occurred that infuriated Southerners throughout the Deep South. First, on October 4, Kansas voters adopted the anti-slavery Wyandotte Constitution by a 2-to-1 margin. Because of the Wyandotte Constitution, Kansas was admitted as a free state. Secondly, twelve days later John Brown, a radical abolitionist who had been involved in anti-slavery violence in Kansas, led a group of seventeen, including five black members to raid the arsenal located in Harper's Ferry, Virginia. Mr. Brown's goal was to start a slave uprising using the captured weapons at Harper's Ferry. However, Brown and his men were surrounded and captured by Colonel Robert E. Lee. Several of his men were killed. Brown was imprisoned waiting to be tried for treason. This event was one of the growing abolitionist movements that helped fuel tension between the North and the South.

It was the middle of October before Audrey, little Charles, and I finally got moved to Twin Oaks. Audrey was one happy lady! She loved Twin Oaks and loved the freedom to ride Millie and do things in the outdoors. She and mother hit it off right away. They both enjoyed gardening, and Mother let Audrey help her in the garden. After moving into Twin Oaks, I saw Penelope every morning for breakfast and every evening for dinner. She was always dressed well and always carried a smile on her face. She and Audrey were getting along very nicely. Penelope shared with Audrey several things about Boston. One particular night as we were going to bed, Audrey brought up some interesting observations regarding Penelope.

"You know, Obadiah, Penelope is very intelligent."

"What makes you say that?"

"Because she is! Have you read any of her stories?"

"No, I've not had a reason to read them."

"You should ask her if you could read some of them. They are quite good."

"I've always known she loved to write but haven't had an opportunity to read any of her writings. I'll ask her if I can read some."

"Obadiah, I feel really sorry for Penelope."

"Why is that?"

"Where do you want me to start?"

"Just say what's on your mind."

"Well, the way I see it, Penelope is wasting her life away. She's probably the most educated slave in Alabama, but she is not allowed to utilize the many talents she has."

"Audrey, that's not totally true. One of her talents is teaching, and she's a wonderful teacher to our slaves."

"You're exactly right about teaching. She's good and enjoys it, but you don't know the half of it. Penelope can play the piano, she can sing, she can dance, she can sew, she can cook, and she can run this household better than most plantation women, including me. Obadiah, she's amazing!"

"You just told me something I didn't know. Penelope sings and plays the piano?"

"She does! She plays for Mrs. Catherine, Mattie, Betsy, and me almost every day."

"Is she good at singing and playing the piano?"

"She's very good!" Audrey said, nodding her head in the affirmative.

"Well, I'll be darned. She's never mentioned playing the piano to me."

"I heard her one day as she was cleaning the piano. She didn't know anyone was around. I walked into the parlor quietly and just stood there listening to the beautiful music she was playing. After she finished, I startled her by applauding her performance. She jumped up and said, 'Oh, Misses Bradford, please don't tell Master Obadiah.'"

"I assured her I wouldn't. She was so afraid you might punish her for her piano talent. Now, Obadiah, do you see what I

257

mean when I say she's got all of this talent, but it's not doing her any good."

"So, what do you suggest?"

"She's a beautiful woman, one who could latch on to any good looking man if given the right opportunity. Men would swarm around her. It doesn't seem right for a woman like Penelope to be a slave. If she was free, she could return to Boston where she could find a nice man, get married, and have a family of her own."

"Audrey, Penelope is enjoying what she's doing right here at Twin Oaks. She's told me that herself. Have you seen how many slaves she's teaching to read and write? I'm telling you, she loves it."

"Yes, I've noticed that, but something tells me that Penelope wants more than just being a teacher the rest of her life. I believe she would love to have children. She's so good with Little Jim and Charles. They love her!"

"I've promised Penelope that someday I would free her and her Mother. Because of the way free slaves are treated in the South, they would have to move North or be subjected to ridicule and abuse. Although they would be free, in a true sense, they would still be in bondage. At this point in time, I believe we give them a good quality of life, one where they have a good roof over their heads and plenty of food to eat."

"Oh, Obadiah, I know you're right. But why do some people hate them? They are human beings just like us."

"I believe that, and you believe that, but the majority of the South does not. I know that we are where we are today because of our slaves. Without them, there would be no cotton crops, no wheat, and no corn. Without them, we would be nothing and could do nothing."

"I've been thinking about teaching Penelope how to ride a horse. What do you think about that?" Audrey said with excitement.

"I think that's a good idea."

"Now that Patience is broken to ride, I'll let her ride Patience."

"Hang on! Let's think about that. I'm not sure Patience would be the horse for a beginner. He's very spirited! I think you need to let George pick out a gentle horse for Penelope to ride at first. I'd be scared for Penelope to ride Patience."

"I'm sure your right. I'll let George pick her a horse. After she gets used to riding, maybe I could let her ride Millie and I could ride Patience."

"I'd feel comfortable with that idea. You are a skilled rider, and if anyone can handle your spirited Patience, you can."

After Audrey fell asleep, my mind turned to Penelope. I was happy that Audrey wanted to become Penelope's friend. Audrey has such a good heart, and she loves people. Much like my mother, Audrey doesn't see color in her relationships. Audrey's friendship with Penelope might turn out to be a good thing. Although I would like to see a good friendship come out of Audrey's and Penelope's relationship, I still had reservations that Audrey might eventually perceive Penelope's love for me, and my love for her. If that ever came out, it would be a total disaster for all three of us. As I closed my eyes to try to get some sleep, I couldn't believe Penelope had learned to sing and play the piano in Boston. It would be a treat to see her perform. Why had she kept this from me?

The Prattville Hospital was finally completed, and Mr. Daniel Pratt threw a grand opening celebration that was second to none. He sent out invitations to residents in Autauga County, to Alabama State officials, and to dignitaries in surrounding counties. The festivities started at ten o'clock on Saturday morning and ended with a dance on Saturday night at town hall. Alabama's Governor Andrew B. Moore was the keynote speaker for the grand event. The new hospital would be a valuable asset and addition to Prattville, one that would play a major role in the county's health care needs.

Dr. Banister was made chief administrator of the hospital. I, along with two of my best friends from the Old Georgia Medical School, Dr. Frank Matthews from Charleston, South Carolina, and Dr. Jim Boroughs from Columbus, Mississippi, rounded out the medical staff at the hospital.

The relationship between Penelope and Audrey turned into a good friendship. It wasn't long before Penelope was riding Millie and Audrey was riding Patience. They were like two peas in a pod, you might say. Audrey needed a good female friend. She still had her old friends but didn't see them often.

One night after dinner, Mother invited me for a stroll through her garden. This was something we hadn't done in awhile. I was curious about what she had on her mind.

"All right, Mother, what's on your mind?"

"Obadiah, I've been watching Audrey and Penelope together. I'm telling you, they have become the best of friends. Penelope looks after little Charles like he was hers. Little Charles loves to play with Little Jim and some of the other slave children. When Mattie has her second child, there will be another playmate for Charles. I guess the reason I'm telling you this is because I'm so happy you and Audrey are living here with me at Twin Oaks. It's been hard losing your father. I don't think I could have survived the pain of being alone."

"Mother, I'm hoping you'll be around for a long time."

"Obadiah, I'm so blessed having you as my son. I ask myself daily how things could be any better than what they are now."

Mother then took my arm as we headed back to the house.

CHAPTER 30

This was our first Christmas at Twin Oaks without Father. Things wouldn't be the same without him, but Mother was determined to make it a good day for everyone. After breakfast, Mother invited our house slaves to share in opening Christmas gifts with us. Audrey and Mother had purchased gifts for everyone. To my recollection, this was the first time our house slaves had been invited to participate in opening Christmas gifts on Christmas day.

Audrey and I decided to get Penelope a fashionable hat to wear with her burgundy dress. Much to our surprise, our house slaves presented us with personal gifts that they had made. Penelope made Audrey, Mother, and me wool scarves. The scarf felt good and warm around my neck. It was a joyous time, full of laughter and excitement to see Little Jim and Charles tear open their Christmas presents.

As I looked at Penelope and Audrey, I told myself I was a lucky man to have two beautiful and wonderful ladies living under the same roof. Penelope had been wonderful in not putting me in any kind of compromising position as she worked around the house. I, too, made an extra effort not to let myself get in an awkward position of being alone with Penelope.

Mother is still the nucleus of the family. As long as she's alive, we will be celebrating Christmas with her at Twin Oaks. The entire Bradford family will be arriving soon. We will conduct our normal activities of eating dinner together, reading the Christmas story, which Dent will take over for Father, exchanging gifts, and having our sharing time together.

Right after finishing Christmas dinner, I touched Audrey's hand to say Merry Christmas and that I loved her. She was shivering as though she was cold. Her hands were cold and shaking. She looked pale, like she might be getting ready to vomit.

"Are you all right, Audrey?" I asked as I took her hand in mine.

"I feel sick. Please excuse me," she said, as she got up from her chair and quickly exited the dining room.

As she passed through the doorway, I saw Penelope following her to the bathroom. I excused myself and went directly to the bathroom where I saw Penelope wiping Audrey's forehead with a wet towel.

"Audrey, what's wrong?"

"She's sick at her stomach, Master Obadiah."

"I'll be all right, Obadiah. Penelope will take care of me. You go back and take care of our guests. I'll be back as soon as I get to feeling better."

"No, I'm not going to leave you," I said, as I led her over to a chair and set her down.

"How long has this been going on?"

"Obadiah, I didn't want to tell you this way, but I've been having morning sickness for the past week. I think we are going to have another baby," she said with a smile.

"Really!"

"I'm feeling the very same way I felt when I was pregnant with Charles. I'm almost sure I'm with child."

I looked at Penelope and said, "Penelope, would you go tell Mother we will join them in the parlor in a few minutes."

"Yes, Master Obadiah!"

"That sounds so awkward for Penelope to still call you Master Obadiah. Why can't she call you, Master Bradford, since your father is deceased? She's more than a slave around here, you know."

"Audrey, every slave on this plantation addresses me as Master Obadiah. To change that would be very confusing."

"Forget it; I'm just angry because I'm sick. I hate this part of being with child. Why does this happen to women?"

"Hey, let's not talk anymore about this right now. How are you feeling?"

"I'm all right now that I've vomited my guts out," she said as she smiled at me.

"Do you feel good enough to join the family for the Christmas story and the exchange of presents?"

"Yes, I do. I want to see Charles's face when he opens more of his presents. He's so excited!"

We joined the others in the parlor. As usual, it was packed, standing room only. The young people didn't mind sitting on the floor. They had done that all their lives. As long as we could seat the ladies, we would make it just fine.

Dent did an excellent job of reading the Christmas story. He put a lot of himself into it. He was gifted in relating the story to his audience. He was the oldest and was respected by all. It was only fitting that he take Father's place in reading the Christmas story.

The exchange of presents was the highlight of the day. Everyone seemed pleased with their presents. My sister Mary Shadrack requested to address the family.

"Of course you may, Mary Ann," Mother said.

"There is something Virgil and I want you to pray with us about. Last Friday, Mr. Daniel Pratt called Virgil into his office and offered him a great opportunity to manage and operate a large general store and cotton gin in El Dorado, Arkansas. If Virgil decides to take Mr. Pratt's offer, we will be leaving Autauga County and moving to El Dorado.

"Where in the world is El Dorado, Arkansas?" Mother asked.

"I knew you would want to know so I brought a map along to show you. El Dorado is located in the southeast part of Arkansas. It's a growing town on the move with a railroad passing through and lots of prime cotton land. Mr. Pratt assures Virgil that he will do well financially, and with the money Father left me, we can buy a nice home in El Dorado and maybe have some money to invest."

"Lord, I certainly didn't expect this," Mother said, as she shook her head in disbelief.

263

"Mother, I know El Dorado looks a long way off, but with the railroads, it's not too far. Please try to understand," Mary said, with tears welling in her eyes.

Someone had to step in and say something positive to reinforce what Mary had requested. That someone had to be someone other than Mother. I looked around hoping that Dent, being the oldest, would step forward and say something supportive. Our eyes met about the same time. I nodded my head as if to say to Dent, "Say something!"

"Hey, listen up, everyone," Dent said. "Mary Ann has asked for our help in praying about this important decision in her family's life. I think we should do as she requested, starting right now. I'm going to ask my brother, Dr. Obadiah Bradford, to lead us in this prayer. Obadiah, would you please pray for Mary's request."

Dent certainly knew how to turn the tables on me. "Let us pray," I said.

It was going to take awhile for Mother to realize that this might be the best thing for Mary and her family. After she gets over the initial shock, she will be able to think rationally, and I'm sure she will be supportive of Virgil's decision.

On January 1, 1860, we awakened with a big snow and lots of ice in Autauga County. The misty rain we had gotten the day before had turned into ice and then the snow came during the night. The road conditions were awful. The snow must be a foot deep in places. I worried about whether our slaves had enough food and enough wood to keep them warm. George assured me he had everything under control.

We were snowed in for four days. On the fifth day, the sun came out and started melting the snow away. We still had some very cold temperatures, however. I'm afraid some slaves on other plantations in Autauga County may have frozen to death. There were several of them living in shacks that had holes in both the walls and roof. I can only hope that the plantation owners had enough sense to move them into barns or better housing. Sometimes the barn was nicer than the shacks they lived in. At least fires could be built on the barn floor to help keep them warm. The plantation I worried most about was Mr. James

Jones's place. I decided to make the Jones's place my first stop. Since Bill had experience driving on ice and snow, I asked him to drive for me.

As Bill pulled up in front of Jones's house, his overseer, Mason, was coming out of the house.

"Doc, where have you been? We've already lost three of our slaves, and several more are sick," Mason said.

"How did they die?"

"I'm assuming either pneumonia or freezing to death."

I mumbled, "I'm not surprised," under my breath.

"What did you say?" Mason asked.

I said, "Where are you keeping the sick?"

"We've moved them to that large cabin over there," he said as he pointed in the direction of the cabin.

"Mason, what about your other slaves. Do they have plenty of blankets and enough wood and cotton stalks to keep them from freezing to death?"

"Yes, sir, after finding those three frozen slaves, I made sure the others had plenty of wood and cotton stalks to keep them warm. I moved several of our slaves to the barn. They've been doing pretty good. This weather caught us off guard."

"Let's go check on those sick ones."

As I opened the door, I was surprised to feel heat in the cabin. A good fire was going in the fireplace and the sick were lying on the floor covered with blankets. I immediately smelled the stink of human feces. As I looked around, I could see several of the slaves groaning, moaning, and coughing. Although they were covered with a blanket, they were shivering. Mason had a mixture of male and female slaves in the cabin. I counted fifteen slaves, four women and eleven men. I started examining the women first. The first one I examined had pneumonia and was in bad shape. The second one had a cold but no pneumonia. When I got to the last one, she was dead.

"Mason, this one is dead. You need to get some help and remove her from the cabin. As cold as it is, we won't have to worry about burying her right now. I doubt if you could dig through this ice, anyway."

I started my examinations of the men. I had glanced over the floor and had noticed one man who hadn't moved. I went to him first. He, too, was dead. He had been dead for at least three hours.

"Mason, we've got another dead one here. You need to remove him as well."

Out of the fifteen slaves, two were dead, six had pneumonia, and seven were sick with colds.

"Mason, these sick slaves need to be sleeping on mattresses or cots. Don't you have some old cots or mattresses around here?"

"No, sir! This is the best we can offer them."

"What a shame, what a shame," I said as I shook my head in disbelief.

"Are these the only sick ones you have?"

"Yes, sir!"

"Where is Teshia and her family?"

"Dr. Bradford, you don't need to worry about them; they are being well cared for."

"I've not seen Teshia and the baby in some time. Do you mind if I take a look at them?"

"I guess not!" he said.

He took me to a cabin near the barn. It was one of the better cabins on the plantation. Since Mason was the father of Teshia's baby, I was hoping they were being well provided for. As I entered the cabin, Teshia and her family were seated near the fireplace. It was still pretty cold in the cabin but not freezing. Teshia was holding her baby boy with a blanket around him. She immediately recognized me and got up to greet me.

"Doctor Bradford, it's good to see you."

"It's good to see you, too, Teshia. Are you and your family doing all right?"

She looked at Mason and nodded her head that everything was all right. I had expected her to be pregnant again but was surprised and happy when I noticed she wasn't. *Maybe he is leaving her alone,* I thought. Teshia and her family were in good shape. Teshia's father had a little cold so I left some medicine for him. I told Mason I wanted to talk with Mr. Jones before I left the plantation. He escorted Bill and me to the house.

"I believe you need to hear this, so you might as well join us," I said to Mason, as we entered the house.

Upon entering the house, we were escorted to the parlor where Mr. Jones was reading a newspaper. He looked up and acknowledged us by welcoming us into the parlor. "You must be freezing," he said.

I took a seat near the fireplace while Bill decided to stand near the parlor door.

"Well, Dr. Bradford, I heard we lost two more slaves."

"You're fortunate not to have lost more, Mr. Jones."

"Them slaves are not nearly as tough as they once were," he said.

"Mr. Jones, if you want those sick slaves to live, you've got to follow my instructions."

"All right, Doc, what would you have us do?"

"First, you've got to clothe them better. Their skin is exposed in all directions. They need shirts and pants to wear, especially during this wintry weather. They need more than one blanket. They need nourishment right now. You've got to get some food in them. Some of them are starving to death. How can you expect them to be tough when you starve them?"

"Doc, I may not like you, but I respect you. You have always spoken what's on your mind. We will do as you request. I'll need those slaves when spring comes. I don't need any more of them to die."

"I do appreciate your cooperation, Mr. Jones. I'm leaving medicine for them, and hopefully, with ample food, blankets, and proper clothing, they might make it through the winter."

"We'll do our best!" Mason said.

As Bill and I left the Jones plantation, I looked over at Bill, who looked really perplexed.

"Are you all right, Bill?"

"Master Obadiah, I've never seen anything like that in my whole life."

"Bill, I'm sorry to say I see some really sad situations on some of these plantations."

"I'm glad you're my master and not that Mr. Jones."

"Bill, you can't tell anyone what you saw here today. Dr. Banister and I had to sign a written oath that we would not mention what we do for these plantation owners. We don't like it, but that's the way it is here in the South."

"Master Obadiah!"

"Yes, Bill?"

"I just got one thing to say. Someday, Mr. Jones and that Mr. Mason are going to burn in hell!"

That was the strongest language I'd ever heard Bill speak. I was somewhat taken aback by his remarks, but in all truthfulness, I agreed with his statement. To show my love for him, I patted him on the shoulder and said, "Bill, I appreciate everything you do for me and the Bradford family. I pray that God will always keep you in his spirit."

CHAPTER 31

The political atmosphere between Southern and Northern legislators in the U.S. Congress has become very disruptive in Washington. The newspapers, on a daily basis, are having a party reporting the day-by-day grumblings, fighting, and heated debates between the Democrats and Republicans. Several issues are being debated across party lines. Just like my father, I am getting caught up in politics and literally have caught myself looking forward to reading the daily newspaper reports.

Today's newspaper had an article on the 1860 United States Census. I found the statistics to be very interesting. The census records revealed that the U.S. population was 31,443,321, which was an increase of 35.4 percent over the 23,191,875 persons enumerated in 1850. The U.S. slave population in the 1860 census was 3,954,174. Autauga County happened to be one of the largest slave counties in Alabama.

Abraham Lincoln of Illinois has quickly become a new voice in the Republican Party. In February, he created a lot of anger in the South with his Cooper Institute speech against the spread of slavery. The newspapers described him as being a new and refreshing addition to the Republican Party. Some said he might even be the nomination for the President of the United States of America. The Deep South, including Alabama, is strongly opposed to Abraham Lincoln. They fear if he is elected, he will try to abolish slavery throughout the South.

Spring has now arrived in Autauga County. We made it through the winter without losing any slaves. Everyone at Twin Oaks is doing well except for Audrey. She is having difficulties with her pregnancy, one being elevated blood pressure. She is also experiencing sharp pains in her head. I'm afraid she will have to be restricted to bed rest soon. I also worry that she may not be able to carry the baby to full term.

Virgil accepted Mr. Pratt's offer to move to El Dorado, Arkansas, to manage the new cotton gin and general store. At the end of May, they loaded up their belongings and moved to El Dorado. Mary, in her letters to my mother, describes El Dorado as being a nice place to live, with lots of things to do. She's been complimentary of First Baptist Church of El Dorado, which they have chosen as a church home. They have already added several acquaintances to their circle of friends.

Mary is helping Virgil run the general store. According to Mary, the store is stocked with every food and general merchandized items that one would ever need. Her working in the store gives her something constructive to do while the children are in school. One letter Mother received last week had a footnote to me. It said, "Obadiah, there is only one doctor for the entire town of El Dorado. They could use you here. Another thing, Union County has some of the richest farm land in South Arkansas. Cotton is the chief row crop here, and there are some large plantations. One plantation is presently up for sale. If you want to invest in another plantation, we can recommend this one."

Things continued to go badly for Audrey. I decided to put her on bed rest. I've asked Penelope to be her chief caregiver. Audrey's back hurts continuously and her blood pressure is still erratic. I need to delay the baby's coming for at least another month, if possible.

Today is the last day of May. I've had a rough week at the hospital. I had three surgeries and several plantation calls this week. As I pulled the carriage up in front of Twin Oaks, Penelope met me on the front porch. She looked scared!

"What's wrong, Penelope?"

"Master Obadiah, I'm worried about Missus Audrey. She's just lying in bed staring at the ceiling. I couldn't get her to eat a bite of food today. In fact, I can't rouse her at all. Her eyes are open, but she doesn't respond."

"I'll go check on her."

I quickly went inside and went directly to her bedside. As soon as I saw Audrey, I knew what had happened to her. She had had a stroke. I checked her blood pressure and it was falling. I had to do something and do something fast. Both she and the baby's lives were in jeopardy.

I looked around and said to Penelope. "Audrey has had a stroke. Go tell Mattie to send me some boiling water and lots of towels. Also, see if Mother is home. If she is, tell her I need her help. I'll need Mattie's and Betsy's help as well."

I started pulling surgical tools from my medicine bag and laying them on a table near the bed. I knew what I had to do. I had to do a Cesarean Section to save the baby and Audrey's life. I didn't have long. I had just finished getting all of my surgical instruments organized when Mother and Penelope entered the door.

"What's going on, Obadiah?" Mother asked.

"I'm afraid Audrey has had a stroke. I'll need assistance from both of you. I'm going to have to take the baby. It's the only way to save the baby and Audrey."

"Obadiah, what are you going to do?" Mother asked.

"Mother, I'm going to have to do another Cesarean Section on Audrey. I've got to get the baby out. The baby is putting too much stress on Audrey."

"Is this the same procedure you used on her before?"

"Yes, it is!"

"Tell us what you need us to do," Mother said.

"Mother, I need you to stand at Audrey's head and hold her shoulders still. Mattie, I need for you to stand at her feet and hold her feet in case she begins to move around. Penelope, I need for you to stand on the other side of her and use these towels to soak up the blood. This procedure isn't pretty, and you are going to see lots of blood. Please don't get sick on me. I've done this procedure before. Trust me; I know what I'm doing."

"Where's Betsy?"

"I'm right here, Master Obadiah!"

"Betsy, I need for you stand by in case we need more water and supplies.

"Does everyone understand what I want you to do?"

Everyone answered in the affirmative.

As I made my first incision blood went everywhere. Penelope didn't flinch one bit. She was wonderful and immediately applied the towel to the opening, soaking up the excess blood. She appeared to know exactly what I instructed her to do. My second incision was made and brought more blood. Again, Penelope was calm and soaked up the blood.

I glanced at Mother, she looked pale. She had seen lots of babies born into this world but not like this. She was shaking her head in disbelief. She was witnessing something she had never seen before.

As I pulled my daughter through the openings I had made in Audrey's uterus and abdomen, I found myself questioning whether I had waited too long. If Audrey dies, I will never forgive myself. I prayed all through the surgery that both the baby and Audrey would live. The baby was perfect. After spanking her on the bottom and hearing her cry, I knew she was alive. I handed her to Mother so she and Betsy could clean her up.

Penelope was wonderful. I couldn't have asked for a better assistant. She kept the blood soaked up as I closed the incisions. She was as solid as a rock.

I took my stethoscope and examined Audrey. Her blood pressure was slowly coming back. It would be awhile before I could tell how much damage had been done by the stroke.

I was exhausted. I sat down in the rocking chair near Penelope.

Mother came over to me and said, "Here's your beautiful daughter. She's perfect!

She was beautiful, just like her mother. She had lots of blond hair and strong lungs. She was crying very loudly when Mother handed her to me. Just as I pulled her to my chest, there was a sudden change. She stopped crying. For several nights when Audrey was pregnant and we were lying in bed, I would put my hand on Audrey's stomach and would sing a song to the baby. We didn't know what sex the baby was, but we didn't really care.

We had always heard that reading and singing to babies gave them a sense of belonging.

After holding her for a few minutes, I took her over and laid her beside Audrey. I whispered in Audrey's ear and said, "Audrey, meet your daughter, Belle."

Audrey and I had decided if it was a girl we would name her Belle Catherine Bradford. We both agreed that we wanted our baby girl to be named after our mothers. Belle is Audrey's mother's middle name, and Catherine is my mother's first name.

One week after Belle was born, we saw some improvement in Audrey. She began to blink her eyes some. She also moved her fingers some. We could talk to her, and she would respond by squeezing our hands or blinking. This is a prayer being answered, I thought. Since Audrey couldn't nurse little Belle, mother and Penelope took turns feeding her cow's milk. Mother said, "I raised all of you on cow's milk, and we can do it with Belle, too."

Since Audrey was in good hands at Twin Oaks, I decided to resume my schedule at the hospital and calling on the plantations.

Politics was still the number one subject on the streets of Prattville. On May 18, Abraham Lincoln won the Republican Party's nomination for President of the United States. The Republicans adopted a concrete, precise, and moderately worded platform, which included the exclusion of slavery from the territories but the affirmation of the right of states to order and control their own domestic institutions. Lincoln's presidential nomination created anger throughout the Deep South. The newspapers were full of statements like, "If Lincoln is elected President of the United States, we will secede from the union."

With the dedicated service of Penelope, Audrey showed improvement daily. Penelope worked daily with Audrey on her exercise and speech. Belle was doing fine. Her development was right on course. She was a healthy little girl. Between Penelope and Mother, Charles and Belle were certainly not neglected.

My visits to the plantations were mostly good. I found that during cotton planting time, the slaves were treated better by their overseers and owners. They were allowed to grow fresh vegetables, which was a good supplement to their normal corn diet.

My mother continued her trips to Prattville twice a week. She went shopping and visited my sisters Tanyua and Sarah on Mondays and played bridge with her friends on Wednesdays. Her health was holding up.

Mattie and Big Jim had another boy. They named him Henry. The birth of Henry gave Mattie and Big Jim two sons. I am amazed at how Mattie looks. Giving birth to two children has not hurt her looks at all. She's still as beautiful as the first time I saw her in Selma, Alabama.

The hospital in Prattville is now up and running. Dr. Banister is doing a great job as its first administrator. My friends Dr. Jim Burroughs, and Dr. Frank Matthews, and I keep busy working at the hospital and making plantation calls.

Daniel Pratt has done it again. The hospital is a big success and was badly needed in our county. Our hospital beds are filled to capacity. I've always admired Mr. Pratt's visionary qualities. He has a way of seeing a need for something and figuring out a way to make it happen. The citizens of Autauga County are blessed to have a man of his vision.

The summer brought good weather to Autauga County, and the cotton and corn were bumper crops.

Audrey was making slow progress. She could now say a few words but was still unable to walk and hold the children. Penelope continued to work daily with her. The children looked to Penelope for their needs since Audrey was not able to attend them. I know it made Audrey sad not to be able to pick up her children and play with them. At times, she breaks down and cries. Although I'm not one hundred percent sure, I believe that someday Audrey will recover most of the use of her body functions and mental capacity. I pray daily this will happen.

On November 6, 1860, Abraham Lincoln was elected President of the United States. His platform included the prohibition of slavery in new states and territories. Mr. Lincoln won all the electoral votes in all the Free states except New Jersey where he received four votes to Douglas's three.

As I read the newspaper article announcing Mr. Lincoln's victory, I was reminded of one conversation I had had with Father. I remember Father saying, "Abe Lincoln from Illinois may someday be President of the United States. He's a clever one, he is." He went on to say, "Lincoln's stand on slavery would be the end to the South as we know it. If he's elected, our country will never be the same again."

What was once calmness across the Deep South was no longer. Plantation owners were fearful that Lincoln would abolish slavery and free the slaves in the South. If that occurred, bankruptcy would be the death of many plantation owners.

The month of December brought on several incidents that made things even worse. On December 4, President Buchanan condemned Northern interference with slave policies of Southern states. He went on to say, however, that states had no right to secede from the Union.

On December 17, 1860, South Carolina called a secession convention in Columbia. On the second day of the convention, the representatives voted to move the convention to Charleston because of a small pox epidemic which was running rampant in Columbia. While in Charleston, the convention's business was held at St. Andrews Hall.

On December 20, 1860, the convention adopted the Ordinance of Secession on a roll call vote. The vote consisted of one hundred and sixty-nine yeas, and zero nays. The convention published a declaration of the immediate causes that induced and justified the secession of South Carolina from the Federal Union.

The document cited several causes to justify their secession from the Union. Among the causes were, "Encroachments on the reserved right of the states," and "an increasing hostility of the non-slaveholding states to the institution of slavery," and "the election of a man to the high office of President of the United States, whose opinions and purposes are hostile to slavery."

The convention also resolved that all previously federally owned properties in the state were now South Carolina's. The Convention called on the federal government to restore South Carolina authority to Forts Moultrie and Sumter, the Charleston Arsenal, and Castle Pinckney.

South Carolina's promise to secede from the Union if Abe Lincoln was elected was now history.

After reading the South Carolina Declaration of Secession, I knew we were in trouble. How could the Union allow South Carolina to take possession of these forts and assume a Union of their own? I had a bad feeling about all of this.

On December 24, 1860, South Carolina Governor Francis Wilkinson Pickens declared the act of secession in effect.

CHAPTER 32

My sister Mary Ann Shadrack and her family arrived at Twin Oaks on December 24, 1860, by train from El Dorado, Arkansas. We had not seen them since their move to El Dorado. Dent and his family and my brother John and sisters Tanyua and Sarah arrived early this morning. Mother had succeeded again to arrange for all of us to be present for another Bradford Christmas.

As the family visited over eggnog in the parlor, we could smell the refreshing aroma of the Christmas meal being prepared by Mattie, Betsy, Penelope, Big Jim, and Bill. These were some of my fondest memories of smelling the mouth-watering food cooking on Christmas morning. While visiting in the parlor, Dent and John approached me and asked if we could go to my room where it would be private and warm. I had a hunch about what they wanted to talk to me about.

"Hey, what's going on?" I asked.

Dent was the first to speak. Being the oldest he normally took the lead.

"Obadiah, John and I have been gravely concerned about where our country's heading. With the election of Abraham Lincoln and South Carolina seceding from the Union, it's looking pretty bad. We're hearing rumors of a possible civil war between the South and the North. Do you think we're headed for a civil war?"

"I wish I knew the answer to that question, Dent. All I know is South Carolina has created a big mess by seceding from the Union. If South Carolina is successful in influencing other Southern states to secede, then Alabama will surely be one of them. I find this scary and dangerous for us in the South. Thursday I attended a business luncheon as a guest of Daniel Pratt. He invited several big businessmen from different parts of Alabama to join him at convention hall in Prattville. The purpose for the meeting was to hear from other businessmen about how Lincoln's winning the presidential race and how South Carolina's secession would affect the economy in the South. The majority of the businessmen felt that the economy would definitely be affected should additional Southern states secede from the Union. They were equally in agreement that President Lincoln's stand on slavery could create outrage throughout the South and eventually lead to a civil war."

"Obadiah, do you really think Alabama will secede?" John asked.

"Yes, I do!"

"Lord help us all," John said as he dropped his head.

"If there is a civil war, do I fight or do I stay at home and farm? If I don't fight, I'll be called a traitor to my country. My boys will want to fight for their country. I can't very well let them go off to a war and me stay home. I'm telling you, brothers, we are in a heck of a mess," Dent said.

"From what I'm hearing in Prattville, people are ready to go to war to protect their state's rights. They think the Northern states are trying to take away their constitutional and state's rights," John said.

"That's what I'm hearing in Selma as well," Dent said.

"I pray there won't be a war. I don't think the South can win."

"Obadiah, don't say that! At least don't say that to anyone in Autauga County or anywhere else. Those words would make you very unpopular in these parts," Dent said.

"Let me tell you why I don't think the South can win a civil war. The North has the manpower. They are better equipped to fight a war. They have the factories to make military weapons and supplies. They have training facilities that we don't have. They have all kinds of resources that we don't have. If the North was successful in closing down river ports and train lines, how would the South get supplies? Are you getting what I'm saying? We are noted for our cotton and that's about it!"

"Lord, what can we do?" John asked.

"Let's pray that a civil war can be avoided — that Mr. Lincoln can work something out with the South so that a war can be prevented," I said.

"Let's start praying right now," Dent said.

We met in the middle of my bedroom. We formed a circle by putting our arms on each other's shoulders and prayed. We made a pledge that we would pray daily that President Lincoln and Congress can work out an agreeable solution so that a civil war can be avoided.

We returned to the parlor and from there went directly to the dining room to enjoy a delicious Christmas dinner. After dinner, we returned to the parlor where Dent read the Christmas story.

After Dent finished the Christmas story, Sarah and Tanyua, with the help of some of the younger nieces and nephews, passed out the Christmas presents. I took a seat near Audrey where I held Belle in my lap while Charles played at my feet. Charles got really excited opening his presents. He was now old enough to enjoy tearing open the packages. He showed much excitement with each present he opened. I helped little Belle and Audrey open their presents. Audrey had regained some movement in her arms and hands, but hadn't regained enough of her strength to tear away the Christmas paper. As I sat watching her, I was happy to see the joy she showed in her facial expressions. I keep telling myself that someday she will be back to her old self.

While Virgil and Mary were at Twin Oaks, I quizzed them about El Dorado, Arkansas. The general store and cotton gin was quite successful for them. They were making good money and investing their money back into the store. The kids were attending good schools and were making good grades. Virgil described the land lying north of El Dorado as being some of the best cotton land he had seen. Most of the cotton was grown on plantations located near Norphlet, Arkansas. El Dorado was also noted for its sawmills and tall pine trees. According to Virgil and Mary, El Dorado was a progressive place to live.

I spent the following five days after Christmas with my family at Twin Oaks. My busy schedule during the fall convinced me I needed to take some time off to spend with my family. Part of each day was spent playing with Charles and Belle, something I hadn't had time to do in the past. As I played with them, I realized that as a father, I had the awesome responsibility to love and teach them how to be respectful and how to become productive citizens. Since I became a doctor, I have dedicated most of my time attending sick folks, which has kept me away from my family. This has to stop. I had to find some way to balance family time with my medical practice. Audrey has given me two lovely children and I need to do my best to help her raise them.

As Audrey and the children took their mid-afternoon naps, I took some time to visit with Penelope. There had been little time for us to visit during the week since I left early in the morning and returned late in the afternoon. For some time, I had wanted to tell Penelope how much I appreciated her helping Audrey with her therapy and the time she spent looking after Charles and Belle. I decided meeting in the parlor would be the best place for us to meet. We could meet there without any interruption and the door could stay open. I still didn't trust myself being alone with her in some secluded place.

"Master Obadiah, you wanted to talk to me?" she asked as she came into the parlor carrying a pot of hot tea.

"Yes, I do. You and I haven't had much time to visit lately."

"I thought I would make us some hot tea. Would you like some?"

"I certainly would. It smells heavenly!"

"I make good tea!" she said as she smiled.

She poured both of us tea and sat down in a chair near me.

"Penelope, I'm very grateful for what you're doing for Audrey and the kids."

"That's my pleasure, Master Obadiah."

"You are so good with them."

"All three are very precious to me. Audrey and I have become very good friends. She's working really hard to get better. I hope it's all right for me to call her Audrey. She has asked me to."

"Certainly, it's all right! I'm grateful you and Audrey are friends."

"She's improved so much since we started the therapy sessions. Don't you think?"

"Yes, I'm in total agreement with you. I see improvement in her by the week."

"Master Obadiah, do you think Audrey will fully recover?"

"I'm praying she will, Penelope. Sometimes it takes a long time for a stroke victim to recover."

"Audrey wants to get better so badly. She feels she's cheating you and the kids by not being able to be a wife and mother."

"Penelope, are you serious? Does she really feel that away?"

"I'm afraid she does."

"I really didn't know she was feeling that way."

"I've tried to encourage her. I reassure her on a daily basis that you love her and that you want her to recover."

"Thank you, Penelope. You are everything I've always known you to be. We are so lucky to have you back here with us at Twin Oaks."

"Master Obadiah, I'm really happy here. I'm with my family and that means everything to me."

"Then you are happy?"

"Oh, yes, I'm happy. I also feel safe here at Twin Oaks. You are here every night and that makes me feel safe."

"What are your nights like, Penelope?"

"I read until I get sleepy. I get up and attend Charles and Belle when they need me. I dream. My dreams are normally good dreams. I consider myself a wealthy slave."

"I don't quite understand the wealthy slave part."

"Oh, I guess that was a poor way of expressing my happiness. What I meant to say was I consider myself fortunate to live in a nice home, sleep in a nice bed, and eat the best food in the world. The only thing missing is that I'm not married and I don't have children. But in one way, I look at Charles and Belle as being my children, too. So the only thing lacking is that I'm not a wife."

"You are really something!"

"I hope I didn't anger you, Master Obadiah!"

"Oh, no! I meant that as a compliment. You are so honest! That's one reason I love you so much."

"I still love you, too, Master Obadiah! Oh, you will have to excuse me, I hear Belle crying. I need to go. I don't want her to wake Audrey. Let's talk again sometime."

"We will talk again, Penelope!" I said as she rushed down the hall to attend to Belle.

My mother arrived home from Prattville with a newspaper in her hand. As she entered the parlor, she said, "Obadiah, I'm so glad your father didn't live long enough to read what's going on in the South. The talk around town is that all the states in the South may secede from the Union. If that happens, I'm afraid we're going to have a civil war. Here's your paper. I've got to go see what the girls are cooking for dinner. Oh, how's Audrey doing?"

"She's resting right now. She's making improvement."

"That's good, Obadiah," Mother said as she left the room.

I opened the newspaper and begin to read as I took a sip of Penelope's tea. Mother was right. The paper predicted several repercussions the South would face because of South Carolina's action in seceding from the Union. The editorial criticized South Carolina for not waiting to give Abe Lincoln an opportunity to work with the South on the slavery issue. President Lincoln had not yet taken office and wouldn't officially become president until his inauguration on March 4, 1861.

As I returned to work on January 2, 1861, I went immediately to the hospital where Dr. Banister had called an early morning staff meeting. Daniel Pratt, chairman of the hospital board, was present for the meeting. Dr. Banister called the staff meeting at Mr. Pratt's request.

"Good morning, everyone," Dr. Banister said. "I trust everyone had a nice, safe, and healthy Christmas break. I want to welcome you back. We've got a lot of sick folks to see this week. We are going to dispense of our regular staff business and give Mr. Pratt an opportunity to address us this morning. Let's make Mr. Pratt feel welcome," Dr. Banister said as we clapped.

"Thank you for that welcome. I asked Dr. Banister if I could have a little of your time this morning to share with you some of the things I've been working on. I'm assuming all of you are aware of South Carolina's secession from the Union. South Carolina's decision to secede from the Union has created a big stir across the South. This could be a big disaster for the South. It is my firm belief the South's economy will surely suffer as a result of secession. What I fear most is that other Southern states will follow suit and secede as well. That will certainly make things worse.

"I've tried to play the devil's advocate and have tried to look ahead should other Southern states secede from the Union. I'm going to be as truthful in my assessment as I know how. I don't think the South can survive without the union. I'm afraid we are going to experience hard times ahead.

"We've just opened one of the finest hospitals in the South and our cotton production has been just wonderful up to now, but this could all change should there be a civil war. I've been told that South Carolina has voted to take over all the federal forts located in their state. If this is the case, I don't think the federal government will allow this to happen. In my opinion, it will be only a matter of time before the federal government will take action in regaining command of those forts. When this happens, I look for South Carolina to resist, and that could be the beginning of a civil war.

"You may be sitting there asking yourself why I'm sharing my thoughts with you. It's because I'm afraid if a war comes, you, as medical doctors, will be called upon to aid the Southern army in hospitals throughout the South where battles will be fought. If you leave Autauga County, I don't see how we can properly keep this hospital open. This truly concerns me. I'm not here today to try to convince you not to serve in the war but to ask you to search your souls for what God would want you to do. None of us know at this time what Alabama will do, but it's my feeling they will secede as well.

"I have been told that if the South goes to war with the federal government, the South will be depending on a volunteer army. At this time, there are no laws on the books that would require a man to serve in the army. Right now, it's strictly a man's choice. I want you to be thinking about what I've said. I'm praying the South will be able to resolve their differences with our new President, and we can avoid a civil war. I hope you will join me on a daily basis in praying that a war can be prevented. Thank you for allowing me to visit with you this morning. I have a few minutes if anyone would like to ask me questions."

"Mr. Pratt, as you are aware, my brothers and I are all plantation owners. Our livelihood has been cotton production. If we go to war, in your opinion, how will the cotton industry be affected?"

"That's a good question, Obadiah! War will most definitely affect the cotton industry, especially in those states that are directly involved in fighting. If we can keep our slave population, I think we can make it."

"What do you mean by 'if we can keep our slave population'?" I asked.

"There will be a big push for President Abraham Lincoln to free slaves in the South. If that occurs, who will pick our cotton? We can pay our slaves to pick, but that will certainly cut into our profits."

Everyone appreciated Mr. Pratt's visit to the hospital. He was a man who was in the know. His business connections were far-reaching. He was known throughout the United States and abroad. His brilliance and success as a businessman have made him respected by many. I'm very proud to be considered one of his friends. I expect the newspapers will keep us well informed on what's going on in the weeks and months to come. It's going to be interesting, I'm sure!

CHAPTER 33

It didn't take long for other Southern states to jump on the band wagon and secede from the Union. This certainly brought on nerve wracking events and situations. On January 9, 1861, Mississippi seceded. On the same day as Mississippi's secession, South Carolina state troops at Charleston fired on the merchant ship Star of the West to prevent it from landing reinforcements and relief supplies for Union Troops at Fort Sumter. The ship was struck twice by South Carolina's guns. After seeing that it was hopeless to land the reinforcements and supplies, the ship turned back toward New York.

Everywhere I went around Autauga County, the plantation owners wanted to talk about a civil war. Almost everyone wanted to go to war to show the North they couldn't tell the South what we could do and couldn't do. Everyone I talked with was strong in his beliefs on state's rights. They were ready to fight. I tried to stay focused on attending to the sick rather than getting into politics. As I made my rounds, I found the cold winter had already taken a toll on the slaves. Because of poor living conditions, unfit clothing, and lack of food, several of the older slaves had died. Every time I found a dead slave, I shook my head and said, "Lord, when will these owners learn?"

During the month of January, I treated twenty-two cases of pneumonia among the slaves, and several cases of bad cold infections. I also delivered six babies. The slave population wasn't the only race of people I treated. We had an unusual number of whites in Prattville who suffered from pneumonia and bad colds as well. I found myself again spending too much time as a doctor and too little time at Twin Oaks with my family. I kept telling myself that I would soon be able to catch up on my medical calls and again be able to spend more time with my family.

By the end of January, six Southern states had seceded from the Union. South Carolina was the first to secede on December 20, 1860; Mississippi on January 9; Florida on January 10; Alabama on January 11; Georgia on January 19; and Louisiana on January 26.

On January 13, 1861, two days after Alabama voted to secede from the Union, the Selma newspaper printed Alabama's Ordinance of Secession in its entirety. I found it amusing in places.

The Ordinance of Secession started by saying, "Whereas, the election of Abraham Lincoln and Hannibal Hamlin to the offices of President and Vice-President of the United States of America, by a sectional party, avowedly hostile to the domestic institutions and to the peace and security of the people of the State of Alabama, preceded by many and dangerous infractions of the Constitution of the United States by many of the States and people of the Northern section, is a political wrong of so insulting and menacing a character as to justify the people of the State of Alabama in the adoption of prompt and decided measures for their future peace and security: therefore, be it declared and ordained by the people of the State of Alabama in Convention assembled, that the State of Alabama now withdraws, and is herby withdrawn from the Union known as 'the United States of America,' and henceforth ceases to be one of said United States, and is, and of right ought to be, a Sovereign and Independent State."

The words *hostile, dangerous infractions of the Constitution of the United States, peace and security of the people, insulting and menacing a character* were phrases used to justify seceding from the Union. If the reader fully understood what the writer was saying, I could understand how the Ordinance would arouse the emotions of the people of Alabama. This secession mess is crazy. The Southern states have blinded themselves to the repercussions of a war. If war comes, there will be thousands of men killed and wounded from both sides. What a tragedy! It's like a wildfire: once it gets going, it spreads. If my father was living today he would say, "Son, the South will never be the same again."

On January 21, U.S. Senators Clement C. Clay Jr. and Benjamin Fitzpatrick from Alabama, David L. Yulee and Stephen R. Mallory from Florida, and Jefferson Davis from Mississippi withdrew from the U.S. Senate. This created another big stir.

On January 29, Kansas was admitted to the Union as the thirty-fourth state of the Union, and Kansas was admitted as a Free State under the Wyandotte Constitution.

On February 1, 1861, Texas seceded from the Union.

On February 4, 1861, representatives from Alabama, Georgia, Florida, Louisiana, Mississippi, and South Carolina met in Montgomery, Alabama, and voted to form the Confederate States of America. Plans were made to make Montgomery the State Capitol of the Confederacy.

Because of my heavy work schedule and my being depressed from reading newspaper articles, I found myself exhausted and ready for a quiet and relaxing weekend at Twin Oaks. I looked forward to visiting with Audrey and playing with our kids. George met me as soon as I pulled up at the house.

"Master Obadiah, I need to talk to you."

"What's going on, George?"

"Master Obadiah, you know I've always been able to handle our slaves, but I'm telling you that all this talk of war and freedom has caused a big uproar here at Twin Oaks. Some of our slaves are talking crazy."

"George, you are going to have to be more specific. What do you mean crazy?"

"Some say that it won't be long before Mr. Lincoln will issue some kind of order and we will all be free. Do you think that's going to happen, Master Obadiah?"

"George, I believe that someday all slaves will be set free, but I don't think that's going to happen in the near future. Who is responsible for getting our slaves all excited about this freedom thing?"

"It's Feather Joe, mostly."

"You go tell Feather Joe that I want to see him at the big house."

"Yes, sir, Master Obadiah!"

I knew Feather Joe pretty well. He had been with us for about fifteen years now. Father had acquired him in a trade with Mr. Ralph Brogdan from Lowndes County. Feather Joe was smart. I'm thinking that he's been reading the papers from somewhere. I'm wondering if Penelope is letting some of our slaves read the newspapers. I need to find out before Feather Joe gets here.

I went inside and said hello to Audrey and the kids before looking for Penelope. After a short visit with Audrey, I excused myself to look for Penelope. I knocked on her door and she opened it.

"Penelope, are you busy right now?"

"I have some children doing some extra work. I can send them home."

"Could you do that? I need to talk to you as soon as possible."

"I'll be with you shortly."

"Meet me in the parlor."

I went to the parlor and sat down. Having our slaves all upset about secession and the talk of freedom is definitely not what we need right now. Dent warned me about letting our slaves learn to read. I know Feather Joe reads because he's read from the Bible in the barn on the occasions I've observed their church service.

I had no sooner sat down when Penelope entered the room.

"Master Obadiah, what's wrong?"

"I need to know what you do with the newspapers after I get through reading them."

"I read the newspapers and then I take them to my class-room. I've been letting some of my advanced students read from the newspapers."

"Is Feather Joe one of your students?"

"Yes, he is. He came to me a few months ago and asked if he could come to my reading class. He's a pretty good reader."

"I'm afraid he's spreading propaganda to our slaves about what he's reading from the newspapers."

"Have I done some wrong?"

"No, I just needed to confirm where Feather Joe was getting his information. Let me ask you one other question. Has Feather Joe asked your opinion on any of the articles that have been printed in the newspaper?"

"Yes, he has. We've talked about some of the things, but he's not indicated he's upset or anything like that."

At this time, Feather Joe came in with George. "I'll talk with you later, Penelope."

"Feather Joe, how are you?"

"I'm doing fine, Master Obadiah."

"Take a chair and sit down, Feather Joe. George, you can sit in that chair."

"Feather Joe, I need to talk with you about your relationship with our slaves."

"Yes, Master!"

"George tells me you've been telling them that our new President Abe Lincoln is going to free every slave in the South. Is that right?"

"Master Obadiah, I don't mean to cause any trouble."

"Feather Joe, I'm not saying you're a trouble maker. I just need for you to stop telling the other slaves all this stuff you read in a newspaper. A lot of that stuff is not true."

"Yes, sir! I'll not say another word. I promise, Master Obadiah."

"Feather Joe, I'm glad you read well. That speaks very well of your ability to learn, but I do believe it's best not to share what you read anymore with the other slaves. When there is something you and the other slaves need to know, I'll tell you in due time."

"I understand, Master Obadiah."

"I'm going to trust you will do as I ask. Are you willing to do that?"

"Oh, yes, Master Obadiah! You can count on me. I won't say another word."

"You can go, Feather Joe. I need to visit with George."

"Yes, sir, Master Obadiah. Thank you, Master Obadiah, thank you," he said as he bowed and left the room.

"I think you scared him half to death, Master Obadiah," George said.

"Then you think he's had enough punishment?"

"Yes, sir! I don't think he will be doing anymore talking. I'll keep my eyes and ears opened. If he does anymore talking, I'll be sure to let you know."

"Thanks, George. How's the family doing?"

"We are all well. My girl, Nellie, and that boy Willie have eyes for each other. I have to watch that situation closely."

"How old is Nellie?"

"She's almost eighteen."

"Well, what do you think of this Willie?"

"Oh, he's a good boy, I guess."

"Well, maybe we should be planning a wedding."

"When Willie comes asking me for my daughter's hand in marriage, we will think about a wedding and not a minute sooner."

"You hang in there, George!"

"Yes, Master. Will there be anything else?"

"No, George. You go and have dinner with your family."

I needed to talk to Penelope again but would wait until after dinner. I believe she was trembling during our conversation. I don't want her to think that I blame her for Feather Joe's action.

Mother was wound up at dinner time. She couldn't slow down from telling us about her day in Prattville. She, Tanyua, and Sarah had shopped most the day for maternity clothes for Sarah. Mother announced that Sarah was expecting her second child. When Mother announced that Sarah was expecting a child, I heard Audrey mumble her first sentence, "I'm happy for Sarah." It was slurred, but I know that's what she said.

I had a fun weekend with Audrey, Charles, and Belle. Bill took us for a ride over to Audrey's folks to visit on Saturday afternoon. Audrey hadn't seen them in a while and wanted to go. Penelope came with us to help with Charles and Belle.

The afternoon at the Dentons went well. The Dentons were happy to see Audrey and the children. Mr. Denton took Charles out to the corral to see the cows and horses. Charles was thrilled to spend some time with his grandfather. Mr. Denton told me how grateful he was that I had brought Audrey over to see them. He felt she had made considerable improvement since the last time he and Mrs. Denton had seen her at Twin Oaks.

After we returned to Twin Oaks, we had dinner together. Audrey was tired, so Penelope helped her get to bed and then put Charles and Belle to bed. After everyone was settled, Penelope met me in the parlor.

"Master Obadiah, I want to apologize for letting Feather Joe read the newspapers. I had no idea he would upset the plantation slaves with what he was reading."

"I know that, Penelope. I don't blame you for any of this. As a teacher, you did the right thing. I know you don't have enough reading materials to teach your advanced students. If I had known what reading materials you needed, I could have purchased them for you."

"That's just it, Master Obadiah. I don't know what's available. I need to go to the library at Prattville and see what they have available. Do you think that's possible?"

As far as I knew, Penelope had never been in the library at Prattville. I wondered how she would know what they had in the Prattville library.

"Penelope, how do you know about the Prattville library?"

"Audrey told me."

"Really!"

"Yes, I was sharing with her about needing some reading materials, and she said, 'Go to library.' I asked her what library, and she said Prattville."

"Penelope, your relationship with Audrey amazes me."

"I don't have any problem talking with Audrey. We understand each other well. When she told me about the library I said, 'Missus Audrey, can't you just see this black slave girl going into that white library in Prattville.' Audrey just smiled at me and said, 'Tell Obadiah!'"

"Penelope, I'm going to ask Sarah to go with you to the library on Monday. She will know what to do, and I'm sure the library will be able to help you select some additional teaching materials."

"Oh, Master Obadiah, that would be wonderful."

"I'll see Sarah tomorrow at church, and I'll get this all set up."

"Thank you, Obadiah!" she said as she threw her arms around me and hugged me.

Immediately, she pulled away and fled from the room.

CHAPTER 34

Sometime during the early morning hours, I was awakening by Audrey calling out for me. I sprang from my bed and was at Audrey's side within seconds. I took her hand as I said, "Audrey, what's wrong?"

Audrey looked up at me with tears running down her cheeks and said, "Obadiah, I had a horrible dream."

"What was it?"

"Oh, Obadiah! I dreamed I was dying. I wasn't ready to die. I wanted to stay here with you, Charles, and little Belle. I asked God to give me time to say goodbye to you and the kids. Obadiah, I'm not afraid to die, but I just don't want to leave you and the kids."

"It's all right, Audrey. I don't think God's going to take you away from us. I can't see him doing that. You are improving daily, and sometime in the future, you are going to get back to normal. You are going to be all right. It was only a dream, Audrey."

"Oh, Obadiah, I do want to get well. I try so hard. Penelope encourages me daily. She compliments me on my efforts. She is such a nice lady and my very best friend. If I was to die, Obadiah, Penelope would be someone I would trust to be your wife and raise my children. She is so good with them. Oh, I know she's got Negro blood in her veins, but that doesn't matter to me. I can't think of a better lady to raise my children. One other thing Obadiah! I believe Penelope loves you."

"My dear Audrey! Why do you think that?"

"Because, I see how she looks at you. I've known from the first time I met her and saw how she looked at you that she loves you."

"Audrey, let's don't talk anymore about this tonight. You need your rest. I'm going to move my chair over here, and I'll sit by you the rest of the night."

"Obadiah, I'll be all right. You need your rest as well. I want you to go back to bed. I'm going to be all right. I love you, my darling, Obadiah. You are my soul mate and my love forever."

As I bent down to kiss her, I felt so ashamed. I felt I had betrayed her. I always knew Audrey was perceptive but had no idea she had sensed Penelope's love for me. Audrey trusted Penelope with her heart. She loved Penelope regardless of her Negro blood. She trusted Penelope with our children's lives. Hearing Audrey's kind words in regard to Penelope gave me a sense of comfort. As I closed my eyes, I promised God I would never touch Penelope again as long as my wife was alive. I would do nothing to endanger Audrey's trust for Penelope. So help me, God, I would keep this promise.

After breakfast, I found Penelope brushing Audrey's hair in our bedroom. I had not seen Penelope brush Audrey's hair before. As I stood there watching her make the slow strokes though Audrey's beautiful blonde hair, I wanted to cry. Here were two of the kindest and most considerate ladies one could ever hope to know. They were great together. God had given them the gift to look beyond the man-made boundaries of prejudice that had been created over generations by Southern culture.

I had previously told Audrey that I had made arrangements for Bill to drive Penelope to Sarah's house and on to the Prattville library to select some reading materials. I reminded Audrey that Mother was volunteering her services to take care of her and the kids today and that Mattie and Betsy would be helping. I looked at the clock on the wall and noticed I was running late. I quickly exited the house, jumped into my carriage, and headed to Prattville.

Since I had not seen Sarah since Christmas, I invited her and Penelope to have lunch with me after they finished their visit to the library. They met me at the hospital, and we walked to Pratt's restaurant, which was about one block away. I was wondering how Penelope would react walking into a restaurant with Sarah and me. Penelope's beauty would certainly turn some men's heads, I thought. Mrs. Adams's Prep School had taught Penelope well. No one could have guessed she was anything but a beautiful Southern white lady. Both Penelope and Sarah stood until I seated them at the table, a custom practiced by most Southern ladies.

Sarah couldn't wait to tell me about their morning.

"Obadiah, Mrs. Jacobs, the librarian, was most helpful in selecting reading and math materials for Penelope's school. When she asked me who Penelope was, I introduced her as Penelope Bradford, a cousin from Boston. I didn't think it was any of her business to know any more than that. Mrs. Jacobs was somewhat of a busybody and wanted to know why we needed the reading and math teaching supplies. I told her that Penelope was working with our children at Twin Oaks. Much to my surprise, she didn't ask any more questions."

"I'm glad everything went well. Are you ladies ready to order?" I asked.

"I am," Sarah said. "I'm so hungry! I'm telling you, I think I'm eating for three people," Sarah said, holding her stomach.

"Maybe you're having twins," I said.

"Oh, wouldn't that be just wonderful!" Sarah said.

"That would be most interesting since I've not known any Bradford girls having twins," I said.

"Obadiah, do we have a limit in the amount we can spend on our lunch?" Sarah asked, smiling.

"No limit for you ladies. You order what you like."

I was anxiously waiting to see what Penelope would order. Sarah ordered first. She ordered a nice Southern dish that included skillet friend chicken, creamed potatoes, green beans, and hot bread.

The waiter looked at Penelope and asked, "What will you be having, madam?"

"I'm going to have the same as Sarah," Penelope said.

"Good choice," the waiter said. "What would you like to drink?" he asked.

"I'll have water," Penelope said.

I was so impressed with her.

"Penelope, this restaurant has great desserts. I like their blackberry cobbler the best, but all their desserts are wonderful," Sarah said.

I hadn't seen Sarah since she found out she was with child. I congratulated her and asked when she was due. She informed me "about four months." When her food arrived, she dug right in and enjoyed every bite of her lunch. She meant it when she said she was hungry.

Penelope used her Southern graces as she ate slowly. No one would have guessed that she was a slave girl who had already dined in some of the best restaurants in Boston and now in the best restaurant in Prattville, Alabama.

While we were sitting in the restaurant, a group of business-men came in and were seated near our table. I recognized Jim Dawson, who was the superintendent of Daniel Pratt's cotton gin factory. I was sitting close enough to hear Mr. Dawson telling the other men that he had just read in the Montgomery Chronicle that the Southern Confederacy of America had just elected Jefferson Davis as provisional president and Alexander Stephens as provisional vice president. All of this took place yesterday in Montgomery, Alabama, he said.

This news was so very disturbing to me. Things were happening too fast. The Southern states that had seceded earlier had voted to take over all the federal forts and river ports located within their respective states. This was something, I'm sure, wasn't going to sit well with our new President Abraham Lincoln. I'm afraid their action will surely cause serious problems when Mr. Lincoln finally takes over the reins as president.

When we left the restaurant, I noticed several of the men turning their heads to take a good look at Penelope. She wore the burgundy hat that Audrey and I had gotten her for Christmas, along with a gorgeous black dress. She was a new face in town, and I'm sure they were wondering who I had been dining with. Knowing Jim Dawson, he will be asking me about her the next time we crossed paths. As far as I know, this was Penelope's first time in Prattville. She had handled herself like a Southern lady.

I escorted Sarah and Penelope to the carriage where Bill was waiting to take Sarah back to her home and Penelope back to Twin Oaks.

I found the next few weeks exhausting. Trying to be a doctor, husband, and father, and trying to keep up with all the things occurring in the Confederacy, was almost an impossible task. I was worried that if a civil war came, I would be caught in the middle. The Confederacy would surely need doctors to attend to the sick and wounded. I would feel bad not to fulfill my duties as a doctor if called upon by the Confederacy. In truth, I didn't want to fight, but I would volunteer my service because it would be the right thing to do.

Each day, I took time to read the newspaper. I had become just like my father. I couldn't stand not to know what was taking place day by day. As each event occurred, I was convinced that it was only a matter of time before we would be fighting a war that we couldn't win.

On February 4, 1861, Montgomery, Alabama, became the capitol of the Confederacy.

On February 18, 1861, Jefferson Davis was inaugurated as President of the Confederacy.

On March 4, 1861, Abraham Lincoln was inaugurated as President of the United States. He stated that his intentions were not to interfere with slavery where it exists and to preserve the Union.

On April 3, a Confederate battery on Morris Island in Charleston Harbor fired upon the American vessel Rhoda H. Shannon.

On April 4, President Lincoln advised Gustavus V. Fox, his representative and former naval commander, that Fort Sumter will be relieved. He drafted a letter for Secretary of War Simon Cameron to send to Major Robert Anderson, commander at Fort Sumter.

On April 6, President Lincoln informed South Carolina that an attempt will be made to resupply Fort Sumter but only with provisions.

On April 8, Confederate Secretary of State Robert Toombs opposed using force against Fort Sumter, but President Jefferson

Davis said that the Confederate States had created a nation, and he had a duty as its executive to use force if necessary.

On April 9, the Steamer Baltic, with Gustavus V. Fox as Lincoln's agent, sailed from New York for the purpose of relieving the Charleston Garrison.

On April 10, the USS Pawnee left Norfolk, Virginia, for Fort Sumter.

On April 11, Confederates demanded surrender of Fort Sumter. After discussing the matter with his officers, Major Robert Anderson refused to give up Fort Sumter but felt the garrison will be starved out in a few days without relief.

On April 12, the Confederates, knowing relief was on its way, opened fire on Ft. Sumter. Federal forces returned fire starting at 7:30 a.m., but the garrison was too small to man all guns, which were not all in working order. After a thirty-four hour bombardment, on April 13, Major Anderson surrendered Fort Sumter to the Confederates since his supplies and ammunition were nearly exhausted. Relief ships finally arrived but couldn't complete their mission due to the bombardment. There were four thousand shells fired at the fort but only a few minor injuries were sustained by the garrison. On April 14, Fort Sumter was formally surrendered to the Confederates.

On April 15, President Lincoln called on the United States of America to provide seventy-five thousand militia soldiers to recapture federal property and to suppress the rebellion. As soon as I read President Lincoln's order to recapture federal property and to suppress the rebellion, I knew there was no turning back. I dropped my head and prayed, "Lord, please help us all."

On April 17, Virginia seceded from the Union. On May 6, Arkansas seceded, followed by North Carolina on May 20 and Tennessee on June 8, 1861.

The Battle of First Bull Run, which occurred on July 21, 1861, was the first major battle of the war. After this battle, it became clear to everyone in the South and North that there could be no compromise between the Union and the seceding states, and that a long and bloody war could not be avoided. All hope of a settlement short of a catastrophic war was lost.

It was now August 1861. The cotton and corn crops were looking good throughout Autauga County. It appeared we would have another bumper cotton crop. So far, Alabama hadn't been affected by the civil war. Right now, Virginia was seeing the most fighting. In the Battle of First Bull Run in Virginia, the Confederacy was able to beat back the Northern army to Washington. This bought the South a little more time. It now appeared that the South was going to be greatly outnumbered if it had to rely on a volunteer army. The North had already passed a conscription law which drafted men into its army. The Confederacy was considering doing the same.

During the month of August, Audrey's health began to deteriorate at an alarming rate. She was now confined to her bed. When she needed to go to the bathroom, Penelope enlisted the help of Big Jim to lift her out of bed onto her chair. We were now feeding Audrey her meals. She had grown so weak that she couldn't even handle a spoon or hold a glass in her hands. Since I left early for work in the mornings, Penelope fed Audrey both her breakfast and lunch meals. During the evening, I fed her dinner. The stroke had done more damage than I had first thought. Unless God performs a miracle, I don't think my Audrey will be with us much longer. It's apparent that she's getting weaker by the day.

On Monday, before leaving for my scheduled appointment at James Jones's plantation, I had a meeting with Penelope and Mother. I reported to them that it wasn't looking good for Audrey. I informed them I had ordered a wheelchair, which was supposed to be delivered today. I wanted Audrey to be wheeled to the front porch at least two times a day. I wanted to see if it might make a difference in her mental attitude. She loved the outdoors, and I thought the fresh air and sunshine might do her some good.

I pulled up in front of James Jones's plantation around ten o'clock in the morning. As soon as I stopped my carriage, Mason was there to meet me.

"Good morning, Doctor Bradford."

"Good morning, Mason! What can I do for you this morning?"

"We need you to look at some of our male slaves who have that impetigo. Some of them have it pretty bad. We also have three female slaves who are expecting in the next few weeks."

"Let's take a look at those female slaves first."

"I need to tell you something before you get all out of sorts."

"All right, Mason, what is it?"

"One of the female slaves is Teshia."

"You've got to be kidding me. Need I ask you who the father is?"

"I think you've guessed, Dr. Bradford."

"Mason, you are the scum of the earth. Why would you do that to Teshia? You know she almost died the last time you got her with child."

"Dr. Bradford, I love that girl, and she loves me. I moved her in with me, and she's been happy. I've taken good care of her and her folks. Our baby boy, Joseph, is doing well also."

"Mason, I gave up on you a long time ago. I won't give up on Teshia and her little boy, however. I think too much of her to give up on her. You better hope she's in good shape so she can give birth to this child. Where is she?"

"She's over there in that cabin. Come on, I'll go with you."

I wanted to choke the life out of Mason. He just couldn't leave her alone. I'm convinced he's a sick man. I wish I could do something about him. If Mr. Lincoln makes all slaves free this might be the best thing for Teshia. As we entered the cabin, Teshia got up from a rocking chair where she had been holding her baby boy. She struggled to get to her feet because of her size. She was really big, too big for her age and body frame. I hope she's in better shape than what I'm observing.

"Dr. Bradford, it's good to see you again," Teshia said, as she slowly walked across the room to shake my hand.

"Teshia, it's good to see you, too. How are you feeling?"

"I'm all right, I guess. I have to stay off my feet because they swell badly."

"Mason, I'd like to examine Teshia alone, if I may?"

"All right, I'll be on the front porch."

"Teshia, is Mason being good to you?"

"He's all right to me, Dr. Bradford. He makes sure me and Joseph get what we need."

"Joseph is a nice looking little boy."

"Me or my Joseph wouldn't be alive if it wasn't for you."

"Let's take a look at you, Teshia. I need to examine you. This may hurt a little, but it's what I do to check to see if you are dilating — that means if you are getting close to your time in having the baby."

I listened to both Teshia and the baby's hearts, and both of them sounded normal. Teshia's blood pressure was normal as well. She was one tough little girl. Teshia had dilated several centimeters and could go into labor anytime. I encouraged her to stay off her feet as much as possible. She indicated she understood. I told her to have Mason send for me when she went into labor.

After leaving the cabin, I told Mason basically what I had told Teshia. At this point in time, I didn't see anything that alarmed me, but I encouraged him to send for me as soon as she went into labor. She was still a very young girl, and anything could happen. He assured me he would send for me.

The other two female slaves would be having their babies any time now. They shouldn't have any problems.

"How's Minnie doing?" I asked Mason.

"Oh, she's fine. She's the head household maid at the big house now."

"Minnie deserves that recognition. Please tell her that I want her to assist me when Teshia goes into labor."

"I'll tell her, Dr. Bradford."

I gave Mason medicine for the impetigo and then left for my next stop at the Campbell plantation.

It had been a long day, and I was exhausted. I couldn't get Teshia and Mason off my mind. What kind of man could continually abuse a girl of Teshia's age? I had anticipated he would try to hit me when I called him a scum of the earth. I was prepared to duck if his fist came my way. I had no respect for a man of his character. My only hope was that someday, Teshia would be free and rid of Mason.

As I arrived home, I found Audrey sitting on the front porch in her new wheelchair. The temperature had cooled down, and she and Mother were sitting together on the porch.

George met me as I drove up; he took my horse and carriage to the barn. As I walked up the stairs and onto the porch, I saw Audrey smiling at me. Although she was frail and weak, she still had the sweetest smile in the world.

"Good evening, ladies!"

"Good evening, Son," my mother replied.

"Good evening, Dr. Bradford," Audrey mumbled as she smiled.

"How are you feeling?"

"I love my wheelchair," she said and smiled.

"I'm glad. I thought you might enjoy sitting out here on the porch watching the animals and the birds."

"Thank you, Obadiah. I have enjoyed my day out here."

"Obadiah, you take my chair," Mother said. "I'll go and check on supper while you and Audrey visit," Mother said as she went inside.

I moved Mother's chair next to Audrey's so I could hold her hand. Audrey appeared to be happy. It was a little warm, but she loved summer. Hot weather never seemed to bother her. We were having a good visit when Mother came out of the house and announced that dinner was ready.

I pushed Audrey to the dining room where Mattie wiped her face and hands with a clean cloth. Penelope entered the room with Charles and Belle. I picked Charles up and gave him a big hug. I then held Belle until Mattie and Betsy started delivering the food. Penelope put Charles in a high chair next to Audrey. Penelope then sat down by Charles and held Belle as she fed her. As I watched Penelope feed my children, I knew Audrey was right. She would certainly be a good mother. While I ate supper, I took time to feed Audrey as well. I enjoyed feeding Audrey. It gave me a sense of satisfaction knowing that I could be of help in looking after my wife.

CHAPTER 35

In early September, a few weeks after purchasing Audrey's wheelchair, my hopes were shattered because Audrey wasn't making any progress. I had hoped for improvement in her health after moving her to the front porch where she could enjoy fresh air and sunshine. Instead, her health was worsening each day. I made the decision not to put her through the two-a-day trips to the front porch. Her heart was weakening, and I wasn't certain how much physical activity she could stand. My medical diagnosis indicated that Audrey's death was drawing near. I estimated that she could live two to three more days.

I sent Bill to the Denton plantation with a note encouraging them to come as quickly as they could. I explained to them that Audrey's health had taken a turn for the worse. I felt they needed to know. I would have found it hard to forgive myself if Audrey died before her parents had an opportunity to say goodbye. Audrey was their only daughter. She had one unmarried brother, Samuel Denton, who lived in Atlanta, Georgia.

I found it difficult to share Audrey's health condition with Mother and Penelope. Like me, they had hoped she would improve and get well. They had dedicated themselves to a momentous task of trying to improve Audrey's physical condition. No one could have asked for better nursing care and physical therapy. Penelope had spent hours upon hours giving Audrey her prescribed physical therapy. I had no sooner finished explaining what was going to happen to Audrey when Mother screamed out, "Oh, Lord, have mercy on our beautiful Audrey." When she said that, Penelope began to cry as well. It was at this very moment that I discovered I wasn't good at calming ladies who were hurting inside. My consoling didn't do much good. Their feelings went beyond anything I could say or do to help comfort them. They loved Audrey with all their hearts and had given their very best to help her.

"Obadiah, don't you think we should inform the family?" Mother asked.

"Mother, I considered that, but I don't think Audrey has the strength to receive visitors."

"Obadiah, if she's going to die, I don't think it would hurt if the family came by to say their goodbyes. I know Sarah would be crushed if she wasn't afforded the opportunity to say goodbye."

I had learned from past years not to question Mother's wisdom. She normally was right. After what Mother said, I prepared notes for Bill and George to carry to Dent and other family members. My note said, "Urgent! Audrey's health condition has turned for the worst. I don't think she will be around more than two days. If you would like to say your goodbyes, this would be the time. Please pray for her and all of us. Love to all! Obadiah."

The Dentons were the first to come. Audrey was in her bed resting when they arrived. I escorted them to our bedroom. They spent about thirty minutes with Audrey. After Mrs. Denton became emotional, Mr. Denton felt it best for them to say their goodbyes. As they came out of the room, Mrs. Denton was crying loudly. She was shaking so badly she was having trouble standing. I asked Penelope to accompany her to the bathroom and stay with her until she calmed down.

"We will be in the parlor when she feels well enough to join us," I said to Penelope.

Mr. Denton had asked if he and Mrs. Denton could spend some time with the kids. I arranged for Mattie to bring the children to the parlor where I had ordered refreshments.

After Mrs. Denton regained her composure, she and Mr. Denton played with Charles and Belle for a little over an hour.

The next two days were emotional for everyone. My entire family of brothers and sisters, except for Mary who lived in El Dorado, Arkansas, came by to pay their last respects to Audrey. The night Audrey went to be with the Lord, she asked me if I would come and sit with her by her bed.

"My dear, Obadiah! Last night an angel of God appeared to me in my dream. He was a good-looking angel. I'm not calling him good-looking to make you jealous, you do understand?" she said with one of her beautiful smiles.

"Yes, my dear, I think I understand!"

"Anyway, the angel of the Lord told me that it was time for me to come to be with my Savior, Jesus Christ. I'm ready, Obadiah! I still hate to leave you and the children, but the angel said I will see everyone again someday. He said that one day in God's Kingdom was like a thousand years on earth, so it would seem a short time before I see my children and you. I was comforted by that thought."

"Oh, Audrey, I love you so much! You have brought joy into my life, and you were just what God wanted for me. I, too, will look forward to that glorious day when we will be together again."

"Obadiah, Charles and Belle need to have a loving mother to raise them — someone whom they can love and trust. I believe that someone is Penelope. She is so good with Charles and Belle. They love her like a mother. I want you to think about Penelope. She would be good for you and the kids."

"Audrey, have you said anything to Penelope?"

"To be truthful with you, yes!"

"What did you talk about?"

"We talked about what we're talking about right now."

"What was her reaction?"

"She first, like you, didn't want to discuss it. But finally she agreed to hear me out."

"What did you say to her?"

"I told her I appreciated everything she had done for me, the children, and you. I told her I felt she was in love with you, and I was pleased about that. I told her I felt you had loved her from the first time you met her."

"Oh, Audrey, you told her all of that?"

"It's the truth, Obadiah. You do love her. It's not wrong to love two women. I've been the lucky one. I've had the pleasure of being your wife. I've had the enjoyment of sharing your bed and having your children. See, Obadiah, I've been the blessed one. I've not been jealous of you and Penelope. I knew in my heart you were faithful to me and have always been faithful to me. I can certainly understand how you could love Penelope, and I fully understand how she loves you."

"Oh, my dear Audrey! God will surely rejoice daily by having you in his Heavenly Kingdom. Your loving spirit will cheer him up when he's sad."

"Obadiah, I'm not afraid to die. I'm ready to see Jesus and all those who we've read about in the good book all these years. The angel tells me it's going to be a joyful experience."

"Audrey, I will miss you so very much," I said, as I began to cry.

I couldn't stop my crying. I had tried to remain strong, but the thought of Audrey dying hurt so badly. My heart ached like never before. I realized then how much I loved her. God had been so good to me. He had given me a wife who had made me happy, and yet, let me love another lady as well. *How many men get this opportunity?* I thought.

"Obadiah, I need to see my children now. Will you please have Penelope bring them to me? Please hurry, Obadiah."

I almost sprinted to the door. I knew she felt something inside that was giving her a warning. I picked Charles up in the hall and asked Penelope to bring Belle. My mother heard the commotion and came in behind us.

"Audrey, the kids are here."

I placed little Belle by her side and put Charles in a chair near her so she could touch him.

She reached and touched Belle's beautiful face. Tears were welling in her eyes, and were soon streaming down her cheeks.

"Daddy, why is Mommy crying?" Charles asked.

"Mommy's sad," I said.

"Why is Mommy sad?" Charles asked.

This is one time I wished Charles hadn't asked. What kind of answer was I going to give him? He had stood up in his chair and was wiping Audrey's tears from her cheeks with his small hands. I began to choke up again. This was one of the hardest things I had ever done. *Lord, please help me to say and do the right thing, right now.*

The words finally came to me.

"Charles, Mommy is going to sleep, and she's sad she won't get to see you and Belle for a long time."

"Mommy, don't cry! I'll see you in the morning," Charles said as he touched her face.

I looked around at Mother and Penelope, and they, too, were crying. I couldn't hold back my tears. I wanted to be strong for both Audrey and the kids, but saying goodbye was too hard.

Audrey closed her eyes as she lowered her hand from little Belle's face. I knew time was near. I quickly picked up Belle and handed her to Penelope. I gave Charles to Mother and asked them to take them out of the room. I didn't want them to see their mother die.

"Audrey, can you hear me?" I asked.

Audrey opened her eyes. She looked up at me and said, "Thank you, Obadiah, for letting me see my children."

"Audrey, I promise you I'll take good care of our children. I'll speak of you often. I will tell them how much you loved them. I will tell them how you loved the outdoors, how you loved to ride Millie, and how you loved fishing. They will know and feel your presence in their lives, that I promise you, my love."

Audrey looked at me and tried to reach up for me but was too weak. I put my lips on hers and kissed her for the last time. I could feel the life leaving her. Her last words she mumbled to me were, "I love you, Obadiah," as she gave up the ghost.

I don't know how long I stood over her with her in my arms. It seemed like a long time. My legs had become numb from bending too long. I couldn't seem to turn her loose. I heard the door open, and my mother came through the door.

"Obadiah, is she gone?"

I gently laid her back on her pillow and said, "Yes, Mother, she's gone to be with Jesus."

Mother slowly walked over to me and leaned her head against my shoulder as we both stood there and looked at one of the greatest women of all times. She was so courageous!

We buried Audrey in the Oak Hill Cemetery in Prattville, not far from where we had laid my Father, James Bradford, to rest. Father had purchased a large burial plot in the cemetery for the Bradford family. It was his and Mother's desire that their children and family members be buried in the Bradford plot.

Audrey's funeral was both beautiful and sad. She was well known in Prattville from her days working at Daniel Pratt's ladies' shop and from her church membership in the Oak Hills Baptist Church. The gravesite service was the hardest part. I was afraid as they lowered Audrey's body into the grave that Charles might ask, "Daddy, why are they putting Mommy in the ground?" What was I to tell him? Fortunately, he didn't ask questions.

The months of September and October brought on the cotton harvest. Again, we had a bumper cotton and corn crop. The rich soil of Autauga County was best suited for cotton. I can't remember a bad year yet for cotton or corn on the Twin Oaks plantation.

Another letter came from my sister Mary Shadrack. She apologized for not being able to be here for Audrey's funeral. Again, Mary spoke highly of her town, El Dorado, and the rich cotton soil there. She also reminded me that El Dorado needed another doctor badly, and the cotton plantation was still up for sale in the Norphlet community a few miles from El Dorado.

It has entered my mind several times to sell my share of Twin Oaks to my brothers, John and Dent, and move to El Dorado, Arkansas. Times have been difficult around the plantation since Audrey's death. I'm torn between my mourning of Audrey and my agonizing feelings toward Penelope. I will have to reconcile this problem before it drives me crazy.

It was now Christmas at Twin Oaks. Again, Mother had the entire family at Twin Oaks for Christmas. Dent, being his normal self, perceived that I wasn't very happy. When he asked me if I was ready for our yearly stroll in mother's garden, I said, "Yes."

"It's been about three and a half months now since Audrey's death. How are things going with you?" Dent asked.

"To tell you the truth, not so well. I miss her."

"Obadiah, I'd like to get personal with you, if I may?"

"Getting personal with me has never stopped you before, big brother!"

"You know me, Little Brother. I can read you like a book."

"All right, what personal things do you want to discuss with me?"

"You've gone a long time without a woman. How are you and Penelope doing?"

"If you're asking me if we've been together, the answer is no."

"Obadiah, you are making this all too difficult for yourself."

"What do you mean by that, Dent?"

"Audrey's gone; she's dead. No one is going to bring her back to life. You need to get on with your life. She would want you to do that, Obadiah."

"All right, Dent! If you want to know why I'm so miserable it's because of Penelope. I agonize over her. I want her, I need her, but yet, I know I can't have her. Yes, I'm very aware that I could sleep with her. She is more than willing. I want to, Dent, but God keeps telling me that it would be wrong. I believe he wants me and Penelope to be together, but to be together as husband and wife and not a slave owner and his slave girl. I've asked God to show me a plan to make this happen. But he's not done it yet."

"Little brother, it's very obvious you love Penelope and have loved her from the first time you laid eyes on her. If you love her and want to marry her, then leave Autauga County and go some place where no one knows you and marry. Don't wait until it's too late. She looks white, and no one would ever know the difference."

"Since you brought up the subject, let's talk about it. Mary has been trying to get me interested in moving to El Dorado, Arkansas. She says there is only one doctor there, and there is a plantation for sale in the Norphlet community, a few miles from El Dorado. I've been thinking this might be just the opportunity for Penelope and me. Virgil, Mary, and the kids are the only ones who know us. Since Penelope looks white, this could be the solution to our happiness. We could be together there as husband and wife."

"I agree with you; Virgil and Mary wouldn't tell anyone in El Dorado that Penelope was once a slave. This may be just the plan God wants you to pursue. It might be the smartest thing you ever did. Little Brother, I'm tired of seeing you miserable."

"Dent, there is only one thing standing in my way in moving to El Dorado."

"What?"

"The civil war! What if I get called up to serve in the war? What then?"

"That's a strong possibility, one that we all may have to face," Dent said.

"I've got to decide soon what to do. The Confederacy is thinking about passing a conscription law, which would force men between the ages of 20 and 35 to serve up to three years. If I were to enlist now, I might avoid being drafted and be able to opt out with a year's service. Daniel Pratt thinks that doctors might be exempted from the war, but this is all speculation right now. I'm really struggling about what to do!"

"What would you do with Twin Oaks?"

"I've been thinking about that as well. I thought I would approach you and John to see if you guys might be interested in buying Twin Oaks."

"I don't know if we could come up with that type of money, Obadiah. I personally know what Twin Oaks is worth. If John was interested, I would be interested in exploring a partnership with him."

"Why don't you two talk about it? I know Father and Mother would want us to keep the plantations in the Bradford family. It's possible that if you two wanted Twin Oaks, we could work out an installment plan. I'm sure I would need money for a down payment on the plantation in El Dorado. But after that, if I could get a yearly payment from you and John, I could make my payment on the property in El Dorado."

"Do me a favor, Obadiah; don't mention this to anyone, especially to Mr. Daniel Pratt. He's always wanted Twin Oaks, and he has the money to buy it."

"I promise I won't say a word to Mr. Pratt."

"Obadiah, are you sure you want to keep denying Penelope. You need her, and she needs you. What happens if you're killed in a battle or injured so badly that you won't ever be able to marry Penelope? Do you think she would want to take care of a cripple for the rest of her life? Are you listening to me, Little Brother?"

"I've been thinking about all of this as well. I don't want to wait, but even if I moved to El Dorado what assurance would I have that I wouldn't have to fight for the Confederacy as a citizen of the state of Arkansas. Then what would I do?"

"Obadiah, since you plan to someday marry Penelope why don't you consider — I mean consider seeing her on the side? I know this goes against everything you believe in, but Penelope wants you as much as you want her. A year is a very long time!"

"I somehow knew you would bring this option up again. I don't know what to do, Dent. It's wrong to do what you're suggesting. I believe God would punish me in some way if I did that. I've asked myself over and over what is more important in life: a life with a clean conscience and walking daily with my Lord and Savior, Jesus Christ or a life filled with sinful pleasures? I believe I will choose a life in Jesus Christ."

"I'm telling you, Little Brother, you are more of a Christian than I am. I'm afraid I would have to have her now."

"Dent, please pray with me on this. Do ask God what he would have me do, not what I want, but what he wants for me."

"I just hate to see you miserable when I know you don't have to be."

"I love you, Dent. You're my big brother, and I'll always appreciate your thinking of my best interest. But I have to do what I think is right in God's eyes."

"All right, let's go get some of Mattie's dessert," Dent said.

CHAPTER 36

The month of January started off with another big snow. We didn't have the ice as we did during last January, but plenty of white snow. It was knee deep in places. I was still in a quandary on what to do about the Civil War. If I waited for the draft, I would have a commitment for three years. If I volunteered now, there was a good possibility that I would have only a one-year commitment. As I continued to ponder these questions, I decided to contact Daniel Pratt. Mr. Pratt had connections in high places. If anyone could help me, he would be the one. Mr. Pratt and I met for lunch at Pratt's restaurant.

When I arrived at the restaurant, I found him sitting at a corner table. He got up from his table and greeted me with a handshake.

"Obadiah, it's good to see you. Please have a seat," he said.

"It's good to see you, too, sir."

"I'd prefer you address me as Mr. Pratt. The sir makes me feel a little strange."

"Okay, thanks, Mr. Pratt."

"Let's order first and then we can talk," he said, as he waved for the waiter.

After we had placed our orders, Mr. Pratt looked at me and asked, "Obadiah, what's on your mind?"

"Mr. Pratt, the last several months has been some of the most difficult of my life. Losing Audrey in September has caused much grief. To complicate things, we are now involved in a civil war, which has further complicated things in my life. I'm now faced with making a decision about either volunteering or waiting to be drafted by the Confederacy. I've heard, as of late, that President Jefferson Davis may ask the Confederate Congress to pass an Enrollment Act in April of this year. If it is enacted, it's my understanding that it carries a three-year service requirement for all able-bodied men between the ages of 20 and 35. Being a medical doctor, owner of a three-hundred-acre plantation, looking after my elderly mother, and most importantly, raising my two small children, I don't see how I can make a three-year commitment."

"Obadiah, first of all, let me say I'm sorry about Audrey's death. She was a wonderful lady, and I know you must miss her a lot."

"I do miss her."

"Obadiah, it's apparent to me you have more than one good reason not to enlist or accept a draft based upon the so-called Enrollment Act. I've seen a rough draft of the act, and it exempts certain professional people, such as hospital personnel. As you are aware, I'm on the draft board here in Autauga County, and if you, or any of my doctors are drafted, I will certainly represent you before the board. We need every doctor we have to staff our hospital right here in Prattville."

"I've been hearing that anyone who volunteers would only have to commit to a one-year service. I really don't want to fight in a battle, but I would feel bad not to serve my country in the capacity of a doctor caring for the sick and wounded."

"Obadiah, I hear what you're saying. Right now, that's what the law says, but come April this can all change. Even if you did volunteer, you would still be faced with the same problem of leaving your family and plantation for a year."

"Mr. Pratt, you're right, but one year is much better than three."

"Obadiah, let me dig a little deeper into this volunteer thing. It might be possible to connect you with a hospital in Virginia or Tennessee. Those states seem to be doing all the fighting right now. I'm hearing they are begging for doctors to attend the wounded. If you feel strongly about serving, maybe we could get you in a hospital setting where you would be safer than on a battlefield. Give me a few days, and let's get back together for lunch. How does that sound?"

"That sounds great!"

"Obadiah, I'd like to remind you that I strongly believe you could be exempted from this crazy war. As I've mentioned already, I believe there will be provisions in the Enrollment Act that will give local draft boards an opportunity to exempt hospital doctors. But because of your interest in serving your country and to utilize your medical skills to save lives, I will certainly do what I can to help you."

I left our meeting feeling good about the whole situation. Mr. Pratt often rubs elbows with people of influence. I didn't mind asking for his help. I decided not to share my future plans with Mr. Pratt. I didn't want him to know that I was planning to leave Autauga County in a year or so. He might decide not to help me if he knew I wasn't planning to return to the Autauga County Hospital.

Since my visit with Mr. Pratt, I'm getting anxious. I need to know something. One thing I've noticed about myself for years is patience is not my best virtue. When I fail to get things resolved in my mind, it drives me crazy. This civil war could very well change the course of my life forever.

Two weeks later, I received a note from Daniel Pratt. The note started with an apology. "Obadiah, please forgive me for not getting back with you sooner. Our project has taken longer than I had anticipated. But I'm ready to share what I know with you. Please meet me for lunch today at twelve o'clock noon at Pratt's restaurant. I look forward to your response. Daniel Pratt."

In my note to Mr. Pratt, I said, "I would be happy to meet with you for lunch. Obadiah Bradford."

For our first meeting, he beat me to the restaurant. This time I decided to arrive early and get us a table. After arriving, I asked the waiter to seat us at the same corner table where we had eaten before because it was a quieter location. Pratt's restaurant was famous for its lunch specials, and drew large crowds. Most days, it was very noisy.

I had just gotten seated when Mr. Pratt came through the door of the restaurant. I saw him talking to the door greeter who pointed in my direction. Mr. Pratt waved at me and headed my way.

"Obadiah, how are you?"

"I'm doing fine," I said, as we shook hands and sat down.

"Have you been waiting long?"

"Not really! Maybe five minutes at the most," I said.

"That's good! It bothers me to be late for appointments. I apologize to you."

"No apologies necessary."

Mr. Pratt recommended a lunch that included an assortment of meats. The meal consisted of two sides, a green salad, and fresh baked bread. "Obadiah, you are going to like this dish," he said with a smile.

"My mouth is already watering," I said.

"Obadiah, I believe I have some interesting news to share with you."

"Please tell me! I can hardly wait!"

"Well, first of all, I can assure you that if you volunteer now, you will only have to serve one year. Secondly, you will get an honorable discharge after the one-year service, but you can only get an honorable discharge if you stay honorable," Mr. Pratt said smiling.

"Here is the part you may not like. To get this deal, you will need to volunteer for Captain James F. Waddell's 20th Alabama Artillery Battalion that is currently being organized. After you become a part of this battalion, you will be transferred to the Army of the Mississippi. The Army of the Mississippi is under the command of General Albert Sidney Johnston. From what I can find out, there will be a great need for doctors in upcoming battles in Tennessee and Mississippi. The Confederate Army is badly in need of doctors. It's my understanding that tents and farm houses are being used as hospitals in most locations where battles are being fought. Obadiah, I'm afraid it's not going to be a pretty sight when these men are brought in wounded, butchered, and bleeding. You will not have a nice clean hospital room to operate in. You will be lucky if you have a decent table to do an operation on."

"Mr. Pratt, from what you're telling me, I'm going to have to act fast."

"I'm afraid so, Obadiah. If this is what you truly want to do, I can help you by getting your paper work processed. Are you one hundred percent sure you want to do this?"

"I don't know about the one hundred percent, but I'm convinced that I need to serve my country. I appreciate your help, Mr. Pratt. How can I repay you?"

"You don't owe me a cent. You've already helped me by being on our hospital staff. You have a wonderful reputation. I don't know anyone who doesn't like you, except maybe that Mason guy, who is the overseer of Mr. James Jones's plantation. But he doesn't count!"

"You had me going there for a minute, Mr. Pratt."

"I know you need a little time to get all this processed in your head. Please let me know when you are ready, and I'll start the paper work. Remember one thing. After you finish your commitment, I'm expecting you back here as a member of our medical staff."

At this time, our plates were served, and we ate the delicious meal with light conversation about non-important things.

The first person I had to talk to was my mother. I didn't know how she'd feel being at Twin Oaks without my presence. She and Penelope would become the caretakers of Charles and Belle while I was away. *How would she feel about this?* I wondered.

I decided I must talk with her after dinner tonight.

After we finished our dinner meal, I asked Mother if she had time to visit with me in the parlor. She looked at me and asked, "What's this all about, Obadiah?"

"I just need your opinion on a few things."

"Certainly, why don't we take our desserts into the parlor and I'll have Mattie bring us a fresh pot of coffee?"

Before we left for the parlor, I watched Penelope feed little Belle. Belle looked so much like Audrey. She had the softest blonde hair and gorgeous blue eyes. Penelope was so good with her. She would eat every bite Penelope gave her. As I sat watching them, I totally agreed with Audrey. Penelope was the lady I should marry to help me raise Charles and Belle. In fact, if

God blessed Penelope and me with children that, too, would be a blessing. I helped Charles with his dessert. He didn't finish it, so like most fathers, I made sure that good dessert didn't go to waste.

Penelope handed Belle to me while she cleaned Charles and his mess from his high chair. I gave Belle a kiss on the cheek as I said, "Sweet dreams, Belle."

I passed her to Penelope as I picked Charles up and gave him a big bear hug. He loves bear hugs. "Good night, Charles! I will see you in the morning," I said as I gave him a good night kiss.

Mother left the room and said, "I'll meet you in the parlor in about three minutes."

As I sat waiting for Mother, Mattie entered the parlor with apple pie and a pot of fresh brewed coffee.

"Mattie, that coffee smells so good!" I said.

"Thank you, Master Obadiah! I brought your favorite dissert as well. I hope you enjoy it!"

It was at this time Mother entered the room. She said, "Mattie that coffee smells so very good." Mattie poured Mother her coffee and exited the parlor.

"All right, Obadiah, what's on your mind?" Mother asked.

"I've got something really serious to talk to you about, Mother."

"Oh, Obadiah, you want to marry Penelope, don't you?"

I almost strangled on my coffee when Mother raised that question. She had caught me completely off guard.

"Mother, that's not exactly what I wanted to discuss with you."

"Oh, Obadiah, I'm so sorry. It just popped into my mind, and I just blurted it out."

"All right, we might as well talk about Penelope right now since you brought her up. Yes, Mother, I do want to marry Penelope. I'm in love with her. I want her to help me raise the children.

"I know we can't be together here in Autauga County, but I was thinking we might move to El Dorado, Arkansas, and start a new life where no one knows about Penelope's background."

317

"What are you going to do with me?"

"That's the subject I needed to talk to you about. I need to explain something to you and get your honest opinion on what I should do. I would never make a serious decision without first discussing it with you."

"Oh, Obadiah, thank you! I was afraid you were about to abandon your old Mother."

"Oh, no, Mother! I would never abandon you."

"All right, what are these plans you want to discuss with me?"

"I found out that in April, President Davis is planning to ask the Confederate Congress to vote on an Enrollment Act. If this passes, and I believe it will, I'm at the right age to be drafted for the Civil War. The act calls for a mandatory three-year commitment to the Confederacy. I don't see how I can make a three-year commitment when I've got a family, a mother, a plantation, and a medical practice to look after. So Mr. Pratt looked into me volunteering my service for a one-year commitment. I would still have to serve the Confederacy for one year, but that wouldn't be as bad as three years."

"Oh, Obadiah, what if you are killed? What would we do without you? Oh, I can't bear even thinking about it!"

"Mother, I wouldn't be in battle. I would be working in a hospital attending the sick and wounded."

"When do you have to make up your mind?"

"Soon. I need to get started in a few days getting the paperwork completed."

"Oh, me! Oh, me! What are we going to do without you?"

"That's where you come in, Mother. I would want you to stay here at Twin Oaks with Penelope and the kids. The kids will need you."

"Obadiah is there not a way you can be exempted from this volunteering or draft or whatever it's called?"

"I'm afraid not, Mother. I'm thirty years old, and the draft is written to include able-bodied men from the ages of 20 to 35."

"Oh, my God, Obadiah! That age would get Marion, Dent's son!"

"Yes, Mother, I've thought about Marion. I need to talk to Dent."

"I'm telling you, our world is crumbling down around us. In a way, I'm glad your father isn't alive to see this happening. He prophesized this thing happening when all that mess in Kansas was going on. He was a smart man, you know."

"I agree with you; Father was a very smart man."

"Obadiah, I want to stay in my home. I can tell you right now, you can count on me to help look after Belle and Charles. Penelope is so good with them and they are never any problem."

"Yes, I agree. She is very good with them. I believe Belle thinks Penelope is her mother."

"Obadiah, let's get back to an earlier subject, Penelope. I've grown to love Penelope. She is one of the sweetest ladies I've known. You will probably keel over in your shoes when I say what I'm going to say, but you have to hear me out."

I sat there not knowing what Mother was going to say. For her to say, "You have to hear me out," was serious!

"Obadiah, I know you loved Audrey, but your father and I knew from the first time we saw you and Penelope looking at each other that you had something special together. I've known for years that you two would someday be together. I had no idea that Audrey's dying would speed up the process. If ever two people were meant to be together, it's you and Penelope. So there, I've said what's on my mind! I hope you like it!"

"Oh, Mother, it makes me happy to hear those words coming from your mouth. I do love Penelope with all my heart. You're right; I've loved her since the first day I set eyes on her in Selma. I want you to know, Penelope and I have never been together. I have respected God's teaching from the Bible and have respected your and Father's teachings."

"Obadiah, I know the temptations you've had to overcome, especially after Audrey had her stroke and couldn't be a wife to you. You had opportunities to go to Penelope, but you never did. I'm so proud of you, Son."

"Mother, time is running out for both me and Penelope. I'm now thirty years old and Penelope is twenty-four. We are in the prime of life. We need to be together."

"So you think pulling up stakes and moving to El Dorado would give you the opportunity to live with her as husband and wife?"

"Yes, Mother, I do. No one, other than Virgil and Mary, knows she is a slave. She looks white and heaven knows she's one of the prettiest and best educated ladies in the South, thanks to you and Father paying for her schooling in Boston."

"Son, I think you have a good plan, but what about me, Twin Oaks, and your medical practice?"

"Mary tells me that El Dorado has only one doctor. I could start a medical practice there and make a good living. There is a cotton plantation that Virgil is looking into for me. The plantation is at a little place called Norphlet, Arkansas, a few miles north of El Dorado."

"All right, that takes care of two of the concerns. What about Twin Oaks? You know your father would want you to keep Twin Oaks in the family."

"I've been thinking about that as well. Dent and John are discussing maybe buying me out."

"Do John and Dent know all that is happening?"

"No, just the Twin Oaks part and the possibility of my moving to El Dorado."

"All right, I guess that leaves one other thing that has to be resolved. What about me? Will you take me to El Dorado with you?"

"Oh, Mother, would you go? Would you leave Sarah, Tanyua, John, and Dent and move to El Dorado with me?"

"Of course, I would. You should know you're my baby boy, one whom I love more than life itself. We have always been the best of friends. You are special to me, Obadiah. Do you think I would let you take Belle and Charles off to El Dorado without their grandma tagging along? No, sir. If you will have me, I'd love to move to El Dorado."

"Mother, you have just made me the happiest person on earth. I was afraid you would throw a fit."

"Obadiah, I love your sisters and brothers, but my baby needs me. My health is still good for a sixty-three-year-old gal, and I'm still active in sewing and bridge clubs. I bet El Dorado will have some bridge and sewing clubs, don't you think? Another thing, according to Mary, El Dorado is just a two day-trip by train from Selma."

"Mother, lots of things are going to start happening in the next few days. I will need your help with the kids more than ever."

"Obadiah, you can count on me!"

"Thanks, Mother!"

"I have one more question for you."

"What is it, Mother?"

"After we move to El Dorado, will I still get my percentage of profits that I'm currently getting from Twin Oaks?"

"You certainly will. That's the only way I will agree to sell Twin Oaks to John and Dent. The paperwork will stipulate that you will continue to get your percentage of the profits as long as you live."

"That's good enough for me."

Penelope entered the room as Mother was leaving. "Master Obadiah, you wanted to see me?"

"Yes, I do, Penelope. Take a seat, please."

Penelope came over and sat in Mother's chair, which was located near where I was sitting in Father's chair.

"Penelope, first of all, I want to thank you for the good job you do with Charles and Belle. They love you."

"I love them as well, Master Obadiah. They are wonderful children."

"You are a big reason for that," I said, leaning forward in my chair.

"Penelope, I have something very important to talk to you about. Please don't discuss what I'm going to say with anyone. Do you understand?"

321

"Yes, I understand. I would never disrespect your wishes, Master Obadiah."

"Thank you, Penelope. I have some good news and some bad news. I think I'll start with the bad news."

"Oh, Master Obadiah, I hope nothing bad has happened."

"Penelope, I have to go away for a year. As you are well aware, the South is at war with the North. The Confederacy is asking all able-bodied men between the ages of 20 and 35 to either volunteer or be drafted into the service. If I volunteer, which I'm planning to do, I'll finish my requirement in one year. If I were to wait and be drafted, I might have to serve up to three years. Do you know what I mean by volunteering and being drafted?"

Penelope smiled at me and said, "Yes, Master Obadiah, I do know what those terms mean. It appears to me that you're planning to volunteer."

"That's correct, Penelope. There are good reasons that I need to volunteer. You are one of those reasons." I pulled my chair close enough to reach out and take her hands.

"What are you saying to me, Master Obadiah?"

"I'm saying that it is my plan to serve one year in the Confederate Army, come home, pack my goods, and move to El Dorado, Arkansas, where Mary and her family live."

"How will that affect me?"

"I'm taking you with me, Penelope. I want you to be my wife. I want to spend the rest of my life with you, and I want you to be the mother of my children. If we have children that will be another blessing."

"Oh, Master Obadiah, you're not teasing me, are you?"

"No, I promise you. I would never mislead you with something like that. This is what I want to do. While traveling to Arkansas, we could get married on the train."

Penelope jumped up from her chair and threw herself into my lap. She wrapped her arms around my neck and whispered, "I can't believe this is happening!"

"If you remember, I told you that I felt someday God would make it possible for you and me to be together. I had no idea it was going to be this soon. I have thought about this day for months now. Ever since Audrey passed on, I have longed for the day to be with you as husband and wife. I know that moving to El Dorado is the solution to our problem. There are too many people here in Autauga County who know you as a servant. Our marriage could not work here.

"Because of your beauty, your blue eyes, and the color of your skin, folks in El Dorado, Arkansas, will never know you're not white. You will be able to live there without someone treating you as a slave. You will be Mrs. Penelope Bradford, and you will surely be the best looking lady in town. This has to be God's plan for us."

"Oh, Obadiah, I've been waiting so long to hear you ask me to marry you. Before Audrey died, she asked if I would take care of you and the children. I reassured her that I would. I would go anywhere with you, regardless of whether we were married or not. All I want is your love and to be treated right."

"Penelope, I would never do anything to hurt you."

"I know that, Master Obadiah."

"I know you must be wondering what will happen to Mattie and her family."

"What is your plan for Mama?"

"I am taking Mattie and her family with us, along with several of our slaves. They will have a new home in El Dorado, Arkansas."

"Oh, Obadiah, I've spent hours praying that something like this would eventually happen. You don't know how much I've prayed."

"I want to make this official. Penelope, my love! As God is my witness, I'm asking you, down on my knees, to be my wife. I promise you I will love you as Christ loved his church. I will take care of you when you are sick. I will provide for all your needs, and I'll be faithful and true to you for the rest of my life. Will you marry me, my love?"

"Oh, yes, I'll marry you, Obadiah Bradford. I promise you I will do all the things you're needing and expecting."

It wasn't long before we were caught up in a passionate kiss, one that neither of us wanted to stop. For some reason, our kiss was distinctly different from the ones in the past. This time, it felt so right. It was like we didn't have to worry about being caught kissing. There was no shame in how we loved each other. We had loved each other from the first day we met at Selma some ten years ago. On that day, Penelope was fourteen years old. Today, she is twenty-four. Today, she's virtually stolen my heart away. I felt breathless!

"Penelope, I need some air. Wow! You've never kissed me like that before."

"You've never asked me to marry you before, either!"

"Penelope, you will wait for me for a year, won't you?"

"Master Obadiah, I've been waiting for you for ten years. I guess one more year isn't going to hurt me. I wished you didn't have to go, but I understand why you must. I have a question; does your mother know about your plans?"

"Yes, she does. That's what I've been discussing with her. She's in agreement."

"You mean she's all right with us getting married?"

"That's right! We have her blessings. She, too, will be moving with us to El Dorado. There will be enough room for all of us. Is that going to be a problem for you?"

"Master Obadiah, I love your mother. I want her to go with us. She loves Charles and Belle, and she would be very sad if she wasn't near them. By all means, I would welcome your mother."

"I, too, love Mattie and her family. I would like for her and her family to live with us in El Dorado. I really don't want to split up our family unit here at Twin Oaks. If President Lincoln has his way, I expect all slaves will get their freedom sometime in the near future. As I see it, Mattie and Big Jim will need a job to survive. It will be hard for slaves to make it on their own. Freedom may sound good, but if the slaves have to go around with empty stomachs, they will wish they still had a good master to turn to. If freedom does come to all slaves, I will continue to work my slaves, but they will be paid wages."

"Oh, Master Obadiah, I'm so happy!"

"I'm happy, Penelope, that you're happy. It's time you were rewarded for your loyalty and dedication to my family. I'm looking forward to a long life with you, my dear Penelope."

"When will you have to leave, and where will you go?"

"I'll have to leave soon. I will probably be located in either Mississippi or Tennessee. It appears right now that most of the Civil War battles are being fought in those states."

"Oh, Master Obadiah! What if you are killed? What will we do without you?"

"Penelope, I don't plan to be in any battles. My services will be in a hospital taking care of the sick and wounded. I should be safe."

"Will you write me?"

"I'll write you at every opportunity I get, but I'm guessing we doctors will be quite busy attending to the wounded."

"Can you tell me what you plan to do with Twin Oaks?"

"I'm going to sell it to John and Dent, providing they can come up with the money."

"What will you do in El Dorado, Arkansas?"

"I'm going to start a medical practice there. Mary Ann tells me that they have only one doctor in El Dorado. She said they need another doctor, badly."

"Then you don't plan to be a plantation owner?"

"Oh, yes! I plan to purchase another plantation with the funds I get from Twin Oaks. Our lifestyle won't change considerably in El Dorado. What El Dorado is going to do for you and me is allow us to start a new life as husband and wife. We will have the opportunity to live out our lives together, to cherish each moment we're together and enjoy watching our family grow up. If God finds favor in our marriage, he might even bless us with children of our own. Would you like that, Penelope?"

"Oh, Master Obadiah, I would love to give you lots of babies. I can hardly wait. When can I tell Mama?"

"I think it's best to wait until everything is finalized. After that, you can tell your Mama, but Mattie must keep all this to herself. Do you understand?"

"I promise you I will respect your wishes, Master Obadiah."

"It's getting late and I need to get in bed. Tomorrow is going to be a busy day."

"May I ask you one more question before you go?" Penelope asked.

"Certainly, Penelope! What is it, my dear?"

"Master Obadiah, since we are planning to marry each other, what would be wrong with us spending some time together? I would be more than honored to give myself to you, if you know what I mean?"

"Oh, my dear, Penelope! You don't know how many times I've thought about making love to you, but every time I try to rationalize why it's all right, my conscience tells me it's still wrong. My God, and your God, our Lord and Savior Jesus Christ, teaches that sex outside of marriage is wrong. You are a virgin, and I want you to stay a virgin until we give ourselves to each other in holy matrimony. I cannot make love to you before we are married. I want our love to be perfect and right before God. Do you understand?"

"Yes, I do understand, but I know how long you've gone without a woman. I just wanted you to know that I'm here, and if you change your mind, I'll be ready. I have saved myself for you and you only, Master Obadiah. I will continue to save myself for you."

"Penelope, our day will come. Our love making will be wonderful. My philosophy has always been that something good is worth waiting for. I do thank you for your offer. I'm so thankful that you've found love in your heart for me. Please know that I do love you with all my heart and soul. Again, our day will come, my love."

I kissed Penelope once again, which was the wrong thing to do. Again, my passion rose. My heart and soul ached for her. I wanted to make love to this beautiful woman more than anything, but I knew it would be wrong. I felt as I prepared to go away to war that my God would protect me. I had to remain strong to my faith in Jesus Christ and what he's taught me through his Word. I will cling to his promises and someday Penelope and I will find blessings and happiness from waiting. In this, I am completely confidant.

CHAPTER 37

Mr. Pratt was very helpful in getting my paperwork to the right people. All I had to do now was to wait until I received word where I would be sent. I continued my duties at the hospital and my visits to the plantations as though I would be there indefinitely.

As each day passed, I found myself getting more and more anxious. As I've stated before, patience isn't one of my virtues. I had spent my free time making preparations for my departure. One major thing I did while waiting was to have my last will and testament prepared by our family lawyer, Mr. Jonathan Beckard. I felt it important that my children be properly cared for should I be killed while serving in the Confederate Army.

In my will, I left my estate to my children. I named Mother as their guardian. If my Mother was to die or become unable to look after my children, then they would go to live with my brother, Dent, who would then become their guardian. I also made provisions for Penelope, Mattie, Bill, and Betsy.

Before I left for lunch on March 10, 1862, I checked my incoming mail to see if I had gotten anything relating to my official orders. Much to my surprise, there was an official letter from General Albert Sidney Johnston's headquarters in Corinth, Mississippi. I quickly went to my office, sat down, opened the letter, and began to read.

Dear Dr. Obadiah Bradford:
General Albert Johnston appreciates your decision
to volunteer your service as a physician and soldier
under his command in the Army of the Mississippi.

This is to notify you that he would like for you to report to his command post in Corinth, Mississippi, on or before March 15, 1862.

We look forward to your dedicated service to the Army of the Mississippi and wish you a safe trip to Corinth.

Sincerely yours,

Lt. Marcus Johnson, Secretary to General Albert Sidney Johnston

I put the letter back in the envelope, folded it, and stuck it in my coat pocket as I left for lunch. As I ate lunch, I begin to wonder where Corinth, Mississippi was located and why Corinth? About mid-way through lunch, Henry Pratt came into the restaurant and asked if he could join me. I said, "Certainly, have a seat. I've got some news to tell you."

"What is this news, Obadiah?"

"I just got my orders to report to General Albert Johnston's command in Corinth, Mississippi, by March 15. Why Corinth, I really don't know!"

"I thank I can answer that question for you. It's my under-standing that Corinth's military importance is that two major railroads — the Memphis and Charleston Railroad running east and west and the Mobile and Ohio Railroad running north and south — cross in Corinth. I'm hearing that the Union Army wants to take control of Corinth so they can stop supplies being transported to the Confederate Army in the South. I'm thinking that's why General Johnston's army is in Corinth."

"That makes good sense to me."

"Obadiah, Is there anything I can do for you?"

"No, sir! You have done more than enough for me already. I've made arrangements at the hospital for someone to take my schedule and everything is all right on the home front. All I have to do now is get to Corinth, Mississippi, by March 15."

"Well, if there's anything I can do, just let me know. I'm picking up your lunch ticket today, young man. If I don't get to see you before you leave, you be safe, you hear? We want you back here in Prattville after you complete your assignment. I wish you well, Obadiah!"

"Thank you, Mr. Pratt. You've been wonderful in every way."

I arrived home just in time to join Mother, Penelope, and the children for dinner. I wasn't looking forward to telling Mother and Penelope about my leaving for Corinth, Mississippi. I knew I shouldn't put it off, however. I had only three days before I had to take the train to Corinth. I wanted to enjoy what time I had left with my family.

After Mattie and Betsy served our dinner, I decided I'd share my news with Mother and Penelope.

Mother, sensing I had something on my mind asked, "Obadiah, you seem to be a little distant tonight. What's going on?"

"I got my orders today, and I have to be in Corinth, Mississippi, by March 15."

"Where on earth is Corinth, Mississippi?"

"I'm told it's not far from Memphis, Tennessee."

"I've been thinking you'd be going to Virginia."

"I've been thinking either Tennessee or Virginia. That's where most of the fighting is. Corinth isn't far from the Tennessee border and it wouldn't surprise me if we didn't end up in Tennessee."

"If you have to report to Corinth by March 15, that doesn't give you much time to say goodbye to the family."

"I'm aware of that, Mother."

"I'll take care of that! We are going to have us a going-away party. I'm sending Bill and George to notify your brothers and sisters. They will want to be here to say goodbye to you."

I had not really expected a party, but knowing Mother, I wasn't going to challenge her. It would be nice seeing everyone before I left. I had not worried about being killed or wounded in the war, but in reality, this might be the last time I would see my family alive this side of heaven.

After Penelope put Charles and Belle to bed, we took a stroll in Mother's garden. It was cold, but the sky was full of stars, and the moon was full. It was just beautiful!

"Penelope, I have something to tell you."

"What is it, Obadiah?"

"I like you calling me Obadiah! It sounds better than Master Obadiah."

"Oh, Obadiah, I would never in the presence of other people refer to you only as Obadiah. I just wanted to see how it felt."

"I like it! I think it is only fitting for you to start calling me Obadiah."

"All right; what do you have to tell me?"

"There's always a possibility that I may be killed or wounded during my stint with the Confederate Army. If I was to be killed, I have made provisions in my will and last testament for you, Mattie, Bill, and Betsy. One of the provisions is to give you and your family your freedom. I also have made some financial provisions for you as well. If something was to happen to me, I would hope you would stay on and help Mother with Charles and Belle. However, that's not a requirement."

"Obadiah, I don't want to think about you being killed. You get that out of your head. We've come too far. I wouldn't want to live should anything happen to you. I want you to promise me, you will come back to us in one piece. You are not to be killed, you hear me?" she said as she put her arms around my neck and we kissed.

After I caught my breath, I said, "I promise you, I'll return to you."

Again, it was hard for me to resist the temptation of making love to this beautiful lady, one I loved and cherished more than life itself. Our love was real. I could search the world over and never find another Penelope. She and my children would be my strength in surviving this war.

CHAPTER 38

My entire family was present for my going-away party. Mother did an excellent job putting the party together. Just as I was headed for the refreshment table, I saw Dent coming across the room. I had been wondering when my big brother would corner me and quiz me about how Penelope was reacting to my departure to Corinth.

"Hey, Little Brother, what's going on?" Dent asked.

"All is well, Big Brother!" I said, as Penelope poured me another glass of eggnog.

"Is there anything I can do for you while you are away?"

"Thanks, Dent, but everything has been taken care of. You might look in on Mother and my children from time to time."

"I'll do that! Hey, let's take our annual stroll through Mother's garden. I could use some fresh air."

"That sounds like a good idea."

"Are you regretting making your decision to volunteer?" Dent asked.

"Dent, I wish I didn't have to go, but as sure as I didn't, I'd be caught up in a three-year draft, and I certainly don't want to have to deal with that."

"I don't blame you one bit, Obadiah. Sara and I have been worried about Marion. We've asked him not to volunteer. We're hoping the war will be over within a year. Maybe he won't have to go!"

"I'm hoping you're right about the length of the war. I'd like to see it end as soon as possible."

"How did Penelope take the news of you leaving?"

I knew this question was coming. Dent just can't stand not knowing what's going on between Penelope and me.

"Like everyone else, she hates to see me go but knows it's best for all of us to get this one-year commitment behind us."

"Have you two been together yet?"

"There you go again, Dent!"

"Well, I know you asked her to marry you, and I know she said yes."

"Who told you?"

"Our dear mother whispered that in my ear tonight."

"Then you probably know everything."

"No, I don't! I was just wondering since you've gotten yourself engaged to Penelope if this has done anything for your love life."

"Dent, our love is still strong and maybe more so than before, but no, we've not been having sex."

"I don't know how you do it, Little Brother."

"Strong will, and respect, my dear brother!"

"I've been trying to figure out why you're being sent to Corinth, Mississippi."

"I wondered that as well until Daniel Pratt enlightened me on the military importance of Corinth to both the South and the North."

"What kind of military importance?"

"There are two railroads that cross at Corinth. One goes east and west, the other north and south. The South wants to keep the railroads open to move supplies to the South, while the North wants control of Corinth to stop supplies from being shipped to the Confederate Army in the South. Does that make sense?"

"So are you saying the North and South will do battle at Corinth?"

"I think that's a strong possibility."

"Obadiah, although you may not be exposed to combat, you will still face danger. You be extremely careful. Don't take any unnecessary chances. Stay away from the battlefields. Concentrate on saving those soldiers who will be brought to you off the battlefield. You will have your hands full. You be alert and be safe, you hear!"

"Dent, by the grace of God, I'll survive this war. I believe in my heart that God wants Penelope and me to be together. She and the kids will be my strong and shining armor."

"Well, needless to say, we will all be praying for your safety."

"Thanks, Dent! That means a lot to me."

"Obadiah, you are one lucky man. Penelope is so beautiful. I know she is going to make you a fine wife. You keep focused on your future plans. Don't lose sight of your goals and objectives. Be smart and pray often! That's the last advice I have for you," Dent said as he smiled and put his arm around me as we headed back to the main house.

It was nice seeing everyone, but things turned a little sad when the goodbyes started. Several were fearful for my life, and that, I can understand. The war has just started and already there have been numerous casualties. Family members are grieving over loved ones who have already died or are badly wounded. Those dead have been buried hundreds of miles from home, and those seriously wounded are presently lying in hospitals somewhere trying to recover from their wounds. Several will die of infection and never again be able to see their loved ones back home. What a tragedy unfolding right before our eyes.

The last one to hug me was my sister Sarah. I knew she was hanging around for a purpose. Sarah and I have always been close. We were not only brother and sister, but Sarah was perhaps my best friend. As she hugged me, she said, "Obadiah, you be safe. You've got to stay alive for Penelope, Charles, and little Belle. The children need their father, and I need my youngest brother. You find some way to stay alive, you hear!"

"Sarah, I plan to stay alive. I'll do everything I can to stay alive. Please look in on Penelope from time to time. Maybe you and she could go shopping together in Prattville. I think she would like that."

"Obadiah, I promise you, I'll look in on her."

"Thanks, Sarah!"

After everyone had left Twin Oaks, Penelope and I took our last stroll through Mother's garden. There was a full moon, and the sky was full of sparkling stars. God's universe was remarkably beautiful that night.

"Obadiah, this is a sad night. I don't think I'm going to sleep tonight knowing you will be leaving in the morning."

I took Penelope in my arms. She was trembling. I held her close to my chest. She looked up at me with those gorgeous blue eyes. It wasn't long before we were kissing each other passionately.

"Make love to me, Obadiah!" she said in a soft whisper.

"Penelope, we have to stop. We can't do this. We have to wait."

"Obadiah, I hate your social and religious beliefs. I don't understand why it's wrong to have sex with the man you will later marry. Oh, Obadiah, I love you so much!"

"Oh, Penelope, my love, we've gone through this time and time again. It's my desire to wait. Please understand that. The passion we feel for each other is not going away. It will still be there a year from now. Please trust me!"

"I do trust you, but I don't understand."

"In time, my love, you will understand. We will be spending our whole life together."

"My greatest fear, Obadiah, is you will be killed, and I'll never know what it was like to have been made love to by the man who has my heart and soul. I don't think I would want to live without you, Obadiah."

"Don't say that, Penelope. I need you to be strong and look after my babies. You will be their mother, and they will always consider you their mother. They need you while I'm away. My God will see me through this war. I promise you, I'll be coming back to you. I will not be killed. When I come back, we will start our lifelong journey together. We will never be separated again. Our days will be filled with joy and thanksgiving. You just wait and see, my love."

"Will you write me often?"

"I'll write you every chance I get. Don't expect to hear often because I'm going to be quite busy caring for the sick and wounded."

"I'll write you every chance I get. I'll make sure that Charles and Belle know where you are and what you're doing."

"Penelope, we better go back into the house. Seven o'clock in the morning will be here before we know it."

"I heard your mother say she was going to have Betsy make you some flapjacks in the morning. I'm looking forward to some of them as well. I know Charles likes them."

I had trouble going to sleep. I couldn't get Penelope out of my mind. I kept seeing her piercing blue eyes and hearing her words, "Please make love to me, Obadiah." I caught myself several times sitting on the edge of my bed telling myself to go to her. Each time I lay back down on the bed, I tried to justify doing what my mind and body wanted me to do. I had never struggled with this type of temptation before. Why was it different? I wanted to believe it was because we are now engaged to be married. The fear of sinning was different. What would it hurt, just this one time? Finally, sometime in the night, I fell asleep.

At seven o'clock, I sat straight up in bed as hungry as I could be. I smelled the aroma of the fried bacon cooking and knew that in about thirty minutes I would be enjoying those flapjacks and sorghum molasses. The bacon would just top everything off.

After breakfast, Bill loaded my luggage in the carriage, and I said my goodbyes to Mother, Charles, Belle, Mattie, Betsy, and Penelope. Penelope hugged me so tightly. I thought she would never release me. She whispered in my ear and said, "You stay alive, my love!"

As Bill drove us away in the family carriage, I looked back through the rear window and waved bye one more time. In about an hour, we would be in Selma, Alabama, where I would board the train for Corinth, Mississippi.

CHAPTER 39

The two-day trip from Selma to Corinth was depressing. My heart grieved for Penelope and my family. I hate this war and what it's doing to my family, other families, and our country!

The wintery scenery, viewed from my train window, hasn't helped things either. Everything from Selma to Corinth looked gloomy and dead. Winter is my least favorite season. To me, it's like life has been lifted from the beautiful trees, grass, shrubs, and other things that grow wild. Winter leaves things looking ugly and desolate. Spring is my favorite season. I love it when trees leaf out and green grass appears. Life springs forward in its full radiant beauty. Well, life goes on; I've learned to live and tolerate the seasons. *It helps sometimes to let loose of one's feelings,* I thought.

I arrived in Corinth on March 14, 1862. As I stepped off the train in Corinth, I was met by Lt. Marcus Johnson. He was holding a sign with my name on it. I walked up to him and said, "I'm Dr. Obadiah Bradford."

"Dr. Bradford, I'm Lt. Marcus Johnson, Secretary to General Pierre Gustave Toutant Beauregard."

"It's a pleasure to meet you, Lt. Johnson."

"I'm pleased to meet you, Dr. Bradford. The Mississippi Army is happy that you've volunteered to serve in our army. We don't have many doctors to volunteer so you will be treated extremely well."

"Thank you, Lt. Johnson, but I don't expect any special treatment."

"I'm just carrying out the General's orders, Dr. Bradford. He's made arrangements to house you and the other regimental doctors at the Tishomingo Hotel here in Corinth."

"Where are the soldiers staying?"

"Right now, we have about forty-four thousand soldiers camped in and around Corinth."

"Did I hear you right: forty-four thousand Confederate soldiers?"

"That's right, Dr. Bradford!"

"How many doctors are here in Corinth?"

"There are twenty-one, counting you."

"Twenty-one doctors are not many for forty-four thousand soldiers."

"That's right, Dr. Bradford. That's the reason you are getting special treatment. You will earn every privilege you get, I assure you of that! Right now, all the doctors work at a hospital here in Corinth attending to sick soldiers who have come down with diseases. You will be very busy; I can guarantee you of that. By the way, are you a good surgeon, Dr. Bradford?"

"I think I am, Lt. Johnson."

"Well, you better be! I expect there will be lots of amputations during and after a battle."

"Who will I be answering to?"

"I'll introduce you to him at the Tishomingo Hotel. His name is Dr. Henry Dotson."

"Would this Henry Dotson be from Atlanta, Georgia?"

"I believe he is from Atlanta."

"Well, I can't believe this."

"Do you know Dr. Dotson?"

"He was my best friend during medical school at the Old Medical School in Augusta, Georgia. He's one of the best surgeons in the country."

"Excuse me, Dr. Bradford; he said the same thing about you."

"Then he knows I'm coming?"

"I wasn't supposed to tell you, so you act surprised when you see him, you hear?"

"Yes, sir, indeed I will!"

As we approached the city of Corinth, I was reminded of what I had read about this quaint little town. Corinth was located in northeast Mississippi and had a population of a little over one thousand people. It was a progressive town with a hospital, hotels, restaurants, several stores, and beautiful homes. The two railroads that crossed in Corinth made it strategically important. The railroads were important to the Confederacy because they extended nearly the entire length and breadth of the South. The Corinth railroads were busy shipping troops, arms, and food all over the Confederacy.

As Lt. Johnson's wagon pulled up in front of the Tishomingo Hotel, I was excited. I couldn't wait to see my friend Henry Dotson. We went inside where I was checked in and given the key to my room. The desk clerk told me I would be rooming with Dr. Dotson. I asked him if there were two beds. He looked at me, smiled, and said, "Yes, Dr. Bradford, there are two beds."

Lt. Johnson had been conferring with another officer as I was checking in. He came over to the desk and said, "Dr. Bradford, your friend Dr. Dotson is over at the hospital. It appears he will be there for awhile."

"By the way, where is the hospital from here?" I asked.

"When you leave the hotel, take a right and go about one block and you will see it on your right. Are you thinking about checking out the hospital?"

"I was thinking I might just do that."

"Dr. Bradford, you will be safe walking around here in Corinth. There are Confederate soldiers everywhere. If you need anything, just ask one of them. Oh, by the way, General Albert Sidney Johnston will be arriving here from Nashville in a few days. After he gets settled in, I'll bring him and General Beauregard around to meet you at the hospital. I'm sure Dr. Dotson has plans to put you to work right away."

"Thank you, Lt. Johnson! You can rest assured I won't tell my friend you let the cat out of the bag."

"Please, by all means, don't. You act really surprised!"

After making myself presentable, I decided to walk over to the hospital and see if I could locate my friend.

Lt. Johnson was right; I had never seen so many Confederate soldiers. They were everywhere. As I approached the hospital, I was stopped at the door by two soldiers who were guarding the front entrance to the hospital.

"May we help you, sir?"

"Yes, you may. My name is Dr. Obadiah Bradford. I just arrived in Corinth and am supposed to report to Dr. Henry Dotson. I was wondering if I might see him."

"May we see some ID, Dr. Bradford?"

The only ID I had was the letter from Lt. Johnson welcoming me to Corinth as a doctor. I pulled it out of my pocket and handed it to one of the guards.

"Sorry about the formality, Dr. Bradford, but we've been asked by Dr. Dotson to screen everyone who enters the hospital. There's a lot of sickness going on right now, and Dr. Dotson doesn't want people coming and going at will. I trust you understand that."

"Yes, of course."

"You may go in now. There is a nurse's desk in the center of the room. A nurse should be able to get Dr. Dotson for you."

"Thank you!"

I reported to the nurse's desk and asked to see Dr. Dotson. The nurse was very nice and asked my name.

"My name is Dr. Obadiah Bradford."

"Dr. Bradford, have a seat over there and we will see if Dr. Dotson can see you."

"Thanks!"

It wasn't long before the nurse returned and said, "Dr. Dotson will be with you shortly. He's making his rounds now but will be with you soon. Can we get you a cool glass of water?"

"That's sounds great!"

I had turned and was looking out the window into the main street of Corinth when I heard that familiar voice of my dear friend, Henry Dotson.

"Obadiah, what in the world brings you to Corinth, Mississippi?"

"Well, I heard you were here and decided if my best buddy can take the time to volunteer his time to the Confederacy, then I could as well."

We hugged each other and patted each other on the back as Henry said, "Follow me, and let's go to my office. We will have more privacy there."

It was so good to see Henry. We never slowed down in talking to each other. Henry answered every question I had regarding why we were assigned to Corinth. Henry had been answering to General P.G.T. Beauregard who was presently in charge of the army at Corinth. General Beauregard had made Henry the chief physician over the medical staff in Corinth. Henry had been working with General Beauregard on military procedures should the North attack Corinth.

General Beauregard had informed all of his ranking officers, as well as Henry, that General Ulysses S. Grant, commander and chief of the Army of Tennessee, was sending 45,000 Union troops to a place in Tennessee called Pittsburg Landing. Pittsburg Landing was only twenty miles from Corinth. General Beauregard felt that General Grant's objective was to attack Corinth and take control of the two major railroads that crossed here. If the North got control of Corinth, they could stop military supplies and the transporting of Confederate troops to different strategic battle areas in the South. If Corinth fell to the North, the Confederacy's chances of winning the war would be greatly reduced.

Henry went on to tell me that General Albert Johnston, commander and chief of the Army of Mississippi, was on his way to Corinth from Nashville with additional Confederate troops. He was expected in Corinth any day.

"Obadiah, we need you here. I would like for you to start tomorrow. We have a lot of sick soldiers here. Some are dying of influenza, some have severe diarrhea, and some have infections from sores, etc. I have only twenty-one doctors on staff, and we are all overworked. I truly appreciate your being here."

"I'm here to help," I said. "I'm ready to start anytime you ask."

"I hope you don't mind rooming with me at the Tishomingo Hotel. All my doctors are being housed there. They take good care of us."

"I'm looking forward to being roommates."

"Oh, by the way, when I saw your name on the volunteer list, I was thrilled. My thoughts began to reflect back on the good old days in Augusta, Georgia. I informed Lt. Johnson that you were my good friend and to take good care of you."

"Lt. Johnson was very nice and treated me well. I like him!"

"Obadiah, after I confer with my head nurse, we can walk to the hotel together. I bet you're starving!"

"I could eat a horse! By the way, how's the cooking compared to Kissy's and Martha's cooking at the Milton House?"

"Well, I must say the food at the Tishomingo is not as good as Kissy's and Martha's, but it's all right. I think you'll like it."

After dinner, Henry and I went to our room and visited for several hours catching up on all that had been going on in our lives since graduating from the Old Medical School in Augusta.

Henry shared with me that he was now the father of three boys. He married Helen Anderson, the daughter of Frank Anderson, who was mayor of Atlanta. He and Helen were happily married and hoped to someday have a daughter to go with the three boys. Henry also told me about his aspirations of someday entering politics.

"Obadiah, I've got a craving to fix things. Our country shouldn't have gotten in the mess it's in today. Greed is what's gotten us where we are. I'm afraid our country is going to pay a terrible price from this Civil War."

"I'm afraid you're right about that, Henry."

"What about you? Why are you here?"

"Henry, you must never reveal what I'm going to tell you. Do you promise?"

"Obadiah, you are one of my best friends. I would never reveal something you asked me not to."

"I'm here because I want to serve my time before the Confederate Conscription Law is passed and implemented. I lost my wife over a year ago from complications of childbirth and a stroke. We had two children whom I love dearly. I want to return to Autauga County and marry Penelope. You remember me talking about Penelope."

"Yes, I believe you were in love with Penelope."

"That love has never gone away since the day my father purchased her and her mother, Mattie. Our love for each other is greater than anything I can describe. Because she is my slave, I could never marry her in Autauga County. I have figured out a way for us to be together, however. After I complete my one-year service here, I will return to Autauga County, pack up our goods, and move to El Dorado, Arkansas, where my sister and her husband live. I plan to purchase a plantation there and start a medical practice. On the way to El Dorado, Penelope and I will be married on the train. We will finally become husband and wife. No one will ever know Penelope was a slave. She's so beautiful. She looks white and the Adams School in Boston has taught her how to be a lady. This is my plan, Henry. I hope you're not disappointed in my motives."

"Obadiah, all the time I knew you in Augusta, I felt your pain and agony over your love for Penelope. I had never seen anyone suffer as you did. You can rest assured I support your goal and objectives. Now, all we have to do is ask God to keep you safe. I'll do my part, Buddy!"

"Thanks, Henry! I truly appreciate having you as my friend."

"We had better get some sleep. Tomorrow is going to be a long day."

"Good night, Henry."

"Good night."

CHAPTER 40

Henry was right. We had some very sick soldiers suffering from influenza and infection of the bowels. The hospital was full. The soldiers who camped in and around Corinth were exposed to severe climactic conditions. There were tents erected to keep the soldiers dry, but this did little good to protect them from the below freezing temperatures at night. To survive, the soldiers often slept huddled together to utilize each other's body heat to survive the freezing nights. Those who were sick, or getting sick, spread the influenza to their buddies, and as a result, several were dying. Since I've been at the hospital, we have been losing an average of three soldiers daily. We need spring to hurry and get here.

Today, I met General Pierre Gustave Toutant Beauregard and General Albert Sidney Johnston. General Johnston is Commander and Chief of the entire Mississippi Army. I was impressed with both. They looked the role of leaders. I'm sure President Jefferson Davis knew what he was doing when he made his appointments.

On April 1, 1862, Henry was summoned to General Albert Johnston's headquarters. The meeting lasted for hours before he returned to the hospital. Upon his return, he immediately called a staff meeting.

"Gentleman, I just returned from General Albert Johnston's headquarters. We will soon be doing battle with the Northern Army of Tennessee. General Beauregard has convinced General Johnston to make a surprise attack on General Ulysses Grant's Army of Tennessee at Pittsburg Landing. Pittsburg Landing is about twenty miles from here. General Beauregard has received classified information that General Grant has some forty-nine thousand soldiers camped at Pittsburg Landing and that General

Don Carlos Buell, of the Northern Army of Ohio, is on his way to Pittsburg Landing with an additional twenty-five thousand troops. With these numbers, the Northern Army could easily defeat us and take control of Corinth. General Beauregard believes a surprise attack on Grant's army now is our only hope in keeping Corinth under Confederate control. If we wait until General Buell arrives at Pittsburg Landing, this wipes out our chance of victory. I believe General Beauregard is right. This is our only hope."

"What is our role in the battle?" I asked.

"I am leaving three doctors here to take care of the sick. The other eighteen will accompany me with the Army of Mississippi to Pittsburg Landing. After we arrive, each of you will be assigned two regiments. It will be your responsibility to care of those who are wounded from those regiments. It's understandable that you will not be able to take care of every soldier that falls, but it will be your job to examine each wounded soldier and determine if he has a chance to survive. If not, don't spend any time with him. Place a red flag by him so the medics will know not to attend to him. Move on to the next fallen soldier. When you find a soldier who has a chance of survival, do what you can quickly and then put a green flag by him. The green flag tells the medics to pick him up and put him in a wagon. You will have a dozen soldiers and some trained medics at your disposal. They will load the soldiers in wagons and bring them back to a safe location for further treatment. Your hardest task will be deciding which ones have a chance in surviving their wounds and which ones don't. Gentleman, this may be the hardest thing you've ever undertaken, but you can do this."

"Will we be fired upon by the enemy?" another doctor asked.

"We will fly yellow flags on our wagons. This will let the enemy know that we are a medical unit attending to the wounded. Normally, the enemy will honor our flags. We will do the same for them."

"What if there are too many soldiers who have fallen who might have a chance of survival, but we don't have room in our wagons. What do we do then?" another doctor asked.

"Put down green flags beside them, and they will be picked up at a later time. Gentlemen, this is going to be your call. You will be the best ones to make that call. You've got to do it. No one else will be available. When the wagons are full, the medics will return to the starting point of the battle and unload the wounded. After doing so, they will return to the battlefield for additional wounded soldiers. Gentlemen, this is our plan; do you have any additional questions?"

Henry told me that General Albert Johnston's original plans were to attack General Grant's Army on April 4, 1862. This didn't happen! Before we left Corinth, there was lots of confusion centered on General Leonidias Polk, a cousin of President James K. Polk, with his ten-thousand-man corps refusing to move his troops without written orders, which were still being composed. Due to General Polk's large corps blocking the muddy main street of Corinth, the departure of the Army of Mississippi was delayed.

When we finally left Corinth, we traveled all night trying to make up lost time. A mighty rainstorm hit us and hit us hard. As we marched through flooded roads, we had to stop and push wagons out of potholes and roads that were washed away by the flooding. The rain came down so hard that some of our regiments got lost from the main army. It became very apparent that we wouldn't be attacking anyone on the fifth. It took the entire day on April 5 to regroup and get ready for battle on April 6.

I spent a lot of my quiet time praying for God's blessings upon our troops as we prepared for battle. It was my hope that General Beauregard was right, and that a surprise attack would be to our advantage. If he was right, maybe it would save numerous lives for both sides.

Finally, General Johnston gave the order to attack. Our troops came out of the woods for a distance of two miles wide and advanced through the open fields toward the campsites of the Army of Tennessee. General Beauregard was right. We caught the Northern Army by surprise. All morning our troops drove the blue coats northward in a carnival of carnage that left the mutilated bodies of both sides strewn in heaps amid great heroism.

345

It was now time for us doctors to take the field. As we approached the area where the Northern Army's guns began to be effective and started to do harm, we experienced something that I hope I never have to experience again. Dead bodies were everywhere. Men were screaming, "Help me!" from all directions. When I came to the first fallen soldier, it didn't take me long to place the red flag by his side. He was dead. He perhaps would be one of the luckiest ones. At least he was not suffering pain. A few steps further, I found a soldier with one arm completely severed from above the elbow. He was bleeding severely. I applied a tourniquet and placed a green flag by his side. I came next upon a soldier who had his head blown off. This almost made me sick. As I waded through the fallen soldiers, I couldn't keep from crying. It was horrible. Almost every soldier I put a green flag by had wounds to the arms, legs, or head. Those I placed red flags by were severely wounded in the chest or stomach. Some had intestines hanging out their lower abdomen. I knew it wouldn't do any good to try to save these men. If they survived any time at all, they would later die of infection.

Our wagons soon became full, and the soldiers began to haul the wounded back to the woods where we had started the battle. I remained examining the bodies and doing everything I knew to temporarily stop some of the bleeding. I had nothing to give them for pain. Their suffering had to be awful!

By midday, the fighting centered on the Union center, a small forest called the Hornet's Nest. When the Confederates overran Hornet's Nest, we found several casualties from both sides in a sunken road. These men died mostly of bayonet wounds and close encounters with bullets. We could only assume that there had been hand-to-hand combat in this forest.

By mid-afternoon, the Northern Army was driven due north from their original camp. Everything seemed to be going well when we got word that General Albert Johnston had been shot and had bled to death from his wound. This damped the spirits of the entire Army of Mississippi. He had been a courageous warrior, one who was out front on his horse leading his soldiers on to victory.

General Beauregard assumed command and decided to call it a day. He was convinced there would be no problem in declaring victory over the Army of Tennessee the next day.

The night of April 6 is one I shall never forget. We eighteen doctors spent most of the night trying to save lives. I don't know how many arms and legs I amputated with a saw. I can still smell the stale blood and the awful odor after I cauterized each limb. Some soldiers went into shock. Some died for lack of strength to endure the terrible pain inflicted upon their bodies in removing a limb. I hated to amputate anyone's limb, but it was necessary in order to save lives.

On April 7, the battle once again started. What General Beauregard didn't know was that the Northern General, Don Carlos Buell, Commander of the Army of the Ohio, with his twenty-five thousand soldiers had arrived during the night of April 6 and had joined forces with General Ulysses Grant. Early on the morning of April 7, the Northern Army and the Ohio Army started advancing forward against the Army of the Mississippi. For a half day, General Beauregard put up a good fight, but the odds in numbers were hopeless because of the larger Union Army. By 2:00 p.m., Beauregard ordered a withdrawal back to the stronghold of Corinth.

Every available wagon was loaded with wounded soldiers who couldn't walk. The wounded soldiers who could walk were assisted by healthy soldiers. We estimated that there were over eight thousand soldiers who suffered some type of wounds that were not life threatening.

After we left the battlefield and headed back to Corinth, we were notified by General Beauregard to step it up because the Union General William Sherman was in hot pursuit. It was General Grant's objective to overtake the Army of Mississippi and defeat us before reaching Corinth. General Sherman would have surely been successful had it not been for a Confederate officer, Lt. General Nathan Bedford Forrest, and his cavalry. Nathan Bedford Forrest was given the duty of being the Rear Guard for the Army of Mississippi when we retreated. It was on April 8 that General Forrest engaged in battle with General

Sherman head on at the Battle of Fallen Timbers. It was at this battle that Nathan Forrest taught Sherman a lesson about the power of cavalry that Sherman would never forget. Nathan Forrest was successful in sending General Sherman back to Pittsburg Landing and this officially ended the Battle of Shiloh at Pittsburg Landing.

It has now been one week since the Battle of Shiloh. We learned that this battle had produced more casualties than all the previous wars of the United States combined. We know the Union Army had 65,085 federal soldiers who were engaged in the battle. Of these 65,085, there were 1,754 Federal soldiers killed, 8,408 wounded, and 959 missing, for a total of 10,699.

The South had 44,699 engaged in the battle of Shiloh, with 1,728 Confederate soldiers killed, 8,012 wounded, and 900 missing.

It wasn't long after the Battle of Shiloh that the Union armies under Maj. General Henry W. Halleck, the Army of the Tennessee, and the Army of Ohio advanced on Corinth. General Halleck had taken great pains to prepare to take Corinth. By May 25, 1862, General Halleck was in position to start the battle.

Henry called a staff meeting and briefed us on General Beauregard's plan. We were to pack three days of rations and be prepared to leave Corinth when the orders were given. Henry informed us that General Beauregard had decided not to stay and defend Corinth. He knew what the outcome of a battle would be. Due to the large numbers of the Union forces, the Confederate Army of Mississippi had no chance of defending Corinth. It would be a massacre, and he didn't want to sacrifice the lives of his men. On the night of May 29, 1862, we made our move. The Mobile and Ohio Railroad was used to carry the sick and wounded, the heavy artillery, and tons of supplies. General Beauregard had dummy Quaker Guns set up along the defensive earth works. He had his men build camp fires that would burn during the night. After everything was completed, we were able to board the Mobile and Ohio train and withdraw to Tupelo, Mississippi.

We later learned that on May 30, the Union troops advanced on Corinth without firing a shot. They were totally surprised that the town had been abandoned. There was a lot of talk that General Beauregard should have stayed and fought for Corinth. I believe he made the right decision. Wisdom teaches us that a life is more important than vain glory!

After arriving in Tupelo, however, we had ample time to relax. I was able to get letters off to Penelope and Mother and received answers. Both Penelope and Mother assured me all was well with Charles and Belle and that my brother, John, was doing a good job managing the affairs of Twin Oaks.

At Tupelo, we continued to work with the wounded from the Battle of Shiloh as well as caring for sick soldiers. There were no military operations going on near Tupelo.

On September 28, Henry came to me and said, "General Beauregard has called me to a staff meeting. I have a pretty good hunch what's developing."

"Henry, can you share that with me?"

"I've been hearing there are plans to recapture Corinth from Union control. I have a feeling that's what this meeting is all about. I'll know more after the meeting. See you later, Obadiah!"

The three hours Henry was away felt like the longest of my life. I was eager to know what was happening. I had always thought the Confederacy would someday try to retake Corinth because of its railroads.

Finally, there was a knock on my door. I quickly sprang to my feet and opened the door. It was Henry. He came in and flung his hat on the bed and said, "Are you ready to go back to Corinth?"

"So it's true. The Confederacy is going to try to recapture Corinth?"

"That's the plan, Obadiah, but it won't involve the Army of the Mississippi, under General Beauregard."

"What? This is really getting interesting. Please tell me more."

"Fifteen of my doctors, including me, are being transferred to Major General Earl Van Dorn's Trans-Mississippi Army. It is

Major General Earl Van Dorn's assignment to recapture Corinth. He is in need of doctors and since things are going well here, we are being transferred."

"I'm assuming I'm one of those fifteen doctors."

"You don't think I would leave my buddy behind, do you?"

"I would hope not, my dear friend!"

"We don't have long to wait. We are to report to General Van Dorn by October 1."

"That only gives us three days!"

"That right, so get to packing!"

"You appear to be very happy about this, Henry."

"I guess I am. I enjoyed Corinth. I do hope we can recapture the town. If we can, it will be of major importance to the Confederacy."

I didn't get much sleep during the night. I was completely focused on what ifs. What if General Van Dorn is successful? What if he's not? What will happen if he's not? What procedures will we follow during the battle? I tried to put all this out of my mind, but the harder I tried the worse it got. I finally got up and wrote Penelope a long letter. I had to be careful what I wrote because if it's intercepted by the Union forces, it could give away General Van Dorn's plans.

General Beauregard furnished two wagons with more than ample food rations to get us to General Van Dorn's camp outside of Corinth. He also assigned a company of soldiers to escort us there. On September 31, we reached General Van Dorn's camp. As soon as we arrived, Henry asked to see General Van Dorn. He handed the clerk a letter from General Beauregard. The clerk, in turn, handed the letter to another clerk who took it into General Van Dorn's office. In a few minutes, General Van Dorn's assistant came out and asked Henry to come in.

Henry was in General Van Dorn's headquarters for about fifteen minutes. When he came out, he was escorted to our wagon by two soldiers.

"Gentlemen, these soldiers are going to show us where we will be staying."

Henry got in the wagon as the soldiers climbed on their horses and headed out in front of our wagon. We were assigned three tents in the middle of General Van Dorn's camp. Before climbing out of the wagon, Henry said, "Gentlemen, in about fifteen minutes I want everyone to meet in my tent. I will fill you in on our responsibilities here in Corinth."

In fifteen minutes, we all crowded into Henry's tent to hear what our responsibilities were going to be. Henry said, "Gentlemen, find you somewhere to sit down. We have been transferred here for the purpose of taking care of the wounded when the Battle of Corinth starts. The invasion will be on October 3. Our procedure is a little different from what it was at the Battle of Shiloh. We will be in the rear when the battle starts, just like we were at Shiloh. We will remain there until I think it's safe to move forward. A lot will depend on how fast General Van Dorn's army advances. You need to know there is going to be a greater danger of being shot than we faced at Shiloh. As you know, there are lots of buildings in Corinth. I'm sure the Union soldiers will be located in every building that offers a strategic advantage to them. We will have to be extremely cautious when we move through the city.

"General Van Dorn has promised me there will be a company of soldiers who will be moving in front of us to intercept any Union soldiers who may have not moved along with the main unit. Keep your eyes open and stay as low as you can. We will be wearing yellow arm bands for identity purposes, but that doesn't assure us that Yankees won't take shots at us. I'll try not to send you forward unless I think it's safe. We will use the red and green flags as we did at the Battle of Shiloh for identification purposes. There will be medics and other soldiers who will be picking up the wounded. Do you have any questions?"

"What about the hospital? It would be nice if we could take control of the hospital quickly," a doctor said.

"That's a good point. I believe the hospital is one of the first places General Van Dorn plans to take, provided he can break through the trenches"

"Do you have other questions?"

351

"What if we get separated? Where do we meet and what happens if we're not at that location at the appointed time?" another doctor asked.

"That's a good question. I want everyone to meet at the hospital, providing we have been successful in taking it. Be there at 3:00 p.m. If we're not successful in taking the hospital, let's meet at the starting point where we entered the battlefield. Does anyone have additional questions? If any of the plans change, I'll let you know. Gentlemen, get some good rest. Oh, by the way, supper is at 6:00 p.m. and breakfast will be served in the big tent at 6:00 a.m."

After the meeting was adjourned, I asked Henry if we could take a walk before supper.

"What's on your mind, Obadiah?"

"This procedure scares me a little."

"To be honest with you, it scares me, too."

"I don't have a good feeling about this."

"Obadiah, all we can do is pray. I'll watch your back and you watch mine. Is that a deal?"

"That's a deal!"

"Let's go get some chow. I'm hungry."

"That sounds good to me."

I didn't sleep well during the night. The cots in our tents were nothing like what we were accustomed to. I guess I shouldn't complain. I doubt if the soldiers have cots. The ground is probably their cot. The battle tomorrow weighs heavy on my mind. I have a bad feeling about this battle.

CHAPTER 41

The Battle of Corinth started around ten o'clock in the morning on October 3, 1862. It was already hot and from all indications, it was going to be a blistering day. Major General Sterling Price's men were the first to reach the rifle pits, which were originally constructed by the Confederates for the Siege of Corinth. The Confederates advanced, pushing the Yankees back toward the city of Corinth. A gap occurred between two Union brigades around one o'clock in the afternoon. Our Confederate soldiers took advantage of this gap and proceeded forward.

The Yankee troops moved back in a futile effort to close the gap, but General Price's men advanced forward with strong determination to drive the Yankees farther back. They were successful and the Yankees withdrew back to their inner line. At this point, things looked good for the Confederate Army.

A little after one o'clock in the afternoon, the medical corps was given the go ahead to enter the battlefield. As I moved through the battlefield, fallen soldiers were everywhere. Just like Shiloh, they were moaning and groaning and were butchered badly. The shrapnel from the exploding cannon balls always does serious damage when coming into contact with its victims.

As usual, I placed my red flags by several soldiers who were not going to make it. The doctor in me wanted to attend to everyone I bent over to examine. I continued my walk through the fallen and placed red or green flags by those who were not already dead. Why did this war have to happen? Did anyone ever really consider the price this country would pay? Did anyone ever consider this type of butchering? Oh, God, please help these men!

The farther we marched toward Corinth, the more fallen soldiers we encountered. We were now seeing wounded and dead

Yankee soldiers who were intermixed with our own. I wanted to stop and help them, too. We were given orders not to administer aid to them, but to make sure we disarmed them so they wouldn't fire at us. After removing the weapons, we turned them over to our Confederate attendants who were accompanying us. I noticed that the weapons I removed from the fallen Union soldiers were better than some of ours; our men were not on equal ground when it came to weapons. I always said, "The Northern Armies will be superior to the South's because of the North's industrial advantages."

The heat was just awful! I had to wipe my forehead constantly with my long-sleeved shirt to keep the sweat from running into my eyes. It must be at least 110 degrees, I thought.

We were not too far behind our advancing troops. I glanced over to my left and saw Henry Dotson examining a Confederate soldier. He was bent over the soldier with his back to me. I then saw a fallen, struggling, Yankee soldier get to his feet with his rifle. He was heading toward Henry with the intention of stabbing him with his bayonet.

I started running toward Henry, yelling, "Henry, Henry, watch out!"

Just as I was about ten feet from the Yankee soldier, he turned with his rifle in hand and fired a shot at me. The bullet entered my chest just under my right shoulder. I remember falling to the ground and that was it. The next thing I remembered was Henry standing over me.

"Obadiah, say something!"

"What happened, Henry? Where am I?"

"We're back at General Van Dorn's camp. You have been badly wounded. I've got to get that bullet out of your chest or you're going to bleed to death. It's going to hurt, my friend."

"Henry, don't let me die."

Those were the last words I spoke for two days. The next thing I remembered was lying in a wagon. I opened my eyes and yelled out when the wagon ran over something in the road and shot pain throughout my body. The pain was awful! A medic bent over me and asked, "Doctor Bradford, are you all right?"

"Where are we?" I asked.

"We are pulling into Tupelo, Mississippi, Doctor Bradford."

"Tupelo! Why are we back in Tupelo? I thought we were still in Corinth."

"General Van Dorn and General Price had to withdraw their efforts to retake Corinth. There were too many Yankees. We did well for awhile, but in the end, they were victorious."

"Where is my friend, Doctor Henry Dotson?"

"Doctor Dotson and the others are behind us somewhere. They sent the worst of the wounded on to Tupelo. We will be at the hospital in a few minutes. You're going to be all right, Doctor Bradford."

After arriving at the Tupelo Hospital, the nurses started cleaning my wound. My chest wound had bled badly and the bandage was now dry and stiff. The nurses were very careful in cutting away the nasty bandage and getting me washed. I realized then how lucky I had been. If the bullet had hit the other side I wouldn't be lying here being attended by nice, dedicated nurses. God had spared my life, and for that, I'm deeply grateful!

It felt strange lying in a hospital bed. I felt so helpless. I lay there thinking about Henry and the other doctors. I worried that they may have been captured by the Northern Army. I prayed for them and hoped that General Grant didn't send an army after them as he did at Shiloh. I was grateful that Henry had not been killed by the Yankee soldier. I was thankful that we had other soldiers with us that day. I learned from the medic that after I was shot, a Confederate soldier shot and killed the Yankee who shot me. He never got another opportunity to go after Henry. I had never once worried about a fallen soldier attempting to do harm to one of us. I guess I should have, but I just didn't think about a wounded soldier getting up and attempting to kill us. After this episode, I certainly will be more cautious.

It was on the second day after I was admitted that word came to us in the hospital that General Van Dorn and General Price's army had arrived in Tupelo. There was nothing mentioned about Henry and the medical staff or the wounded. There had to be many wounded that would need hospital attention. It wasn't long before a doctor stuck his head in my room and said, "Obadiah, you will be happy to know that Dr. Dotson and his staff will be arriving shortly at the hospital."

"Thank God! Thank you, Doctor, for that information," I said with much relief.

The first thing Henry did after arriving at the hospital was to visit me.

"Obadiah Bradford, get up out of that bed. We've got work to do. I need you!" he said, kidding around with me.

"I'm at your command, Dr. Dotson," I said, smiling.

Henry came over and stood by my bed. He looked down at me and said, "Obadiah, you gave me a big scare when I was operating on you. You died on me, once. I had to revive you. I was praying like you had never heard me pray. God heard me, Obadiah, and the rest is history. He spared my good friend's life," Henry said with tears welling up in his eyes.

"Henry, I knew I was in good hands. I've got a nasty wound, but in time, I imagine I will heal," I hoped.

"Let me take a look at it. That is nasty!" he said, shaking his head.

"Do you think I'm going to be all right?"

"Obadiah, this wound is going to get you home to Prattville. I've decided that after you are well enough to travel by train, I'm discharging you and sending you back to Autauga County."

"Are you serious?" I asked with great interest.

"Yes, I'm serious. You will eventually recover from this wound, and again practice medicine, hopefully in El Dorado, Arkansas. You will have the opportunity to marry Penelope and live happily ever-after."

"Henry, what about the new conscription law that's increased a soldier's service time from one year to three years? How do you plan to get around that?"

"Obadiah, you let me worry about that. I'm going to do this for you. You and Penelope need to be together, and I believe that God spared you for more than just Penelope and the kids. He wants you in El Dorado, Arkansas, saving lives. That's what we're going to do. You be patient, my friend!"

"Henry, I don't know how to thank you."

"You saving my life on that battlefield in Corinth is thanks enough. I would be dead if you hadn't called out and taken that bullet. I will always be indebted to you, my friend. I can pull this off, so don't you worry about anything. You just concentrate on getting better and being ready to travel when I give you the word."

"Henry, since I can't use my right hand, could you arrange for a nurse to write a couple of letters for me? I'll dictate the letters if someone will write them. I want to write Penelope and Mother and let them know I'm all right."

"I think I can arrange that!"

"In your opinion, how long do you think it will take for me to heal enough to make the trip home to Autauga County?"

"Knowing how tough you are, maybe two weeks. Let's see what two weeks from now looks like."

"Thanks, Henry! Oh, by the way, do you know how many soldiers were killed and wounded at Corinth?"

"The information that General Van Dorn shared with us was that there were 473 men killed, 1,997 wounded, and 1,764 captured and missing. It could have been worse! Our men were brave. On the second day of the battle, our soldiers moved forward to meet heavy Union artillery. They stormed Battery Powell and Battery Robinett inside of Corinth. I believe you know where the batteries are located. Anyway, our soldiers were successful in taking both batteries after hand-to-hand fighting occurred.

"Unfortunately, this success didn't last long. The Union soldiers recaptured both batteries, and General Van Dorn ordered a retreat. No one seems to know why, but General William Rosecrans who was in charge of the Union Army didn't immediately pursue our army, and we escaped death or capture."

"Henry, I'm afraid the South is going to lose this war. Corinth will now be completely controlled by Northern forces. The North will now be able to stop shipments of weapons, supplies, and other resources to the South. They will eventually control the waterways as well as the railroads."

"I believe you are right, Obadiah. I guess I've always felt the same way as you have about our slim chances of winning this war. But being from the South, I wanted to prove to the North that we weren't going to let them push everything down our throats. It's now my belief we got in too big of a hurry to prove our point. This war will be known as a war of all wars in America. You and I have already experienced seeing thousands of soldiers die and we've just been in two battles. I'm afraid this is only the beginning of many sad and hard times ahead. I can only hope that God will have mercy on our souls."

CHAPTER 42

My last two weeks at Tupelo were the longest of my life. Henry was successful in getting my release approved by the Confederate government. I was pleased to see on the release papers the statement, "Approved with Honorable Discharge."

Henry had not yet released me from the hospital. He felt it best I take the necessary time to heal before making the long train ride to Selma, Alabama, and then home to Twin Oaks. It was going to take a few months for me to fully heal. The bullet that Henry removed from me had done extensive damage to my shoulder muscles and ligaments.

There would be countless hours spent in exercising to rehabilitate my shoulder and right arm. The good part about my rehabilitation is I will be at home with my family, and Penelope would be there to help me.

On the morning of October 17, 1862, Henry came to my room smiling from ear to ear.

"What's up with you today, Henry Dotson?"

"Well, to tell you the truth, I'm ready to send you on your way to Autauga County. We need your bed for someone sicker than you. How do you like those apples?"

"Henry, you're not kidding around with me, are you?"

"Maybe a little, but I believe you've healed enough to make the train ride home. How's that sound to you?"

"I'm ready, Henry. I've been wondering when you were going to give me the word. I'm more than ready to give this bed up to someone else. I'm telling you, it's one of the hardest beds I've ever lain in."

"Quit your complaining. Let me take a look at your wound. Yep, it looks much better! I believe it's going to heal nicely. I'm going to miss you, my friend."

"I will miss you as well, Henry."

"Obadiah, I decided to let you make your own arrangements for the train ride to Selma. I'm assuming you're up to that?"

"I'm sure I can handle that!"

"The only favor I would ask of you is to keep in touch with me. I want to know how all these plans you've made pan out. I'm hoping to hear that you and Penelope were married and have reached El Dorado, Arkansas, sometime in the near future."

"I will certainly write you, Henry. I will worry about you, and I assure you that I will be praying for you and your staff. Please promise me that you will be extra careful. I want to be able to visit with you back in Atlanta when this war is over."

"Obadiah, I'm so grateful we've had this opportunity to renew our friendship these last several months. You will always be my best friend. If something was to happen to me, I would like for you to stay in touch with my family from time to time. That would mean a lot to me and them."

"I promise you, I'll do that, Henry."

"I need your signature on this form. It's our responsibility to get every soldier's signature when we dismiss him. So sign your John Henry on the line that has the X."

"I am going to have to use my left hand."

"Oh, I forgot all about your right hand. As long as you can scribble, the signature will be fine."

"There is one more thing, Henry Dotson!"

"What's that, my friend?"

"I need a big hug. Remember, I can only hug with my left arm. I appreciate what you've done for me, Henry. Please always know you will be in my thoughts and prayers."

"Thank you, Obadiah! Now, you best get dressed and go make those arrangements. You take care of yourself while you are out. I don't want to have to put you back in this hospital. If you feel faint or weak, go somewhere and sit down. Don't push yourself. Take it nice and easy. I'll see you tonight at the hotel. I'm assuming you won't be leaving until tomorrow?"

"You're right! I've got to send Mother a telegram of my arrival time in Selma."

As Henry turned and left the room, my heart grieved for him. I can only pray that God will wrap his gentle arms around Henry and shield him of dangers that lie ahead. I will pray daily that he will survive this cruel and bloody war, and someday be united with his family in Atlanta. Henry is such an outstanding doctor and one of the kindest persons one could know. He has taught me so much about life, and our friendship is like having another brother. I look forward to hearing wonderful things about him in years to come.

Henry was right. My little energy was sapped when I finished making arrangements to return to Autauga County. My bed at the hotel felt good as I lay down. It wasn't long before I was sound asleep.

Henry and the hospital staff gave me a going-away party at the hotel. We had a wonderful time. I would miss everyone. They are a great group of professional men who came here as I did to offer their services in saving lives. I will pray for their safety as well.

Henry and I had breakfast and then he walked me to the Tupelo train station where we said our goodbyes. My train was leaving at ten o'clock. Again, it was hard leaving my best friend behind in Tupelo. I was the lucky one who was returning home to a county that had not yet experienced the effects of the war. So far, Autauga County and other counties around Autauga were still enjoying the fruits of the harvests.

I spent most of the train trip lying in bed. I was able to get more comfort lying down rather than sitting up. As we approached Selma, I heard those familiar remarks from the train attendant, "Approaching Selma, Alabama."

As I stepped off the train in Selma, I saw a large group of people running toward me. I immediately recognized my brothers, Dent and John. My mother was directly behind them, and a large group was following. It appeared that my entire family had come to welcome me home. I was hoping they wouldn't give me bear hugs because of my wound. It made me feel alive as we started hugging and kissing each other, just like old times at family reunions. My family had always been huggers, and they always brought inspiration to me. The first person to reach me was Mother. I would normally pick her up and swing her around, but today, she would have to be satisfied with just a soft hug and kiss. After she hugged me, she looked into my eyes with tears streaming down her face and said, "I didn't hurt you did I?"

"No, Mother, I'm fine."

"Obadiah, my sweet, Obadiah. It's so good to have you home."

"Mother, it's good to be home. I've missed you so much."

Dent and John were carrying Charles and Belle. Knowing I was hurt, Dent let Charles lean forward for a hug and kiss from me. Charles's gentle, warm touch made me cry. It had been almost nine months since I had held him and little Belle and told them I loved them. John passed Belle to me. She was not nearly as heavy as Charles and I was able to hug and kiss her as I stood holding her. She was such a pretty little girl. She looked just like Audrey. In fact, she was a spitting image of Audrey. I passed Belle back to John as I sought getting hugs and kisses from other family members.

"Obadiah, there is one other person you will want to see as well," Mother said.

Penelope, who was waiting her turn, stepped out from behind Sarah and politely said, "Welcome home, Obadiah."

She was so beautiful! Never in my life have I seen such pure beauty in a woman.

"Thank you, Penelope," I said as I gave her a hug and kissed her right before everyone. I could hear laughter and clapping of approval behind me. My family loved Penelope and looked forward to our marriage. The kiss was nothing of a surprise to any of them. The next familiar voice I heard was that of Bill. He stepped forward and said, "Welcome home, Master Obadiah."

"Bill, it's so good to see you," I said as we embraced.

"Good to see you, too, Master Obadiah. I'll put your bags in the carriage."

The October weather in Selma was just right. It wasn't too cold or too hot. Mother had rented the Selma community build-ing for a homecoming reception. There was food everywhere and lots of cold milk. I hadn't had good cold milk since leaving for the war. How thoughtful of Mother to arrange for cold milk, I thought.

When I thanked her for serving cold milk, she looked at Penelope and said, "Penelope is responsible for the cold milk. She remembered how much you love it."

I looked at her and whispered, "Thank you, my love!"

After spending a good two hours at the reception, I was ready to head home to Twin Oaks. The train ride plus the two hour reception had drained the energy from my body. I needed to sit down and rest. Bill helped Mother and the children into the family carriage. I took Penelope's hand and helped her. After we were seated, Mother took Belle and Charles and seated them by her. She knew Penelope and I would like to sit together.

Penelope grabbed my left arm and laid her head on my left shoulder. Her warm body next to mine felt good. I've always known that Penelope was going to make me the happiest man on earth. She and I were meant to be together, and God had done his part. We had both experienced heartaches and heartbreaks over the years but had never stopped believing that our day would come. In a few months, with God's blessings, our day will come. That day will be a day filled with joy and jubilee.

ABOUT THE AUTHOR

As a young, migrant boy, growing up in the Ozark Mountains of Cleburne County, Arkansas, Carl J. Barger spent fifteen straight summers in Benton Harbor, Michigan, harvesting fruit crops and picking cotton in Leachville, Craighead County, Arkansas. While laboring in the fields, Barger used daydreaming as a means of entertainment in passing the time away. His daydreaming became his passion. Some days he dreamed of becoming a great inspiring actor, one who won more Oscars than the great Spencer Tracy. Other days, he dreamed of becoming the greatest basketball coach in Arkansas. Barger even dreamed of becoming a well-known author.

Strangely enough, Barger's daydreaming of becoming a basketball coach and writer become a reality. Barger spent thirty-seven years in the field of education, coaching and being a public school superintendent in Arkansas. After retirement from public schools, Barger has written and published three books: *Swords and Plowshares*; *Mamie, an Ozark Mountain Girl of Courage;* and *Cleburne County and Its People.*

Barger is married to his childhood sweetheart, Lena Dollar, also of the Ozark Mountains of Cleburne County. They make their home in Conway, Arkansas.

CPSIA information can be obtained
at www.ICGtesting.com
Printed in the USA
FFOW02n0514100418
46196246-47449FF